20   with
Mr Rochester, not Mr Darcy. Drawn to his darkness, she longed to find a tortured hero of her own ... until she realised the ramifications of Rochester locking his first wife up in his attic. Discovering the error of her ways, Máire now looks for a real-life Darcy and creates deliciously dark heroes on the page. Oh, and she wants everyone to know her name is pronounced *Moira*. Her parents just had to give her an Irish Gaelic name.

Praise for Máire Claremont:

'*The Dark Lady* has as much romance, adventure, passion, torment, and triumph as any one love story could deliver' Grace Burrowes, *New York Times* bestselling author

'Real, intelligent, and gritty but above all deeply romantic. In my opinion Máire Claremont is the stunning reincarnation of the Brontë sisters' Delilah Marvelle, award-winning author of *Forever a Lady*

'Will keep you hooked to the very last page' Anna Campbell, award-winning author of *Seven Nights in a Rogue's Bed*

'Intense, bold, gripping, and passionate' Leanne Renee Hieber, bestselling author of *The Strangely Beautiful Tale of Miss Percy Parker*

The Dark Lady

MÁIRE CLAREMONT

A novel of Mad Passions

ETERNAL
ROMANCE

Published by arrangement with NAL Signet
a division of Penguin Group (USA) Inc.

First published in Great Britain in 2013
by ETERNAL ROMANCE
An imprint of HEADLINE PUBLISHING GROUP

1

Cataloguing in Publication Data is available from the British Library

ISBN 978 1 4722 0475 2

Offset in Times by Avon DataSet Ltd, Bidford-on-Avon, Warwickshire

Printed and bound by CPI Group (UK) Ltd, Croydon, CR0 4YY

Headline's policy is to use papers that are natural, renewable and recyclable
products and made from wood grown in sustainable forests.
The logging and manufacturing processes are expected to conform to the
environmental regulations of the country of origin.

HEADLINE PUBLISHING GROUP
An Hachette UK Company
338 Euston Road
London NW1 3BH

www.eternalromancebooks.co.uk
www.headline.co.uk
www.hachette.co.uk

For my father.

You gave me my love of reading by spending hours every day on the sofa reading massive novels and World War II books.

When I longed for the stars, you gave me a ladder.

I miss you, Dad, and I know you're proud.

Acknowledgments

This novel would never have happened without some absolutely amazing women. Delilah Marvelle drove me hard and never let me give up my dreams. Helen Breitweiser, my agent extraordinaire, took a chance on me and gave *The Dark Lady* her blood and passion, I swear. Jesse Feldman, my dear, dear editor, offered darling Eva and all my other characters a home, for which I will be eternally grateful. I must also give my deepest thanks to my friends who encouraged me to follow this passionately mad story: Lacey Kaye, Erica Ridley, Lenore Bell. And last but not least, thank you, Katrina, for holding my hand and loving me when things were dark. This book never would have found its way to the light without all these incredible and inspiring women.

The Dark Lady

Chapter 1

England
1865

The road stretched on like a line of corrupting filth in the pristine snow. Lord Ian Blake clutched the folds of his thick wool greatcoat against his frigid frame as he stared at it.

If he chose, he could simply keep on.

The coach had left him at the edge of Carridan Hall a quarter of an hour past, but if he took to the muddy and ice-filled road, he would be in the village by dark and on the first mail back to London. Back to India.

Back to anywhere but here.

For perhaps the tenth time, he faced the untouched wide drive that led up to the great house. Snow lay fluffed and cold, crystal pure upon the ground. It dragged the limbs of the fingerlike branches toward the blanketed earth. And after almost three years in the baked heat and blazing colors of India, this punishing winter landscape was sheer hell.

Despite the ache, he drew in a long, icy breath and trudged forward, his booted feet crunching as he went.

Eva hated him.

Hated him enough to not return his letters. Not even the letter begging her forgiveness for her husband's death. But then again, Ian had failed her. He had promised her that he wouldn't let Hamilton die in India. But he had. He'd made so many promises that he'd been unable to keep.

Now he would go before his friend's widow, the woman he had held in his heart since childhood. To make amends for his failures, he would do whatever she might command. His soul yearned for the ease she might give him. For, even as he walked up the drive, following the curve to the spot where the trees suddenly stopped and the towering four-story Palladian mansion loomed, he didn't walk alone.

The unrelenting memory of Hamilton's brutal death was with him.

He paused before the intimidating limestone edifice that had been built by Hamilton's grandfather. The windows, even under the pregnant gray sky, heavy with unshed snow, glistened like diamonds, beckoning him to his boyhood home.

The very thought of standing before Eva filled him with dread, but he kept his pace swift and steady. Each step merely a continuation on the long journey he'd set upon months before.

Even though the cold bit through his thick garments and whipped against his dark hair, sweat slipped down his back. Winter silence pounded in his ears, blending with his boot steps as he mounted the brushed stairs before the house, and as he raised his hand to knock, the door swung open. Charles, his black suit pressed to perfection, stood in the frame.

That now greatly wrinkled face slackened with shock. "Master Ian." He paused. "Pardon. Of course, I mean, my lord."

Ian's gut twisted. It had been years since he had seen the man who had chided him, Hamilton, and Eva time and again for tracking mud from the lake upon the vast marble floors of the house. "Hello, Charles."

The butler continued to linger in the doorway, his soft brown eyes wide, his usually unreadable face perfectly astonished.

Ian smiled tightly. "Might I be allowed entrance?"

Charles jerked to attention and instantly backed away from the door. "I am so sorry, my lord. Do forgive me. It has been—"

Ian nodded and stepped into the massive foyer, shaking the wisps of snow from his person. He couldn't blame the old man for his strange behavior. After all, the last time Ian had seen the servant had been when he'd been invested as Viscount Blake, just before he'd left for India. The title should have prevented his traveling so far and risking his life. But life didn't always unfold according to the dictates of tradition.

Three years had passed since his departure with Hamilton. Now, Hamilton would not join his return. "I should have informed you of my visit."

As the door closed behind them, it seemed to close in on his heart, filling his chest with a leaden weight. Not even the beauty of the soft blue and gold-leafed walls of his childhood home could alleviate it.

Charles reached out for his coat and took the wet mass into his white-gloved hands. "It is so good to see you, my lord."

The words hung between them. The words that said it would have been preferable if he had not returned alone.

He pulled off his top hat and passed it to the butler. "I should like to speak to Lady Carin."

Charles's mouth opened slightly as he maneuvered the coat into one hand and stretched out the other to take the last item. "But . . ."

Ian glanced about as if she might suddenly appear out

of one of the mazelike hallways. "Is she not in residence?"

Charles's gaze darted to the broad, ornately carved stairs and then back. "Perhaps you should speak to his lordship."

Ian shook his head, a laugh upon his lips, but something stopped him. "His lordship? Adam is not three. Does he rule the house?"

A sheen cooled Charles's eyes. "Master Adam has passed, my lord."

The unbelievable words, barely audible in the vast foyer of silk walls and marble floor, whispered about them.

"Passed?" Ian echoed.

"Was not Lord Thomas's letter delivered to you in India?"

The world spun with more force than his ship had done rounding the Cape of Good Hope. "No. No, it was never delivered."

He had never met the boy. Nor had Hamilton. They had both only heard tales of him from Eva's detailed and delightful letters. In his mind, Ian had always imagined the child to be an exact replica of Eva. Only ... he was gone. He shifted on his booted feet, trying to fathom this new information. "What happened? I don't understand."

Charles drew in a long breath and stared at Ian for a few moments, then quickly jerked his gaze away. "I shall leave it to Thomas, the new Lord Carin, to inform you."

What the devil was going on? Charles had never avoided his eyes in all the years he'd known him, and now ... 'Twas as if the old man was ashamed or fearful. "Then take me to him at once."

Charles nodded, his head bobbing up and down with renewed humbleness. "Of course."

They spoke no more as they turned to the winding

staircase that twisted and split into two wings like a double-headed serpent.

They followed the wide set of stairs that led to the east wing. Their footsteps thudded against the red-and-blue woven runner. Ian blinked when they reached the hallway. Hideous red velvet wallpaper covered the walls and massive portraits and mirrors seemed to hang upon every surface. "Lady Carin has redecorated?"

Charles kept face forward. "Lord Thomas is undergoing renovations, my lord. He began with the family rooms but intends to alter the ground floor this spring."

Decorations should have been the lady of the house's domain. Another mystery. One that added greatly to his unease.

The place looked little like the house he had left. Gone were the cool colors, beautiful wallpapers of silk and gold or silver, framed with stuccoed accents. Once, this house had been the height of beauty, with airy hallways and bright colors. Now dark, rich tones wrapped the house in melancholy. The elegant honeyed oak had been ripped out and replaced by mahogany to match the red velvet wallpaper. In the brief days since his return, he'd noticed the change in society's fashion, the departure from light and the acceptance of oppressive furnishings.

But he'd never thought to see Carridan Hall so changed.

At last, the two men paused before the old lord's office.

Charles knocked. Quickly, he opened the door, edged into the room, then shut the door behind him. The panel was thick enough that the voices were muffled. But Ian didn't miss the sharp silence that followed the announcement of his name.

The door opened and Charles announced, "Lord Blake, my lord."

Ian strode into the space. As he entered, Charles made a swift retreat, shutting the door with a thud.

Tension crackled in the room. So thick Ian was sure he could reach out and grab it.

Hamilton's little brother, Thomas, sat behind a solid desk of walnut. His brownish blond hair thinned out over his pale scalp and a light brushing of hair curled at his upper lip. His sunken green eyes watered as he stood. 'Twas hard to believe the man was not even five and twenty.

Slowly, Thomas reached out his hand in offering, the crest of the Carin family on the gold ring displayed prominently on his finger.

Thomas was lord at last.

How Thomas must have longed for it these years in the shadows of the house, separate from everyone and everything, watching for any chance to betray Hamilton, Ian, and Eva's adventures to his father. Desperate for any sort of attention from the old lord.

But that was hardly charitable of Ian. Perhaps in the years since he had left, Thomas had improved. Perhaps he was no longer the jealous—and often cruel—boy he had been.

Ian doubted it as he allowed the young lord's hand to linger in the air.

Though every instinct told him to push away the nicety, a man never made an enemy out of a source of information. And right now Thomas held all the information Ian needed.

Ian forced himself to take Thomas's hand. It was cold and limp. Thomas had not cared for sports or outdoor activities. But nor had he cared for studies. Even now, Ian was uncertain what it was that Thomas had ever enjoyed.

"Ian, I am so glad you have come back."

'Twas a voice he hadn't heard in three years, and the reedy, affected sound struck Ian as distinctly strange for such a man not yet of middle years. Had it always been so thoroughly unpleasant? Or had it slowly become thus?

"Thank you." Ian pulled his hand back, resisting the urge to wipe it on his coat. "I regret that I was unable to bring your brother."

Thomas lowered his head, half nodding, seemingly unable to quite hide the satisfaction that he had at last superseded his brother in something. "A true tragedy."

"Indeed." If you could reduce a man's passing, his guts ruptured by a blade, to such a simple word. "Tragedy" really just didn't seem to express the horror of it.

Thomas eased himself into his leather wingback chair.

Ian remained standing, taking in the crowded room, willing himself to accept this strange reality unfolding before him. But still, he could not.

This room had once been another man's. A great man's. Hamilton and Thomas's father had undoubtedly ruled with an iron fist. Perhaps he had not known how to love as a father should, but he had managed his estate and fulfilled his duties with admirable skill.

Ian could only hope that, now, he would do the same for his own tenants and lands.

And once, this room had been remarkable in its serenity, the green silk walls slightly reflective of the skittish English sun, encouraging study. It had been uncluttered, allowing Hamilton, Ian, and Eva to play out mock battles with toy soldiers on the simply woven rugs from the East as the old man read over the estate reports.

Now every space was littered with round and square tables, lace and fringe covering them. Bric-a-brac filled their surfaces. It was a veritable explosion of trinkets.

The chamber was choking Ian, and he suddenly knew what a tree surrounded by encroaching ivy must feel. He swung his gaze back to his cousin. "This family has known a great deal of tragedy, it would seem."

Thomas's fingers rested on the edge of his elaborately carved desk. "It has been a very bad few years for the Carins."

A bad few years?

Ian arched a brow and glanced to the glaring windows. Snow fell slowly in heavy flakes. And even though a fire blazed in the hearth not ten feet away, the cold wouldn't leave his bones. He wished he hadn't given up his coat. But even he knew the cold he felt had little to do with the ice feathering over the glass panes. "Where is Lady Carin? I wish to speak with her."

Thomas cleared his throat and shifted in his chair, the creak of leather piercing the silence.

Ian returned his gaze to Thomas. The man's face creased into a series of lines. Still, Thomas said nothing. Ian waited, unrelenting, as he gazed upon his cousin.

Thomas swallowed, fidgeting slightly, then waved a hand at the empty cushioned chairs just behind Ian. "Forgive me. Do sit." Thomas stood and slowly made his way to a table standing near the fire. "Very rude of me. The shock of seeing you, you know."

"I prefer to stand."

"Certainly. A drink then?" Crystal decanters reflected the bare, dull light. Thomas's shadow fell over the tray of libations and he quickly pulled the crystal stopper free of the brandy bottle and poured out two drinks.

Thomas cradled the two snifters, then crossed over to Ian. His dark blue suit drank in the darkness of the late afternoon, making it appear black. "Here."

Ian took the glass, fighting the desire to reach out and tug it away. "Thank you." He tossed the contents of the drink back in one quick swallow, the taste of expensive brandy barely registering on his tongue. "Now, please tell me the whereabouts of Lady Carin. I wish to see her."

Thomas turned his back to him, facing the fire. "Seeing Lady Carin isn't a possibility."

"Bullocks." The coarse word gritted past his teeth before he could stop himself.

Thomas's shoulders tensed, his pale hair twitching against his perfectly starched collar. "No. It's not."

The bastard didn't even have the guts to face him.

Ian gripped the glass in his hand, the intricate crystal design pressing deep into his skin. "Where the hell is she, Thomas?"

Thomas whipped back to him, that damned ring winking in the winter's gloom. "She's not here. She's—"

Ian tensed as fear grabbed his guts. She'd never returned his letters, something entirely unlike the Eva he'd always known. Christ, he hated his sudden uncertainty. Even more, he hated the words he was about to utter. He had lost Eva to duty once; to lose her again would be beyond what he could bear. "Has she died?"

Thomas shook his head. "No, though it would have been better if she had."

Ian slammed his glass down on Thomas's desk. The crystal cracked, a nearly invisible line snaking the length of the snifter. "That is a damn despicable thing to say."

Jumping, Thomas edged away. "You say that now, but if you had seen—"

Ian locked eyes with his cousin. "I haven't traveled halfway around the world to play this out with you."

Thomas took a sip of his brandy; then his mouth worked as if the words in his throat tasted of poison. "Eva is in a madhouse." He took another quick sip of brandy, his shoulders hunching. "Or rather, an asylum."

The air in his lungs flew out of his chest with more

force than any rifle butt blow could induce. For a moment, Ian could have sworn that Thomas hadn't spoken at all. The blackguard's mouth still worked, twisting, then pressing into a tight line as if that refuse he'd just spewed truly displeased him. "Explain," Ian bit out, barely able to contain the sudden rage pumping through him.

Thomas took a long drink, his Adam's apple bobbing as he gulped. He wiped his mouth with the back of his pale hand. "It happened after the boy. She simply went mad."

Ian took a step forward. "What happened to Adam?"

"It was horrible. Absolutely horrible." Thomas fiddled with his glass, then walked abruptly back to the silver liquor tray and poured himself another drink. As he dispensed another two fingers' worth, he muffled, "Was her damn fault, you see."

Her fault?

Ian dug his fingertips into his palms, tempted to go over and shake Thomas like the little rat he was. He'd imagined a thousand different outcomes to his homecoming. It had even struck him that Eva might throw him out of the house. "Thomas, I'm a military man. I need facts, not ramblings."

"The facts?" He nodded. "It was November. Eva insisted on taking her curricle to the village for heaven only knows what reason. The stable hands tried to convince her the roads were bad from the rain. Only she wouldn't listen. I think she was distraught over Hamilton's death. Even then she wasn't behaving quite right."

How was a grieving widow supposed to behave? "Go on," Ian said, breathing deeply to keep his voice even.

"Somehow she lost control. The wheel came off, I think, and the curricle crashed."

Ian closed his eyes for a moment. It was almost easy

to envision. The bodies flying in the air. The shriek of the crash and breaking metal and wood. "And Adam?"

"He was in a basket beside her on the front seat. The boy was flung from the vehicle. They found him not even ten feet from Eva. Her leg was broken and she was screaming for him." Thomas coughed slightly. "All she did was scream."

Opening his eyes, Ian swallowed back vomit. "Christ. But she was distraught. Her husband dead—her son, too." Ian paused, barely able to believe the list of horrors unfolding before him. He'd thought nothing could shock him after his years in India. "Why is she in a madhouse?"

"Oh, Ian," Thomas said softly. "You should have seen her. She walked the halls of the house nights on end. She screamed in starts. Sudden, violent fits. She insisted that someone else had killed Adam."

Lord, he couldn't even imagine. The little boy dead, thrown from a vehicle before the mother's eyes. "Why would she do that?"

Thomas shrugged. "Guilt, no doubt. She couldn't bear that if she had just listened, her boy would still be alive. After a few upsetting occurrences, I refused to be responsible for her. I could no longer guarantee her safety."

"What in the hell does that mean?" Ian snapped.

"The gardeners found Eva walking into the lake. You know as well as I that Eva does not swim."

"She tried to destroy herself—"

"Shh. To say such a thing . . ." Thomas took several steps forward and his shoulders tensed. "Most of the servants don't know. The gardeners were paid and dismissed." Thomas grimaced. "You may think I did wrong. But I had no wish to come across Eva hanging from a chandelier or sprawled at the bottom of the stair. Where she is now she can be protected."

Ian lowered his gaze to the thick rug, woven no doubt in the land where he had just spent so many years. In the end, he'd betrayed both of his best friends, then. Hamilton and Eva. He closed his eyes for a moment, pain shooting through his skull. Ian crossed the room in a few short strides, towering over Thomas. "I want to see her."

"Impossible."

Ian grabbed Thomas's lapel, his body so tense he thought it just might shatter. "You're going to tell me where she is." He shook Thomas hard enough that the man's head snapped back. "And you're going to tell me now."

Chapter 2

The room tilted in never-ending ups and downs. So much brown. Brown above. Brown below. Brown on her skin. Brown ceilings, walls, and floors. Brown clothes. She knew that once even her hair had been brown. No. Not brown. Black. Her hair had been black.

It might be still.

She hadn't seen it in over a year.

Eva swallowed, her mouth certainly drier than the vast deserts Hamilton had described in his letters so long ago. She'd gotten used to the awful taste. The bitter taste. But the taste meant that forgetfulness would soon offer itself up to her, wiping her mind clean of a little body, lifeless in the mud.

The bed itched and gnawed at her. It always did. Little enemies running about. Even when she slipped away from the present, she couldn't quite rid herself of the disgusting tickle of a thousand little legs running up and down her skin.

She knew this room so well. Even without a jot of light, for there were no windows or bars. Why would one need bars with endless walls?

In the silence, Eva could hear Mary breathing. It wasn't the peaceful breath of dreaming. Mary breathed in starts. Gasps. Many of the girls did, herself included.

Mary rolled over toward her, her cot creaking. "Eva?"

"Mmm?"

"Tell me about the sea."

"You've been to the sea," Eva murmured, waiting for her medicine to roll her into the deepness of a different sea. A sea free of memory.

"Please. I want to hear it."

Eva blew out a breath. "If you wish it, Mary." She opened her eyes to the darkness, trying to sharpen her dull mind. "When you go down to the sea, the first thing you will notice is the scent. The air is heavy with salt and the wind whips against your skin, clean and crisp."

"Not like here," Mary interrupted.

"No. Not like here." They had this conversation at least twice a week and it was almost always the same every time. It was comforting. Once, she'd loved the sea above any place on earth. "Then you hear it. Before you even see it, you hear the waves crashing and roaring to the shore, making you feel as if you are a part of its wildness."

Mary let out a contented sigh. "We'll go to Brighton, won't we? We'll walk along the promenade?"

Eva half nodded in the darkness. "We'll buy ices and eat just a bite before we toss them away."

"Because we can."

"Exactly." But they never would. Neither of them would ever leave this place.

Footsteps thudded down the hallway, drawing close. Lone footsteps. Boot steps. Eva froze, her voice dying swiftly. It was important to know what shoes made what sound. If one knew what shoes, then one knew who was coming.

Mary tensed, her sheet rustling. "Do you hear that?" she whispered.

"Yes."

"God, not tonight," Mary whimpered. "Not tonight."

"Shh." Eva's fingers clutched her raspy sheet. If they just lay still enough, quiet enough, he would pass.

"I hate him. I hate, hate, hate—"

"Mary!" she hissed, reaching across the short space between their cots and grabbing the girl's hand. Their fingers intertwined for a moment.

The boot steps paused before their narrow cell and the ghoulish light of a lantern drifted in through the small cracks lining their door.

Eva's heart thudded painfully. Even her medicine couldn't dull the sudden fear that crawled along her neck. Fear for herself . . . but even more fear for Mary, who endured the keeper's advances.

Keys chinked together and the keeper Matthew coughed. It was a loud, wet cough full of phlegm. The light swayed, doubtless as he looked for the key he wanted.

Mary's fingers tightened around hers, and Eva willed her to be silent. If they were quiet, he would not pick them. He wouldn't. She had to believe that.

The squeal of long-neglected hinges drifted through their door. They could hear his boots as he entered the room next to theirs. The girls on the other side of the thin wall scrambled on their cots.

A shriek followed, then the smack of human flesh to human flesh.

The girl's continuous cries filtered down the halls, mixed with Matthew's grunts. Every girl would hear it, Eva knew. She'd stayed in many of the rooms. She had heard many a cry. And tonight she was just thankful the cry was not hers. Or Mary's. She'd cried enough, her body beaten and bruised. But such were the punishments of fighting off the keepers. 'Twas perverse the way the keepers had their favorites, and though Matthew beat her regularly he did not care for her body, bearing as it did the traces of childbirth. So she had never been touched in such a way at the asylum. Matthew and his fellows preferred a slight, young body like Mary's, unmarred by anything but their corruption.

And so she and Mary clung to each other. Listening. Listening to the sounds that would be their own some other night. For the battle they would have to fight to retain whatever was left of themselves.

Eva stared into the blackness, thoughts of the sea fading away with all the other memories that had died in this place of punishment.

No one would come to free her. And after what she had done, no one should.

The burning scent of lye assaulted Ian's nose, stinging his eyes. He wiped at the water abruptly lining his lids and looked up at the house. If it could be called a house. Blackened brick walls stood in austere determination against the muddy, grave-strewn yard. There were no windows, except for a few on the first floor. Smoke curled like devil's forks from a series of chimneys lining the crown of the slate roof. Even the snow piling up against the sides of the building could not purify the misery leaking through the mortar.

Ian marched up the worn, uneven stone steps and slammed his gloved fist against the wood paneling. Moans filtered from the other side of the door, and then high-pitched laughter cackled from above. The kind of wild laughter that came with minds lost and broken.

A shiver twisted down his spine. He'd been to madhouses before, brought poor chaps whose brains had just shattered after battle, but those places had been different. They'd been unpleasant, filled with chained-up men scratching at themselves, but there had been a cleanliness and air of concern.

This place? Out in the middle of the Yorkshire moors?

Ian fingered the burgeoning sack of gold guineas tucked in his coat and then slipped his fingers to the pistol secured at the back of his trousers. This place was meant to suck the hope out of a soul. To render a person silent and lost.

And there was no way in hell he'd let that happen to Eva.

Metal clattered and chinked on the other side of the door. At last it swung open. The man before him was a good six feet tall and his chest was as broad as a bull's. A dark brown coat covered his shoulders, swinging open to reveal a dirt-streaked shirt. Lank brown hair slicked the sides of his pockmarked face. The stink of grease and slop buckets rolled off him. His piglike eyes roved up and down Ian. He rolled black iron keys in his sausage grip, contemplating what appeared to be exceptionally rare: a visitor. His thick lips worked for a moment before spitting out, "Whot?"

Ian stood his ground, knowing his nobility would at least see him inside. "I've come to see the head of this establishment."

The man blinked vacantly as if he had never seen an outsider, then squared a belligerent chin. "You have an appointment?" he challenged. "If not, shuffle on."

Ian lifted an imperious brow, calling upon the innate air that came with title, estates, and an education at one of the high-brow Thomas Aquinas philosophical institutions in Oxford. He may have been born to a second son, but fate had dictated his ascension to the title of viscount upon his uncle's death. And as his uncle's heir, he'd been raised to wield authority. A lackey was not going to stand in his way now. "I didn't think an appointment was necessary. I am hardly checking myself in."

The man hesitated, shifting awkwardly from one lardfilled leg to the other. "Whot name?"

"I am Lord Carin." The lie slipped past his lips with ridiculous ease. One learned to lie swiftly in the army and with as much conviction as a Methodist protesting the evils of liquor.

"Fine, then." The servant edged back from the door, his body eclipsed by shadows. "Follow me."

Ian nodded and stepped into the asylum. Instantly, he was bathed in shadow. It took a moment for him to adjust to the gloom. And as his eyes adjusted, the scent assailed him. Lord, the smell of lye was far preferable to the wretched stench of unwashed human and raw fear permeating the stagnant indoor air.

A chain slithered down the hall, its big, sooty links heavy upon the floor. Ian followed its length with his gaze and his heart slammed in his chest. A girl, no more than twenty, sat upon the floor, her blond head shaved but with errant tufts sticking in wiry brushes. Her ratty dress hung in stained scraps about her thin frame. A big, black metal cuff circled her ankle. And as any chain would do, it had cut sores into her delicate flesh. Unattended, blood slipped down to her foot. Absently, she picked at the loose splinters in the floor.

"Why is she tied?" Ian whispered, his voice sticking in his throat.

The servant laughed. "Well, they will try to run away, won't they? There're only five of us keepers, and there's more than a baker's dozen of them." He walked over to the girl, who cringed and pulled back as far as she could to the wall. Patting her head, he crooned, "You've tried to run three times, haven't you, pet? But Matthew caught you."

Ian had seen enough horror for one lifetime, enough innocents slaughtered, but this was an entirely different level of hell. Ian cleared his throat. "I'm by no means a patient man."

Matthew shrugged his hulking shoulders, then gave the girl a chuck under the chin. She didn't jerk away and, after her earlier cringe, remained bizarrely still as if she'd slipped away to some unseen world. The keeper laughed softly, then straightened. "Come along, my lord."

God, he needed to see Eva, to see that she was unharmed. But in reality, he knew he might see her terrorized like the poor creature on the floor.

Perhaps . . . The thought hit him hard enough to make him sick. Perhaps Thomas, the true Lord Carin, was correct. It might have been better if she had died than be condemned to a place such as this.

They headed down the dim, austere hall, scratching sounds coming through the walls. "Why are there no candles?" Ian finally inquired.

"They're more quiet in the dark."

Or more afraid in the dark.

They remained silent as they wound down the halls to the back of the establishment.

"Here we are." The man knocked on the paneled door.

A light voice called, "Yes? Do come in."

As the door swung open, Ian prayed that Thomas had never met the master of this interminable place. If he had, the ruse was up. But he had a strong feeling that Thomas wouldn't want to have dirtied his hands with such a place or transaction.

Surely, even Thomas, Eva's legal guardian, had soul enough not to knowingly deposit her in this pit?

As golden light slid over his boots and he crossed the threshold, he realized he had been mistaken: there was no master.

A mature woman of about five and thirty sat behind a simple desk. Her large, wine-colored skirts flowed around her, and a snowy lace cap covered auburn blond hair. She stood with surprising grace, completely at ease in the office filled with paintings of pastoral scenes and little shepherdess statuettes. "Good afternoon." Her voice was soft. Comforting. Like a deep flowing river.

Ian forced himself to give a slight bow. "Good afternoon. Mrs. . . . ?"

"Mrs. Palmer, of course." She gestured with a delicate yet capable hand to the chair before her desk. "Do sit down. And you are?"

"Lord Carin," Ian announced as he crossed to the plain wood seat, polished to a sleek finish. It positively gleamed. In fact, everything in the room was in exacting order. There was no clutter atop her pristine desk or ornament on the table before the window. Everything was in a perfect place, just like the folds of her gown and the strands of her contained coiffure.

Ian lowered himself onto the chair, keeping his gaze fixed upon her.

"Tea?" she inquired.

"No." Somehow the very idea of tea while sitting just a few feet away from such misery seemed especially disgusting. Though he had known a few generals who sipped their champagne as battles unfurled before them.

She closed the ledger before her, careful of the spine, then set it aside like a well-loved child. "We rarely receive visitors."

Ian rested a brown-gloved hand over his knee. "Yes, I understand it's not best for them."

She laughed softly, folding her hands before her on the desk. "Or for their guardians."

It felt as if he'd been thrust into some topsy-turvy world. The woman looked as if she should be surrounded by a host of teasing admirers, not be the mistress of a madhouse, its victims tortured and harried. "I'm afraid I don't quite understand your sentiment."

"Please, my lord, this is a house of secrets." She smiled, a tight, calculated gesture. Not too broad, not too small. "You need not worry. I take very good care of my clients."

Just exactly how did she take care of them? Or what, rather, did she do for them? "I do appreciate your discretion."

She inclined her head modestly. "Thank you. My discretion is what ensures my prosperity. Now, I must admit your presence is . . . odd."

Ian braced an elbow on the chair's arm, forcing himself to nonchalance. "I've come to see Lady Carin."

Her brows lifted ever so slightly. "Have you?"

"Yes."

"I assure you she is quite happy here."

"I am not questioning her happiness or your ability to provide it. I simply require that I should see her."

Silence stretched between them for several seconds. "Of course." She eyed him carefully. "Our dear Eva is still very beautiful." A strange smile tilted the woman's mouth and her eyes lit up. With hunger. With anticipation. "Would you like me to arrange a private room for the two of you?"

Ian's first reaction was to reach over the desk and throttle the woman with his clenched fists. A direct assault, however, would not likely free Eva. But what was this? A bordello? To Ian's disgust, he admitted that it very well might be. After all, it was a house of secrets. And secrets came in many forms. Well, he would rip down every shred of wood before he left Eva here. "Yes, a private room would best suit my needs."

She gave the barest of nods. Her hand moved to rest

lovingly on her ledger. "You contribute generously to keep your ward safe and that is much appreciated."

Oh, he contributed generously, did he? Thomas was paying this woman to keep Eva's existence a secret. Still, Ian had to admit, to a man like Thomas a madwoman was indeed a horrible secret to be kept from society. After all, the ton would worry such a scandalous thing like a dog with a bone until there was no more marrow to be had. The Carins would forever be known as a family touched by madness. A family to be shunned.

Ian shifted in his chair and smiled at Mrs. Palmer. A reassuring smile. The same kind of smile a man wore when facing the evil sights of an enemy. Cocky and determined. "Lead me to her, then."

She tutted, leaning back into her chair. "We shall first have to collect her from the yard, my lord. She is being exercised. As soon as she is presentable, we will ensure you are brought to her."

Fury burned in his throat, acidic and harsh, but he controlled himself, focusing on what he truly wanted: Eva's release.

Eva had always been beautiful and full of life, the first to play games, to ride, to run, despite the lack of female virtues attributed to such actions. Now she was being exercised—as one might walk a dog or put a horse through its paces.

Mrs. Palmer tilted her gleaming head to the side. "Would that be satisfactory?"

"Indeed." He forced himself to remain calm. As satisfying as it might be to rip this woman to shreds, the only thing that mattered now was freeing Eva.

No, he would stick to his course, keep his reserve. Mad or no, Eva would be gone from this place.

Chapter 3

When he had stepped aboard that ship in India to set sail for his mother shore, Ian had felt certain he had left the worst horrors of his life behind him. He had been certain nothing could be worse than watching the blood pour from Hamilton's body, his friend's eyes wide, panicked . . . betrayed.

He'd been mistaken.

With every step he took, his understanding of horror altered. He had not even known what it was. He'd assumed it was dead men, their bodies ripped apart. This place changed all that.

He struggled for air. If the oppressive nature of the hellhole was any indication, the body was nothing compared to the soul. And the walls of this asylum seemed to shudder with the souls of destroyed innocents.

This was horror in all its destructive glory.

Worse than this realization was the growing knowledge that his guilt had not let him return sooner. Because of pride, he'd condemned Eva to damnation. Even one day sooner would have been better to take her from this place.

He swallowed, trying to rid himself of the acrid taste of misery that drifted in the very air about him.

Nothing was as it should be any longer.

Even doors were no longer doors. They were portals

to hell. As he neared this newest one, behind which Eva waited, he knew without a doubt that there were levels of perdition and he had surely descended into the most despicable.

The sodding keeper opened the splintered wood door for him. The heavy panel creaked as it swung. "She's been medicated, my lord. Though she's not a violent one." He laughed. "Leastways, not anymore."

"Thank you." How he wanted to burn the damn place down to a cinder, or perhaps rip that thick throat out. It would be hard for the bag of filth to laugh without a windpipe, but such an action would not be conducive to his immediate plan to keep Eva safe.

Dim light filtered through the room from the lone lamp that hung from the ceiling. There were no windows. No chairs. Just a bed, wide enough for two.

Ian drew in a slow breath and stepped in. The door swung shut behind him and it locked with a solid thud. Once again, his eyes struggled against the weird light. Shadows tossed themselves over the floor. Strips of yellow-gold light bathed the bed.

He narrowed his eyes. Where was she?

A shuffle echoed in the silence and he whipped around. A slight movement caught his eye. There by the door, hiding by the hinges, stood a woman. She half faced the wall. A brown sack dress hung on her emaciated frame. Black hair caressed her cheeks, so short it could never be pulled back. And her eyes?

He could barely see them in the murky light. The pupils were so small all he could see was blue. The blue of piercing indigo and long-forgotten summer.

She swayed slightly and Ian darted forward, ready to catch her. But she floated away. Her body moved like the most delicate butterfly in the breeze. If he touched her, she would shatter, wings broken, earthbound.

She wasn't here anymore. She wasn't in the room, and it broke what remained of his heart. "Eva?" he whispered, tears stinging his eyes.

She tilted her head toward him, but she stared into the distance, her eyes wide.

He ached to take her in his arms. To fold her up in care as no one had done in a very long time. To catch that once perfect essence that had captured Hamilton's heart, and his own, so long ago before everything had changed. "Eva, love, do you hear me?"

Her motions were slow, as if suspended in water. She blinked, then turned to him. She stared at his face.

Ian frowned. She stared, but was she even looking at him? She appeared not to see beyond her own nose. Perhaps not even that far. Perhaps she saw nothing but the nightmares of her own mind.

He didn't know for certain. But he had to do something, anything, to make her remember.

Ian took a step forward, his hand outreached.

A whimper strangled her throat as she wrenched back from his touch so fast she nearly tripped. "N-no. N-no!" she shrieked, panic shooting her voice up an octave.

He pressed her to his chest, pain at her thinness coursing through him. Lord, he could feel every one of her ribs. "Eva, oh, love, don't you recall? Remember Ian? Remember the sea and ices? And running through the grass?" He spoke quickly, firmly, determined to bring her back. And if he held her, if he kept talking, she would remember it all, remember who she was.

She tensed in his hold, angling her body away from his, but she stopped struggling. Her breath came in sharp, shallow gasps.

Ever so slowly, she lifted her gaze to his. Light sparked in them and her brows drew together. "I—I know you."

He nodded. "Oh, yes, Eva. You do." His heart burned

with the pain of it. Shadows smudged her eyes and he could smell the laudanum upon her breath. How bloody much had they given her?

Enough to leave her lost in the nightmares of the past. Enough to torture her for an eternity. Her fingertips dug into his biceps. Her lips pursed as if she was trying to say something. She swallowed. "Ian?"

He nodded quickly. Relief pummeled him so fiercely it was painful. "Yes, Eva, yes. It's Ian."

"Why are you here?" She pushed at him slightly, hands moving from his arms to press against his chest. "You have to go," she whispered urgently. She pushed at him again, her touch more desperate, more forceful. "They might try to keep you here."

Even now, she thought of others before herself. Even now, she placed his safety before her own. He clasped her to him, careful lest she break right before his gaze. "No, Eva. They could never. I'm taking you with me."

Her eyes darted to the door, then back to him as if she didn't understand. "Leave? Here?"

"Yes," he said firmly. "Forever."

Tears filled her eyes. "You're lying again. Please don't lie. They told me I'd never be well enough to go."

His heart wrenched. He'd told her only one lie in all the years they'd known each other. To hear her mention it now in her state was nearly his undoing. He had told her and Hamilton's father that he would protect his friend. It had not been true. Hamilton was never coming home.

That venture, meant to recapture friendship and honor, had ended in death and misery. But he wouldn't allow his own shortcomings to dictate Eva's fate any longer.

He commanded the pain away and smoothed her hair back, short though it was, and murmured against her temple, "Sweetheart, you never should have been here at all."

"Oh, yes." She nodded jerkily against him. "Yes, I should." Her voice shook and her slender fingers twisted into his linen shirt. "I did something terrible, Ian. Terrible." Her lashes and tears brushed against his neck. "You must leave me here." Her entire body tensed against his. "To pay for what I've done."

"None of that. Come, now," he soothed, not daring to think overlong on the accident that had broken her mind. He took one of her icy, soot-marked hands in his and enveloped it lightly. "I promise, I will help you."

She nodded again, but strangely, at the same time, she said, "No one can, Ian. No one."

He drew her carefully back against his chest. She was wrong, so very wrong. Never in his life had anything felt more right than his helping her. Even here, where so many women had been left to die, with her pressed against him, he knew that he would rescue her—no matter the cost.

Chapter 4

England
Sixteen years earlier

*I*an's fingers curled, empty of his toy elephant. It had been a gift from his father after a long journey with the new governor general of India. His father had said that they'd hunted many tigers, but the elephants had been the most interesting. Big, funny-looking things with noses as long as flagpoles.

Ian missed the gift very much, but he'd given it away to someone who needed it more. He stared up at the wide stairs, half hearing the whispered voices of his new guardian, Lord Carin, and the solicitor making the last arrangements for his stay at Carridan Hall.

Ian looked down at the dirty gray light that poured in the tall parlor windows, spilling over his feet. He had a scuff on his boot. Mama would not have liked that at all. Swallowing back the ache in his throat, Ian bent over and rubbed at the mark on his black shoe, but it wouldn't come free. He frowned. And much to his dismay, a tear slipped out his eye and down his cheek.

"Hello?"

Horror-struck to be caught crying like a baby, he whipped his head up and dashed a hand over his eyes. He blinked as he spotted the girl standing not more than two *feet away. She'd sneaked up on him like a fairy creature. She looked like a fairy creature, too. Great big blue eyes stared out of her pale small face and her black hair was a wild riot of curls down her back. In her arms, she held a stuffed black dog with a red bow about its neck.*

He drew in a shallow breath, wishing that he was that little toy tucked carefully in her arms; she looked so kind and only a little younger than himself. "Who are you?" he said, far more rudely than he'd intended.

"My name is Eva. I live here." She cocked her head to the side. "Why are you crying?"

"I'm not."

"You are indeed. Your eyes are all red."

He looked away. He wasn't going to argue with her. So the best thing was just to tell the truth. That's what his papa would have said. "My parents have died."

Her dark brows lifted and her pink mouth opened slightly before she nodded matter-of-factly. "It's a very good reason to cry. I cried all the time."

"Your parents, too?"

"They died when I was four. Ages ago now. Lord Carin liked my papa very much and so took me in because I haven't any other family. He says I'm to marry Hamilton when we are of age. And then I shall always be a part of the family."

"Oh." For some reason, this struck him as most unpleasant. And a brief, sharp jealousy of this Hamilton boy flared in his chest. "Do you want to marry him?"

She looked at him as if he'd sprouted a second head. "It's my duty," she said, though she looked a little confused by the word.

Duty. He'd heard that word so many times. His nanny had said he mustn't fail in his duty to his mama and papa and must not cry. Gentlemen didn't cry. So he understood. Duty was important but hard.

"*It's very sad about your mama and papa, but you shall be happy again.*"

So many people had told him that, but when she said it, he knew she spoke the truth. It was a funny feeling in his belly, like butterflies doing a springtime dance. He pointed at her toy, not wanting to speak of sad things any longer. He'd never seen anything quite like it. "That's a very nice dog."

"*My mama made it for me. Before she died,*" *she said softly, then smiled.*

All his limbs seemed to suddenly seize up. Why was it so hard to move? Even his breath seemed to do a strange little skip. Her smile—it made him want her to look at him that way always. Ian brushed his hair out of his eyes so as not to appear a complete dunce. "What's his name?"

"*Magilicutty.*"

"*That's a funny sort of name.*"

"*He's a funny sort of dog.*" *She squeezed the little fellow tight, looked down at it, then looked back up at Ian. "I say, haven't you got a toy?"*

He shook his head.

"*Everyone should have one,*" *she said most seriously.*

He bit his lip, his throat tightening up again. "I had an elephant."

Her eyes grew big with delight. "Really? I've seen them only in picture books. Hamilton has a book of animals and I should like to see one made up. Such a thing would be much more interesting than my Magilicutty, love him as I do. May I meet him?"

Ian shook his head, trying to not let the image of his mother lying quite still and cold in the polished wood box linger in his head.

"*Why ever not?*"

"*He's—he's with my mama.*"

"*Oh.*" *She breathed. "To protect her."*

"I thought she might be lonely . . . in the ground."

"That was very good of you. But she shan't be lonely. There are far too many angels for that. But she will most likely like to have something of yours in heaven. So that's good."

He hadn't thought of it like that. "Yes."

The sounds of running feet echoed through the hall and Eva sighed. "Hamilton."

Another boy of about Ian's age came running into the foyer and stopped suddenly at the sight of them. His dark brown hair glinted in the sun and he had dirt smudged on his nose. A mischievous glint warmed his eyes. "Are you Ian?"

Ian nodded, staring at the boy who would live with Eva forever. After all, that's what husbands and wives did. Or, at least, that was what his mama had said.

"You must be bored witless. Standing here talking to a girl. I've been waiting ages for a mate. So let's go fishing."

Ian shifted on his feet. Fishing? He'd dearly love to go. He glanced at Eva. "Can she come?"

Hamilton scowled. "Eva? She's a girl."

Ian drew himself up and said, "She's my friend."

Hamilton threw up his hands. "Oh, all right." Then he pointed at Eva. "Don't get in the way."

"Of course I shan't. I'm quite good with worms."

Ian laughed. Something caught his attention and he looked up, spotting a small sandy-haired boy peering down at them from the landing. "Who is that?"

Hamilton glanced up, then shrugged. "That's just Thomas."

"Does he want to come?"

Hamilton hesitated, then called up, "Would you like to come, Thomas?"

The boy jerked back from the stairs and ran down the hall.

Ian listened to the retreating steps, a funny feeling wobbling down his spine. There was something strange about the sandy-haired boy.

"Here, now." *Hamilton's face grew serious, drawing Ian's focus as he crossed the short space between them. Hamilton placed his hand on Ian's shoulder.* "You've had a bad time of it, but Eva and I will sort you out. Just you wait and see."

Then, without another word about it, Hamilton marched off, waving his hand for them to follow.

Eva scooted up to Ian and whispered. "You can have Magilicutty sometimes, if you want. No one needs to know. He's a very good dog."

"Thank you," *he whispered back, his heart lighter than it had been since a very horrible day in a very horrible cemetery.*

England
The Present

Someone had come for her.

Ian. Ian had come for her.

The black room wrapped her up in its crushing embrace as she allowed her gaze to adjust to the shapes and shadows. But this night she clung to a sliver of hope. More than half of her was certain her medicine had made her believe Ian had come.

Yet it couldn't be her imaginings. For he had not been the Ian of her childhood. The Ian she had once loved. The Ian who had told her he wasn't coming back. Nor was it the Ian who had stood pale and distant on her wedding day, promising that he would bring Hamilton back.

No, this Ian's face was lined with hardship. With pain. And his body . . . he was so large and strong. He could break her in a moment, but he had held her so gently. As if he knew that she might run at the first touch.

He had come back. Against all hope, he'd come back to her. But now it was too late.

"Who was it?" Mary's innocently rich voice penetrated the dark.

"Pardon?"

"It was all over the yard." Mary shifted on the bed, rolling onto her side. "Beth saw a man enter the house. You saw him. Didn't you?"

Eva swallowed. She was afraid to speak of it aloud. If she spoke of it, it might make it not true. At last she confessed softly, "Yes."

"What did he want? Did he hurt you?"

"No." He had touched her with such kindness. Then again, he couldn't possibly know why she was here. He could not know that she alone was responsible for . . . She shook her head furiously, fighting back the memories.

No. If he had, he would have hurled her to the ground. And left her here.

Instead, he'd promised to take her from this place.

For the first time in years, her heart swelled with something besides dread. His eyes had been so green. The green of limes and malachite.

"You're going to leave me, aren't you?" Mary's voice was dead.

Eva closed her eyes, the pain licking back into her heart. "I don't ever want to leave you."

"But you will," Mary said flatly as she rolled onto her back. "I am glad of it."

Tears stung Eva's eyes. The thought of leaving her only friend penetrated the haze that drifted about her. "Oh, Mary. I'll find you. I'll—"

"Shh!"

The *clink, clink, clink* of keys echoed down the hall, accompanied by the steady thud of boots. Matthew's.

Eva's eyes snapped wide against the blackness. Praying that Matthew would pass their door, she stared at the flat panel. She willed it to stay shut.

Mary's hand flew across the small space between their beds, grabbing at her fingers.

The lantern light stopped right in front of their cell. There was a muttered curse as Matthew fumbled as he always did with his keys. The yellow-gold beams slid through the cracks and threw bright lines on the dark floor.

No. It wasn't fair. Ian had promised to take her away. Now she was here, unable to escape. Unable to escape the beating that was about to come. Defending Mary. Defending herself.

A key slipped into their lock, tumbling the mechanism.

Eva slipped her feet over the side of the bed, not caring that the floor was frigid against her bare skin. She sucked in several slow breaths, ready to receive a beating like no other. But she would not let Matthew touch Mary. Not tonight, when hope was on the horizon.

Mary's fingers slipped away and she reached under her mattress. Her small hand clasped something, then pulled. It was a long piece of iron. A rusty old blade that looked as if it had been pried off a door. "Leave him to me."

"No." Eva stood and faced the door. "We'll do this together."

And the door creaked open.

"I am removing Lady Carin this evening." Already, night had fallen, the gaslights sputtering in the small office. With every passing shade of night, Ian grew more furious. The damn woman was prevaricating.

Mrs. Palmer glared at him as though he was the one

who was mad. "I cannot just release her to you, my lord." Calmly, she poured tea in a steady stream. Steam wafted about her delicate fingers as the liquid filled the blue-and-white china. "You committed her for a reason."

"Yes," he clipped. And though he longed to smash the cup, he took the delicate bone china in his large hand. "And I paid you for upkeep these months and now I will take her with me."

"But—" Her eyes darted about the room as she clearly realized she was about to lose a great deal of money. She drew herself up, cold and determined. "She is not cured."

He held his cup, frozen in the air. Cured? The only thing a soul might be cured of here was sanity. "It matters not to me. Not anymore."

"But you cannot possibly oversee her well-being," she scoffed. She slammed down her own teacup. The little silver spoon jumped on the saucer. She drew in a quick breath, then righted the spoon, angling it so it sat delicately along the saucer. "She must be guarded. Controlled."

It took every ounce of control he had to remain seated. Ian had agreed to be civil and drink tea. If he'd had his way, he would have brewed it out of a bottle of laudanum so the woman might live and die in the same torturous dreams she delivered to her wards. He had seen the effects of laudanum over a prolonged period of time. They were neither attractive or kind. "I am sure I shall cope and I certainly have the means to hire private keepers."

Mrs. Palmer's composed features tightened, her lips pursing. "This is most irregular. When patients come here—"

"They don't leave?" he challenged. He leaned forward and very slowly placed his cup down upon her desk.

"Your premises are obviously questionable, madam. Do you even employ a physician?"

Her silence hung in the air and, for one brief moment, Ian could have sworn there was a thread of regret in the woman. Finally, she lifted her teacup to her lips. "It is a waste of funds," she said, her voice hard and uncompromising. Final.

Anger throttled through him. He'd seen this attitude with more frequency than he cared to admit. Generals, fellow colonels, and Hamilton had all believed that certain people were expendable. "They are not even human to you, are they?" His fingers curled, hungry to strangle the woman so piously sitting across from him. "They are but numbers in your ledger and coins in your purse."

"It is important to remain detached from them." She took a delicate swallow, then lifted her eyes, completely unmoved in the face of his anger. Only sheer confidence glittered in her gaze. "I shall release Lady Carin. But only on one condition: one hundred guineas."

There it was. Exactly what he'd expected and at present what he wanted. "Is that your standard fee?"

"My lord, my husband taught me well the value of commerce. Do not abase me."

He inclined his head. "I bow to your business acumen."

"Thank you."

"Best be wary, though. Someone might report you to the authorities based on such corruptions."

She laughed. A brittle, amused laugh. The lace at her throat shook slightly, causing her cameo brooch to wink in the light. "Oh, my lord, do you think they care for the fate of these women?" Wiping her eyes, she looked up at him. Harsh reality replaced her amusement. "Men do not bring women here because they are mad." She shoved back her chair, her wine-colored skirts whooshing against the floor. "They bring women here to silence them. If you wish me to keep your secret, I will not do so gratis." She planted her palms on her desk and leveled him with an unyielding stare. "My customers pay or I send a letter to the authorities intimating their business."

Ian folded his arms across his chest, fascination for this cold jailor mixed with his disgust. It galled him that her words rang true. "Is that so?"

"It is the good fortune of having some very powerful friends with wives and daughters who even now live under my roof. I do think they would protect me from such threats as you have posited. Don't you?"

The muscles in his jaw tightened with contempt. Contempt for the inhuman thing before him profiting off her fellow women's heartache and loathing for the men who had the power to send a woman here without question. "Yes. They would. Your services are in high demand, no doubt."

She smiled as if they had just agreed on the sale of a splendid horse. "One hundred guineas and you can take your lady anywhere you please."

Ian grated his teeth for a moment. "Certainly." He reached into his cloak.

Slowly, she eased her position, standing fully. "And if this clears you of ready cash, we have a remarkably resourceful bank in the village. Give them my name and they shall certainly extend credit in your honor."

"My thanks." He pulled the heavy leather purse from his coat and tossed it with a clunk onto her desk. It sat between them. To him, it was nothing. A small pile of his many piles of coins stacked in some bank somewhere. To the women in this establishment, such gold was either salvation or the metal that kept them imprisoned. "Have her made ready. We leave in a quarter of an hour."

"Out of the question. The girls are sleeping and Matthew and the other keepers are—"

Screams echoed overhead. Heartrending battle screams.

Without a moment's hesitation, Mrs. Palmer yanked open her desk drawer. The wood shrieked at the harsh treatment. She dug into the drawer and pulled out a pistol. "Matthew!" she shouted, marching for the door.

Ian darted after her and locked his hand onto her wrist. In one swift motion, he twisted the pistol from her fingers. "I don't think so."

Her eyes flared in alarm. "I will have order," she hissed.

"I won't give you a chance to shoot one of them." He slipped the weapon into his belt and strode to the door. "Lock yourself in if you are so afraid."

He ran out into the dim hall.

Screams ricocheted off the walls. He darted forward and immediately tripped on the long chain draped down the hall. He plunged forward in darkness and his knee cracked on the wood floor. Pain spiked up his thigh.

He ignored it. Didn't care about it. He shoved himself to his feet and charged down the hall and to the winding stair drenched in darkness. "Eva!" he shouted.

He tore up the stairs, then turned down the loudest hall. One door stood open. The faint glow of a lantern filled the empty space. On the floor, a long pool of black liquid fingered its way over the wood.

Blood.

Oh, God. Eva.

"Mary!" Eva scrambled forward, her hands shaking.

"We've done it!" Mary exclaimed, her voice shrill with triumph and adrenaline. "At last! We've done it! We go to Brighton!"

Mary stood over Matthew's body. Her frayed brown

shift was torn down the shoulder, exposing one pale, small breast. Her hand was still up in the air, the iron blade tightly clenched. Even in the yellow light, Eva could see the whiteness of her knuckles.

Blood dripped from the dull blade. It splashed onto Mary's toes. "He'll not hurt anyone again. Not you. Not me. Not anyone." Mary shook her head, her soft hair ghostly in the lamplight. "Never."

"They'll be here soon." Eva bit down on her lower lip as she stepped closer to the body. What were they going to do now? She crept toward Mary's hand, ready to take the weapon. Matthew groaned, his body shuddering. Eva bent to kick his head, but before she could Mary let out a ferocious cry. She dropped to one knee and drove the blade into his chest.

Eva watched with horrified fascination at the fervor brightening her friend's face. Matthew deserved to die. No one deserved it more, except perhaps the bitch downstairs. Yet still, the terror of it. The reality. The smell of iron in the air, the stench of his fluid. It should have made her long to faint. Instead, she was all the more awake.

"We're free now," Mary muttered, lifting her face, her eyes closed with peace. "Finally, we're free."

Matthew jerked once more, then stilled.

Letting go of the blade, Mary stood. She wiped a blood-streaked hand over her face.

Eva remained standing by the body, her gaze fixed upon the blade whilst listening to the escalating sounds outside their little cell.

Screams and banging surrounded them and Mary's hands slammed up to her ears. Blood smeared her opalescent skin. "Why are they screaming?"

"They know," Eva stated. Dread weighed her stomach, replacing the exhilaration. "They know we've done it."

Footsteps thundered up the stairs. Different steps. Steps she didn't know.

Quick. Quick. What were they to do? For sure they'd be killed for what they'd done. No one would ever think twice about two more graves out in the courtyard.

"Someone's coming!" Mary cried. Terror creased her face into a mask.

"Hide. Under the bed." Some strange stillness came over Eva. An old courage she could not recall drove her to grab the slippery blade.

Wordlessly, Mary dropped to her knees, then tucked herself under the small bunk.

The steps grew closer. Slowing. They paused just outside the door.

Eva swallowed, her palms wet with sweat and sticky now with Matthew's blood. She could do this. She could protect them.

Chapter 5

Ian skidded into the room and scrambled to a halt as his boot nearly slammed down onto the keeper's skull. His eye caught a flash of movement, and he twisted toward it. A dull blade came down. He seized the small wrist driving it, halting it midswing.

There she was. Her panicked face white in the sparse light. Fear and resolve glowed in her wide eyes. "Eva!"

She winced at his imprisoning arm, struggling to drive the blade down; then she looked at him. Recognition flared in her gaze. "Ian?" she rasped.

"Yes." Sure that she knew him, he loosened his grip and snatched the rough weapon from her. Wet, warm blood slicked his fingers. He grimaced at the familiar liquid.

More steps thundered on the floor below. The other keepers. He had to get her out—and now. God alone knew how Mrs. Palmer would react to this. Most likely she'd demand more money, which in itself was not a significant problem. But she wouldn't let Eva go until she had it. And there was no way he was leaving her here for another moment. "We're going."

He dropped the blade and it clunked on Matthew's fleshy body. The filthy, ballooned figure sparked no pity in him. He started forward and his boot squelched. More blood. A thick pool of it.

God, what kind of hell had Eva endured that she would kill so brutally?

"Wait!" she hissed.

"Come now," he snapped back. Ignoring her protests, he yanked Eva into his arms, lifting her off her feet and cradling her against his chest. "We have to go."

"Eva?!" a girl's fragile voice called out. Her gaunt frame darted out from under the bed and sprang with surprising speed to her feet. "This is him? The man who came to save you?"

Nodding, Eva forced herself out of Ian's embrace, her feet thunking on the floor. Quickly, she glanced up at him, clutching fistfuls of his dark coat. "We have to take Mary. We must."

He snapped his gaze from one woman to the next, unsure how the hell he'd gotten into such a situation. "Christ, this is a debacle."

Mary drew up beside Eva, her wiry body crackling with ferocity. A sharp little cackle of exultation tumbled from her mouth. "I killed that bastard and he deserved it. I'd kill every one of them."

Ian blinked at the tigerish voice echoing from Mary's small frame. "Later. You can kill them later."

Mary's eyes glowed with such ferocious courage that he had to yank his gaze from them before he could formulate his thoughts.

He should just leave this other girl. He was here to save Eva. But one look at Eva's imploring face and the other girl's elfin one, so frail from neglect, and he found himself saying the words he should not: "We all go."

"Thank you." Eva gasped. "Thank you."

They hurried out into the hall, their harsh breaths like a wild chorus of wind. But they had gone only a few feet when they heard the heavy, furious clomp of boots tearing up the stairs.

The keepers. They were coming.

"Back passage?" he demanded. There was no time for softness. Later—he could be soft with her later. When she was safe.

Eva didn't even flinch at his abruptness but rather whipped a finger toward the end of the hall. He grabbed up both girls' hands and ran toward the dark stairwell, racing them to escape. The three of them, an incongruous sight, dashed down the hall.

The girls in their ratty shifts, animated with a mad sort of hope, could not dim his own fury and awareness that they were but a heartbeat away from capture.

As they ran down the passage, the screams and pounding registered among his controlled thoughts. The others. The other girls locked up behind the doors in the long passage. How many were imprisoned here in never-ending hell? He scrubbed the thought away, knowing what he must do, resolving to return. To save them all after the two firmly at his side were safe.

They clattered down the last of the back stairs, not giving a whit for silence, all of them knowing pursuit was on their heels like devil dogs. His shoulders banged on the wooden walls, the stairs were so narrow, but the girls were fleet as they charged downward and spilled out into a small hallway that led to a door.

Mary's hand tore from his and she flung herself at the door. "Locked!"

He'd never seen anything like her madness, her body flailing passionately against her barrier to freedom. "Step back," he ordered.

She didn't listen but rather raked her hand down the wood.

Eva tried to grab her, but Mary wouldn't stop.

Not allowing himself to regret the use of force, Ian seized Mary's shoulders, pulled her away, and shoved her into Eva's waiting arms. He raised one booted foot and slammed with all his might. The hinges screamed and then the cheap wood shredded, the panel giving way and swinging open drunkenly. "Go!"

If they could just reach his carriage, they would be away from this place.

They tumbled out into the frigid air, the wind tearing up the walled yard. In the distance, the arched gateway onto the moors beckoned, open. Snow swirled fiercely, blurring the air.

His carriage sat not twenty feet away, his coachman shivering in the blistering wind. "Make ready!" Ian shouted.

The coachman shook himself, his movements slow before he realized what was happening. He yanked up the reins, his whip coming to attention.

When they were mere inches from the carriage door, a pistol shot cracked through the air.

Ian stopped and looked back to their pursuers. As he turned to face Palmer's men, he pushed the two girls behind him and slowly inched backward, the door to his coach so close they could reach out and touch it.

Four keepers stood at the ready. Their big bodies were a shapeless mass of mindless aggression. In their hamlike hands they held ropes and cudgels.

Mary leaned forward, her teeth bared. "Come on, then, bastards. I'll eat your damn hearts out!"

Ian's innards shook at the promise in her rough voice. What a powerful young woman she was. He couldn't help hating the audacity of men for locking her up.

Indeed, her words seemed to shake the keepers. They shifted on their mud-caked boots, glancing at one another.

One of them, russet haired with a pinkish scar running down his cheek, stepped forward. "Step away, my lord. You cannot escape and we must put them back in their cell until this matter can be sorted."

Ian willed Mary and Eva to slowly move to the coach door as he stared the piece of filth down. The keeper, sensing the head of a pack challenging his weak authority, retreated slightly. Ian stood stock-still, his eyes narrowing as he said very quietly, his voice as hard as iron, "You touch either of them, and you'll be no more than a wet spot on the snow. I'm taking them. Both."

"No, you are not." Mrs. Palmer pushed her way through her keepers. The full length of her wine red skirts, dark as blood amid the pristine snow, swished as she tucked them around her to avoid the trousers of her men. In the dark night, she stood powerfully, unafraid and livid.

"I will take them both," Ian repeated, praying that his sheer presence and a strong bluff would get them out of this.

Mrs. Palmer snapped up a finger and pointed it at Mary, her gaze piercing through the night. "She is mine and she is a murderess."

"She belongs to no one." Ian locked gazes with the woman, quickly trying to calculate a plan of escape. Mrs. Palmer had her brute squad ready to charge and he had two small women to protect. It was an impossible position. "It was self-defense."

Unflinching as a battle-hardened general, Mrs. Palmer countered, "She has no self to defend. Quite simply, she is owned by others."

A small growl came from Eva. Ian reached out, curling his fingers around hers. "Well, I own this one, do I not?" His guts twisted. Negotiating for human life was all too familiar. Then he nodded to Mary. "I will give you another hundred guineas from your bank on the morrow for this one. Something for something, yes?"

Mrs. Palmer lifted her brows and a muscle twitched in her smooth cheek as strands of hair flickered about her face. "A tempting offer, my lord, but I must refuse. She is a secret far too valuable to part with. She stays. But don't concern yourself. Murderess though she may be, she won't be harmed. She's the daughter of someone far too important for that, no matter how mad she is, no matter if she happened to slay one of my fellows." Mrs. Palmer slipped a pistol easily from her skirts, triumphant. "You see, I am a woman prepared. Now, no matter what you say or do, I swear Mary stays."

"Fine," he said flatly, swiftly plotting how to get Mary out without them all being shot. "We'll go. And quietly."

"Mary?" Eva questioned, her eyes luminous and large as twin stars in her pale face.

Ian tore his gaze from Eva's. But Mary's was worse. With her pale skin and short black hair, she might have been Eva's sister. In her pale visage was a grim resignation that she would now never be freed. 'Twas a look for an old woman. "Get in the coach," he mouthed. "Do it now."

Mary's eyes flared, but she needed no second telling.

Ian jerked his own pistol free, ready to shoot. He spun back toward the pack of disgusting inhumanity. He would gladly kill Mrs. Palmer, woman or no.

Eva yanked the door open and sprang in, Mary fast behind her.

Mrs. Palmer's eyes flashed with fury. "Close the gate doors!" And just as Ian vaulted toward his coach, another pistol shot cracked and wood splinters exploded from the swinging, still open door.

He didn't waste a second glance back, but threw himself into the vehicle as his coachman struck up the horses. They were too slow. He knew it in his gut. Yet they had to make it. The fear of losing Eva to this nightmare of a place uncoiled in his innards. He would do whatever it took to protect her.

The cool steel of the pistol weighed heavily in his palm, a familiar companion. He'd use it if necessary. And, damn it, it was about to be necessary. He swung his gaze to the door, but before he could start for it, he caught sight of Mary.

Mary held herself rigid in the darkness of the rattling coach, her gaze traveling from Eva to Ian, then briefly back toward the asylum. She'd found some mysterious calm. Her delicate features were serene as she smiled slightly. God, she couldn't be more than eighteen.

"No matter what, Eva," Mary whispered, "remember, I'm free now. I'm free."

"Mary?" Eva demanded, her voice twisted with confusion.

Mary shoved the coach door open. As she threw herself forward, Ian grabbed wildly for her. His guts dropped as she tumbled back out into the yard, his hand grasping at empty air.

"Mary!" Eva screamed.

As the coach raced forward, Mary's slight body rolled along the snow-covered earth before she was up again, her little feet planted on the frozen ground. "Come on, then, you bastards!"

And she ran . . . in the opposite direction of the gate.

The keepers, all of them, sensing the most important prize was within reach, turned and bolted for her. Mary's body flickered across the yard, her little shift as fragile as the snow falling about her. A wild creature desperately trying to break free of its trap.

The sudden feeling that all the carnage of battle would never compete with this one moment of savagery swallowed Ian.

He watched, horror-stricken and in awe, as Mary tore across the landscape.

Eva's arm tugged at the socket as Ian attempted to jerk her away from the swinging door. She couldn't bear it. She couldn't tear her eyes from the heavy hands of the keepers as they twitched, bearing their rope.

"Don't look," Ian commanded, his voice raw.

But she did.

Mary darted back and forth, a cornered animal, her feet sliding over the icy patches, a wild and defiant figure. "Mary!" Eva's heart splintered at the sight before her, though she knew her friend couldn't hear her scream.

One animal grabbed Mary's arms. Another seized her feet and in an instant they had her on the ground. The third yanked out a rope.

And on the faint wind, she heard Mary cry, "Go!"

The world exploded around Eva in pain. She couldn't leave her friend. She couldn't. Not after they'd survived so much together. She couldn't look away, or draw breath.

Suddenly she was in the air, yanked up by strong arms.

Her body jostled as she met contact with Ian's hard chest.

"I'll come back!" Eva shouted over the din of carriage wheels flying onto the rough road. She screamed with all her force, though Mary would never hear her proclamation. "I will!"

The door slammed shut so hard, she thought it might suddenly drop from its hinges.

With Ian cradling her tight against his unyielding chest, the coach raced off into the night. Away from hell, away from Mary, and back into the world.

A world full of memory.

Chapter 6

Eva couldn't speak as they flew over the Yorkshire moors. The moon hung like Matthew's lantern, throwing its rays down on the snow. The cold white surface glittered hard as diamonds and rolled on for miles.

The little iron charcoal burner tucked in the corner on the floor couldn't penetrate the cold. It couldn't penetrate the veil she'd woven so thoroughly over her past.

And the sway of the coach. Oh, God. The sway of the coach made her sick.

If she closed her eyes for a moment, she'd feel the rain. The panic. The mud sucking her down. The curricle in the mire . . . and the feeling of flying before she crashed down hard to the earth . . . lifted her eyes and saw.

She gulped back sickness and her eyes snapped open. "We have to stop." She panted.

"We can't." Ian gazed fixedly out the other window. Every muscle in his face was hard, his lips a rigid line.

"Yes." She gulped again, saliva filling her mouth.

"No, Eva." Each word bit out of his mouth. "We must go—as far as possible."

Her stomach rolled with each bob of the vehicle over the rough terrain and the thought of the little white bundle. The little white bundle so far from her grasp. Unmoving, soaked by cold, lifeless rain. She lurched forward and twisted the brass door handle.

"What the hell are you doing?!" He slammed his fist to the ceiling and they came to a jerking halt.

She shoved the door open. Without even climbing down, she pushed her face out into the cold air and vomited. Her body heaved and her arms could barely keep her from falling face forward into the snow.

"Damn it," Ian hissed behind her, grabbing her and trapping her against his strong body.

She groaned, her mouth acrid and her body clammy despite the sudden ice cold circling her.

His large hand caressed her back and his other hand came to support her head, brushing back her feathery hair from her face. "There you go, love. There you go."

Eva leaned out the coach a little farther, her hands braced on the door ledge, and savored the cleansing sensation of the bitter cold. White flakes piled up in the banks before her. She let her eyes trail to the miles of it stretching out forever. It was so frozen, so perfect. So unlike the pain and wild unhappiness flooding her.

Why had she been so stupid? So foolish? That reckless stupidity of hers had ruined her life ... and her baby's. Pain racked her heart and her face twisted into a grimace before she shook the hideous thoughts out of her head.

Ian slipped a handkerchief before her face and she took it. "Thank you," she murmured as she dabbed it at her mouth. She pressed the square of linen to her lips, then leaned back into the coach. His hands helped ease her back onto the soft seat.

"Forgive me," he said softly.

She blinked at his words, hardly understanding how he could speak them. "Why? You've saved me."

"It wasn't enough. I should have come sooner."

She could have sworn the words *I never should have*

left passed his lips. They hadn't. It was only a phantom. A wish, made by her wrecked brain.

She stared back, finally capable of truly seeing him. On the last edges of her medicine, her mind was almost fully sharp. His black hair teased his forehead. The only boyish thing about him now. Slightly almond-shaped green eyes probed her. There was nothing soft about his face. His cheekbones were two hard slashes and his jaw looked as if it dared one to punch it. A slight shadowing of black beard dusted his skin.

His white linen shirt was mussed, as was his burgundy cravat. He'd opened his champagne-colored waistcoat and his black coat was unbuttoned and splayed about him like great wings. Muscles filled out those clothes. He was almost twice the size of the young man she recalled.

This was not the wild and carefree youth she remembered. The boy she'd wished she could marry though duty forbade it. But it was still Ian. She could see it lingering in his eyes. He really did believe he hadn't done enough.

This was the new Ian. A man never content. A man driven to the edge—not unlike herself. Except he had kept his demons imprisoned. "You have done enough, Ian."

A grim resolution shadowed his visage. "I will not have done near enough until I have you entirely safe," he said firmly. "I don't care what I have to do."

Safe. The word mocked her. Once, she had known what it meant. "I don't think I shall ever be safe."

His dark brows drew together. "Why would you say that?"

"What I've done. Tonight. And before . . ." Somewhere in the back of her mind she knew why she would always be in danger, but she couldn't recall it. An image of Thomas, his envious face, white lipped and angry, hovered in her vision. She blinked and it vanished. "I don't know. I just won't be."

Ian hesitated for a long moment.

Eva struggled not to shift under his unrelenting gaze. She knew what he was thinking. He loathed her. Loathed her for letting Adam die through utter foolishness. How could he not? Her stomach churned again. She swallowed back her pain and fear. It had been the one sacred charge in her life, the protection of her son. And was she responsible for his death?

The answer was a resounding yes, though she could not give utterance to it. It was she who had insisted on taking the curricle out into the rain. On lashing the horse with the whip, to hand deliver a letter to the post, a letter that she could no longer recall. And it had been she who had tucked her son in his basket beside her. Despite the warnings, despite the roads, she had driven out and her son had not come back.

Ian didn't move, his body like a statue when he broke the silence. "I swear, as long I breathe, I will dedicate myself to your safety."

She opened her mouth slightly to protest and then she realized, with a stunned and selfish gratitude, that he was in absolute earnest. It burned in his eyes with a terrible brightness. It struck her he was just as mad as she. Perhaps his demons did indeed own him, too. "Thank you."

"It is an honor and my duty to you."

"Duty?" she echoed. Duty had destroyed them. Duty had married her to a man she didn't love. Duty had sent Ian halfway around the world to protect an unworthy friend.

Once, they had been friends and would have done anything for one another. She, Hamilton, and Ian . . .

they'd been inseparable. The "Merry Band," as Hamilton's father had called them. But as they'd grown older, cracks had formed in their perfect friendship. And slowly, over time, Ian and Hamilton had begun to compete against each other for so many things. For marks at school, for Hamilton's father's affection. But Hamilton had never been quite as good as Ian.

And because Hamilton had not been able to bear that, their unbreakable friendship had cracked amid lies, disappointment, and the desperate wish to recover that which could never be had again. She narrowed her eyes, wondering whether Ian would ever forget the night Lord Carin had admitted to loving him more than his eldest son. How that love had first twisted Thomas and then had driven Hamilton away from the path of right. It was that night Ian had promised to protect Hamilton in India and the night she had promised to uphold her arranged betrothal. A sharp wave of sadness crashed upon her at such memories, and she swallowed back the misery. "Why are you here?"

He shifted uncomfortably on the seat, abruptly looking away. "I—I promised."

She drew in a slow breath, her limbs growing heavy. An unfortunate side effect of her medicine, even if it had been some time since her last dose. It wouldn't be long till she hungered for more. "Promised who?"

"Hamilton, Eva."

She could have sworn he wasn't telling her the full truth. But once again, perhaps it was just her imaginings. She nodded. Hamilton. She'd tried so hard to love her husband, even though her heart had always belonged to Ian. But Ian had not wanted her heart.

He had abandoned it.

Sweat broke out on her skin and she closed her eyes. God, she hated this part. The moment when she realized how much she needed her medicine. Especially at the mention of the past. "You make too many promises."

He blanched.

It was a cruel thing for her to say and her heart cried out at the way she could wound him now. Her savior.

"Do you wish to talk of him?" he asked, despite the tension marring his face.

Eva licked her lips. Her hands were beginning to tremble. Not a propitious sign. "Who?"

"Hamilton," he bit out. "Do you wish—do you wish to know how he died?"

"No," she whispered, averting her eyes. "I have no wish to speak of him." How she wished tears could sting her eyes. But she didn't cry at the past anymore. She couldn't think about it. Or she would drown. "Or anything else."

"Should I restrain my comments to the weather?"

She opened her eyes, no mercy left in her soul, not even for her savior. Not when she was unraveling so quickly. "Do you wish to talk about the war? Do you wish to tell me about the people you killed?"

His lips pressed into a hard line and then his hands balled into fists. "No, Eva."

"The weather," she said evenly, forcing herself to form every word perfectly even though she longed to let her head loll back against the cushions, "is a very fine topic."

Then she closed her eyes against his questions.

Against the past.

She wasn't mad. At least he prayed she was not.

She certainly was unstable. Of course, even if she were as sane as Plato, that place would have addled her brain. She was definitely fading in and out of laudanum-induced thoughts.

That would end. Never, absolutely never would he see

that filth cross her lips again. It would be a long road through her withdrawals, which would not even begin until every last drop of laudanum was burned from her stomach. And then ... then she would be driven wild with need for days, if not weeks.

Ian tried to relax against the coach seat, but he couldn't quite bring himself to do it. He'd done what he'd set out to do. He'd found her. He'd freed her. But now what?

How could he tell her about the circumstances of Hamilton's death? Should he even try, given her state? How could he explain now that he'd failed his friend so utterly and, in turn, had failed her? She wasn't ready to hear that she would have to live on. Even if her son and husband were dead.

And he would have to live with his dark secret, a dream that would never leave him peace. A truth that rang in his head with such vicious repetition that he would never hope for redemption. Though he would never have peace or forgiveness, at the very least he could make amends.

Ian lifted a hand to his face and rubbed it over his eyes. God. Mary had killed that keeper, but blood had slicked Eva's hand, too. It didn't bear imagining, the way she had had to fight for her freedom.

The keeper had deserved his brutal death. No question. But such things couldn't be done without affecting Eva's beautiful, battered soul.

In the last five years, he'd killed. Blood was on his hands, and they would never come clean. He'd borne witness to things he never would have believed possible. It would be unimaginable for him to judge Eva if she had killed Matthew, but for a jury of men? She'd swing for it.

A vision hit him of her small body swaying at the end of thick rope knotted about her slim throat. With how light she was now, she'd be lucky to die in five minutes. Would he be able to have done as he'd seen others do for their loved ones—pull on her feet to help her strangle all the faster?

Thank God Mary had claimed the blame. And he prayed that she was indeed too important to be harmed or given over to the authorities.

A heavy knot formed in his throat. He swallowed quickly before letting his attention wander unrestrained over Eva, taking his time on her face. The hollowed cheekbones, faint shadows beneath her eyes, the pallor of her skin and the slight parting of her full lips struck his heart. Even like this, she looked as she did when he had first met her and she was all of six years old. An elfin creature who had wandered into this world from some magical place. She didn't belong among mere mortals.

She looked so familiar, even if she was no longer that girl—the girl who had stolen both his and Hamilton's hearts.

If only he had not been such a fool. If only he had known that leaving her would rip his guts out and leave him an empty shell. At the time, he'd had no other recourse. Not after what the old Lord Carin had said on his deathbed. But in fact, leaving had been the greatest mistake he had ever made. And he was paying for it.

Eva had already paid for it. Dearly.

Now all that mattered was how he could help heal the woman across from him.

Especially since a particularly strong feeling ached to ease her off the opposite seat and curl her against his protective body. Christ, he longed to comfort her, but so much had passed, he no longer felt the right to draw her into his arms.

Eva's face should have appeared childlike in sleep, what with her short hair and her nightshift of a dress.

There wasn't a damn childlike thing about her.

Instead, her eyelids twitched and a frown pulled at her full mouth. Every now and then her fingers fluttered as if searching for something. Nightmares. Laudanum would help her sleep, but it would fill her dreams with specters. Did she dream about Adam, her infant son, even now?

Or perhaps Hamilton?

The very thought bothered him, and that fact bothered him even more. He had no claims on this woman, except those of a protector over his ward. It didn't matter that once he had secretly longed to make her his. But he couldn't go back. In his mind, she would always belong to Hamilton.

The man he had betrayed.

Yet a disturbing, possessive tug urged him to claim her for his own forever. It mattered not that he would never be able to touch her. All he longed to do was give her safety and shelter for the rest of her life.

He'd fought these protective feelings all his life. All his life he'd longed to break the expectations of the old Lord Carin and fight for her hand, but obligation had compelled him to silence.

Now she was Hamilton's widow. She belonged to the dead man. He could never allow himself this wanting. Dropping his head back against the velvet cushions, he tried to turn his gaze from her face, but was unable.

It was as if he were a man who had searched for water for days and finally come upon an oasis. Eva Carin was more trouble than he might find in any rebelling village or bigoted officers' camp, but he felt drawn to her.

Drawn in the manner in which a moth flies to the flame only to die, anguished and burned. Even with such knowledge, he kept looking. He was certain that somewhere deep inside this shell of a woman was the Eva he had known all his life.

If he could find that Eva, perhaps the part of himself he had left behind in India with Hamilton's corpse could be found as well. It was a dangerous game he was playing, this all-consuming need to alleviate the grief of his dishonored soul.

He plunked his elbow against the side of the window and leaned against his fist.

Thomas had claimed she was stark raving mad and guilty of rash action resulting in her son's death. But what was madness? He had seen men kill themselves, their brains splattered against their tent walls because they spent too many coins at cards.

That was madness.

And Hamilton . . . When he'd arrived in India, he'd begun to change even more. That swift shift in Hamilton's moral attitude toward the natives had shocked Ian. It had been remarkable and horrifying the way Hamilton had swallowed the swill that the Indians were somehow subhuman.

To grieve over a child? Over a husband? Could such a thing be construed as madness? Perhaps. To someone who had never loved, who had never lost.

Smallpox had claimed Ian's parents while he'd been at Eton. He thought he might go half mad himself. But the old Lord Carin, his father's best friend, had taken him in, not committed him to the madhouse. Still, Thomas had intimated that Eva had attempted to drown herself, the final straw before her committal.

No doubt in a few days Thomas would know what Ian had done. And Ian had no idea how Thomas would react. After all, Ian had used his name and liberated the very woman he had locked up. There were no other words for what Thomas had done—that asylum rivaled Bridewell Jail for horror.

Eva shivered in her sleep.

Without giving it a thought, Ian took his thick wool coat and slipped it over her small frame. For the briefest of moments, her frown eased and she rested.

It was the most relieved his heart had felt since before Hamilton's brutal death.

There was no question he'd made a bold and irrevocable move. He was certain that Thomas would not have approved. In fact, he very much expected a detective from the Bow Street Runners upon his doorstep within days.

But when they came, he would be ready.

Chapter 7

England
Six years earlier

Ian braced himself up on his stirrups, keeping his chest low, adjusting his weight with the pound of his stallion's hooves against the hard earth and bright green grass of the country.

He could almost taste the win.

In the distance, the two trees that marked the finish line and a crowd that included Lord Carin had gathered. They hollered and called to him. Ian's stallion, Dragon, sensed it, too. The white beast charged forward, his stride smooth and perfect, mane whipping through the air. A thrill at the speed and grace pumped deep in Ian's heart. He let out a laugh at the wild joy working as one with Dragon gave him.

Just behind, perhaps two horse lengths back, Hamilton shouted.

Ian couldn't quite make out the words his friend was yelling, but the intensity penetrated the thundering of the horses' gaits. Ian narrowed his eyes against the wind, focused on the finish. Focused on winning. Ahead the crowd waved wildly, their cheers piercing the air. Ian leaned in, his cheek dancing against Dragon's mane. "Come on, boy," he urged. "Come on."

At those soft words the stallion stretched his neck, increased his stride, and tore across the remaining distance to the finish. The shouts of the crowd boomed around him as he raced between the two trees. He caught Lord Carin's face, beaming, his gray beard framing his broad smile.

On an undignified but triumphant whoop, the old man lifted his top hat and waved it.

Ian pulled gently on the bit and Dragon immediately eased back, coming to a slow walk. Ian patted the stallion on his graceful neck. "Thank you, Dragon."

"Well done!" Lord Carin shouted, walking up beside the seventeen-hand-high horse. "Well done, son."

The whole crowd was pressing in to congratulate Ian, and a smile of pure triumph pulled his lips. All that mattered was winning Lord Carin's approval. "Thank you, sir."

"You could always outride Hamilton," boomed Lord Carin. "Foolish boy, to try and best you."

Ian swallowed, though his heart beat wildly at the praise. He glanced back over his shoulder and spotted Hamilton's stricken face as his friend reined his horse in. "He rode well," Ian said.

Lord Carin waved a dismissive hand. "He rides adequately. Doesn't understand horseflesh. Not like you, my boy."

Ian froze atop his mount as a snaking feeling of dread grabbed his gut. He hadn't intended to so thoroughly outride Hamilton.

Red tinged Hamilton's cheeks, and he seemed to shrink atop his horse. "Are you not proud of me as well, Father?"

Lord Carin hesitated, as if searching for words. "Of course. Of course. But Ian here . . ." His voice trailed off, the meaning clear to all.

The crowd began to slip away, moving toward the manor in chatty groups, eager to partake in the cake and cider provided. Only a few curious bystanders remained to watch the scene unfolding between the lord, his son, and his ward.

Dragon shifted nervously and Ian stroked the stallion's neck.

Hamilton's throat worked, apparently to hold back his emotions, but the beginnings of tears glazed his eyes. "I tried, Father."

Lord Carin looked away. "'Course you did. You always do."

"And I always fail," Hamilton said bitterly.

"Don't," Ian said, his gloved hands tightening on the reins. "You know—"

"What?" Hamilton snapped. His russet horse danced at Hamilton's agitation and he gave a sharp yank to his bridle. "That you will always best me? In everything?"

"That's enough now," Lord Carin said darkly. "Apologize to Ian."

Hamilton's eyes flared. "Apologize?"

Lord Carin drew in a long breath before he said, "It's not Ian's fault you're not as skilled."

"Father—"

"Enough now. You lost." Lord Carin's eyes turned steely. "Don't disgrace yourself. And wipe those damn tears out of your eyes. To think you're nearly a man grown."

"But, Father—"

"I do not wish to hear your excuses. I sometimes wish—"

Hamilton's lips went white. "Wish what?" His focus whipped to Ian. "That he was your son?"

Lord Carin looked away, the lack of contradiction a powerful reply.

It was what Ian had always longed for. Strove for. He'd sweated blood and tears over the years to prove himself worthy to be the old man's son, a real part of the family, but he never thought it would be at the expense of Hamilton's place.

Hamilton nodded. "I understand."

Lord Carin's silence stretched out.

Ian started to speak, but Hamilton swung his horse around, riding back over the small hill in the distance.

Ian looked down at the man he'd respected for so long. "Why?"

Lord Carin shook his head. "There's something weak in him. Something dangerous. He needs to understand that."

"But he desperately wants your respect."

"Then he must earn it. If—"

A pistol shot cracked through the air. Dragon reared, his ears snapping in the direction of the hill.

Ian's guts twisted. Hamilton. He squeezed his calves against Dragon's barrel and the animal sped forward. With every beat of his stallion's hooves, panic thundered through Ian's veins. Lord Carin had driven his friend too far. He'd known. He'd known how important it was to Hamilton to appear strong in his father's eyes.

As he mounted the hill, he braced himself, but what he saw seized his breath and burned his eyes despite his resolve.

Hamilton stood sobbing, his arm outstretched and a pistol in his hand, and his own steed lay prone upon the earth. Blood stained the bright green grass about the stallion's dark mane.

Dragon let out a fierce whinny, his eyes rolling wildly.

"What have you done?" Ian yelled, swinging down off Dragon. He ran to the animal on the ground.

"He failed me." Hamilton sobbed.

Ian's hands hovered above the once vibrant, beautiful creature that had graced God's land with pride. Now its gaze, framed by soft lashes, was void of life and its sleek body seemed dull of the magic that had warmed its blood. "Failed you?" Ian whispered, a raging ache growing inside him. Why did the innocent always have to pay?

"I needed to win, Ian."

Ian closed his eyes, feeling the stallion's flesh cool beneath his palms. It took every bit of strength he had to reply calmly, "I know."

"But you won."

The earth seemed to slip beneath him and his stomach lurched. "Yes."

"You always have to win."

When Ian looked up, he longed to see the friend who had eased him through his childhood griefs, the third member of the Merry Band. But he saw only a stranger. A man willing to kill an innocent animal to ease his pain. "How could you?" he asked, his throat tightening around the words.

"How could I?" Hamilton echoed. "How could you? You've stolen my father's esteem. As long as you are here, he will never love me," he railed. "Do you understand?"

"I— You wish me to go?" Ian asked, incredulous. They'd been together, inseparable, since that day he'd come to Carridan Hall ten years before.

Hamilton hesitated, then said, "No. No matter how angry I am, Ian, I could never wish to be separated from you."

Ian closed his eyes for a moment, then gently rested his forehead along Hamilton's stallion's neck. "Go with God, my friend," he whispered.

Slowly, he stood and pointed at the dead horse. "You know this changes everything."

"What?"

"This," he said, pointing from the dead stallion to the pistol in Hamilton's hand. "You. What you did. It changes

everything. You're becoming someone I don't know. Someone I don't wish to know."

Hamilton's eyes flared. "Ian ..."

"No. I—" Tears stung Ian's eyes. "We can't let this happen. To you. To our friendship."

Hamilton nodded. "I know. I promise." He swallowed, his face ashen. "I promise I'll do better. Somehow, I'll make you and Father proud."

Ian longed to shout that none of that mattered, that honor mattered. But Hamilton wasn't listening. His friend was staring off into the distance, tormented by demons that even Ian couldn't see.

England
The present

They came into the city of York at dawn. The gray-pink light of morning was obscured once again by the heavy white clouds that heralded another batch of snow. Ian glanced out the window, then back at Eva. They were about to arrive at the coaching inn. One of lesser repute, the Norseman's Arms.

They rattled over icy cobblestones, passing the medieval wall protecting the city from ghostly marauders. The harsh metropolis bore a quiet welcome at such an early hour. Certainly, at the heart of the old city there would be the cry of street hawkers. But here on the outskirts and in this ramshackle bit of town at this hour, one would turn one's head before raising a hand in greeting.

But even with so few people about, Ian couldn't deny that Eva was a sight. Any Bow Street Runner would be able to track down a woman of such a description. Only ladies struck by illness had hair shorn to such a degree.

The last thing they needed was undue attention.

The coach rumbled to a halt and his man jumped down. The snick of the carriage steps being unfolded heralded the door's opening. Ian nudged Eva, but she didn't move. Heavy sleep had taken her. Although he wished he could let her rest, it would be difficult to make a quiet entrance with her in his arms. He might as well shout their presence from the rooftops.

"Eva," he prodded.

"Mmm?"

He stroked her arm, savoring the touch. For years, he had not been able to do more than imagine her. Now all he longed to do was drag her into his arms, to hold her, to know she was real. Hunger stirred within him, shocking hunger for the woman who was before him. Just that gentle touch was enough to send his blood pounding. She was his to care for now. His to ensure that nothing ever harmed her again. Carefully, he stroked his fingers along her shoulder, tempted to cup her cheek. He hesitated, unwilling to frighten her. "Wake up."

"Don't want . . ."

Gently, Ian drew his cloak back from her slight frame. "We've arrived. Wouldn't you like food?"

She shivered at the cold and her fingers stretched out, searching for her lost blanket.

He glanced to his manservant, Digby, who stood just outside the door. Servants had long been a part of Ian's life. In India, he'd adjusted to the personal service of a single batman, but now . . . Now he was returning to the ever watchful eyes of an army of servants routine to a man of his station. Digby and the two other liveried servants—their names Ian couldn't recall—craned their necks, trying to get a glance at Eva from under their matching black-and-gold braided hats. No doubt the men were stunned by the events of the night and this strange addition to Ian's vehicle.

Only Digby had dismounted; the others kept their respectful distance, one at the back of the coach and the other up on the driver's seat.

Ian threw a warning glare at Digby, who stood too close for comfort. Immediately the man stepped back.

"Come, Eva," Ian said more firmly, shaking off the strange sensation of being surrounded by those ready to aid him. Ready to secretly judge, even as they bowed and scraped. "There will be a bed."

She snuggled deeper into the soft bench.

Christ, it would be so much easier if he could just sweep her into the damn inn. "A bath?" he tried.

Her eyes fluttered. "A what?"

He smiled despite his unease. It was as obvious as day what would please her. "A nice hot bath, Eva, love."

She uncurled and stretched. "Oh, yes." But in a moment, the languid movement vanished. Her eyes widened and her indigo gaze darted left to right. "Where—?" She gulped, the color draining from her face. She scrambled to the corner of the coach. "I don't—"

The intensity of her sudden alarm shocked him. He reached out, but instead of moving toward him, she jerked back.

"What's happening?" she asked in near panic.

"Remember." He remained so still it almost pained him. "It's Ian," he said, as softly as he would to a spooked horse. "You're free."

Her eyes alighted on his face, her countenance as pale as the snow falling outside. The tips of her fingers dug into the seat. Her entire body tensed as if she expected a blow. For several seconds she stared at him; then she drew in a slow breath. "I thought it was a dream. I thought you were a dream."

"No."

"There are times when I am never quite sure." She

pressed her lips together and her gaze darted away from his. "The difference between dreams and reality."

"It's only going to get better," he lied. If anything, the next days would be agony for her. She had not faced the world in two years, and she would have to face it now without laudanum. Within the next twelve hours, she would begin to feel the very serious effects of being without her drug. He'd seen it. Officers and enlisted soldiers alike desperately trying to wean themselves off opiates after prolonged injuries. It was no pleasant thing.

"I—" She peered out the coach; then she sat back, her eyes wide and glassy with fear.

"Eva, we must go in." Soon they would start to draw attention, not to mention freeze in the morning chill.

She stared at the opening and the street just outside it as if it were a living beast. "I—I understand." Nodding to herself, she slid forward. "Of course."

He smiled reassuringly. He took his greatcoat from the seat and placed it across her lap. "Put this on. And—" Reaching behind him, he slipped a long, thick burgundy scarf from a neatly stitched pocket in the coach wall. "We'll wrap this about your head."

She laughed softly. Then slowly her hand came up to touch her chopped hair. "I do look bizarre."

"Eva, you will always be beautiful." Gently, he placed the wool scarf over her head. His fingers caressed her cheeks, marveling at the reality of her cool skin against his rough fingers.

"Do you need help?" she whispered, her own hands lifting. Touching his.

Swallowing, he pulled his hands back and lied. "I can't tie a knot or bow to save my soul."

"Luckily, I can." Her fingers shook and it took her several seconds to work one end of the scarf around the other. But she did it. Then she took the greatcoat and slipped it over her own shoulders. "Ready now."

"Good." Ian stood, hunched, and swung down out of the coach. His boots squelched into the icy mud. Mud. His gaze turned to her slippered feet. The rattiest bits of leather covered them. "Come, I'll carry you just a little."

She nodded from the shadowy interior, then inched forward. Her face came out into the morning light and she blinked repeatedly. Who knew how long it had been since she'd stood in sunlight, despite Mrs. Palmer's claims of "exercise."

Quickly, he lifted her and carried her to the cobbles. From there it was but a few steps into the inn. The building was quiet as they walked in through the door and into the wide, sparsely decorated common room.

A stout man of about fifty, his gray hair wild and curly, stood by the fire. His white apron was pressed and folded to perfection over a light brown waistcoat. "Good morrow," he said brightly.

Ian held Eva's hand reassuringly in his. "I require a room for myself and my wife."

The man's eyes swung to Eva and his brows twitched for a moment at her odd attire. Confusion shaped his face into a surface of fatty creases until he smiled knowingly. "Certainly."

"Of the best you have," Ian clarified. It was strange to be at home, among the English, who while respectful had not been coerced into subservience. "I want a good, clean room," he emphasized.

Eva had slept in enough vermin-infested beds for a lifetime.

"Of course, sir," the man said genially.

"And I'd like a bath," Eva added.

"Whatever you require, ma'am."

"And food. A great deal of it, I should think." Ian eyed Eva's frail frame. She needed to eat. In fact, if she ate for two days straight it would only be a beginning to setting a healthy amount of flesh to her body.

"Me wife will send up a breakfast. Now just follow along." He hefted his bulk out into the hall and up a set of narrow, creaking old oak stairs.

Ian followed, keeping Eva close behind. She was quiet as they meandered down a whitewashed passageway. At the end of the hall, the man opened a black Tudor-style door. "Our best room for you."

Ian guided Eva inside. Well, it wasn't Carridan Hall or even his own estate, Blythely Castle, which he hadn't seen since just before he'd left for India. Even so, it was quaint and thoroughly English. Muslin curtains lined the one window and the walls had been painted a cheerful buttercream. A four-poster stood at one end, the empty fireplace exactly to the opposite. A round table for two had been placed in the center. "It will do."

The man backed out and shut the door.

The latch thunked shut, leaving them in solitude.

Eva slipped the deep ruby scarf from her head. In the faint light, the wild blue of her eyes glowed and she lifted a single black brow. "Your wife?"

Ian approached her slowly, still unsure how she would react to his presence after her fear in the carriage. Lifting a hand, he watched her face for any sign of distress, then slipped the scarf from her hand. He looked down at her, a good foot difference in their heights. "Would you have preferred I called you my prisoner?" he teased.

A small smile curved her colorless lips. "That does sound overly dramatic."

He tossed the scarf in a flutter of wool to the bed. "I'm sure Mrs. Radcliffe has written something to this effect."

The smile dimmed from Eva's face. "I haven't read a novel in . . ."

He placed a finger to her lips. "There are many things you haven't done. There are many things I haven't done since I took my commission." To his astonishment, he could feel nothing but the softness of her mouth beneath his touch and a vibration of heat slid along his skin. Her eyes, dark and lonely, called to him for assurance. "We shall learn to do them together."

Frozen, she parted her lips ever so slightly beneath his finger, forming a tentative O of astonishment.

Before he could think, he lowered his mouth to her forehead in the chastest of kisses, as he had once done when she'd fallen, bruising her knees or cutting her palms. It was the barest touch and the most innocent, but he no longer felt innocent.

As if she needed to feel something, anything, her arms flung up and two fists hit his shoulders; then her palms flattened and she grabbed on to his coat. She didn't shake or cry but merely held on, drawing strength from his gentle gesture. In turn, he wrapped his arms about her back. He lifted his face and took in her shocked features.

This was what he had wanted for years. To kiss her. Even if it was but on the forehead for now. In all that time they had spent together as children and then as adolescents, he had never understood the intensity of his affections for this woman. He had convinced himself long before, when he'd left for India, that theirs was a bond that would never be broken, a bond of friendship. Why in God's name had he not claimed her? Why had he not taken her lips in a fiery kiss, ensuring that she would never be anyone's but his? Duty and honor be damned.

The breath-stealing revelation was the most painful

and beautiful feeling he had ever known, because he had not claimed her. Their youthful selves were gone, incapable of being recaptured.

She still held on to him. But not out of pleasure. Her face was a mask of paralyzed fear. "Please let me go," she murmured.

Ian's soul cracked. The woman before him was a woman that couldn't be touched. Not with the way she had been brutalized. He couldn't—but, oh, how he wished to make her feel cared for.

Unable to stop himself, Ian stroked a hand up to her short hair, the tendrils soft and blunted against his fingers.

At the caress, her face twisted into an unwelcoming mask and she jerked her head away.

Horrified by his own audacity and thoughtlessness, he released her so fast she stumbled.

"My God," she rasped. Her pale hands flew up and pressed against her cheeks.

"Eva—" His body shook, furious that he had so terrified her.

"No." She licked her lips and lifted a shaking hand to her forehead. "But I—I don't like to be touched."

"I should apologize," he said, his voice rough with a sudden need to be consumed in the fire that tortured her. To seize her from it or be consumed with her in it. "I didn't mean to scare you. I should have known better."

The room seemed to expand at her silent perusal of him. Wariness darkened her eyes, deepening the shadows just above her cheekbones. "But you're not going to?"

He drove his hand through his hair. "No. It was done of care. I felt compelled to kiss you, as I did when we were children."

"Children?" She cocked her head to the side, a lock of black hair caressing her cheek as she contemplated him.

She let out a slow sigh then. "I know, Ian. It is just . . ." Her throat worked for a moment before she breathed. "I can't explain."

"You don't have to. I promise that I will take care of you . . . and I won't touch you again." He wouldn't. Even if it killed him, he wouldn't . . . until she asked. But would she ever ask?

The sort of friendship they had had so long ago was over. There would be no dancing, or hugs that threatened to crush one's ribs, or hands entwined on long walks. Those days were done and could never be reclaimed.

They were strangers.

They had been since the day they had both made promises to Lord Carin, choosing his wishes over their own.

Slowly, she turned from him and faced the window. The light of it silhouetted his big coat dwarfing her small frame. After a moment, she lifted her hands to the lapels and eased the heavy fabric from her shoulders. As it whooshed to the floor, her ribs expanded in a deep breath, as if the coat had been far too heavy for her.

Ian suppressed a gasp at the surprisingly erotic movement. There should have been nothing to tempt him about this moment. But the sight of her vulnerable, baring herself to him? It stole his breath away, stirring instincts within that had no right to exist.

He wished he could ignore the light peering through the window, emphasizing the transparency of her frayed shift, giving light to the curves of her waist, her bottom, the shadows that hinted at her most intimate places. A good man would not have noticed such a thing.

Nor would he have noticed how the rough fabric of the shift hung on her shoulders, skimming her body, leaving that fragile, unearthly silhouette for him to study. His fingers curled into fists, as if he had to deny his need to cross the room and touch her. To rend the formless fabric that caressed her legs, so that she was never touched by such rotten stuff again. God, even in such a hideous dress, even having undergone such foul treatment, she was the most beautiful woman he had ever seen. And when he had his way, she would be dressed in silk, a fabric that would kiss her skin with its softness, not punish it with its every thread.

It took all the self-will he had cultivated in the last five years to stop himself from reaching out to her, from claiming that beauty, so that he might fan it to a life bursting with power. But he couldn't, and the pain of it crushed him.

In careful steps, she walked to the window and braced her hands against the panes. The heat of her breath blossomed against the cold glass. For a moment he wondered whether she had entirely forgotten him, she was so absorbed.

"Ian?" Her voice hummed through the space.

"Yes?"

"I don't know myself anymore." Her slender fingers curled as she lingered, looking out to the street below. "How do I find myself again?"

Ian rooted his boots in the floor, still resisting the desire to go to her. To try once again to wrap her in his arms and soothe all her fears away. He would have to be far more clever to accomplish such a thing. "Eva, you are who you always were."

She laughed. The brittle noise bounced lifelessly off the plaster walls. "Oh, Ian. Don't lie, even if you do it with such conviction."

"It's not a lie," he ground out, another lie thick between them. "Underneath it all, you are still the same. The woman your husband loved." It didn't matter that, in the end, Hamilton had proved himself unworthy of her. So he continued. "You are the girl who raced horses with me with more confidence than any man I've met. Nothing can take that away."

"Horses." She sighed.

He flinched. How thoughtless could he be to bring them up? A horse had changed their lives forever. He had never told her about Hamilton and the horse, having harbored a secret hope that his childhood companion had not already been ruined in that moment. He'd lied to himself about the truth of his friend's heart and, as a result, he'd lied to Eva. To protect her. He wondered now who he'd truly been protecting. "Eva, please—"

A shallow laughed echoed from her. "Please? Please, what? Pretend it never happened? Pretend you kept it from me?"

"Yes," he whispered. Neither of them could face the choices he had made.

"Then you are in good luck. Pretending is what I do best these days."

"I am sorry. But I had thought . . . I had thought he still was good at heart, that I could change him."

She sighed. "I suppose we both did. We paid a heavy price trying to save him."

The pain in her words lacerated him, and if he could have undone all that had transpired, he would have, but that power was not within his grasp. "Eva, you will be yourself again. I promise."

"I don't think so, Ian." She glanced back over her shoulder. Her fingers slid off the glass, leaving long trails in the soft clouds, marring the panes. "That woman you speak of is gone. She died."

"What?"

"On a muddy road." Eva gave him her back, perhaps unable to look at him. Her stance was severe, unforgiving. She lowered her head and rested her forehead against the window before she breathed. "In the rain. With her son."

Ian's chest constricted. There was nothing he could say that would give her comfort. Adam was dead. And perhaps Eva had indeed lost herself that day among the wreckage of a twisted curricle in the rain and the mud.

Chapter 8

The world made no sense. Just hours ago, she'd been locked away in a dark cell and now here she was in this room of winter light and sprightly furnishings.

She forced herself not to think, because if she did, she would think of him and then the pain would eat her up. And she would not be able to push away thoughts of her other man. The little one.

Her boy. Her Adam. How she had killed him with one mad decision to race off into the storm. She paused. How she wished she could recall why it had been so imperative to dash out into the rain and race to the village. But such memories had dimmed to soft gray edges that could no longer be made out.

Ian stood not ten feet away from her. She sensed his eyes burning into her back. It was the most she had felt since Thomas's doctors had given her the first doses of laudanum hours after Adam's death. She hated it. "Ian? I am so confused—"

"I know." His voice was strong and deep, hypnotic even. "But I will see you right."

Eva was sure that if she closed her eyes, she could fall into his voice and be safe forever. If she let herself believe . . . But she would never be right again.

His steps echoed on the wood floor, a clear sign he meant to close the gap between them. She had no idea whether she should run or simply meet him. Perhaps she should let herself be consumed by his strength.

A knock shook the door and the latch clicked. "Breakfast, dears!"

The door popped open and Eva swallowed back the fear and anticipation beating through her veins. Even though she was sweating slightly now, confused at her sudden escape from the asylum, she forced herself to at least physically acknowledge the bouncing voice of the woman with a small nod.

"I'm Mrs. Marlock—if me husband hasn't already given our name." The older woman bustled in, her arms straining at the weight of the tray before her. Her belled calico skirts twitched about her ankles like a cat after a ball. "He said to me, 'Missus, there's a young woman upstairs what needs feeding.' And so I fetched up all my best vittles."

Mrs. Marlock, apparently completely oblivious to the tension in the room, scooted the tray onto the circular table. It gleamed with dishes fit not for the best of lords, but certainly suitable to those with a hungry appetite.

Eva eyed it with no desire. Hunger was a distant memory that had eluded her for years.

The older woman hesitated, her peppery sausage curls bobbing as she looked from Ian back to Eva. Her smile brightened with emphasized cheer as she clasped her hands in front of her. "Now, my dear Mrs. . . . ? I'm sorry I don't believe my husband caught the name."

"Blacktower," Ian blurted.

"My!" Mrs. Marlock exclaimed. "What an ominous name! Now, Mrs. Blacktower, you look a little worse for wear. May I provide you with a gown or robe? Mr. Marlock said you had no luggage."

Eva had absolutely no idea what to say. She had

owned but one shabby piece of material in the last two years. Before that, she had filled her closets with more gowns than half the women in Mayfair.

"That would be most kind of you," Ian said. He beamed at the woman as if she were the most fetching creature he had set his eyes upon. Indeed, he sauntered forward and took the woman's crinkled hand in his own. "Our luggage was lost. Our footman—new boy, don't you see—didn't secure the straps properly. They must be tossed about the moors around Harrogate."

Mrs. Marlock gasped, then tittered like a schoolgirl as she slipped her hand back from his. "What a disaster! I can recommend some very good shops for you and your wife." Mrs. Marlock's mobcap fluffed as she dipped her head slightly to the side. "The items are ready-made, mind you, but—"

"Thank you, madam," Eva cut in, more sharply than she'd intended. But suddenly exhaustion pulled at her muscles. All she wanted was to lie upon the bed. "My husband shall inquire when we have need."

Mrs. Marlock smiled as if Eva hadn't stopped her short. "Certainly." She gave a quick curtsy. "My boy will be up in a moment to light your fire. Now excuse me and do enjoy."

The woman left as quickly as she had come and Eva's shoulders sagged with relief. She had become accustomed to the strange comings and goings of the asylum. Cries in the night. Scratching at the door. The grunts and shouts of the keepers. But this strange exchange of pleasantries mixed with a barely veiled line of questions . . . 'Twas too much.

"You are upset?" Ian asked.

"No." She eyed the bed, her limbs as heavy as the cobbles on the street below. Every sinew cried out to stretch upon it and close her eyes in forgetfulness. Without her medicine, however, forgetting was an elusive phantom. "Indeed not. I am merely out of sorts."

Ian let out a humphing sound. "She is right, however."

"How so?" she said, because she knew he expected her to say something in response.

He raised a gloved hand and gestured to her loosely clad body. "Your clothes."

Eva glanced down at the threadbare fabric against her skin for several moments; then a wry smile split her lips. "Shall I not be presented? The court would be most amused by my dress." She swept a shaky court curtsy. "All I need is a few feathers for my hair." She waved her hand behind her head, wiggling the fingers in a mockery of ostrich plumes. "Don't you think?"

Ian's lips pressed into a hard line. Obviously he was at a loss as to how to react to her gallows humor. Perhaps he'd left his sense of humor in India. He crossed to the table and eyed the items on the tray. One by one, he lifted the lids from the porcelain dishes. Steam puffed up toward his face. "It looks surprisingly appealing. You should eat."

The scent of sliced bacon and kippers filled the air. Her stomach spasmed with displeasure and she grimaced. "I have no appetite."

He scowled and picked up a china plate painted with Dutch windmills. "Despite this, you shall eat."

The very idea was loathsome. Her body ached and the scent of the meat sent her stomach to jumping and twitching, and he had the audacity to suggest she eat? "Food is not what I require."

As he ladled a helping of fried egg onto a plate, he contradicted, "It is exactly what you require."

"No." She fisted her hands, driving her short nails into her palms. A strange snaking fire slid through her. It had been hours since her last dose of medicine. And she wanted it now. No, not wanted . . . *needed*.

"I—I—require." Eva bit down on her lower lip. She knew exactly what she desperately required. Lord, but she was not quite willing to tell him. Not yet. It was shameful enough, letting Ian see her like this. Broken, a shambles of her former self.

She shouldn't be ashamed. Laudanum in large doses had been prescribed for her by doctors, and then she'd been fed the stuff by Palmer's keepers. But she was horribly ashamed. And the unpleasant emotions hardly helped the slight shaking of her hands and the perspiration beading her brow.

"Eva," he said firmly, "you shall eat. Strength comes from such sustenance."

In pure, irrational defiance, she folded her arms under her breasts. "Will you order me?"

The words were petty, childish, but it was all she could summon considering how tormented she was by the growing nausea. Along with the sickness, an alarming clawing sensation raced along the inside of her skin, demanding she do whatever need be done to secure her next dose.

His face grew stony and his strong fingers on the plate so visibly tightened she was sure it would shatter. "Yes, damn it." He squared his jaw, screwing down his temper. "I most certainly will if it is in your best interest."

"I will not be ordered!" she snapped back, hating the sting in her voice. Knowing she was being stubborn, yet unable to stop herself at the frustration and unfulfilled need ruling her. But was it not also a matter of will? Did her will not matter in this? He'd given her freedom, but she hardly seemed free. His to command. His to be protected. Protection was a blessed thing, but not if it came in the guise of a prettier prison, surely?

Ian's face darkened. His entire body rumbled with bridled tension and he crossed very slowly to her. "If I have to, I shall feed you myself. For I swear to God, I will not stand by and watch you destroy yourself."

"I don't need food—I need medicine," she hissed. "I'm not well."

He glared down at her. "That odious swill is the last thing you need."

Eva blinked and her arms slowly lowered as she studied him. Resolution fixed his features, and as she realized it, panic slid right into her potent need for laudanum. Strengthening the intense demand ruling her.

He couldn't mean it. He must understand how important laudanum was to her. Even Thomas had understood. The doctors. The keepers, too. It was what kept her from pain as grating as ground glass. "But—"

He pointed a determined finger at her. "You are never going to have that poison again."

It was tempting to bite the appendage directed at her face. "I am not a child!" she shouted, even as her eyes burned and panic ripped up her innards.

"No, you are not. And I will not humor you like one." His voice softened and he lowered his accusatory hand. "I cannot allow you to damage yourself further with laudanum."

Allow? The word struck a chord. It resonated with a fierce sort of warning. *Allow.* He had rescued her from one set of keepers, but Ian clearly couldn't see that he was setting himself up as another one. One with the mask of mercy on his face. "You can't be serious."

"Deadly serious, Eva."

She let out a frustrated cry. "You can't. It's the only thing that gives me peace."

A muscle in his cheek twitched. "Not anymore. Whatever it takes, you are going to be well. Now," he said softly, his voice irritatingly rational as he crossed back to the table. He lifted a porcelain bowl and dished out a helping of porridge. "You will eat this."

Rage and fear at the uncontrollable need possessing her body sent her trembling. He couldn't. He couldn't take her medicine from her. How else would she forget? Even now she was beginning to remember. Remember how Adam had screamed and cried as she'd shoved the basket down beside her feet and whipped up the horse despite the driving rain. Determined to post a letter. Determined to vent her fury at Hamilton's death. Thomas had told her what happened and it had to be true, for she remembered her hair plastering to her face, her gown sticking to her skin, and Adam wailing in his basket.

Eva shook her head against the memory, then rushed up to Ian. She grabbed the dish of porridge away from him. "You don't know what is best for me!"

It came free of his hands so quickly the bowl flew from her fingers. The white, pasty food splattered over the wood floor and rug. Panting, she felt the anger inside her begin to dissipate. What had she done?

She had acted like a madwoman. A desperate woman. But how could Ian do this? How could he steal her will away as all the others had done?

Ian stared down at her, silent. Slowly, he turned, his shoulders bowed.

"Ian?" she whispered, wishing she could apologize. Wishing she wasn't so harried by her need. Wishing that they were both different than the people they had become. She wished so hard she thought her heart might burst from her chest.

A short, harsh sound came from him; then he straightened his shoulders and strode to the door.

Eva wiped a hand over her mouth, dread pooling in her heart. "Where are you going?"

"I need . . . a moment," he said, so quietly she almost couldn't hear. "Lock the door. I will return within the hour."

And then he was gone, the door clicking behind him.

Eva eyed the closed door. She was unsure what had just happened. He had seemed so completely in control . . . but she could have sworn there was a ragged edge to him as he had left.

There was nothing to be done now. She could not take back her rash action. His desire for her to eat was understandable, but she couldn't bring herself to want to.

Turning back to the silent room, Eva stood still, regret washing over her at her weakness. There were no tears. She'd none to cry. She'd cried them all out.

Slowly, she lifted her fingers to her lips, contemplating the brief, strange feel of his mouth upon her skin. For years she had longed for his kiss, imagining it time and time again. So many times when they'd been young, she'd been sure they were but a breath away from the kiss that would seal their fate. It had never come.

And now, years later, while she was half mad on laudanum and running for her life, he'd kissed her. Just on the forehead, but it had left her shaken, and it had awakened something inside her she'd thought long dead. Every instinct within her had demanded she yank herself from his person. But her heart? Her heart had longed to offer herself up to magnificent strength and to capture that blessed innocence that had long ago abandoned her.

Pain stifled her breath as she recalled the years she'd been so certain she'd never see Ian again. Even though he had written, it had been clear the boy she loved had drifted away, vanished under the revelations of manhood. She shook her head, unable to contemplate the brutal past any longer.

So, instead, she surveyed the room.

He'd left her alone. She swallowed carefully and drew in a slightly shaking breath.

It suddenly occurred to her that she had not actually been alone in years.

She had no idea what to make of it. Always, there had been someone within a foot or two of her. She turned in a slow circle, taking in the luxury of solitude.

Slowly, sounds of the street pierced through the window and worked their way through her distracted thoughts.

"Milk!" a ripe female voice called, puncturing the din. "Fresh milk!"

Another voice joined the cacophony. "Buy some flowers, madam! A penny for a flower!"

"Cabbages!" someone else shouted. "Fresh cabbages!"

The voices lured her back toward the window, but she couldn't quite bear to look down at the bustle. Once, she'd loved the city. Loved its life and wildness. London had been her favorite place in the world.

Frowning, Eva wound her fingers together. Somehow she had to make Ian understand that she had no desire to truly reenter society of any kind. All she wished to do was hide and pay for her sins. But . . . Eva swallowed and forced herself to step to the window and glance out.

In just the last few moments, dozens of carts laden down with wares had plowed onto the narrow street, pushed by men and women swathed in layers of scarves and wool. All of them selling something or other despite the cold weather.

Once again, she lifted her fingers to the cold glass panes and smiled slightly. It was so beautiful, this hustle-bustle of life.

The sellers lifted their heads, their mouths wide as they shouted as loud as they may.

At one time, she would have gone down to the street in the place of her maids, despite her status, and picked the best flowers. Now? Now she stared through a pane of glass unsure whether she would ever feel the call to venture among them again.

Eva let out a guttural breath, the mist of it icing the pane in frigid feathers, then turned back to the room. She eyed the food again and the spattered porridge on the floor. A part of her, the last wise part, knew she should do as Ian had said and try to eat, but she needed something very different, and no matter how hard she tried to ignore the craving, she was going to need it very soon.

Sweat slipped down her back and she grated her teeth at the physical compulsion of her need. Another woman would have lain down upon the large bed, covered herself with the thick patchwork goose down, and prayed that the feeling would pass. But she understood all too well that wouldn't happen. In fact, the feeling would worsen until she was a whimpering ball.

It had been one of Mrs. Palmer's favorite punishments: the abrupt withholding of laudanum, and then its blessed return.

There was but one choice. And she would now take it.

She fingered her shift. There was no chance of going out thus. Even she knew she looked worse than a street urchin grown to adulthood.

Eva closed her eyes for a moment, wondering whether she was truly going to do this. She opened her eyes and walked to the bellpull by the small fire, purpose in her step. Freedom only moments away.

Chapter 9

England
Three years earlier

*L*ord Carin's labored breath drifted through the room,
a grim harbinger of death. Ian clenched his teeth, willing back tears. He wouldn't cry. He'd been taught long ago that gentlemen didn't allow such indulgence, but, God, it hurt so bad he felt certain his entire body might fracture under the pressure.

The man who'd become his father was but a shell of the big, larger-than-life lord who had shaped his destiny. The old man's beard, now white, matched the transparent hue of his skin. Lord Carin's eyes stared, vague from the laudanum poured down his throat to ease his suffering.

It had come on fast, this illness. Less than three weeks had passed since his decline had begun. And now his big body had wasted away, barely taking up any significant space of the ancient oak four-poster bed. The curtains were drawn, bathing them in darkness.

"Ian?" the old man rasped.

Ian swallowed in a deep breath, then crossed to kneel by the bed. They'd been warned Lord Carin would begin to call them in. To make his peace. He'd called Ian first.

The bed shifted slightly under Ian's elbows as he leaned forward. "Lord Carin?"

The old lord turned his head, the slight move a painful effort. "You're a good boy."

Ian's heart warmed at the kind words. It was all he'd longed for since his parents' death, this man's approval and love. And Eva, but she belonged to Hamilton. "Thank you, m'lord."

Carin nodded slightly and reached out slowly, his swollen hand shaking. "Good boy, indeed. The son I wish . . ." Carin closed his eyes, his paper-thin lids twitching ever so slightly.

"Please, my lord," Ian whispered. "Don't trouble yourself. You've been a father to me. More than I—"

"It was a damned mistake," the old man cut in abruptly.

Ian stilled, his breath catching.

Lord Carin's eyes snapped open and his gaze was hard as he glared at Ian. "I love you, boy, and it has been the greatest mistake of my life. Loving you."

Ian shook his head, shocked. "Sir?"

"I—" Lord Carin drew in a gasping, haunting breath, as if one foot were already in the next world. "I have ruined Hamilton. Ruined him by loving you more."

Ian couldn't reply. The words hit him, hard slashes to his soul. How had he done such wrong? For, surely, this had to be his fault. This sudden censure. "I only wanted to please you."

"And you did. You always had to be better than Hamilton. Always. And I c-couldn't help admiring you."

Ian's hands pressed into the counterpane as the meaning of those words became clear. Was it true? Had he tried to come between father and son, not even realizing it?

"You've seen the man Hamilton is becoming. Shallow . . . unkind."

Ian had seen it. The last months had been difficult, their friendship stretched after the incident with the horse.

Lord Carin glanced to the door. "Call in Eva."

Ian hesitated, but then stood and went to the door. He peered out into the dark, quiet hall, where Hamilton, Thomas, Eva, and the doctor stood.

The awkward strangeness of it seemed to fill the large space, the four of them standing silently in the corridor, waiting, unsure. "Eva, he's asking for you."

Her face, always pale, shone nearly translucent in the low light and a track of tears glimmered on her cheeks. She nodded and moved forward. The swoosh of her skirts rustled through the booming silence. He waited for her to pass, then closed the door behind them.

She lingered for a moment on the edge of the room, but after a moment she fearlessly approached the bed and knelt. That peaceful beauty of hers lightened the room. Then she smiled, even through her sorrow. "My lord?"

"Darling girl." Lord Carin breathed.

She caressed his arm, bent, and pressed a kiss to the top of his hand.

"Ian," his lordship said, his voice still commanding despite its weakness.

Ian knelt beside Eva, careful not to crush her gown.

Lord Carin looked first at Eva, then at Ian. "I have loved you both well. You were the brightest, the best, outshining my own children—"

"My lord—" Eva began.

"No," Lord Carin said roughly. "To my shame it's true. I failed my sons. You two were so easy to love that I failed to labor for my sons. I gave you all my love and left them in the shadows and I cannot die in peace knowing what I have done to them."

Eva frowned, her brow furrowing with distress. "I would not have you die so."

"Then promise me something." Lord Carin's gaze burned with desperate fervor. "Both of you."

Ian had never thought to shirk from anything Lord

Carin might ask, but suddenly he felt his future in the balance. Yet there was nothing he would not do. Not for the man who'd given him everything. "Whatever you wish."

"Hamilton is going to India. Joined the Khyber Rifles."

"Yes." Ian knew this. Everyone did. Despite being the eldest son, Hamilton was to go two months after his wedding to Eva. It was largely hoped that service in such a prestigious corps would set him to rights. Lord Carin had pulled in many favors to buy his son's commission in that hallowed group of men.

"I've arranged for you to go with him, Ian. An officer in your own right. And I want you to help him." Lord Carin shifted on the bed, suddenly agitated. "You must. You must put your own pride aside. Help him become the man he was meant to be. Hamilton must . . . must find himself." Lord Carin's hand shot out, grabbing Ian's. "Swear you will do all in your power to save him."

Ian stared at the man who could have been his father and felt a roar of anger and helplessness charging up his throat. He swallowed it back. He owed this man so much. But more than that, he loved him. And if he had indeed stolen Hamilton's place, the least he could do was help him now. "I promise."

Lord Carin nodded, his body relaxing. "And you, sweet Eva? You will be a good wife to Hamilton. You will marry him, and shape him as only a good wife can?"

She paused for a moment, her gaze flying to Ian. But that resolved look didn't linger. Her spine straightened. "I shall do my duty, my lord, and be the best of wives."

Ian fought the burning urge to shout no. But Eva had been on this path her whole life. She'd made her choice, and no matter what he said, nothing would change that. Not even if he told her what had happened with the horse. She'd chosen her duty, and so he couldn't tell her. Ever.

He wouldn't ruin her marriage before it had even begun.

Lord Carin rested his head back on the pillow. Peace eased his features. "Thank you, my children. Now go. I love you both. And I am sorry that I have failed you. I never should have loved you above my own children. I should have loved you all equally. If I had, I would need not ask such things of you now."

Ian looked down on Eva, her face smooth and unreadable as a statue. She didn't love Hamilton. She couldn't. Oh, she could never be his . . . But somewhere deep in his heart, Ian had always secretly hoped that a corner of her heart was just for him. Even if she had to do her duty, fulfilling a promise made long before to marry Hamilton.

Duty was a hard master.

And this promise made on a deathbed was even harder.

"Send in Hamilton and Thomas," Lord Carin said on a sigh.

Eva rose, her skirts rustling. She left without a backward glance for Ian or for Lord Carin, but given the straightness of her spine, Ian knew, her heart wept for what she was losing: her father figure and her independence.

Ian stood for one long moment in the room, suddenly feeling as if his childhood was racing away from him, that all the days of summer were fast slipping away and that a very cold winter was about to sweep him up. But like Eva, he knew his duty and his duty he would obey.

England
The present

Mrs. Palmer stared down at the blank sheet of cream-colored parchment sitting next to a letter from Lord Thomas Carin warning her about the arrival of a cousin who would insist on seeing Eva. The letter explicitly stated she was not to permit such a visit.

The foul note tainted her usually meticulous world.

She'd been outthought—outmaneuvered—by a bastard of a man who had led her a merry dance. She drew in a sharp breath, desperate not to let her calculations fall to baser emotion, emotion that would cloud her vengeance.

Her fingers inched toward the quill, half ready to write the necessary letter. A letter that would make her look an incompetent woman.

Rage, an emotion she'd known full well since she'd been a little girl, threatened to break free of its carefully built prison. That rage howled for blood and punishment at her humiliation.

She smoothed her fingers over the parchment, ensuring there were no wrinkles in its surface. Feeling the thickness of it soothed her for a moment, gave her purpose. She was going to hurt Eva Carin for this. She was going to make Eva pay in blood and flesh and terror for disturbing her carefully constructed world. And then she'd deal with the bastard who'd stolen her away. Perhaps there was a room here in the asylum she could find for him, until a hole could be dug out back with all the other holes that had been dug over the years.

It was a fantasy, of course.

Viscount Blake couldn't be killed so easily. But Eva could. Her destruction was surely the best way to pay back the high-and-mighty lord who had so played her for the fool.

But first, she had to write the letter.

She jerked her hands back from the parchment and eyed the quill as if it were a mortal enemy.

It was almost impossible for her to admit, but she had made a mistake. A significant one, which was even more infuriating because she did not make mistakes. She was an impassable gate through which lies could not slip.

Lord, she should be, for she was a prodigious liar herself. A creator of ephemeral and delicately spun half-truths to ease the minds of her clients who, though brutal, longed to believe they weren't quite as inhuman as they indeed were.

Monsters, the lot of them. Men who ruined the lives of their women. But she had got the better of them. Finding a place of power over even the most powerful. Yes. She was untouchable. Or at least she had been, until the man who had come to collect Lady Eva Carin had sneaked under her gate. His lies had seemed like perfect truths to her well-trained ears, and now . . .

She ground her teeth down, her gaze blurring.

One hundred guineas seemed an insubstantial sum in the wake that had been left behind Eva Carin's abduction.

Her very safety was threatened. The asylum was threatened. And she had not outlived her own brutal husband to be destroyed now by a laudanum-addled woman and her brave, but no doubt hypocritical, white knight.

There was nothing for it but to let loose her dogs. She shoved the blank parchment aside, not yet ready to set pen to paper and write Lord Carin that his ward was missing. Oh, no. Mrs. Palmer rose, heading for the door. That was something she could not yet confess.

There were other avenues she could first pursue, crueler, more permanent avenues, before she took that humbling step. And pursue them she would.

Chapter 10

After having sent Digby to buy a simple gown and a pair of traveling boots for Eva, Ian had tromped around in the muddy snow for an hour. It had taken that long in the insidious cold to ease his grating frustration and return to the inn. He was uncertain whether he would ever adapt to England's climes again after being so long in India's heat.

He clapped his frozen hands together, desperate to invigorate his blood flow.

The inn's sign, a Viking helm, swung in the chill breeze. He headed toward it, easily avoiding the shouts and wavings of the Yorkshire hawkers. The local street vendors certainly could have learned a thing or two from the far more determined bazaar tenders of Calcutta.

After all, he'd yet to have something living shoved directly in his face.

Ian stopped a few feet before the entrance of the inn and stared up at the windows. Despite his frigid limbs, he didn't go directly in, because something entirely foreign held him back.

Hesitation.

Seeing Eva consumed by the need for laudanum had nearly undone him. It was only going to grow worse. And he would have to watch, unable to do more than simply take care of her physical symptoms. For the longer she went without drinking the stuff, the more she'd rail, until she was finally free of it.

He'd been hard with her today. But his dear Eva had not even seen the lengths he'd go to keep her safe, even if it was from herself.

Finally, a flower seller stepped in front of him, her tattered skirts sweeping against his leg. Her worn face became hopeful at his slowing. She thrust a bouquet of bedraggled white and red flowers before his face with her mittened fingers. "Blossoms, sir?"

No played at his lips, but he gave pause. When was the last time Eva received flowers? He thought back to the filthy yard of the asylum. Eva deserved beauty in her life. Nodding to the seller, her lips blue with cold, he reached into his pocket. "I'll take the lot."

The woman, her gray bonnet bound about her head with a thick brown scarf, blinked at him. "Th-the lot, sir?"

He nodded and pulled two sovereigns out. The coins clinked as he put them in her gloved palm. "Here."

A ridiculously brilliant smile pursed her chilled lips at so much money for a bunch of buds. The grin bared chipped and browning teeth. "Thank you. Thank you, gov."

Ian nodded, swiped the flowers from her fingers, and marched into the inn.

Heat from the fires enveloped him and he let out a contented sigh, feeling momentarily transported. He would never be quite as warm as he'd been in India, but this would do. For now.

He stomped the snow from his boots in the entryway and then headed up the narrow stairs. Hopefully Eva had eaten a bit of porridge. Then again, she might have thrown the entire lot on the floor.

She'd always been stubborn. Something he'd always loved about her, even if it could be infuriating. He prayed they wouldn't war with each other. Surely, she'd see he only had her best interests at heart?

At present, he hoped she'd drifted off to sleep. Rest was the only thing she needed as much as food. She'd be upon the bed, her body entwined in the covers. God, but he wanted to strip that horrid piece of cloth from her body, slip her into a hot bath, and massage the worry and pain from her muscles.

He slipped the key Mrs. Marlock had given him from his pocket, balancing the packages and flowers with one arm as he stuck the bit of iron into the hole.

The door swung open and he entered quietly, not wanting to wake her if she slept. But the moment he stepped in the room, his gut clenched.

The blue quilted covers of the bed remained in perfect place. The few chairs were empty and the food lay untouched, though the porridge had been cleaned from the floor.

In short, the room was empty with barely a sign that anyone had been there at all.

Ian dropped the packages and flowers, the pale petals scattering at his feet. He whipped around, panic blurring his vision.

He thundered out into the hall, not bothering to shut the door behind him. "Mrs. Marlock!"

Could Thomas be onto them so quickly? Had Mrs. Palmer's henchmen taken her?

"Mrs. Marlock!" he shouted again, rushing down the stairs and into the main hall. The sound of a clock ticked in the silence, mixing with his ragged breath.

"Ah! Mr. Blacktower." Mrs. Marlock hurried toward him, her face beaming beneath her cap.

"Where is she?" he demanded, coming to an abrupt halt.

Mrs. Marlock's brows creased ever so slightly, her lips

still arranged in her smile. "Mrs. Blacktower? Why, she went out, sir."

"What?" His heart thudded hard in his chest, drowning out the panic rushing through his brain. It was all he could do not to commence yelling at her as if he were still at Khyber Post supervising drills.

"Yes," she replied, her voice slowing with confusion. "She borrowed a frock and a cloak. She went out about an hour ago." Mrs. Marlock nibbled her lower lip. "She said it was most important, I assure you."

Ian snapped his gaze to the door. An hour. And she was not yet returned. "Did she say anything else?"

Mrs. Marlock's smile vanished at his panicked tone. "She did say she needed an apothecary. Is the young lady not well, sir?"

Ian closed his eyes. Christ! He should have known this would happen. And he'd been a damn fool. The damnedest fool. "She is quite well. 'Tis my mistake. She'd mentioned she planned to step out."

Mrs. Marlock's smile returned, though it didn't reach her eyes. "There, now." She folded her hands before her assuredly. "I knew all was well."

"Yes. Of course." Ian nodded, his mouth drying. "Which way did you direct her?"

"Johnson's Apothecary. It's just a few lanes over." Mrs. Marlock's smile flitted from her face as she started to fiddle with her gown.

"Yes?" Ian urged. There was something the woman didn't wish to disclose.

"Now, you mustn't be angry." She looked up at him, her eyes wide and pleading. "I tried to convince her to wait for you or my kitchen boy, Ned, to come back from the shops."

Ian took a step toward her, narrowing his eyes. "What exactly are you trying to say?"

"I told her she must be wary at Bickling Lane. Some rough men do hang about there." Mrs. Marlock rushed. "But it's morning and most likely they'll be sleeping off the night—"

"You let her go?!" he roared, fear gripping him so hard he barely caught himself from grabbing her.

"Well—" Her voice pitched up to a squeak. "I could not make her wait. She was most insistent, and what with her ways of a great lady, I didn't feel I could order her to stay—"

Ian lifted a finger and pointed it at the ridiculous woman. "If anything happens to her—" He couldn't quite finish. Good God, what had he done? This was his fault, not this poor woman's. "Forgive me."

"I am sorry, sir, if I am to blame," she rambled pathetically.

"You are not." He shouldn't have left Eva alone. He shouldn't have trusted her to stay. "You are very kind."

Praying to God that after all this he wouldn't find Eva in the snow, knocked down by toughs, he whipped around and ran for the door.

The very image of her bloodied on the ground shot him down through the street, oblivious to those around him. Heading as fast as he could in the direction Mrs. Marlock had indicated. Praying he wouldn't be too late.

Eva clutched the small brown bottle of laudanum in a fierce grasp. In less than a quarter of an hour she'd measure out a tincture and the world would be right again. Then she would not feel as if she might crawl out of her skin at any moment.

Her feet made fast dips in the snow and she stared straight ahead as she avoided the looks of strangers. There were few people on this street, which was only the more comforting. In truth, she could barely stand the abrasion of being out amid the bustle of life.

Gritting her teeth, Eva picked up her pace. The thin leather shoes she had borrowed didn't fit. With each stride, she clenched her toes into the bottoms to keep them from catching in the snow.

She looked ahead. Only three more lanes up, a right turn, and then a short burst to the inn.

The apothecary had looked at her quite strangely when she'd insisted he send the bill to Mrs. Marlock, but he hadn't argued, recognizing the quality of her speech if not her clothing and appearance.

Now, which lane had Mrs. Marlock said to avoid?

Eva stopped at a crossroads. Carriages and carts choked through the small yet busier way. Blicker Street. This must have been the one to avoid. Yes. Her mind fluttered as she tried to recall exactly what the woman had said.

Goodness, she had not been so long without her medicine since . . .

Balking at the hint of remembrance, she shook the thought away before it could take root. It mattered not. In a few moments, she would slip away from such things.

She waited for the heavily laden coal cart to pass and then she darted across the narrow intersection, avoiding piles of steaming horse leavings. With a healthy measure of relief, she charged up the street and turned down the next lane. She didn't even look at the narrow street sign screwed into the building. If she went this way, she'd be heading to the inn.

It took her several moments to realize the surrounding silence was broken only by the distant rattling of carriage and cart wheels.

Once it occurred to her, she slowed and came to a halt. The strangeness of it gave her pause. The sides of the buildings were tall, blackened bricks. Windowless, they stretched just like the never-ending walls of the asylum.

Her eyes widened and her breath increased. She'd made a mistake. There were no doors in the walls, either. But there were little lean-tos of oddly put-together pieces of wood. Smoke drifted up from the cracks of the makeshift homes, proving that there were indeed people who lived in such hovels.

She stopped. This was not right. A hunted feeling crept over her, worse than the feel of needing her medicine. Quickly, she turned to go back, but she stopped at the sight before her.

There was a single figure standing near the entrance to the alley.

A man.

Eva clutched the laudanum bottle. The same fear that had slithered inside her when Matthew would come about snaked down her spine. She snapped her gaze back over her shoulder to the other end of the lane. If she kept walking, she'd have to pass the lean-tos. And the Lord alone knew who might be inside. On the other hand, if she turned back, she'd have to brush by the man.

Steps crunched in the snow. She was obsessed with steps. Steps she didn't know, but the same dreadful, heavy sort of steps that had echoed on many a night in the asylum. Eva ground her teeth down and twisted toward the man at the end of the alley.

Slowly, he sauntered forward. A bent top hat sat atop his greasy black hair. Coal and dirt smeared his face and hands. Just like a streak of blood, a jaunty red scarf circled his thick throat.

He stopped, his legs braced wide, stretching his ratty black trousers. "You lost, luv?"

That rough voice rumbled down the alley.

She glanced right, then left, her skin crawling as she desperately looked for any form of escape. "I—"

"Sad to see a girl lost," another voice boomed from behind Eva's back.

Eva reeled around, her body pulled toward that other voice, her situation becoming all too clear.

Another man, shorter, squatter, emerged from one of the lean-tos. He wasn't wearing a coat, his once white shirt a dingy yellow. His stained mud brown breeches were half undone, hanging on stocky hips.

She stood still, desperately trying to will them away. But that would never happen. Experience had taught her such hopes seldom—if ever—bore fruit. She lifted her chin and said as firmly as she could, "Sirs, I am merely trying to find my inn."

"You feel tired, then?" the short one asked, taking a few steps forward. "We've a place you can rest."

The tall one closed the distance a bit more. His unwashed scent filled the cold air. "My word, yes. You can have a lie-down. And George and me, we can keep you warm."

George grinned, baring his scum-covered teeth. "We'd hate for you to be chilled, wouldn't we, Ed?"

Why had the laudanum been so important? She knew why. For heaven's sake, she was shaking with need for it. But then she realized that wasn't the only reason she was shaking. Anger pulsed through her veins. Anger at Matthew, who had terrorized her, and anger at these bloody animals who were terrorizing her now.

"Let me pass," she gritted, shifting from foot to foot.

George laughed, a hacking, cruel little bark. "Of course, luv."

"But first," Ed said jauntily, his black-stained hands going to the fold of his trousers, "you must pay the toll."

Chapter 11

A cornered animal couldn't have felt any more aware of its surroundings than Eva did in that moment. Her blood pumped viciously, slamming through her ears. The air tasted sharp and bitter with coal. She could even smell the rank sweat and dark ale off the two men.

Ed and George began to slowly close in. Clearly, they weren't overly concerned about such a small woman as herself fighting them. Without thinking, Eva tucked her bottle into her borrowed coat, then jerked the fabric from her shoulders, letting it drop with a thump to the muddy snow.

She didn't feel the icy wind. She felt nothing but the foreign, and all-powerful, will to survive. No one was going to hurt her again.

George laughed again. "You hungry for it?"

Eva snapped her focus from man to man. They were large, their steps relaxed, but then, they thought she was just going to meekly accept her fate.

Ed reached out, his fingers like long, stained hooks.

Eva forced herself to remain still. She had to let them get just close enough.

"Look at her, George. I think she might beg for it." Ed touched her chin.

Eva winced, sucking in slow breaths. She could do this.

Ed's eyes narrowed, lust darkening the pupils. His fingers dug into her skin. He bent in.

The smell of sour beer and urine surrounded her, and she fought back vomit. Though Ed held her head rigid, she spotted George out of the corner of her eye, a grin on his pockmarked face as he watched. She sensed in his jackal-like smile that he would be the harder, crueler of the two. The years in the asylum had attuned her to the cruelty of men. Of how deep it was rooted in their hearts.

Ed arched her neck back a little farther, and she let her arms dangle at her sides. George whistled and clapped.

It was worse than Matthew. God, at least he had bathed now and again. Ed reeked of last night's drink and months of decaying food. She was sick of such men.

Anticipation shot through her veins before she flexed her hands and drove her rigid fingertips into his throat.

Ed choked, his eyes rolling back for a moment, and his grip released.

George gaped.

Eva took the opportunity. Darting forward, she grabbed George's shoulders, glaring into his stunned eyes. With all her might, she drove her knee up into his groin. A howl of pain tore through the air and he bent, gasping. But as she twisted to run, George grabbed hold of her, his ragged nails so sharp against her flesh she cried out in surprise at the sting.

"You ruddy little bitch!" He gasped, his eyes blazing down at her.

"That's right!" Eva struggled like a frenzied rat in a cat's claws before she sucked up some spit and spat in his face with all the force she could muster.

She felt Ed come up right behind her, the heat of him touching her shoulder blades. Without thinking, she threw her head back. The world exploded in sparks as the top of her head connected with his nose.

"Jaysus! Shit!" Ed screamed. The snow crunched under his boots as he staggered away.

George's face grew red with fury. "Fun's done, you little whore." He threw her to the ground.

Her breath barreled out of her as her elbows hit the icy ground. She blinked, trying to focus on the men.

George towered over her. "You got grit, girl."

Eva scrambled back, terror and the raging urge to fight ruling her. She wasn't done by half yet, even if they were strong and tough.

George stepped forward and Eva shot her foot out. Her heel rammed into his knee and he groaned, falling to the ground.

Frantic now, Eva tried to get up, but Ed, whirling back to them, pressed his boot down on her hand. A scream tore from her lips. The pressure of it rocked through her. She could almost feel bones creaking and splintering.

Eva swallowed back bile, then thrust two rigid fingers at Ed's eyes. He twisted fast and her nails grazed his cheek.

Terror stole over her and, finally, she did what had never worked before.

She screamed. Again and again. Her voice pierced the air like a possessed thing. There was no chance she would make this easy for them.

Ian hit Bickling Lane at a run, and what he saw threw him into instant battle response. Everything slowed and sped at once.

Eva struggled on the ground, fighting like a wild thing. But she was losing. Her dress was ripped to shreds, her pale breasts and long legs exposed to the freezing air.

Rage, unlike any he had ever known, shook him to his core.

As the sensation settled in his heart, an unbelievable stillness took him and he charged forward, spotting a slab of wood on the snow. He bent, clasping it up. His boots ate up the ground so fast the two bastards didn't see him coming. He wound up the thick piece of wood like a cricket bat and swung.

The edge of it smashed into the short one's head. The man's neck jerked to the left and he yelped as blood shot from his mouth.

The tall one vaulted to his feet, whipping a knife from his pocket.

Ian ignored the danger. All he could think of was Eva on the ground. He shot forward, grabbed the man's wrist, and yanked back. A scream gurgled from his throat as his wrist broke in Ian's grasp and the knife fell to the ground.

The short one staggered off, clutching his face, his breeches barely about his hips. Ian focused on the tall one and closed the distance between them.

He grabbed the man's filthy shirt. "You like to hurt women?"

The buggering scum swallowed, his Adam's apple bobbing. "She's a whore. Look at her."

"She's mine," Ian growled. And then he slammed his fist into the piece of offal's face. The man collapsed to the ground and Ian fell onto him, punching.

Hands grabbed his shoulders and he whipped around, ready to defend himself.

"Stop!" Eva shouted. "Stop."

Ian's arm stopped in midswing. He looked back at the man, limp in his grasp. But he didn't want to stop. The gut-wrenching fear of seeing Eva completely vulnerable still held him in some invisible prison. He dropped the man to the ground, his hand still clenched, ready to belt the tosser again.

Eva's fingers pressed into his shoulder, a light but insistent weight. "You're going to kill him."

"I want to."

The man whimpered.

"No, you don't." Eva tugged at his arm. "Let's go, Ian. Let's go!"

Bubbling fury still held him in its sway and he had no desire to walk away, but neither did he wish Eva to witness such a scene. At last, he dropped his raised fist. He'd never lost control of himself like that before.

Unable to speak, he lifted his gaze to her. His innards seized up with another dose of rage. God, she was a sight. She tugged at the scraps of fabric that had once been a frock. Her thighs and stomach peered out from the shreds and her left arm was clasped across her bosom.

"We need to leave now," he said flatly, his body still alive with anger at the beasts who had hurt his Eva. "Can you walk?"

"Yes," she muttered as she staggered to her discarded coat. She pulled it on, largely hiding the evidence of her assault. Except for her face. She couldn't hide the bruise blooming on her cheek.

Ian paced away from the crumpled body in the snow, desperate to pull Eva into his arms and make all this disappear. Where were the tears, the shaking that would send any other woman into his arms out of fear and relief? But then it hit him. This was not the first time Eva had fought for her life. He began to reach out to pull her to him, but he stopped, his own heart aching. He couldn't touch her. Not as he wished. He might never be able to touch her. And it nearly broke him anew not to wrap her in his embrace so that he might feel she was still alive and safe. "You are too damned brave."

"The only alternative is to lie down and die," she drawled with a surprising dose of sanguine humor.

He hated how right she was. "Come."

She gave a barely noticeable nod; then they headed quickly back down the alley, leaving the mess behind. But Ian knew the memory would stay a long time. With both of them.

Chapter 12

India
Two years earlier

*T*he heat only made Hamilton's head pound all the harder with the growing recognition that his friendship with Ian was dead. Cradling his aching skull with his hands, he choked back the unavoidable nausea that followed a night of gulping wine and playing too many cards.

And losing far too much coin.

He fisted his hands, pulling at his hair, desperately attempting not to panic. He'd lost nigh on five thousand last night. That in itself was nothing. But the look on Ian's face?

God, why had his father bought Ian that commission? His father hadn't trusted him. Hadn't trusted that, after his death, his son wouldn't make a complete disgrace of himself. So he'd sent Ian to ensure he behaved.

Hamilton forced himself to stand, readying himself for the routine inspection of his troops. He blinked as his body shook from the adverse effects of too much alcohol. Still, such things were the common lot of soldiers. He enjoyed the long drinking bouts and laughter he and his fellow officers partook of, but what he could no longer tolerate was the self-serving superiority of his once closest friend.

Hamilton held his head up high as he stepped out into the blistering sun and dusty parade ground. He loathed India. He loathed the burning sun, loathed the marauding tribes of men that lurked not far over the borders into Afghanistan, and he loathed the way the natives behaved like animals in need of dominance. But he'd needed to come. To prove to his father, dead or alive, that he was a brave man. Not a failure.

Anger and humiliation burned through Hamilton as he swallowed against his dry throat. Ian thought himself better in so many ways. Ever since they'd gone to Eton, it had begun to show. Ian had pandered to his father's affections, pushing Hamilton to the side with his accomplishments. And no matter how hard Hamilton had tried to compete, Ian had come out the victor one too many times. Though his father had tried to hide it, it had been inescapable, that slight preference he had held for Ian.

Eventually, his father had stopped trying, giving his affections to Ian alone.

But at least Eva was his. He'd seen the way Ian looked at her. He couldn't have borne it if she'd thrown him over for Ian. It mattered not that their marriage was hollow, that she would never fully return his love. She belonged to him. Not to Ian.

England
The present

Hours after they arrived at the Norseman's Arms, Mrs. Marlock's screams still echoed in Eva's ears. Who knew the older lady could be so shrill? Then again, it was likely the woman wasn't presented with such drama on a daily basis.

Steam drifted up from the bath, caressing Eva's face. Thankfully, she sank lower into the hot water, savoring

its soothing cocoon of warmth. Mrs. Marlock had wanted
to fetch a physician, but both Eva and Ian had been firm
that it was not necessary.

Bright man that he was, Ian had handed the lady innkeeper a bag of coins, asked for the bath, another tray of
food, and linen for bandages if needed.

She didn't need bandages, thankfully. On the other
hand, she was going to ache for days. Beneath the lapping water, she was a veritable map of cuts and bruises,
from her scratched knees to her bruised wrists.

Before she'd been left alone with Ian, she'd surrepti-
tiously managed a small drink of laudanum, which had
eased her nerves considerably. She no longer felt the
driving hunger for it, and the knowledge that it was
tucked away in the top drawer waiting for her also eased
her mind.

Ian sat on the other side of the room, his back firmly
to her. She studied that back. It was the same back she'd
known as a girl, but it was different now. When Ian was
a boy, he'd been whip thin. Strong and slender. But now?
His shoulders had fulfilled the promise of their youthful
breadth, and he'd filled out with a shocking display of
muscle that shifted under his linen shirt with each patient breath he took. The sometimes unsure, slightly
awkward boy was gone, replaced by a man of liquid
grace and a strength that could be used to kill . . . or to
comfort.

To her dismay she found her own breath had hitched
in her throat and the heat of her cheeks did not come
from the bath. Was it possible she still found him to be
beautiful? She dared not linger on such a thought.

Years earlier, they'd run about half dressed together,
no fear of proprieties. Much had changed since then.
They weren't children any longer. But she longed for the
carefree ease they had experienced so long ago.

It wasn't that she wished Ian to see her nude. But everything had changed when they'd chosen duty over love, when he hadn't told her that Hamilton had shot a horse simply because he'd lost a race to Ian. She'd learned the truth herself from a groom in passing after Ian and Hamilton had gone to India.

And she'd certainly learned that duty was a dangerous companion, treacherous and ready to steal one's only joys. In the end, she'd failed in a woman's most important duty. She'd failed to protect her son.

Eva squeezed her eyes shut, then looked back to Ian, wishing he could somehow magically take them back to when they'd been happy.

Still, now she wasn't sure if she'd ever truly known Ian. She was grateful, of course, but he was so different. So much larger, so much more dangerous . . . even his voice. His voice was now a rich timbre that danced upon her skin in the most subtle of ways.

Spinning her fingers in little circles on the water's surface, Eva continued to study the back of him. Hoping he wouldn't notice. Where had the Ian who'd disappeared from Carridan Hall without a backward glance gone? Certainly, he was still there—she saw it in the color of his eyes, the fall of his hair. But what of his virtues? The things that had made her girlish heart surrender to him? The Ian she knew had rescued martens and foxes. He'd tended sick and wounded creatures, stealing her affections with his tenderness to birds and squirrels.

And once, when she'd been no more than eleven, he'd promised to kiss her, if she wished it. It had been so real when she was a little girl, the fear that no one would. Hamilton had refused time and time again to give her the smallest of kisses. It had been a heady fear indeed to think that even her husband should not kiss her.

But Ian had assured her that if no one had stolen a

kiss from her by the ripe age of nineteen, he would do it. She could still see the laughter fading from his face as he'd realized how vital it was to her. Despite how it must have made him feel, knowing she was to be Hamilton's, he had made the solemn vow to ensure she wouldn't die unkissed.

They'd been standing in the library, and Eva had hoped he'd kiss her right then, even though they were so young. He hadn't.

But she had been kissed. At eighteen on the day of her wedding and then in the following nights, when she had once again embraced her duty. Hamilton's kisses had proven most disappointing. Passionless things that did not live up to her romantic girlhood notions.

If she asked Ian to kiss her now, would he remember his promise? It was difficult to say, since he was nearly unrecognizable as the boy who had given his word.

Now he rescued madwomen and beat men to bloody masses in narrow alleys. God only knew what he'd done in India. She could hardly countenance it, he'd so abhorred violence.

One summer, as they'd played in one of the tenants' farmyards, Ian had punched Hamilton because he'd had the temerity to feed a salamander to one of the chickens. Eva could still recall how Ian's face had gone red. Tears, though he'd tried to hide them, had tumbled down his cheeks. She'd attempted to comfort him with a gentle embrace, but even then he didn't accept comfort, only gave it.

He'd been such a keeper of the innocent and good. She could hardly pair that young man with the man in the alley. The one who had beaten Ed till he was nothing more than ruptured bone and blood.

Not that the man hadn't deserved it. And it was not as if she was still that girl who raised a hand to no one. Indeed, sometimes, she could hardly believe she'd ever been so trusting and naive.

"What happened to you?" she asked simply.

He leaned back in his plain high-backed chair, his white shirt playing over hard muscle. "I beg your pardon."

"Ian?" She waited, hoping he would turn away from the blazing fire of his own accord. When he did not, she demanded, "Look at me."

When he still didn't turn, she splashed the water. "Everything improper is beneath the bath, you know." She didn't add that he'd virtually seen her naked in the alley in any case.

With what seemed to be Herculean effort, Ian twisted in his chair. And then proceeded to keep his eyes lowered. He crossed his booted feet and rested his strong hands on the armrests. "Yes?"

She snapped her attention down to the steaming water. If she opened this line of questioning, he would no doubt feel the right to inquire about her recent past. Still, she longed to know. About him in the years past. Enough to take the chance. "Tell me, please. About India."

"About Hamilton?"

Eva closed her eyes, guilt burning inside her. She'd married Hamilton because of duty. Because it had been her guardian's wish to keep her protected in a dangerous world and because Lord Carin had believed she'd be able to help Hamilton. It was laughable, it had been such a mistake. A mistake that had led to a dry marriage in which she couldn't fully return her husband's love. A husband who had been desperate to possess her.

Now she couldn't truly bring Hamilton's face to mind. When she closed her eyes, she sometimes saw his dark brown hair and the idea of his confident eyes. But that was all, really. She opened her eyes and began to shift her position in the tub.

A muscle in her neck clamped. Agonizing pain stabbed her shoulder. Gasping, she slipped down into the water. The hot liquid lapped against her face and she winced as she tried to right herself, but she could not.

Her arm refused to move.

"Eva?" Ian shot to his feet and crossed to the tub. "What is it?"

"My neck." She breathed out as she struggled to keep her head above water. The pain wrenched the whole right side of her. She couldn't move. Only her legs and eyes seemed to obey her commands.

Instantly, Ian knelt down beside her. "May I touch you?"

A strangled sound of frustration gurgled from her. The complete gentleman. Of course he wouldn't touch her after this morning. "Yes." She panted, the pain so intense she could barely speak.

His strong hands hovered, then brushed her neck. Easily, he worked the pads of his rough fingers against the strained muscle.

More pain twisted her arm and she yelped. "Ian . . ."

"Wait a moment."

Then he dug his thumbs into the mass of muscle and rubbed them about. Eva nearly slid down into the tub as her entire body relaxed. She let out a relieved sigh. Very carefully, she looked up at him, afraid that the muscle would seize up again. "How did you do that?"

"I learned many strange and useful things in India. No doubt you pulled something fighting off those bastards. Sometimes it takes a while for muscles to spasm when they've been injured."

He crouched down by the tub, his hands still resting

on her shoulders, now massaging gently. "Eva, how did you learn what you did?"

She glanced away, focusing on the fire, watching it jump and cast light and shadow throughout the darkened room. Trying not to think about the delicious and reassuring warmth his touch created or the way his voice surrounded her and filled her up with a warmth she hadn't known since they had been sure of each other and inseparable. Good Lord, just the deep timbre of his voice resonated with such painful pleasure she longed to drown in it. "Learn what?"

"How to fight like that?" His voice was full of hesitation, as if he might not truly wish to know how she had become this creature. Despite his wariness, he gently stroked his fingers up into her short hair.

They both had changed so much, their paths diverging wildly. All because of Hamilton. It was still nigh impossible for her to understand how it had happened. How she had had so little determination to disappoint her guardian. How Ian had left. The painful thought squeezed her heart and she gasped against it, masking it with a hollow little laugh.

He had to be able to see her entire body beneath the warm water. Unless he was staring fixedly at the ceiling. She should cover up. Or roll onto her side. But she didn't. For some inexplicable reason it felt completely natural to bare herself to him.

He wanted to know what had happened to her. She pressed her fingers into the sides of the tub. He thought he wished to know. But what if he left her again when she learned how far she'd truly fallen? He'd left her once out of his sense of right and good.

Her nails raked the tub and she clenched her hands into fists, wishing she could make all the pain and doubt disappear. While it was true that men had treated her foully, she could not ignore the need to open herself to someone. To finally not feel so terribly alone. But could Ian be that person?

"Eva?"

"Hmm?" She could trust him. Couldn't she? Or had she lost her ability to share herself inside the asylum walls? She didn't know. Perhaps trust had been lost, just as so many parts of herself had been lost.

"Fighting?"

She blinked, trying to gather her thoughts. "Yes." She leaned her head back into his hands and gazed up into his bright green eyes. "If you must know, not all the girls are nice in a madhouse."

A dry laugh rippled from Ian's throat, though only grim understanding filled his malachite eyes. "I imagine not. Tell me more."

Eva frowned, wondering whether she should. She'd kept so much to herself for so long. To her shock she began to speak quietly. "Matthew was bad enough. But the other patients—they were either severely medicated or had finally gone mad with imprisonment."

She forced her eyes as wide as they would go. She didn't wish to close them and see the wild, almost doglike faces of the girls who had fought for position just like animals in a pack. "Frequently, it was a struggle for blankets. Mrs. Palmer never had enough. Or for food. And, well, whatever was in demand went to the most ferocious."

"And you were fierce," he said simply, his gaze unwavering and without judgment.

She'd had to be or else she would be dead. But no, she'd not been that tough. Not when compared to the brutal girls who would beat and cajole others into their submission. "I was strong enough to be left alone."

"And Mary?"

A sharp stab of grief grabbed at her heart. What had happened to her friend? Mrs. Palmer had promised she would not be killed . . . but that left a myriad of fates for her friend to endure. No doubt Mary would have been drugged and locked in a small, dark room, lost. "She taught me many things. She'd been there for two years before I got there."

"Good God. How old is she?"

"Eighteen."

"Why would anyone put such a young girl in the madhouse?"

At that, Eva laughed. She couldn't stop herself. Strong, capable Ian was in many ways innocent to the evils of the world.

She'd been innocent once, too. Innocent to the ways of the willful who would use their power to control everyone around them. She shook her head, not knowing how to sweeten her answer. "Because of families. A family might place a girl in the madhouse because she was pregnant. Or there was a botched abortion. Because she wanted to make love to the stable boy. Because she would not marry the man her father insisted upon. Because she followed politics or wished for independence. Because she had too many emotions."

Completely silent now, Ian continued to work his fingers at her muscles. She could feel his frustration through his hands. She found herself adding, "Or because she did something truly unforgivable."

"Eva," he said gently.

She tried to pull away. "No." A faint vision of a little boy bouncing on chubby legs filled her vision. She sucked in a sharp breath. She'd perfected keeping such thoughts away. And now . . . even with the small dose of laudanum she'd just taken, she could not fight it off. "I shouldn't have said anything."

"Yes, you should."

He didn't understand. He couldn't. She pulled away from him, water sluicing down her back. "I cling to my life by a small thread, Ian. Knowing what I've done ..." Her mind struggled for a moment. 'Twas easy to recall the mud and the screams. But there was something else. She frowned, struggling to remember through the haze of years of laudanum, of so much pain and so many unpleasant memories. What couldn't she recall?

She glanced down at the water, seeing her face reflected up at her. "I don't know."

"Don't know what?"

She slapped her hand down on the smooth, glassy surface, eradicating her reflection. "I can't, nor do I wish to, bare my soul at this particular moment."

Slowly, he lifted pain-filled eyes back to hers. Compassionate eyes. "It's true, you know." His voice rumbled softly in the quiet. "What they say."

She eased forward along the tub and placed her hand on the rim. "What do they say?" she asked, her own voice a mere rustle. Matching his. Desperate for any change in their doomed conversation.

"The air is full of spices."

She stared at him blankly, wondering whether perhaps he was being a bit barmy, but then ... spices!

India. He was telling her of India. She clung to the chance to think of anything else besides the past and its torments ... and the dreadful anticipation of knowing such thoughts would indeed drive her to madness. "Tell me."

"I loved the air in a way I never knew one could love it. Cardamom, curry of every kind, wonderful smoky or fruit teas waft through the bazaars and street markets." As he crouched by the tub, his brow furrowed in concentration. Carefully, he lifted his hand and tentatively held it beside her face. "May I?"

He wanted to caress her cheek. She eyed his hand. Masculine hands were brutal, killing objects. Ian's bore the external signs of a man who could destroy with them. They were rough, patched with a hundred lines, nicks, and healed cuts. But there was a gentle gracefulness to them, too, in the way his fingers curved and his palm beckoned to fit itself to her. Putting her misgivings aside, she nodded.

Ever so lightly, he grazed his thumb over her cheekbone, then cupped her chin in his hand. "And the color, Eva." He breathed.

His free hand came to rest on hers. His skin was so much darker than her own pale shade. No doubt he'd gained such color from the months under the Indian sun. It should have terrified her, that touch. But it didn't. Instead, his touch gave her a sort of liquid calm, stilling the room about her, allowing her to focus on him and him alone. "I've known so little color," she murmured.

His fingers curled around hers. "Women wear the brightest hues you can imagine." He knelt by the tub, his eyes growing vibrant. "And fabrics are hung high above head and at every possible spot."

He painted a veritable picture with his words, transporting her. She listened but all the while marveled at how much she enjoyed the feel of his protective hands upon her. "And?"

"Flowers fill the markets, bright yellow and pink. They string them and hang them. The very sky is perfumed."

Eva ached to see something so beautiful. Surely, there in the midst of so much color and beauty one couldn't feel pain.

Then there was this moment with him. How could she feel suffering right now? Here with Ian, who had rescued her. To her surprise, she didn't suffer. For the first time in years, her heart ached not with pain, but with need. The need for the comforting and consuming embrace of another.

His soft touch, compounded by the warm water lapping at her skin, left her hungry with want. "Do you remember your promise?" She whispered as if the words weren't even her own. "To kiss me one day if I asked?"

His breath hitched in his throat. "Eva, I don't think . . . after what happened in the alley."

"You promised." She swallowed. All she desired was to wipe away the memories of evil men. Surely, Ian's pure kiss would do that.

For a moment, he hesitated, and then there was nothing in the world but them.

Ian's lips came down over hers so softly she was unsure he had kissed her in truth. It was strange, unlike anything she could remember. Gentle and giving. She leaned in toward him carefully and allowed her shoulder to rest against his chest. Her wet skin rubbed against his white linen shirt, plastering it to his hard muscles.

The heat of his mouth was hypnotic, drawing her in like the moon pulls the tide. Still, after several moments, she drew back. There was no danger to him, only gentleness, the flicker of hope, and the soft glow of affection.

Perhaps Ian could never quite erase the past for her. Perhaps even worse, he wished to pull it to the surface, but that look . . . that look—which seemed to see her as the most beautiful woman in the world—nearly undid her.

Eva smiled softly up at her rescuer, and for the first time in a great deal of time, she felt that there might just be a bit of joy in the world.

Chapter 13

There was no question. Ian had flung himself onto the bonfire of sinners. But he was bloody well going to make the most of his burning. With just the barest caress of her lips, Eva drew him further and further into her beautiful, broken heart. It was impossible to explain the way he knew she belonged to him. She'd always belonged to him.

Despite the past.

Despite his betrayals.

"Kiss me again?" he murmured. He trailed his fingertips along her delicate jaw, tilting her head back, feeling as though they were still bonded in a kiss, though their lips were no longer touching.

Good Christ, he wanted her kiss, but he would take no more than she would give. A kiss could do no harm, could it? Not when they both needed comfort.

Her lips parted slightly as she contemplated his request. Even now, her skin was flushed, from the bath or from his presence it was impossible to tell. She drew in a soft breath and lifted her mouth to his. Sliding his hand into her shorn black hair, he savored the glorious feel of her mouth on his.

A harsh knock rapped the door, shaking it on its hinges. "Sir!"

They broke their embrace, but neither of them moved

away. Their faces lingered close together, sharing breath and the first blazing tendrils of terrifying passion. A passion forbidden to them by their loyalty to the dead.

"Sir!"

The moment broke and Eva pulled back, her face ashen.

Regret for the loss of her touch and for the growing horror on Eva's face snaked through his gut. Ian snapped his gaze toward the door. "A moment!"

This was not supposed to be happening. He was not supposed to be kissing Hamilton's widow. Not after . . . How could Eva ever trust him if he behaved in such a manner?

"Who is it?" Eva demanded, her voice brittle.

"Mrs. Marlock, I think." Ian grabbed his coat and pulled it over his damp linen shirt. With one last glance at Eva in the bath, he made sure she was decently submerged. The warm water lapped at her chin, and only her wary face and dark hair showed over the edge of the tub.

Smiling with an assurance he didn't feel, he tried to convince himself that this sudden desire for Eva humming through his veins did not bode disastrously ill. He cracked the door.

Mrs. Marlock stood, a gas lamp in her hand. Her wrinkled face seemed to float in the darkness, reflecting the fiery yellow. "Oh, sir," she hissed. "I thought it only right to warn you."

The familiar feeling of impending danger rammed through him, dispelling any illusion that they were safe. "Warn us?"

She glanced right to left and she stepped even closer. "My friend Mrs. Levler, she runs an inn just two streets over. Well, she came over a quarter of the hour ago all in a bother."

Ian nodded, barely able to stand the collection of words it took the woman to impart a small bit of information. "What upset her?"

Mrs. Marlock's lips pursed. "I never saw such doings, if you ask me, but you've been a gentleman despite the carryings-on. And you've contributed handsomely to me and my husband."

Ian resisted his pressing inclination to shake her. "Thank you. What have you learned?"

"Two men," she confessed. "Quite rough and unpleasant they are, going from inn to inn looking for a young woman of your lady's description." Mrs. Marlock nodded to herself. "Unusually pretty, and odd, short hair. Possibly strange dress. And then there was you. A strong, big man with the airs of a gentleman."

Mrs. Palmer, no doubt, had sprung into action. She wouldn't implement official inquiry, even with the death of her guard. She would not wish to have outside sources questioning the manner of her establishment or start probing into the lives of the lords she worked for. But that would not stop her from sending out her less savory associates, associates with no moral qualms about murder or abduction.

Christ, perhaps he should have shot Mrs. Palmer and been done, or at the very least offered up his entire fortune. But now that the damn woman had had enough time to contemplate her position, he very much doubted that anything but Eva's return would placate her. She'd clearly begun to suspect, if not discovered, Lord Thomas Carin had not been the one to come and free Eva from the madhouse.

"Mrs. Marlock, I cannot tell you how I appreciate your assistance." His fingers dug into the wooden grain of the door as he realized they had no time to waste. "Send down to the coaching house, and have my man—"

"I've done it, sir. The minute Mrs. Levler left. I knew you'd want to be off."

Ian gave her a grateful look. Despite her ramblings, the woman had sense. Quickly he reached into his pocket and pulled out one of his few remaining guineas. "You are a gem. A true diamond."

She bobbed a curtsy and gave a quick grin. "Thank you." Her jovial countenance vanished. "Now we best get your lady dressed and ready for travel. I can tell the poor dear has been through a great trial."

Ian stepped back and opened the door just wide enough to let the older woman in. He had experience at getting women out of clothes. Getting them in was quite another matter.

When he turned back to the room, Eva was already on her feet, a long piece of white bath linen wrapped about her slight frame.

Water dotted the floor before the pool and the bed-sheet was a damp mass beside the tub.

Mrs. Marlock hurried into the room. "Make haste. We must be away immediately."

And then he spotted it. The small brown bottle in Eva's frail hand.

Laudanum. He hadn't even thought to ask if she'd managed the purchase this morning. His stomach clenched. How could he have forgotten that Eva was no ordinary woman? That she was a woman half possessed?

It should not have surprised him. She wouldn't be over such an addiction from a kiss, but still . . . It was almost as painful to see her clutch that bottle as to know a half dozen men might be coming after them.

It was all he could do not to cross the room and knock the poison from her hand. He was tempted to shout, "Don't!" He bit back his demand and strode out into the pitch-dark hall. There was no time for that.

Such duels between them would keep for later.

He only prayed she wouldn't drown herself in the stuff while being dressed.

He rushed down the stairs and out to the back alley, where the coach would be waiting. The savage thought that all of this was his fault raged through him. Hamilton was the precursor to all this. And while Ian hadn't driven the blade home, he'd been the instrument that killed his friend. He still felt the hot blood on his hands and the traitorous desire to see justice done.

But there was no turning back now. The dead were dead, and he had enough concerns with the living.

Chapter 14

The back stair creaked.

Eva hoped that in the future Mrs. Marlock might use a pittance of her funds, perhaps the funds Ian had contributed, to fix it. As it was now, she treaded on light feet, the iron floorboard nails making a horrid racket against the old wood. 'Twasn't easy descending so carefully. Her limbs were beginning to shake again because she hadn't taken quite enough laudanum before her dressing. A fine sheen of sweat had broken out over her skin and her stomach was an angry tangle as she forced herself to move.

Every instinct demanded she lift the small vial and drink, but just now she needed her attention as sharp as possible.

She gathered her strength and hurried down the last few stairs. Each breath she drew echoed with an unnatural harshness in her own ears.

She had to get to the coach.

She came out into the windowless back hall. Darkness enveloped her and she blinked, hoping her eyes would adjust quickly. As soon as she was able to make out the gray shapes of furniture she darted past the table and cupboards and started for the back door.

Voices echoed from the hall leading out to the foyer. Eva suddenly felt her feet hesitate. Instead of walking out the door to the coach as she should have done, a voice inside her demanded she quietly pause at the hallway.

Mr. Marlock's rich Yorkshire tones rippled through the air. The sound of rough voices echoed back.

There was a long pause and Eva wished she could see what was happening. Then there was the solid chink of a large amount of coin. The sound of a sizable purse being flung down on a table.

The innkeep's voice eased into a tone of awe. One of the other men laughed.

The saliva dried in Eva's mouth. She backed away from the hall, bolted around, and scrambled for the door. If only Mr. Marlock had the fortitude of his wife.

Footsteps rumbled in the hall behind her. Heavy, booted steps, making a quick pace. The swaggering stride of men who were no better than dogs.

Eva didn't look back, even when she reached a trembling hand for the door. She grasped the black iron latch and lifted. The heavy panel resisted her tug. She gritted her teeth and dragged it back. It gave way, opening with a groan. The cold north wind swirled around her, infiltrating her cloak, freezing the sweat upon her skin.

Eva rushed into the deepening night, searching for any sight of Ian.

The coach light swung just a few feet off in the narrow alley. Ian's silhouette pierced the light like a devil in the dark. His gloved hand stretched out toward her.

She took it with more purpose than she had known in years. Sliding his hands about her waist, he bundled her through the door and dropped her unceremoniously onto the cushioned velvet seat. He shouted something to the driver and then he was beside her, slamming the door.

He didn't settle back, but instead remained at attention, his hands twin fists on his knees.

Eva seized his forearm, his body angular under her fingertips. "They've paid the Marlocks," she said tightly.

"What?"

"Mr. Marlock. They've paid him." Ian's face was nothing more than a pale oval in the darkness, but she had to make him understand. "I'm sure of it."

A muscle worked in his cheek. "How can you know?"

"I heard the chink of coin, and then boot steps were heading for the back kitchen."

"You're certain?"

Did he truly not trust her ability to understand what happened around her? "Yes, Ian," she snapped. "I am certain."

His doubt seemed to linger between them; then he spoke with intensity. "We must make haste from this damned place."

She turned her face away from him, confused and angry. Angry that she should have to run and be so afraid. And confused by her feelings.

She wanted nothing more than to hold on to Ian, to feel his touch. For the first time in years, she truly wanted to be caressed. Terrifying though it might be, she was sure she desired it, but only from Ian.

Such treacherous thoughts were dangerous. Whether she wished to say it aloud or not, she was a monster. And whatever faults Ian might have, he deserved far more than a monster . . . or a woman who could never be more than a burden and risk to his very safety.

She pried her fingers from his arm and clenched her shaking hands. She stared out the coach window, watching the night streets race by, swallowing back her returned nausea, unwilling to show him how desperately she needed to reach for her laudanum. It would be so easy to make all this vanish, but not now. Not when he so loathed that particular weakness in her.

Instead, she focused upon the knowledge that another coach followed them. That it might be a mere few hours before she was taken again.

Ian wouldn't allow that.

She wouldn't allow that.

Even as her brain felt it was rattling apart, of that she was sure. Nothing would make her go back. She'd rather die.

She couldn't shake the feeling that she had not known what danger was. Even in the asylum she had been safe. Locked away, half mad, but safe in a fashion. And now that she was free . . .

The danger seemed stronger. For it was no longer simply she who could be damaged. Oh, no. She could now destroy the man who had come to save her.

He had been a damned fool. A fool to be so soft. A fool to think that he could let Eva rest. His stupidity had very nearly got them caught. And that would be the end of everything.

Eva was Thomas's legal ward. The prick controlled everything about her. Who she could marry, where she could live, how much money she could spend—and when all was said and done no court in the land would let Ian keep her, not until he proved her sane.

The coach rocked on the winter road, jostling them brutally. Ian ground his teeth together, staring out at the outskirts of the city racing by. He couldn't look at Eva. He'd let lust—lust—seize his reason.

He'd made so many mistakes. He was still making them, allowing his emotions to turn into a riot in his staid body. He sucked in a sharp breath and nearly gagged.

Even inside his pristine coach, he could smell the slums just on the other side of the lacquered wood. No matter how frozen the earth, that smell of rancid death would prevail if he did not steel his mind and heart to the task.

There was no questioning the resolute truth of it. The softness in his heart had to be hardened. He could no longer be merciful. Not in his need to keep her safe, not in his resolve to destroy those who had brutalized her, and not in his absolute certainty that she would never drink laudanum again.

Chapter 15

India
Two years earlier

*T*he letter from Eva had been full of descriptions of baby Adam—his firstborn son and heir—and it had, for a moment, filled Hamilton's heart with such relief that he had been certain that all of the confusion between him and his wife would dissipate. But then, slowly, it had struck him that the letter had not truly been written to him. Though his name was on the parchment, it had been written to Ian. The subtle description of the forest in the fall, the animals going into hibernation, and the state of last spring's colts were all meant for Ian. Ian cared about such things. Not him. It was as if she were tearing his guts out. Didn't she understand that? She'd been promised to him since their childhood and God and the law had sealed that promise. She'd never been for that moralizing prig who only played at their friendship now, unwilling to join him in cards, drinking, or the occasional trip to a heathen whore.

Anger pumped through Hamilton as he stared at his men marching over the dusty ground. They had been marching for well over an hour beneath the high sun. And they wouldn't stop sweltering until he deemed them perfect.

These men needed discipline. They were certainly raised without it, with no care for order, or law, or that *which was right. When he looked at his men, all he could see was the grasping hands of the bazaar sellers, the filth in the streets, and the smell of the latrine in the heat.*

These people had no idea how to govern themselves, but, by God, those who came under his rule would come up to snuff, even if a few of them had to pay dearly for his satisfaction. He had learned long ago from his father that anything less than perfect would condemn him to shame. And he wouldn't let his men shame him.

He'd known enough shame from his father. And just because the old man was dead didn't relieve Hamilton of the looming hand of hundreds of years of familial expectation.

The straight lines wavered as one man stumbled and fell to the earth. His tan uniform blended into the puff of dust that spiraled up around his body.

Hamilton ground his teeth together as two men pulled the fallen soldier away from the ranks. "Lazy bastard," he muttered.

Sergeant Ames snapped his attention toward Hamilton and said, "Perhaps the men should cease drill. This heat—"

"I don't give a damn about the heat," Hamilton snapped. How hard was it for Ames to understand that he would settle for nothing less than perfection from these heathen dogs? "Drill them harder." Hamilton turned his gaze to the retreating figures of the men carrying the fallen soldier away. "And have that one flogged."

Ames's eyes flared. "Sir, you—you can't do that."

Hamilton snorted and raised his brow. "The man is negligent, lazy, and attempting to free himself from duty. As such, he must be punished."

"But he is not one of us."

Hamilton paused, then blew out a frustrated breath. "Fine, then. Reduction of pay and extra duties."

As the drill continued, Hamilton forced himself to stare straight ahead. It was a travesty, the lightness of discipline given to the natives. But it was law. A native could not be flogged, not like the men from British soil.

It mattered not. The man would pay for his indiscretion. After all, there were worse punishments to endure than a mere flogging.

England
The present

The bitter wind whipping across England penetrated every crevice of the coach. The charcoal burner had long ceased to warm Eva and the worsening jittering of her body was not of the cold but of need.

And bloody Ian, who had offered her such comfort not so very long ago, sat at a distance as if finally awakened to the truth. She was a leper. Figuratively if not literally. If he touched her, he too would be caught by the horrid shame contaminating her soul.

She could not recall when last they stopped. Hours? A day? In fact, they raced on so cruelly she could not bring herself to ask him to stop. Driven. 'Twas the only word to describe him. His face, which had seemed like that of an angel of mercy at the asylum, had changed into the brutal visage of an avenging beast who would not relent.

He stared out the window, his profile cold. Angry. Eva dug her fingernails into the tops of her thighs to the point of pain. The sharp sensation was welcome; it distracted her. With each rocky groove in the wintery road, her body ached . . . but it was not the ache of simple discomfort. It was the ache of fever, the ache of her body screaming out for its medicine. The shock of every surface of her skin feeling utterly alive.

They had traveled all through the night. Faint blue light insisted on lighting the interior of the coach. The icy fingers of the early sun touched them.

More than anything save laudanum, she needed water. Water to alleviate the sandpaper cruelty of her throat. Water to bathe her itching skin. She let her fingers fidget over her lap. "Ian?"

He didn't turn from the window. "Yes?"

She licked her lips, shocked to find they were hot, feverish. "I . . . need to stop."

"No."

Something, in the middle of the night, had changed. She could not stop the impossible feeling that the moments she had been cared for and not judged were gone now. "Fine, then."

Only the eternal thunder of horse hooves against icy earth penetrated the silence that commenced.

Until finally he burst out, "I will not stop. Not for you. Not for God. Not for any man."

In answer, she fingered her laudanum bottle. She lowered her eyes to the jar hidden by her pocket. "Fine, then," she repeated. She yanked the smooth pottery from her coat, determined to swallow but a drop so the wild, skin-scratching call for peace would stop.

His eyes jerked toward her, the jade green orbs snapping wide. His entire body seemed to enlarge in his sudden rage. "What in the bloody hell are you doing?"

"You give me no comfort and you will not let me rest." She lifted the bottle and gave him a mock salute. "This gives me both. Beautifully." She lifted her cold fingers to the stopper and pulled it out. The pop echoed and she locked gazes with him, defiant.

"Give it to me," he commanded.

She laughed, the sound frightening to her own ears. "Stop the coach," she countered.

He sat so still one might think his muscles had turned to the rock that filled the moors. "Give it to me, Eva."

"Go to hell," she retorted, then lifted the bottle.

"God damn you!" he hissed.

And before she could move another inch, he darted over to her and yanked the bottle from her grasp.

She slammed her fist against his shoulder. "Bastard!"

"Addict," he snapped, holding the bottle far out of reach.

Desperate now that he'd risen to her taunting anger, she bit out, "It's my bottle."

He leaned over her, his face but a few breaths away. "It is in my possession. You'll never have it. Never again."

His nearness only exacerbated the tingling of her skin. If only she could come out of her fleshy envelope. If only she could find some release ... And the only release she knew, he'd just denied her.

She'd pushed too far in a war she could not win, and panic grabbed her guts. But she needed what was in his hand. Needed it to still the voracious animal tearing at her insides. "Please, Ian. Give it me."

"Never."

"Please!" she pleaded, hating the hungry note in her own impassioned voice.

"Never!" he roared.

They sat in silence, staring at each other like two dogs eyeing the other before the attack. Until finally she couldn't bear her hateful feel of her demanding flesh, and the drive to find release. This was compulsion. There was no other word for how she felt. That damn bottle compelled her to act as mad as Thomas accused her of being.

"Ian," she began. Her stomach tightened with what had to be self-revulsion. But it didn't feel like that. It felt ... She stared at his beautiful face, then let her gaze travel to his broad shoulders. Shoulders that had shielded her from danger ... This thing now urging her felt like anticipation.

She bit her lower lip, slowing her suddenly uneven breathing. She'd made bargains before. Not of a sexual nature, but she'd seen the other girls do it. It always worked to their temporary advantage. And Ian was a man. A strong, undoubtedly virile man. She allowed her eyes to soften with the promise of pleasure. His pleasure. To her shock, it did not take much for her to feel the liquid heat of wanting when she looked on him. "I ... I will do anything."

She closed her eyes as a wave of intense want hit her. For him? For her laudanum? Slowly, oh so slowly, she placed her hand on his broad thigh and, amazedly, her body thrilled to the hardness of his leg. Would he be just as hard farther up his thigh? She let her hand trail up his leg toward his hip, seeking answer. She glanced down to her fingers. It would be so easy to believe it was someone else's hand. But it wasn't, and she liked seeing it there. She flicked her gaze back to his, her breath growing ragged. "Anything."

Ian stared at her, completely still. At his lack of response, she dared herself to venture farther. To give in to the sudden interest of her own body. She'd known so little pleasure. But something whispered inside, something that turned her heart and core into molten desire, that Ian could give it to her as no one else had. She slipped her hand up the soft material encasing his muscular thigh until she cupped his length in her hand. To her surprise, he was not aroused. Even so, her hand could not contain him through the fabric.

He'd be large. A size that some women would give anything for. Lovemaking had always been a duty to her; she'd never understood the girls who'd spoken of coupling as bliss and size as an advantage.

In her agitated state, she suddenly realized how much she wanted to understand.

"Please," she moaned, massaging her fingers over him, feeling him harden. What would it feel like to have that hard length inside her? Would it stroke her to the release she so needed? The only release she'd ever known was in the rolling of laudanum. Would it be better than the opiates?

Cupping him, the heat of his cock caressing her hand, she had no doubt. Yes. Yes, it would be far better because Ian was unlike any other man she knew. And so the pleasure would be unlike any other.

Dark emotions turned his eyes emerald, and for a moment Eva was certain he would catch her up and let her have her release—and her laudanum.

She didn't dare think how far she had fallen to be on her knees before her childhood friend, the boy she had loved, begging . . . for pleasure . . . begging for release.

Ian's free hand, large and rough, came to rest on her fingers. He pressed her harder against his cock and his head dropped back against the cushions. He ground against her palm, a moan of lust escaping his lips.

She had him. And she had her laudanum. Yet it wasn't relief she felt. She wanted this, even if she didn't truly understand.

The feel of his hand over hers felt alarmingly right. As did the urge to lean forward and to place her mouth over the fall of his trousers. Her breasts grew tight at the thought, leaving her heavy with the drug of desire. She longed for him to take her in his arms. To devour her. To drive everything away but their bodies, united against the cruel world. With that image in mind, she reached with her free hand to undo the buttons at his front.

Ian's hand suddenly enfolded hers and jerked it back

with a punishing twist. Regret raked his features as he choked. "What are you doing?"

Shaking his head wildly, he yanked the window down and tossed the bottle of laudanum out into the cold.

The desire that had consumed her died a quick death as a shriek tore from her lips. She scrambled toward the door, ready to fly out of the moving vehicle to retrieve it.

Ian grabbed her face, his fingers pressing into her chin and jaw.

Instantly, she stopped.

Slowly, as slowly as she had dragged her hand up his thigh, he turned her face to his. Gazing down at her, his dark gaze blazing with intensity, he forced her face up until their lips were but an inch apart. "You are not a whore."

The pain of his words sliced her to the bone. "How can you be sure?"

His entire body tensed as if she had hit him.

Her lips curled back from her teeth, wishing to hurt him now with the impossible desire he'd taken from her. "Do you imagine I was in a nunnery all this time? I learned a number of tricks from the other girls."

The taut muscles in his face eased, but a shadow tinged his skin. "I don't give a damn what they taught you." His thumb caressed her cheek, but he didn't let go. "I will not let you be a whore of another's making."

As the fight diminished from her shaking body, she grimaced. How could she explain that she would whore herself every day if it meant she didn't have to remember? "It was mine," she insisted.

He gripped her chin, those hypnotic eyes of his a war of agony and fury. "I don't care."

"I risked my life for that bottle!" Eva grabbed his arm with both hands and lurched forward. Her body rocking harshly against his hard chest. The pressure eased as he wrenched his hand away from her jaw.

"I don't give a devil's damn," he growled, his hands coming up around her back, pulling her against him.

"You don't—" She sucked in several breaths, her body pressed against the contours of his hard chest and flat stomach. She'd felt nothing in her life like that hard wall of masculinity. "Do you know what happens—?"

"Yes," he hissed. "You'll shake and scream and feel as if you are losing your mind." His capable hands wrapped around her arms and bound her to him. "I have promised myself that I will protect you, even if I have to protect you from yourself."

Eva gaped at him as it hit her. "You think me pathetic and weak." Suddenly, an unbidden hot tear slipped down her cheek, followed by another. The first true tears she had known in years as she saw herself in his eyes.

He didn't pause but worked his fingers into her hair and pulled ever so slightly. "You have no idea what I think." And then he slanted his lips over hers.

Eva struggled against his powerful embrace, her lips crushed under his. The touch of his mouth to hers shocked her for a moment and then, as tinder struck, her body burned with flame. She'd longed for his kisses once, and now she had them. They were everything she'd ever dreamed and more. So much more.

One of his hands moved to angle her head so that he might deepen the kiss; his other hand splayed over her back, pressing her to him as if he might somehow make them one.

The kiss, harsh and full of need, stole every thought she possessed. Any doubt. Any fear. Gone in a whirlwind of desire and promise. She gasped against him and his tongue delved into her mouth, tasting her.

She moaned softly, marveling at how her body longed to yield itself up to him. Every muscle in her frame was liquid heat, intent on receiving something it barely understood.

But as she held on to him, she felt herself slipping away, losing control. She couldn't forget. She couldn't forget that he had denied her just moments before, and that this kiss was not out of love, but rather fear and anger.

With his skill and her wildness, it was so tempting to give in to this kiss, to give in to his will. A jolt of fury overwhelmed the temptation. He had stolen what little control she had, what few choices she had.

She tried to pull away, bucking harshly against his arms. "Enough."

He only held tighter and his imprisoning embrace spilled ice down her spine. Madly, as if he could somehow reach her with his kiss, he lowered his head to catch her lips again.

Gasping, she twisted her face away, still awed by the pleasure of their kiss. Still tempted to betray herself for the pleasure he could give. But she would never betray herself again, so she snapped, "Are you no better than them?"

Instantly, he pulled his head back, staring down at her with enraged astonishment.

"Remember, I am no whore," she whispered, the words harsh against her closing throat.

His grasp eased. His eyes filled with a matching self-disgust. "Eva—"

"Not even your whore."

Slowly, he pressed her shaking body against his until their heartbeats thrummed together. "Forgive me."

"I'll forgive you if you give me what I need."

Ian pushed her hands from him and he threw himself

back to his own seat. His gaze slowly returned to hers with a terrifying clarity. "You shall have nothing that I don't give you and certainly not laudanum."

Whatever demon had got hold of him showed its face, turning the sweet young man that she had known into the hardest of men. "I don't know you anymore. We are not even friends," she said.

"No. We are not, and I don't know you, either. Not any longer." He leaned back, his face shuttering.

Eva gulped at the sudden swelling of her throat. For in the finality and stone-cold intent in his eyes, she knew he didn't lie. But she was his now, and she was as much a prisoner as she had been in the asylum. Worse, she and Ian were strangers now. Connected by nothing but the past. "Where do you take me?"

"To Blythely Castle."

So tired now, so beaten, her body felt as if it were sinking into the floor. "Devonshire?"

"Nothing but the hills and sea shall see you until I can prove you are not mad. We will prove to the world you are nothing more than a grieved woman addicted by force," he declared adamantly. "You aren't mad. You aren't."

Yet, in his voice, she heard it. There in the deep tone of it was the worst thing she had ever known. Doubt.

Chapter 16

Ian's boots hit the ground hard. He relished the feel of frozen earth jarring his bones. Sooty air invaded his nostrils and he flexed his palms, sure he might tear apart the first person he spoke to. He'd called her a whore. She'd acted as a whore. He'd been a bastard of the first order. Christ, he'd forgotten how to be around ladies, and Eva was no ordinary lady. She'd been to hell and was not yet out of it.

How had he descended into such depths of cruelty?

Worse, he'd been so tempted. So dangerously tempted to let her do as she had wished. Would he have given her the laudanum just for his own goddamn growing need to feel her? To meet with her on some plain that was far afield from that of friendship?

He would never shake this new self-revulsion. He'd been far too close to lacing his hand into her hair and guiding her mouth not to his cock but to his own lips, and then he would have made slow, careful love to her.

Far too close.

So he would have to be as cruel to himself as he was to her.

Crueler.

He strode up to the inn. Perhaps he should have sent Digby to collect their necessaries, but he longed for the normalcy he'd once known. The simple instruction of men, of organizing, something that had come naturally to him in India. But this wasn't India. He doubted whether anything could ever be normal again.

The Tudor structure sat like a tired old woman, half slouched into the earth and snow.

The sign of the Rose & Thistle swung drunkenly above the scratched wood door, its rust-hewn hinges creaking in the wind.

Wordlessly, he walked into the premises. The narrow hall was dim in the morning light, the whitewashed walls unwelcoming. Immediately the scents of dark ale and cooking meat mingled with rosemary assaulted him. God, what wouldn't he give to stride up behind the bar — wherever that was — grab a bottle of whiskey, and pour the peaty liquid down his throat. He'd be done with it all for at least a day. But drunken oblivion was not in his near future.

Hell was on his horizon and one didn't face hell three sheets to the wind. Not if one wished to defeat it rather than join it.

Eva would hate him more and more and he would see more and more of the dark side of her heart that had taken hold in these ravaging years. Striding deeper down the hall, he swung his gaze to a doorway, praying the keep was awake.

A pathetic fire burned in the hearth of the sparsely furnished sitting room. Empty of life, ratty brocade chairs were interspaced over the cracked wood floor. It was barely later than dawn and no one was in sight. A black pot hissed and sputtered over the poorly banked fire and Ian drew in the smells of thick porridge.

His stomach growled, and he forced himself not to go over and eat straight from the spoon still in the pot. It was almost a certainty that Eva was not hungry. Years of laudanum use was a particularly good means of suppressing the appetite. He, on the other hand, might eat an entire boar if it were placed before him.

"Keep!" he barked, not giving a pox-ridden damn if he woke the entire establishment. Ian headed into the frigid room. If he concentrated, he could just barely feel tendrils of heat slipping through the cold air.

"Keep!" he shouted again, his voice echoing off the white-plastered walls.

Footsteps scurried above his head, shaking dust from the low wood-beam ceiling, then scuffled down the stairs at the back. "Sir," an alarmed voice called just loud enough that he might hear. "Sir, please. I've guests. They're sleeping and I can't—"

The short little man of about fifty nearly tripped on his long, flour-covered apron as he hurried forward. His mouth froze as he took Ian in. Bushy white whiskers framed the keep's face, and he squinted up at Ian through myopic blue eyes. For several moments, those fat lips worked and his Adam's apple bobbed as he contemplated him in exaggerated shock.

Apparently, gentlemen didn't make a habit of stopping at the Rose & Thistle.

"Do you require a room?" he finally managed.

Ian shook his head, already desirous of departing. In fact, the fast-brewing impatience in him would not dim until he was safe in his castle on the clean and untouched sea. "Fresh horses. This is a coaching inn?"

The man bobbed his hanging chin up and down. "Indeed. Indeed. I shall fetch my man."

Ian turned toward the window, squinting at the sun's first real rays gleaming through the dirt-smudged panes. "And while you're at it, I'm going to need several other items for quick transport."

"Certainly. In a few hours—"

"Now," Ian barked, his gloved hands fisting as he

snapped his gaze back to the short little man. A man who no doubt had never known a life-threatening day in his existence. "I will give you five guineas if you can make all that I wish happen within the hour."

The innkeeper wrung his calloused hands. "F-five?"

"Five," Ian said firmly. "I need horses. Coal for a burner. Blankets. Water, food. And anything that might relieve—" Ian hesitated. How was he to say it? "Shivering."

"Shi—" The man nodded as he stopped himself. "Of course. Of course."

Ian didn't smile or nod; he was beyond such reassuring measures now. He'd wasted those on Mrs. Marlock. In turn, Mr. Marlock had taken his coin and sent Mrs. Palmer's dogs on Eva. "Good. I shall return within the half hour. I expect all to be done." With that, he charged back out into the cold.

As he came outside the old inn, he slowed his step, eyeing his solitary coach standing in the quiet yard. Something wasn't right.

The door stood ajar.

Eva.

Unruly fear grabbed his guts. His eyes darted to the coaching box. The coachman was gone. Ian ran across the snow, his feet slipping in the icy slush. Windmilling his arms, he just barely kept from sliding headlong into the earth. He stopped at the vehicle and ripped the door open.

The velvet seats stared back at him. Empty.

Bloody hell.

Ian reeled around, his breath coming in strangled intakes. His vision intensified until his pupils burned. Again. He'd made a mistake again. A horrendous mistake. Since Hamilton had shot that horse, his life had been nothing but one mistake after the other. "Eva!" he shouted.

His desperate eyes searched the horizon, then swung back to the inn. "Eva!" he shouted again.

"Yes?" she called sweetly.

He stopped and whipped around at her disembodied speech.

Snow crunched on the other side of the coach. Then Eva emerged from behind the vehicle, straightening her skirts. Dark smudges blossomed under her eyes, but there was a definite relief to her face. Her tension seemed to have dissipated as if she'd been holding her muscles taut these last hours.

For a brief moment, he was certain she'd somehow gotten her hands on laudanum, but there was hardly an apothecary here on the open land.

"Where the hell did you go?" he demanded. Terror still ricocheted through his limbs and stole his reason. He crossed to her in two short strides and grabbed her upper arms, feeling the ridiculous need to have her body under his touch. To know she hadn't been taken. "I told you to stay in the coach."

She narrowed her cobalt eyes, then jerked back from his grasp. "You don't need to handle me."

Her warmth vanished from his now empty hands. Anger and fear rumbled inside him. "Eva, I cannot allow—"

"Oh, yes," she mocked, her hands shaking slightly. "I forgot. My safety is your primary concern."

"Exactly," he said softly, wishing he hadn't reacted with such impulse. "I'm sorry you dislike my behavior, but you are behaving rashly. You charge off without thought—"

"I had to relieve myself," she mumbled quickly, her eyes leaving his. "I believe your servants needed to do the same."

Ian gaped at her, his intense, fury-tinged worry fading

at her practical and yet frustrating words. "You could have waited."

She turned her face back up to his, her bold chin thrusting at him. "No, I couldn't. And you gave me no indication as to how long you might be gone."

"There are men looking for you, Eva." He closed his eyes for a moment, attempting to collect his mixed thoughts. He couldn't decide whether he should shake her for taking such a chance or drive his own head into a nearby stone wall. "Do you understand what will happen? If they find you?"

Instead of the immediate contrition that he had expected, she snorted. Tendrils of short hair bounced against her face as she propped slender hands upon her equally slender waist. "Oh, Ian." The admonition came out as a rich, frightening laugh. "I understand better than you possibly ever could. I lived in that madhouse. Not you. I know what Mrs. Palmer and her men are capable of."

"Then why—?"

"Because you wouldn't stop the coach when you would have been but a step away from me. I have been in severe discomfort for over an hour." Those indigo eyes glinted under the morning sun, cold, empty, furious. "I don't know about you, but I had no desire to ride all the way to Devonshire with the scent of—"

"Yes, thank you," he growled. He had never traveled with a woman and certainly not at breakneck speed. In the military, men had picked up and run without hesitation. With her, there was a host of troubles. Aside from her addiction, there were common necessities that would simply slow them down.

Perhaps he could permit her a few moments' rest inside the inn. As he opened his mouth, the rumble of another coach approaching filled his ears. The brief temptation to let her go into the inn with him vanished. Foolishness could not mislead his heart. Nor pity. Not when so much was at stake.

At any moment, that woman's men could come racing down the road. He might not be able to fight them off, for all his fine experience in killing. "Get in."

She blanched at his harshness, her cheeks even paler than usual. Her skin glistened with the fine touch of perspiration despite the chill in the air. "Ian, I merely wish to walk. My legs—"

"You can walk to Land's End and back when we reach my estate." The last thing they needed was someone to see her. She stood out like a lily among slug-eaten petunias. If Palmer's men came asking questions, he wanted as little information left in their wake as possible. He took a step forward, towering over her. "Are you waiting for something in particular? Another invitation, perhaps?"

She drew in a slow breath, her breasts pressing against the thin gown. "Ian, you cannot mean to—"

Without a word, he picked her up, ignoring her tense muscles. There was no time for words, for explanations or assurances. Her light form barely weighed his arms down as he readied to shove her back inside. It seemed to be a ritual in the making, his depositing her without due manners into his coach.

Still, needs must.

A feral growl came from her throat and her body turned into the harsh angles of an angry cat. "Put me down," she snapped. "You cannot treat me thus."

He said absolutely nothing as he thrust her into the vehicle, bum first. "Digby," he shouted.

His man ran from the back of the inn, his hands at his breeches, buttoning them swiftly.

"My lord?"

"We're leaving. Now," Ian ordered.

"Yes, my lord." Digby turned about and called over his shoulder, "I'll fetch the others."

Ian gave a sharp nod, adjusting his hold on Eva.

She dug her nails deep into his shoulders, but he ignored the sharp pain as he eased her back onto the cushioned seat. Despite being so thin, she struggled and twisted against him with a force worthy of the fiercest grenadier. With each thrust and twist of her, her bottom curved into his hips.

Ian swallowed, grabbing her hands and wrapping his arms across her chest. A double embrace. An embrace one made after making love. Not for subduing women on the brink of madness.

At last, he could take it no more. "Stop fighting, woman."

She glanced back at him, her teeth bared. "I'll stop fighting if you stop being an ass."

His arms tightened about her as he yanked her tighter against him, her back to his front, her breasts soft yet firm under him, and the thin curve of her hip pressed against his. "Don't be mad, you little fool," he gritted against her ear.

Instantly, she stilled. Her eyes lifted to his and his heart slammed against his ribs. Those cool blue depths stared up at him as if he were an enemy. "I am not mad. Nor am I a fool," she said, her voice so low it rang through the small space like a tragic bell.

Suddenly, he felt stricken, as if somehow she had delivered a mortal blow to his heart. But it was he who had delivered the blow. A verbal one. "I—"

She turned her face from him, her entire body held rigid against him as if such a pose were the only thing keeping her inside her skin.

"Eva?" he coaxed, suddenly wishing she still thrashed

against him. Anything but this. "I—I didn't mean it. You must know that?"

As horse hooves, harnesses, and the soft talk of servants loading supplies onto the coach echoed through the yard, she didn't relax against his chest or yield to his words.

The animation of her spirit slipped away from him, even though he held her in his arms. With each painful moment that slipped past, he knew whatever trust she might have had in him was gone. Shattered as easily as spun glass. With careless words.

Chapter 17

*M*ad. It had pained her more than any beating to hear the word slip past Ian's lips. Worse even than *whore*.

Slowly, Eva inhaled and the tangy salt air stole into her lungs.

Soon they would arrive at his castle. Moments, really. After all, Ian had claimed they'd rolled through the gate-house leading to his estate. Though she had said nothing, a part of her rejoiced. They would reach their destination and she would finally be free of this horrid box racing across England.

He'd been tense since the inn, as if he were as wary of returning to his life as she. Would he find it easy to be the lord of the manor? Would he delight in the return to his castle?

As if in answer to her thoughts, the coach rattled over gravel and came to a halt.

"We're here," Ian said, his voice wary. He lingered, staring out the window, his hand on the door handle. A brief look flashed over his face. A look that brought to mind the sweet boy who had come to Carridan Hall afraid and alone.

She resisted the urge to comfort him. He was a man who would not likely accept such a thing now.

Eva didn't move. For all that she longed to leave the coach, she was unsure what awaited her outside it.

The door sprang open and Ian vaulted down into the damp gray light of lowering evening. His hand reached back into the coach. Expectant. "Come, Eva. It's time."

She gave consideration to staying in the coach in the hopes that reality might just let her fade away as it had done many a time before. But in truth, no such thing would occur. It took more effort than she liked, but she forced her stiff limbs to move. She inched forward until her feet brushed the edge of the coach. Head high, she took the barest tips of his fingers and stepped down.

Ian stood just behind her as she paused on the sweeping drive.

Twelve servants stood upon the steep steps of the castle front. Their pristine gray-and-black uniforms flickered in the cold breeze. As if a single being, the servants stiffened at her shocking appearance. But as good servants, they averted their gaze, staring at the intricately patterned white-and-gray cobbled steps.

She had not seen the castle now in almost a decade. Long before, they had visited Ian's aunt and uncle often. And of course, they had come three years earlier, upon Ian's vestiture as viscount.

As a child, it had seemed enormous. Perfect, the stuff of legend. A legend she had played in, often pretending to be Lady Marian to Ian's Robin Hood and Hamilton's Sheriff of Nottingham. Nothing untoward could happen in this place; it had been such a place of love and dreams.

Now it still towered, but it was an earthly domain, its surfaces touched by the encroaching years and sea wind. Strange plantlike creatures pressed like barnacles to its mammoth walls. The stone edifice still towered high above her, though not as high as she remembered. But the turrets, resplendent and majestic, as if waiting for knights of old to guard the keep, were just as she remembered.

The castle dated back to well before the Tudors, and the family had added onto it in the madcap fashion of aristocrats. If she were to wander the gravel path to the other side, she would face a French chalet facade with high windows and butter yellow stone.

Eva squared her shoulders under the staff's pressing eyes. They all must have thought Ian was the mad one, bringing a scrawny rat into their pristine, orderly world after so many years away. Unwilling to face their censure, she focused again on the place that had been a haven, struck by the immensity of it.

The power of the castle was unlike anything she had known in so much time now, it was daunting. Once, such a house would have felt as normal as the rain in the fall months. Now normalcy was a dark room in a brown dress surrounded by loneliness.

"My dear!" a bright voice cried.

That voice rang out, an echo from the past. Eva froze.

Ian turned toward it, and for the first time in days a true smile turned his strong, sensual lips upward. A deep, booming laugh flowed over his lips, and he strode toward the woman, his greatcoat flapping behind him. "Aunt Elizabeth."

The lady, her soft silver blond hair floating about her face, came forward, her pace as elegant as a queen. And by her side charged a great, slightly drooling mastiff, his tawny body almost as large as a small pony. The animal's tail wagged excitedly, beating against Elizabeth's skirts as she opened her arms.

"Dear boy!" Her slender embrace extended, her sapphire day dress pristine yet feminine. "Welcome home!"

Home. It was indeed his home, but he hadn't seen it in years. Did that perchance make him as she was? A stranger but not a stranger, daring to look in and pray for the peace of acceptance?

Ian swept his aunt in his arms and whirled her around as if she were a young girl. The massive folds of her skirts belled out. "It is so good to see you."

The dog let out a booming bark but bore no aggression, just a sort of canine joy at its mistress's pleasure.

"Indeed!" Aunt Elizabeth exclaimed as she staggered a little, patting her hair, then patting a hand on her dog's massive head. "It is too long. Too long since you left us. And how different you look. So strong and so dark. And so impertinent."

Eva swayed ever so slightly on her feet, unsure what to feel. Her hands shook slightly as her throat tightened up.

"You shall be glad to know, I've kept the estates in good order with you away," Elizabeth said.

Ian replied, but Eva was not certain what he'd said as memories consumed her.

Lady Elizabeth Blake, dowager viscountess. Oh, lord, the woman had been at her wedding to Hamilton. At Adam's christening. Eva sucked in quick breaths, the memories hitting hard and fast.

For the briefest moment, the ground beneath her feet swung on a heavy axis and she had to close her eyes to keep from tilting.

Lady Elizabeth had always been so kind, her eyes glinting with mischief. The older woman had teased her about the pleasures of a husband such as Hamilton, fluffing her bouquet of flowers as Eva had received guests after the ceremony. And she'd been right: despite Hamilton's defects, he had been a good husband. Perhaps distant, even in the bedroom, but he'd fulfilled his duties.

It had always been a disappointment, that lack of feeling between them. But once she had learned that he had brutally killed an innocent horse over the loss of a silly race, she'd found it hard to appreciate him, to trust him, and most certainly to love him as Hamilton's father had so wished.

But even with the distance between them, they'd created together the most beautiful boy. For that she would always be grateful. Even though she had lost him. Eva's throat closed. The one only true thing that had come from her marriage was gone.

And these memories? A tide of emotion threatened to crash down upon her, but she couldn't stop them.

At his christening, Elizabeth had brought a perfect silver rattle to shake in front of Adam's bright eyes. She'd watched with delight as Adam had been taken to church in his little white gown with lace embroidered by Irish nuns.

Elizabeth was a figure who'd brought brightness wherever she went.

Eva's lungs clamped tight as the world whirred faster out of focus. She couldn't do this. She couldn't go back into this horrid world where everything would remind her of what she had lost. Of what she had so foolishly and easily destroyed with her rash decision to not listen to Thomas, the grooms, or even the coachman. Perhaps Ian was right. Perhaps she was a fool.

Just as her whole body cramped with sadness, the velvety brush of a damp nose and canine cheek rubbed against her hand. The big dog pressed into her as if it somehow sensed her distress and wished to offer up his Herculean body as a source of refuge.

She swallowed back the tears that the animal's pure and affectionate presence brought forth. Truly, didn't the dog sense she was not worthy of such gentle love?

After all, she'd been determined to go on her own. And ... why had she gone? The letter. The letter to whom? Hamilton was already dead. To Ian?

Yes. The letter had most definitely been to Ian. She blinked, shocked at this new information taking root in her thoughts. Why had it been so important for her to hand mail a letter to him?

She opened her eyes and dared to stroke her hand over the soft, velvety ears the size of her palms.

Ian glanced back over his shoulder, his smile gone. A white sort of worry masked his dusky features. "Eva?"

She met his gaze, returning to him after an unbidden journey through an unwelcome landscape of thought. Then she looked to the older woman. How strange her silence must have been to them, but she couldn't help it.

Once, years before, Lady Elizabeth had known her, known the Eva she had been. They had been equals in joy, in gossip, and in joie de vivre. She had no wish for this still glorious woman to know the Eva she had become.

Clearly, Lady Elizabeth had not noticed her at first. Not in her delight to see her nephew. Now, as those clear eyes turned to Eva, her shining blue gaze darkened with shock and her lips parted. "Ian, what—?"

"Aunt, you know Lady Eva Carin."

Lady Elizabeth snapped a smile back onto her features and padded toward Eva with dainty steps. "Of course, my dear."

To Eva's growing panic, Lady Elizabeth leaned in as if to kiss her on the cheek.

Eva lurched back and quickly murmured, "How do you do?"

Ian's aunt remained leaning forward for one more moment, as if her kiss were hanging in the air. She recovered quickly, as any lady worth her salt would. "Very well."

But when Lady Elizabeth looked away and then glanced back, her soft blue eyes shone wet. There was nothing to say, it seemed, and the lack of words pressed down on them, flattening out the beautiful world that was Blythely Castle. Lady Elizabeth's face creased with sadness. "I am so sorry—"

"There is nothing to be sorry for." She couldn't do this. She couldn't. She could not talk of her past with this woman. No matter how kind. If she began, she might never stop, and then? As if the dog, now leaning heavily against her leg, were a lifeline, she continued to stroke her fingers over his head. "I am tired," she said firmly, hoping Lady Elizabeth would perceive her blunt hint without insult.

Lady Elizabeth's face paled as she slowly took in Eva's frame and then her face. "Of course you are." She glanced down at the dog and smiled as if there were nothing wrong in the world. "And it certainly looks as if you've made a friend."

"A friend?" Eva whispered.

"Falstaff," Elizabeth said.

Eva studied the dog, who tilted his massive head back and gazed up at her with dark, adoring eyes. All the while his tongue slipped out the side of his mouth as he took great panting breaths. There was something completely accepting in that soft brown face. As ridiculous as it sounded, she longed to throw her arms around the mastiff's thick neck, press her face into his fur, and cry. Instead, she pulled her hand back from the dog and squared her chin. She couldn't fall apart. Not here, before Ian, his aunt, and all their servants. She lifted her chin. "Does he love the ladies and drink ale?"

Elizabeth laughed. "No ale, I'm afraid, but he does prefer ladies to gentlemen, and he's a jolly soul." Even as Elizabeth spoke, the older woman carefully studied Eva, and the hints of knowing glinted in her eyes.

In a few short looks, Elizabeth had learned so much,

Eva was sure, and that fact terrified her. She didn't want Ian's beloved aunt seeing the agony darkening her soul. If Elizabeth did, she would surely see Eva's sins. The sins that rightfully condemned her to a raging, soul-ripping damnation.

The older woman smiled another gentle, undemanding smile. "Come, my dear. We shall ready a guest room for you and you shall lie down."

To Eva's distress, Lady Elizabeth took her hand in hers. As if it hadn't been ten years since she'd played here as a child, the society hostess led her into the house.

Shockingly, Eva did not wish to fling the hand from her. The soft touch was warm, calm, and assuring, as if a soft blanket had been tucked around her, defying the general dislike she had for contact with another person.

Falstaff hefted himself up from the ground and followed closely behind, never out of reach as Eva made her way back into Blythely's world. Ian trailed behind, perhaps as careful of all this grandness as she.

They both had much to face, here at the end of England, where the sound of the sea crashing filled the brisk air.

Without words, the older lady seemed to communicate silently to the servants.

As soon as they were inside the large hall, their feet treading on the perfectly checkered black and white marble, Eva knew she was indeed a prisoner. But a prisoner of kindness. A prisoner of those who would save her.

She had no idea what to make of it. So she remained silent as they walked past the towering windows that gazed out onto the immaculate English garden and as they finally entered a salon that overlooked the white-capped sea.

The ice blue and ivory room was the most stunning

tableau she had seen in years. She knew she shouldn't sit on the settee. Not in her horrible gown and short hair and black soul. She'd stain the striped silk and mar the intricately carved marble mantel. The gilt mirrors that reflected the chandelier dripping with crystal and the delicate Chinese porcelain placed carefully about the room would surely be blackened by her presence.

But Lady Elizabeth guided her solidly and simply, finally easing her down onto a chair and placing her hands on the delicately carved pale arms. Falstaff, in the strangest sort of immediate devotion, plunked himself down beside her, resting his jaw on her toes.

The animal's touch seemed to ground her. A blessing, considering how completely unreal this all felt.

She perched on the French furniture, so fine it seemed made of spun sugar, and was terrified it would break. She'd known nothing but dark brown rooms and dirty cots for the longest time. This lavishness? It made her feel out of place, stretched her nerves with anxiety.

The moment Lady Elizabeth lowered herself onto an Empire chair of ivory silk, her skirts masking its gold claw-feet, a servant bustled in with a heavy silver tray laden with an ornate silver teapot and matching cream and sugar set. The nearly translucent pink cups, painted with gold and ruby roses, seemed to float beside the small, tiered silver plates of sugar-dusted scones.

Eva glanced at Ian, and she felt the sudden and bizarre desire to grin. He looked like a man unsure whether he was about to be hanged or given reprieve. Standing at the edge of the room, he watched silently. Without his greatcoat, his shoulders seemed broader, his whole body too big, like a bull that had been suddenly set down in the middle of a china shop. And surely, wherever such a big man stepped in such surrounds, carnage would ensue. In fact, his aunt had most emphatically insisted he remove his high boots and replace them with a pair of embroidered slippers, more suited to a man's dressing room than a drawing room, lest he traipse mud upon the scrolled Turkish rug.

In this salon of feminine confection, he looked terribly out of place. This battle-hardened man seemed far more ready to be in a scarlet coat, blade at the ready and a battalion of men at his command, than standing uncomfortably about to receive a fragile china cup. Yet he owned this castle, the lands around it, and was responsible for every soul who graced it.

Perhaps he did feel just as out of place as she.

"Place the tray on that table, Anne," Lady Elizabeth ordered, her voice melodious yet firm.

Efficiently, Anne placed the tray on the table underneath the windows. Ian's aunt bustled to it, her full moiré silk skirts rustling in the silence. "Now, my dears, this summer the black currants were particularly sweet. I have known no better thing myself." She spoke easily as she filled a plate with a single scone, jam, and butter. "The village children made quite the penny picking them, though I do think they ate a vast deal more than they brought to our cook, Mrs. Anderson."

Eva fidgeted on the seat, sensing some sort of coup. And yet she couldn't run. She was hypnotized by the dowager countess.

And Falstaff's remarkably heavy head kept her feet pinned to the floor. Was this, too, some magic of Aunt Elizabeth's?

Ian seemed fixed, too, for he continued to stand quietly, his body far less tense than Eva could recall in the last days.

Lady Elizabeth poured out a cup of steaming tea. "And I do think a bit of black currant is the only way to taste a bit of summer in our drab winter."

As soon as the teacup was made, she picked up the saucer and the plate with its single prepared scone, then slowly made her way to Eva. "Now, you must taste it, for I and all the children who labored so happily this summer will be greatly offended if you don't."

Eva ground her teeth as her fingers dug into the chair arms. The woman was a witch. A white witch. But a witch no less, with her calming presence and enchanting words. Eva had no hunger in her. She still didn't, not even after the days crossing the country in Ian's coach, away from laudanum. But she knew without a shade of doubt that her hand was going to lift and take the offering.

The traitorous appendage did.

It was ridiculous. She could have sworn Ian gasped. Eva ignored him and Elizabeth smiled easily as if it weren't some triumph.

Slowly, certain she would hate the pastry, Eva took it in her free hand. She grasped the scone covered in butter and jam. The sweet scent of sugar and currant wafted toward her and her mouth filled with saliva. The rich scent was divine. It was the first time she could recall a desire for food in God only knew how long.

Half with fear and half with anticipation, she bit into the scone. The flavor of summer sun and warm, loving kitchens burst in her mouth, and her eyes closed with pleasure.

"There, now," Elizabeth urged. "Is that not nice?"

Eva nodded slowly, chewing pointedly, savoring every morsel. Even as she swallowed, she knew she didn't want another bite. Falstaff peered up at her, snuffling the air, no doubt hopeful some errant crumb might tumble toward him. An irrepressible smile pulled at her lips. She was tempted to toss him the rest of the scone, and only just managed to prevent herself from doing something so scandalous. "Thank you."

Elizabeth slipped the plate away, took the remaining piece of scone, and as if she had read Eva's very thoughts, dropped the morsel.

Falstaff gobbled it up quickly, delighted sounds rumbling from his throat.

Eva couldn't help the laughter that spilled past her lips and barely noticed Elizabeth hand her a steaming teacup and saucer.

Elizabeth folded her hands together. "Now, this is the best Earl Grey, the perfect remedy for such a dreary day."

Eva could have sworn Elizabeth had said *dreary life*, but she knew better.

"Good, now, dear. All shall be right with the world."

As Eva leaned toward the fragrant steam, grinning down at the masticating hound, she could almost believe her.

Chapter 18

"This is pure foolishness, Ian."

Ian stared down into the flames of the fire as if he might find the elusive answer to this mess somewhere in the crackling tongues. Ian's hands itched. He could have sworn Hamilton's blood slowly trickled down his palms. His friend's shocked eyes flashed before him. Shocked and betrayed. But why hadn't Hamilton listened? Why hadn't he returned home to London when he'd still had the chance? If only Hamilton had ceased being such a monster, Ian's hands wouldn't be stained with blood.

And Eva would never have faced the madhouse.

He picked up the poker and stabbed it fiercely into the coals, jabbing the recollection from his mind. Embers burst up into the air and wafted up to the chimney. "It is necessary, what I have done."

His aunt stood half the long gallery away, her presence as strong as it had ever been. It mattered not that he could not see her clearly. He could envision her in the cool blue room, dimmed by the fading light of the day, her back straight, her hands folded, and her chin slightly lifted up.

She was strong. A paragon. Without her, who would have run Blythely? Who would have overseen the running of the estate while he had chased Hamilton halfway across the world in a ridiculous attempt to change his friend?

And now he would have to run Blythely. He'd been raised for it, yet the prospect daunted him.

"Necessary?" A sharp sound of derision filled the room, right up to the pristine white plasterwork upon the high ceiling. "Oh, Ian."

The rustle of her skirts fluttered as she lowered herself into a chair. "Face me, if you please."

Slowly, he placed the poker back on its brass hook. Even though she had been as a second mother to him, he refused to feel as if he were a boy brought to task. He already felt the slight fear that he had made a mistake somewhere along the road. That he would not be able to fulfill his aunt's expectations, let alone Eva's. Anger at his own feelings brimmed in his heart, turning him toward Elizabeth. "Did you know?"

She folded her slender hands in her lap. "Know what exactly? That Eva was in need of doctors?" She did not waver with guilt under his accusatory glare. "My dear, Thomas made it very clear that she was unwell. And in truth—"

"You did know, then?" Damnation, how could she have let this happen? How could any of them?

"We all knew," she said sharply. Even as her voice cut through the dusky light, her face softened with grief. "It couldn't be hidden. For God's sake the boy died in the village just off the Carin estate."

"And did you all think her mad?" he challenged.

For the first time he could recall, his aunt's shoulders bent slightly. "None of us knew what to think. I was not with her at the time. I should have gone to her." She remained silent for a moment, then continued: "To hold her hand, but I did not. And I am sorry for it. But you must understand, Thomas made it very clear that the physicians gave strict orders for her rest."

"I see." Damn, but it was a tangle. He needed to understand how all this had come to take place, but no one seemed to have the answers he sought. "And what did you say, then, to her imprisonment halfway across England in a house not meant for dogs? Did you know what to think then?"

That shook the grief out of her eyes, replacing it with a razor's edge. "I beg your pardon?"

"Locked up." He drew the words out slowly, emphasizing the harsh consonants. As he took decisive steps toward his aunt, the lush carpet muffled his advance.

His debt toward her was great, but he wouldn't make this easy for his beloved aunt, oblivious in her own protected world. Not when Eva had suffered so much. "Chained, drugged, and, I daresay, beaten regularly." He plowed a hand through his already wild hair, on the verge of saying "broken," but he could not bring himself to utter the word aloud.

Disbelief pulled at her features. "No, she was sent to a sanitarium on the Continent." Aunt Elizabeth's delicate hands unfolded and she gestured into the air, searching for words. "Austria, I believe."

Ian snorted. "Who told you this? Thomas?"

"Yes. So you see, you must be mistaken." Her own belief in her declaration blazed upon her regal face. "Can you trust what Eva says? She's been through so—"

Feeling half mad himself, he cut the little distance between them in fast strides. Without thinking, he took his aunt's shoulders in his hands and lifted her to her feet, compelled to make Eva's position understood. "I saw it," he spat out, his breath shaking her curled hair. "Do you understand that? I saw that hell they call an asylum. The place Thomas condemned her to."

Her gaze searched over his face. "W-what?"

Ian released her arms but left only a few inches of space between them. "When I arrived at that excuse for Satan's playground and demanded to see her, the matron offered me a private audience with her." His own torment at Eva's abuse poured out of him, breaking his voice. "They arranged a bed. As if I might come and visit and take her. As if coming and fucking the wards were perfectly normal."

Aunt Elizabeth shook her head with confusion; then her visage twisted with revulsion. "I cannot hear—"

"You will, madam. You will hear every damn word of it." He let out a low groan, the grief in him eating at his heart. "When I saw her, she was so drugged she didn't even recognize me."

"Ian . . ." Elizabeth swallowed, her eyes closing and her lashes pressing to her paper white cheeks. A tear slipped down, and then another.

That tear forced him to realize how harsh he was being with his aunt. So he softened his voice. "Open your eyes. You've been blind long enough. We all have."

Instead of sobbing or shrieking, as another woman might have done, his aunt swiftly wiped the tear away and lifted her eyes determinedly back to his. "Well, that would explain it."

Ian straightened. Had his aunt listened to anything he had said? "Explain what exactly?"

She sighed, then let out a sad sound. "The laudanum, Ian."

He glanced to the clear window. It was his turn to avoid her probing eyes. The night had descended and it was quite a surprise that the servants hadn't come to light the candles. The wild terrain had turned to black shadows. Rather like his life. But there was no way he was about to pronounce Eva's problem to his aunt. They had to keep it secret. For if the world knew of her addiction they might indeed consider her a candidate for an asylum. "I don't understand."

"Don't prevaricate," she said quietly. "You've been brutally honest so far. Let us not revert to polite discourse. She is suffering withdrawal from laudanum."

Instantly, he jerked his gaze from the window back to his aunt. He knew the signs of addiction. He had seen it often enough among the soldiers, many of whom who had had their flesh ripped apart as no man should. "How are you aware of this?"

His aunt shrugged, then turned slightly away from him, the light of the fire bathing her face in a yellow glow. "I simply am."

"As you said, Aunt. No polite discourse."

Her shoulders twitched slightly, the thoughts in her head causing her some measure of distress. She squared those shoulders, facing her demons. "Your mother's death was more than I could bear. Though she was my sister only by marriage and not by blood, she'd become as my other self." Her hands stroked down her skirt before they came up to press at her temples. "I was desperately unhappy after she and my brother-in-law passed. Almost inconsolable. The viscount, your uncle, was often certain I might do myself a mischief, I was so stricken. The doctors came with their miracle cure, their method to soothe my nerves. They gave me laudanum. It became my dearest friend. And my prison. And it is the reason you were Lord Carin's ward and not your uncle's. They would not have you grow up in a house with a woman ravaged by opiates. You had suffered so much already."

Her voice grew flat. "I almost disappeared from this world, a doll who moved about but focused on nothing, lost in a sea of forgetting. When your uncle died, I had to fight with every last strength I had not to return to that cursed bottle. But I did not. I wished to be able to aid you in familiarizing yourself with the duties of your title, but you disappeared."

Guilt, an emotion he was all too familiar with, raised its ugly head. He had left Elizabeth alone to face his responsibilities while he'd thrown himself into the lives of the Carins. That would have to change. Now he would lift the burden from her. He sneaked a glance at the woman who'd always seemed stronger than one of the pillars of St. Paul's.

He had always wondered why Lord Carin had taken him in, but he had assumed it was some legal matter a child could not understand, and so he'd never pursued it. He hesitated, wishing to go to his aunt, to take her in his arms and tell her he understood. That it mattered not. But he knew she wasn't finished with her tale. So he waited.

She glanced back at him, the usual mischief that brightened her eyes vanished to a harsh reality. "So, you see, I know the effects. I, too, have wasted away to nothing, possessed by need. Breaking myself of that need was the hardest thing I have ever done . . . And there are still days, even after having resisted in my mourning, when I think to myself how easy it would be to take my medicine and never feel sorrow or grief again."

Hope suddenly took root within him. He would lift the weight from his aunt's shoulders, and she? She would have knowledge of how to recover from Eva's state in ways that he could only imagine. He could barely speak, he felt such relief. "You can help her?"

The nod was curt, almost pained. "There's no laudanum in the medicine cupboards. I don't tempt myself and so she won't be tempted." She probed him with a demanding glance. "Does Thomas know what you've done?"

They stood in awkward silence, surrounded by the history of their family hanging upon the walls.

Elizabeth's lips pressed into a thoughtful line, her glare probing. "Ian?"

"I did not inform him of my intent," Ian admitted. "When I met with him, he was unwilling to discuss releasing Eva into my care. He acted most strangely. Delighted to have the title, of course, though he tried to hide it."

"He always was a strange boy, never recovering from his mother's death, envious of Hamilton's position as the eldest son. And envious of you, too, I think, your uncle's only heir."

Too true. Thomas had watched Ian, Eva, and Hamilton's play with a sort of incessant envy . . . yet he'd been unwilling to involve himself in their games, as if afraid any sort of friendship would endanger the little peace he had.

At present, Thomas was not the immediate worry. The woman at his employ, as well as her puppets, commanded that dubious honor. "It is worse," he confessed.

"How?" Her hands splayed over her gown, the diamond ring winking in the firelight. "How could it possibly be worse than your taking her without Thomas's approval?"

He rubbed a hand over his face, wishing that he could as easily rub away the long sense of fatigue that had been weighing his muscles since his return to England.

"Perhaps a glass of brandy is in order?" his aunt suggested, her gaze watchful and assessing.

Though the world was crashing around him, his aunt's pragmatism was welcome. "Yes."

Wordlessly, Ian crossed to the table laden with Waterford bottles of amber liquid. He'd brought danger to his aunt and the castle. But he didn't regret it. Not when Eva's survival was in the balance.

This was his home and, as such, it was now Eva's.

He poured out two liberal glasses. Palming the snifters, he remarked, "This will not begin to mitigate the displeasure I feel."

"But it cannot hurt," she parried, a faint smile urging him as she took the offered glass. "I remember when Eva was a little girl . . ." Her voice trailed off, as did the smile. "So beautiful. So full of life. In fact, I would have sworn she could have outdone either of you boys."

The fury dimmed inside him ever so slightly and he placed his hand gently on her shoulder. "I abducted her."

His aunt's eyes widened. She tensed beneath his touch, then lifted her glass and downed half the contents. She echoed him: "Abducted?"

"I pretended to be Thomas. I paid the woman who runs that prison. And I took her." He let his hand trail down her shoulder; then, too tired to keep upright, Ian collapsed into one of the delicate French sofas embroidered in gold and blue that his mother had so cherished. Dropping his head back, he looked up at the pale ceiling painted with the goddesses Aphrodite and Artemis. "Given the events of the last few days, I'm certain she has deduced that I was not Thomas."

Aunt Elizabeth crossed to the sofa and lowered herself down beside him. The hem of her full skirts brushed his boots. "Then we must assume Thomas will know soon?"

"Without doubt word has been dispatched." He lifted the crystal glass to his lips and took a drink of the full-bodied liquor. Swallowing carefully, he savored the feel of it sliding down his throat. "And Eva's friend, a girl named Mary, killed one of the keepers the night we left. Eva could be implicated if Thomas or Mrs. Palmer wished it, but I doubt they will. Not when the chance of their own nefarious behavior could be forced to public scrutiny under a murder trial."

"Good God." She gasped. She stared blankly until her voice shuddered out, "And Eva lived at the asylum for over a year?"

Ian merely raised a brow in acknowledgment.

Elizabeth's fingers whitened as her hand tightened around her glass. "How could Thomas do such a thing?"

"He claimed she had gone mad, that she tried to drown herself in the lake."

"At the time, I didn't wish to accept Thomas's assertion. But given what had happened to her, I believed that it would be possible." Aunt Elizabeth reached up and clasped Ian's hand, seizing it like an avenging angel. And then, with the fire of said seraphim, she said, "She's lost such a great deal."

Ian didn't reply. He didn't need to. At last he asked softly, "What exactly did Thomas say?"

"About the sanitarium?"

Ian nodded.

"Everyone who is anyone believes her to be taking the waters in some private spa." She leaned forward, her lips pursing with disgust. "Though secretly, Ian, I think all society believes her to be mad. Thomas has whispered it about that she is not entirely well, that she is now in his guardianship."

Ian ground his teeth together. Eva had been the toast of London, the greatest beauty and the most sought after. Now, if they all thought her mad, she would be a pariah or, worse, a spectacle meant for entertaining gossip. "We must do something about that."

"Why?" she asked forcefully. "Hasn't Eva suffered enough? Can't we just care for her here? Battling with a hunger for laudanum is not easy, Ian. Even when she has no physical need for it, the emotional and mental need for it may consume her for years. We can hire assistants who are specialized—"

"No." He took hold of her delicate hand as if he could will her by touch. "Thomas will come for her. There is no question. He sent her away for some reason that he hasn't given light to and he is legally her guardian. It is within his right to send her back to that place. So we must show the world that she isn't mad and thereby revoke his power over her."

"But, Ian . . ." His aunt's voice lowered. "What if she can never recover?"

He ground his teeth together. "She will. She must."

"We will protect her," Aunt Elizabeth added calmly, her bright eyes racing with plans.

"We must instruct the staff that Thomas or men on his behalf will come."

"But surely Thomas would let us care for her?"

Ian scowled. "I have very strong doubts."

"Why?" she exclaimed. "We—as family—wish to protect her from scandal."

"I'm not certain, but when last I saw him, he seemed unsettled about Eva. And why would he lock her away in such a place if he wished her to be cared for?"

"It doesn't bear thinking about. That Thomas could do such a thing to his brother's wife."

"It does not." But Ian wondered. Thomas had always chosen to live on the outskirts of life, feeling little for anyone or anything. It had been unnatural, his isolation and independence from any sort of affection.

But there had to be some reason aside from indifference that Thomas would do such a thing to Eva. Perhaps he did not know the horrors of Mrs. Palmer's establishment.

And yet . . .

"What will you do, Ian?"

He tapped a finger against his glass, the crystal ringing dully. "Bring Eva back. Whatever it takes."

"I see."

There was a provocative note to her words. "Yes?" he questioned.

"Nothing." She took a sip of brandy. "Nothing. Only, she needs kindness just now, Ian."

"What she needs is to be proven sane."

His aunt nodded quietly. Yet her concern filled the air around them, as if she didn't quite agree.

"I will do what is best," he promised. He would. Nothing mattered more.

She hesitated, then tilted her head slowly to the side, her features assessing him. "For you or for her?"

Ian drew back, his eyes narrowing at her insinuation. "Explain yourself."

Grief softened her face. "You couldn't change Hamilton, could you? Nor could you save him. Oh, his father wished you to, but I never expected such a thing, both of you being soldiers and reckless. And Hamilton. Well, Hamilton had a streak—"

"Aunt Elizabeth . . ." His voice trailed off, a warning tone insisting she not pursue the subject. She had no idea about the circumstances of Hamilton's death.

"Eva is not Hamilton," she said. "You cannot save a dead man by saving her."

"Don't be ridiculous," he said curtly. The words hung between them, ringing as loud as a slap. "I am sorry. Forgive me."

"Of course, Ian." She stood slowly, for once her movements slow and tired, evidence of the fact she was no longer a young woman and that she had worked hard over the years of his absence. She paused. "I always hoped my boy would come home, but now I see he is as dead as Hamilton." She glanced back over her shoulder, regret filling those kind, intelligent eyes. "And that is as it should be, I suppose."

Somehow, somewhere he had walked down some unseen road that had diverged from Hamilton's. "I am still your nephew."

"You are a man now," she said simply. "No boy left within you." She whisked from the room, her skirts trailing just behind her as she stepped briskly into the hall. Leaving him. In silence. In the growing dark.

He couldn't contradict her. It was true. The boy in him had died, in the stench of death and the heat of injustice. But that boy had been deluded with illusions of a kind and beautiful world.

Now he understood the world to be the ruthless place it was. And only those who confronted the ugliness of it would survive.

India
Two years earlier

"You must cease this behavior."

Hamilton held the wine bottle by the neck and resisted the urge to launch it across the room. Instead, he lifted the mouth to his lips and drank deeply. The thick red wine coursed over his tongue and he choked it back, desperate to feel nothing. He wiped his hand over his mouth, then arched a brow at Ian. "Cease what exactly?"

Ian's gaze crackled with fury and impatience. "That soldier. He killed himself."

Hamilton shrugged and took another swig of wine, wishing he and Ian weren't alone. He had no desire to be made to feel inferior yet again. He'd dogged the young Sepoy for months, determined to teach him the importance of discipline. The importance of deference to the

English. He'd used every tactic he could think of to make the boy's life hell—singling him out for punishing drills, latrine duties, night sentries, reductions in pay, lack of leave while his companions were given free time. In fact, by the time the soldier had killed himself, he'd had no friends, as Hamilton had ensured that whenever he'd made a mistake his comrades had been punished in conjunction. A good man would have risen above it, but not the native. "He was weak," Hamilton retorted.

Ian's face contorted into disbelief. "He was deprived of sleep, abused beyond all human capacity, and utterly isolated. And you're doing it again! To another soldier!"

Hamilton looked toward the screened window and the dark night beyond. Somewhere out there was England. He never should have left it. Never should have tried to be what he wasn't. He'd wanted to show his father, even after his death, that he was worthy. But it was never going to happen now. And it seemed he was never going to have Ian's friendship again. Well, Ian bloody well should have stayed at home. Be damned his father's last wishes.

After all, Ian was right. He was doing it again.

Another soldier's indolent nature had been brought to Hamilton's notice recently, and, well, he'd been giving the native special attention. It was the only thing Hamilton excelled at, the instruction of discipline. It served as a warning to others to keep in line. And Hamilton was more than willing to use whatever means available him, no matter how degrading or torturous, to project that message. "It's for the boy's own good."

Ian stepped forward, the line of his mouth hard. "He's not a boy. He's a full-grown man who deserves respect."

A half laugh bubbled from Hamilton's lips. The idea was absurd. These natives were children who needed one hell of a strict father. He stumbled forward and pointed. "They need an example."

"An example?"

Hamilton gave a sharp nod, his mind swimming slightly. "To show these brown buggers what will happen to them if they step out of line."

Ian's shoulders tensed, and he took a long, slow, disgusted gaze up and down Hamilton. "Who the hell are you?"

That judging look seemed to peel Hamilton's skin from his already burning body. "I'm your goddamn friend, though you never show it now."

"My friend?" Ian whispered, his voice so quiet it was lost in the soft wind blowing off the mountains. "He doesn't exist anymore."

"Yes, he does." Hamilton pounded a hand against his chest. "I'm standing right here."

"No." The emotion drained from Ian's face, replaced by a crushed sort of acceptance. "He disappeared a long time ago."

Hamilton swallowed convulsively, suddenly feeling sick. "What? Is this still about that bloody horse? I made a mistake."

Ian's hands balled into fists. "You shot him. Over petty jealousy."

Hamilton took another step forward until they were but a pace apart. He wanted to throw a punch. To make Ian understand that this was all about needing to win. To be the best. But Ian was oblivious—as always—to the way Hamilton's heart was ruined, so he kept his fist at his side and drawled, "If I upset you so damn much, you should have stayed at home." He sighed. "It was a horse, Ian. A horse."

"Your father asked me to come. I was glad to, but"—Ian looked down, his green eyes pulsing with regret—"is that what you will say about this soldier who killed him-

*self? That he wasn't a man? Is that how you justify your
behavior? By not giving a damn for living things?"*

*"For God's sake, Ian, he was just a worthless piece of
native shite."*

*Ian nodded slowly, then took a slow step back. "He was
a man who needed guidance. You are just a bigoted, sick-
minded bastard who has to be stopped before you kill
anyone else."*

"I didn't kill him!"

*"Didn't you?" Ian turned away and started for the
door. He stopped. "I can't make you resign, and you do
well enough that your sort of violence is overlooked by
command. But I can't overlook it. I can't. I've failed you
and the promise I made your father."*

*"Come back." Hamilton grabbed Ian's shoulder and
tried to whip him around, but Ian was too strong and
Hamilton lost his footing, tumbling to the floor. Wine
sloshed out over his hands and spilled down his trousers.*

*For one terrifying moment, Hamilton was sure it was
blood from the way it spread and darkened the tan fabric
of his trooper uniform.*

*Ian paused but didn't turn back. "I warn you. You must
cease. If you keep driving men to their deaths, you may
meet a similar fate."*

*Hamilton scrambled over the floor, his guts clenching.
"Is that a threat?"*

*Ian remained standing still for one long moment, let-
ting the silence fill up the space between them. And in that
space was Ian's answer. Yes, it was a threat. "I have tried to
have you sent home. Failing that . . ."*

*Hamilton closed his eyes for a moment. He wouldn't
abandon his commission, as much as he hated India. Sol-
diering was the one thing he was actually good at. "Do
you see nothing good left? Between us?"*

"The good I still see is why I have yet to act further," Ian said roughly.

With that, Hamilton's onetime friend, onetime brother left him on the floor covered in wine and indignity.

Something took root in Hamilton's heart at that moment. A sort of hate that he'd never experienced. He hated Ian so much for his own weakness and for the fact that Ian had to be so damn good. Well, if Ian insisted Hamilton was a villain, then he would damn well play the villain. And no one would play it better.

Chapter 19

England
The present

For the first time in a long time, the world was bright and absolutely, gloriously beautiful. Every hue of yellow filled Eva's vision as she floated in the sleek warmth of beautiful linen. She hadn't dared close her eyes, terrified that if she did she would awaken to the browns and shadows of the asylum.

She burrowed deeper into the luxurious covers. But the feeling of soft sheets and warm blankets didn't fade. Indeed, she felt cocooned like some exotic butterfly. Not once had she allowed herself to drift into slumber. Not once through the wind-howling, rain-pounding night. Not once when she was surrounded by a waking dream.

The yellow silk walls glowed, even though the winter sun was veiled by unending clouds. Cheery white snowdrops and lavender crocuses, their throats teased with streaks of orange, filled vases on every possible surface that she could see. Even the walls were painted with white dogwood blossoms. Blossoms that seemed to float down from the crystal chandelier hung at the center of the ceiling.

Eva drew in a slow breath and drank in the soft scent of lavender. It was hard to trust. Perhaps she had paid for her sins? But an insistent voice kept whispering over and over again that she should indeed still be with Mary. Thomas had made it plain that it had been her rash decision and hers alone that had led to the death of her son.

Footsteps thudded down the hall and lingered outside the door. Ian's steps. She already knew their firm clip.

Anticipation mixed with a hint of wariness tingled along her skin. She never knew what to expect from him. Except that he would defend her until his death. Even if in the process he drove her wild with aggravation.

The heavy oak door creaked open, and Ian eased his large body into the room. No doubt, just as she did, Ian looked completely out of place. His black hair, overlong now, hung about his face in jagged waves. Dark shadows deepened the hollows of his defined cheeks, emphasizing his brutally green eyes.

Eva shifted on the bed, grabbing at the covers, suddenly aware she was nigh naked, her body barely covered with a thin chemise. Though he'd seen her thusly before, there had been an openness at the time between them. That openness had vanished somewhere on the brutal road between York and Blythely Castle. She cleared her throat before beginning: "I see you didn't sleep, either."

Ian's eyes darkened with surprise as his gaze locked on her. His chest expanded in a large breath before he shut the door behind him and crossed to the bed. "You should still be sleeping."

She arched a brow, feeling remarkably vulnerable in his home, under his linens. "As should you. Yet here you are."

"A point to you." Easing his big frame onto the bed, he sat like a gargoyle guarding precious secrets.

Immediately, Eva grabbed on to the thick coverlet so she wouldn't roll toward his body.

He smiled briefly, a forced concession on his weary face. "I have not slept through a night for some time."

Eva eyed him. What demons kept such a strong man from his rest? Did they torment him through the night as hers did? If so, she pitied him. Only the damned deserved the thoughts that kept her from slumber. "I suppose that is something we have in common, then."

Despite her best efforts to cling to the mattress, his added weight to the feather bed sent her rolling toward him. Her hip brushed his thigh and her shift eased off her left shoulder, almost baring her breast. Eva quickly tugged the fabric back into its proper place.

"How do you feel this morn?" he asked, his voice as impersonal as a Bath physician.

"I—" In truth, she felt ill. Her stomach twisted and jumped as if a wild dervish. But she would not give him the satisfaction. She would not play into his ideas about her weakness. "I am well."

A softer smile turned his lips. Slowly, he leaned forward. His long, strong fingers, a soldier's fingers, reached out and brushed a lock of her hair back from her face. "Brave of you, sweetheart, but you look a trifle green."

Nodding slightly, Eva dropped her gaze at his touch. God, he could be so tender. At this moment, she could wrap herself up in his strength. Yet, mixed with the passion in his eyes, it was there.

Eva sighed, her eyes wide as she stared blankly at the crisp white sheets. When he looked at her, he saw a damaged woman who needed to be saved. 'Twas heartbreaking to be relegated to such a creature when once she had been his equal. She turned her head to the opposite wall, pulling more firmly at the covers to twist her body away from him. "Well, Ian, we all know the cure for my ill humors, do we not?"

"Indeed, we do," he said with a brittle cheer. "I need

your advice on running this blasted estate and I need you up and about to give it."

The sheets and covers flew away from her body. With one quick move, Ian whipped them to the floor.

Advice?

Eva jerked back toward him. Her shift twisted about her body, exposing her legs all the way up to the apex of her thigh. "What—?"

"Get up," he said, his voice still full with seeming cheer. The cheer a governess supplies before a mathematical lesson. "We begin."

Eva narrowed her eyes, unsure of this new tack. The day before, he'd been as stubborn as a bull. Eva pushed herself up onto her elbows, her garment hanging about her shoulders, the thin string bow precariously tied. She pulled her bared legs ever so slightly toward herself. "What are you about? I thought I wasn't to be trusted."

A hot lick of defiance running through her was wonderful. She hadn't felt so many emotions in an age.

Ian's face tensed as he scanned her half-bared body. His gaze intensified with a curious expression until his eyes glowed the blue-green of a hot spring. "Perhaps, when it comes to your own health, no. But in regard to the running of the estate and the house? Who could guide me better?" This time, his voice was softened, reaching her on a whisper. "Would you deny me help?"

He eased back down beside her, his hand resting only inches from her body.

"I—" Eva buried her fingertips into the sheet as longing coursed through her limbs. God, she desired to reach out to him, to have him hold her as he had done before. Nor could she forget the warmth of his kiss. Had he forgotten? "Elizabeth would be best—"

"Elizabeth is skilled, but I'm afraid I'll bark at her and

send her running down the halls of this castle. You aren't afraid of me. You tell me exactly what I need to hear."

Ian's hand slowly slid across the bed toward her. She held her breath, every nerve aware of that rough hand that could stroke so softly. It would take only one touch. They would be in each other's arms. They could leave the world behind if he pulled her to him. No, she wasn't afraid of him. She never had been and she never would be.

A sudden flash of deep brown hair and blue eyes in a laughing face flashed before her and she gasped at the sudden pain. Hamilton. She had not truly remembered him so clearly since ... Eva jerked her leg away from Ian's touch. "Don't," she whispered, her voice ragged.

Every trace of desire vanished from Ian's face. His hand curled into a fist as he rested it on the bed. He closed his eyes and the lids tensed, pain tightening his face. "I—I apologize."

She had not thought of her husband. Not since she'd drowned in a sea of opiates. In these last days, Ian had been the center of her world ... but now, as the laudanum left her, the world was coming back with an intense clarity of memory. It would only grow worse. "Ian, we—"

The door cracked open and Elizabeth's bright voice cut off her words as did the pad of Falstaff's paws. "Good morning, my dear—"

Ian's eyes snapped open. With the speed of a wet cat, he sprang from the bed.

But not before Elizabeth had swished into the room, followed by her dog and a pert young maid. The older woman wrenched her attention from Ian to Eva's barely covered form on the bed. She held up her ringed hand and waved brusquely at the maid. "Alice? Leave, now."

The young maid glanced down at the pile of bright

fabric and crinoline in her arms. In a panic she simply set them down on the floor and scurried away, shutting the door with an abnormally loud bang.

Falstaff, on the other hand, circled over by the window and lowered himself with a great harrumph.

Elizabeth ignored the flurry of activity and stood with unapologetic authority as her verdant silk gown glinted emerald in the morning light. "Explain."

Eva smoothed down her shift as quickly as her hands would allow. She had no idea what to say. Even she recalled enough about the rules of decorum to know that what Ian and she had been doing was completely unacceptable.

Ian turned his probing gaze on his aunt. "I am a gentleman, and that should be explanation enough."

Elizabeth's face set to unmoving stone. "I see." She took a bold step toward her nephew, her stance just as arrogant as his. "And how am I not to assume that you are taking advantage of a woman in a precarious situation? Ian, you are here alone with her! She's in bed, undressed, for the sake of all the angels."

Eva squeezed her eyes shut against the simple yet ugly words. This was her doing. She was the one driving this wedge between aunt and nephew. Try as she might, she couldn't recall Elizabeth once throwing angry words in Ian's direction.

"Please." Eva forced her limbs, still aching with the unforgiving ride and withdrawal from her drug, to the edge of the bed. Slowly, determined, she stood. "Ian deserves more respect than that."

Ian's rigid stance softened as he turned toward her. "Eva, you don't have to—"

"No." Eva shook her head, her own distress dissipating under the conflict between him and Elizabeth. "He has risked everything for me." Her throat tightened.

With all the conviction she could muster, she swung her gaze to Elizabeth's. "And he does not deserve your censure."

The anger slipped from Elizabeth's eyes, replaced by something unreadable. "That may be so," she said softly, "but you and he cannot carry on in such an intimate manner."

"And how should we carry on?" Ian demanded. "Should we be as strangers?"

The words hung in the room. That he had seen her at far worse. That though they were in many ways strangers, a long-forged bond ran between them.

Their eyes met and the whole world seemed to disappear. It was absolutely true. There was not a soul who could understand the way their lives had turned so furiously and cruelly. It mattered not that his dreams had died in India and hers in a small English village.

Only together could they mourn.

Eva took a step toward Ian. How she longed to place the past behind them. The terrible words of the last days. The memories of perfect summers with them all together. Ian. Hamilton. Eva. And the memories of their chance at happiness vanishing as each of them changed from innocent children to conflicted, disappointed adults. If she could, she would erase it all and start anew. In this moment.

But before she could take another step, Ian turned away. The openness about him vanished, the vulnerability shored up behind a wall of resolve. "You are ever right, Aunt. I have overstepped the bounds of propriety. See to Eva's dress." He moved brusquely to the door. "I am—I am going out."

In a rush of boot steps, he was gone.

Eva sucked back the desire to cry. So long ago she had learned that crying did nothing. Now her traitorous body longed for the release of hot tears. Standing by the bed, her feet bare, her white gown hanging loosely about her, she felt so small. So alone. Ian had rescued her. He had saved her from hell. But now she realized she had found another place of damnation.

The one he had clearly chosen to dwell in.

Oh, she and Ian were together in this fight. But there was someone else watching. Someone else making sure they remained strangers. Eva let out a harsh breath. Hamilton. Hamilton was compelling Ian down this path. Hamilton had been driving Ian away from her for years, and it seemed that even her husband's death would not end his power over Ian.

Lord knew she should also be driven by thoughts of Hamilton. A good woman—an honorable woman— would have been, even if her husband had not been the most honorable of men. But as she stood in the wake of Ian's coldness, all she could think was that he needed saving as badly as she. And Hamilton was dead. Nothing could be done for him. Wasn't life for the living?

"Eva?"

The soft voice penetrated her reverie. "You shouldn't be so harsh. He has already suffered a great deal. I think he will suffer more on my account."

Elizabeth arched a silvering brow. "Indeed? If I am not harsh with him, dearest, who will be? You?"

A smile pulled at Eva's lips. If only Elizabeth knew the words that had passed between them. The way they had exposed each other's weaknesses without the least bit of mercy. The way he admitted fearing for his aunt's feelings. "Yes."

Elizabeth tsked as she bent, picking up white garments from the floor. "You two would defend each other to the devil." She pushed her hand through the folds of a painstakingly embroidered chemise, bringing it to Eva. "It was always the case."

Falstaff lumbered to his feet, tail wagging, and he interjected himself between the two women, stretching his face out for an expected scratch.

Instinctively, Eva reached out, tickling the mastiff behind his ear. Falstaff thumped his tail appreciatively. "Really? I don't truly recall."

Elizabeth circled around the dog, rather than attempting to move him, and gestured for Eva to slip out of the thin gown that she'd slept in. As Eva pulled the fabric away and Elizabeth slipped the new garment over her head, the older woman rolled her eyes. "You two. Not even Hamilton could keep up with your antics." She smoothed the white fabric down Eva's form, just like the most detailed of lady's maids. "And then, of course, you two thick as thieves would convince anyone you were as sinless as angels."

Eva kept silent, listening as Elizabeth handed her a pair of lace-edged pantalettes.

"Remember the day Ian broke his arm?"

Eva thought back and flushed. She had dared Ian to match her climbing up one of the great oaks on the outer boundaries of the estate. They'd sprinted to the top, but she, weighing considerably less, had danced out onto the thin whipping branches at the top. Unwilling to be left behind, Ian had followed and cracked a branch ... plummeting to the ground. At first he'd tried to take the blame, but she'd insisted they tell everyone they'd gone after a wounded squirrel. Ian had been put to bed, and she'd been denied sweets for a month for the fib. Falstaff licked at her fingers, a silly tickle. "I remember," she said softly.

"I think that bond between you never died." Elizabeth smoothed her hands down the front of her blue silk gown, her eyes growing distant, lost in memory. "But then Ian needed a girl like you, especially after his mother died."

Swallowing, Eva stepped into the smalls. "I never thought about it."

"Well, of course not." Elizabeth blinked and turned her gaze back to Eva. "You were children. What with his parents dying so suddenly . . . he always needed you. It is no surprise he needs you still. In fact, even though it had been settled between you and Hamilton as children, for many years I was sure it would be you and Ian that marr—"

"Ian doesn't need me," Eva said quickly, unwilling to hear more. Unwilling to confirm that she, too, had once wished for something other than what duty had dictated. Duty had kept her away from the boy she'd loved. Hamilton had been her intended since she was five years old. It had been an unbreakable match. At least in her eyes. She'd owed the Carins so much.

Hamilton should have felt like a catch.

So many other young women found Hamilton to be the perfect ideal, and she had cared for him greatly. But she'd never loved him. Never understood what it was about Hamilton that had made her hold her heart back.

When she'd learned about the race and its aftermath from a groom, she'd known why Hamilton's father had voiced such fears on his deathbed. Why the old man had begged her and Ian to save Hamilton from himself. Hamilton had gone to India to prove himself a man, and Ian had followed to protect him.

She had stayed behind. Nine months after Hamilton's departure, she'd become a mother. Alone.

If only they had faced who Hamilton truly was before the marriage or before the two young men had departed, things could have been different. She blinked away the sudden burn lining her lids. No, the very idea of her and Ian was absurd. He would never love her. Not like that. He could not need a woman so . . . "He can't."

Pausing, Elizabeth lifted a beautiful pink brocade corset from the fabric on the floor. At last, she asked gently, "Why ever not?"

Eva turned her gaze toward the window. Gray light shone through the window as heavy clouds raced in from the sea. The dimming light spilled along the floor, barely touching her toes. Maybe once. Years ago, if things had been different, she could have been his wife. When she was still innocent. She would have given the world for that place. But now, neither of them was immune from the ravages of deceit and broken trust. He needed someone good and whole. Someone who would not drag him down deeper into darkness. "Simply because."

Elizabeth said nothing for a moment. Then she said plainly, "We must get this corset on you."

Eva took in the older woman, surprised she had not remarked or insisted that she explain. So she held her arms up and Elizabeth slid the partially laced corset down her frame. It drooped about her slender waist. The beautiful material shimmered and Eva resisted the urge to touch it lightly. It must have been Elizabeth's. It was a corset meant to please the eye, but Elizabeth's husband had long since departed the world. Eva's heart ached for Ian's aunt. How many years had she battled the loneliness of solitude in a castle on the sea? Well, not entirely alone. She'd had Falstaff, which as far as Eva could tell was better and more loyal company than most people.

"Bend down," Elizabeth said firmly.

Eva blanched. She had not worn a corset, or a gown for that matter, in nigh two years. "Couldn't we start a little less—?"

"No. We will do all this properly. You must become used to looking like Lady Eva Carin again."

Lady Eva Carin.

"My darling girl." Lady Elizabeth's blue eyes were shadowed. "I have been down a similar path as yours, and I will not leave you to it alone."

The tears that had but a moment ago threatened to overrun Eva's defenses returned with such a vengeance, it was all she could do to keep them at bay. Falstaff pushed himself upward, straining his neck and licking his lips as if he might ease her tears.

"He's such a sweet dog and he's been my loyal companion these many years," Elizabeth said, stroking Falstaff's muzzle. "If you need to cry, my dear, he makes an excellent pillow . . . as do I."

Elizabeth's kindness overwhelmed Eva. With each moment that passed in silence, her heart swelled with gratitude toward the older woman. Perhaps she needn't be alone any longer.

Could she find herself with some help from Ian and his aunt? A little at a time? Was it possible that she might be whole again?

She bent, Falstaff licking at her face. She pushed the dog down and rubbed his back as Elizabeth laced the corset tightly.

If she thought back, Eva could recall the woman who was unafraid of anything, who had charged into London society, winning it over with her love for fun. Today she was unsure of who exactly Eva Carin was.

In truth, she had no idea how to find her again. She seemed unalterably lost. Distant. A ghost now to the world Eva had lived in.

Eva gave Falstaff one last pat, then forced herself to stand upright, her body restricted by the metal corsetry. This was what Ian wanted. The return of a woman who no longer was. Somehow she would find a shadow of her. For Ian. For the memory of the woman she used to be.

She swallowed back the growing nausea and waited, ready to accept the next garment that would lead her ever closer to the world of the sane.

Chapter 20

Eva stroked her hands along Dragon's withers and drew in the earthy scent of stable and horseflesh. Elizabeth and Falstaff were on a long walk. One of the walks they took every day, and which Eva had taken with them over the recent days of her slow recovery.

She'd been tempted to accompany them, but for some reason the stable had called to her. It had been years since she'd been close to horses one might actually ride, and she'd found herself desirous of their company.

Underneath her hands, Dragon felt silky, muscled, and supple. A body well over a ton in weight. A body that could bear all her suffering without any thought.

It would be so easy to give it to him. There was something peaceful and still about a horse. It might have been her imaginings, but she would have sworn a horse could see beyond this world and offer their wisdom to those quiet enough to listen.

Dragon had always been strong and kind, even if he was a bit wild. He'd take her sadness and pain, then toss his head and stomp his hooves into the earth, passing those paralyzing emotions into something eternal and far more powerful than she.

He tossed his head, then looked back at her with his liquid dark eyes, sensing her distress. "Oh, Dragon." She sighed, tears stinging her eyes. "What am I to do?"

The stallion let out a great sigh that shook his barrel chest, Eva's hand moving with the shiver of his white coat.

She laughed, even as a tear slipped down her cheek. And at the stallion's suggestion, she drew in a long, slow breath, then blew it out. And she did feel better. Foolish or no, she allowed tears to flow down her cheeks, unchecked. They were silent, coursing tears. Dragon whickered softly, his eyes soft as he waited patiently under the torrent of her sorrow.

Carefully, she rested her head along the stallion's massive shoulder. Dragon leaned his massive shoulder in toward her, pressing lightly against her body.

It felt like a gentle acceptance of her need. A pillar of strength that wouldn't crack under her mourning.

She stroked her hand along his neck, wishing she could give away all her pain to the beautiful horse that had been Ian's for a decade. It didn't surprise her that Ian had not taken Dragon with him to India. Most likely, Ian hadn't been able to bear the idea of uprooting the horse that was the alpha of his stable, taking him to a land far away that bore no resemblance to the green fields of England.

Closing her eyes, she allowed herself to go back. To envision riding Dragon with Ian. The way she had clasped her arms about Ian's waist as they tore across the countryside. They had been at one with each other then. No worries. No fears. No idea of ever being parted.

Dragon whinnied and shifted on his large hooves.

Eva lifted her head as Dragon's soft ears twitched toward the stable door.

"Eva?"

Her breath caught in her throat. Ian. She'd thought to be alone, but the horses had always been a siren call to both of them. "Yes?"

Ian walked carefully into the stable and Dragon immediately stretched out his beautiful face, nuzzling Ian. Ian laughed, a soft, gentle sound. "I missed you, too, boy."

Eva held her breath, feeling witness to a sacred moment as Ian leaned his own face toward his stallion. For one brief moment, their foreheads touched and all Ian's cares slipped away from his face, leaving behind the gentle, carefree young man she had once loved.

Her own heart twisted at the sight, wishing they could disappear back to that time. Knowing they could not.

Ian stroked his own hand along Dragon's neck until his fingers slipped over Eva's, entwining with them and Dragon's mane. "Did you wish to ride?"

Her breasts rose and fell in quick, short breaths at the touch of his hand. She tore her gaze away from his fingers over hers and glanced toward the stable door. Rain began pelting down, turning the earth a russet brown. "Now?"

He smiled, a slow and boyish smile. "No. I suppose not. I've only just got back from walking the estate with Mr. Harrow."

"Your estate manager?"

"Yes. He's a good man." Ian let out a strange bark of a laugh. "Knew more than I could ever know about cattle and sheep."

"He's had a great deal more experience, I should think," she teased.

"True." His laughter hadn't added humor to his countenance. Quite the opposite. The weight of his responsibilities seemed to strain his features.

Eva nibbled her lower lip. He seemed unsure in this moment. So unlike the confident man who'd stolen her out of the asylum. "You will be a wonderful lord."

He blinked. "I don't know."

"There is something about you that inspires strength, Ian." With her free hand, she stroked Dragon's shoulder, focusing on the powerful muscle beneath her hand. "Your tenants will love you."

"I've no idea how to talk to them," he said, his fingers slipping more firmly about hers and Dragon's silken mane.

A laugh bubbled from her throat. "You can talk to anyone."

He squeezed for a second, then let go, dropping his hand to his side. Defeated. "I— Not any longer."

She hated to see him so full of self-recrimination. It was so misplaced. Eva hesitated, then said quickly, "If you are in such doubt, I shall accompany you when you make your rounds. We can visit your tenants together, and if you feel awkward at all, I shall assist you in conversation."

"Truly?"

She smiled up at him. "Of course. I have much experience with tenants. As Lady of Carridan Hall I was frequently amid those who lived on our land."

He lifted a bronzed hand and gently placed it over hers again, trapping her fingers in his. "I would greatly appreciate your help. I feel ... I feel a bit lost in all this."

She stared at their fingers. Hers pale. His dark. And the way they fit together so easily. "Well, between Elizabeth, Harrow, and myself we shall see you the best landlord in all England."

His gaze softened. "I should like that."

She looked away, her own heart suddenly racing at the intimate idea of helping him in such an important task. "I'm glad."

Ian paused. "Listen."

She frowned but then realized that Ian was mesmer-

ized by the sound of the rain falling upon the roof, a re-
petitive, hypnotic beat that soothed her aching nerves.

Dragon whinnied and nickered.

"Do you suppose he likes the rain?" Eva asked.

Ian laughed, finally, a full, relieved sound. "I think
he'd like a treat."

She grinned. "Of course."

"Shall we?"

Eva nodded and followed Ian out of the stable and
into the hay room. He started for a loose leaf of it, but he
hesitated and glanced back over his shoulder. "You
looked happy just now."

She wove her fingers together. "So did you."

He smiled, then held out a hand to her.

It felt so strange, as if he was asking her to trust him.
Just like he had done to wild and wounded animals so
long ago. And like all the wounded creatures he had
reached out to, she couldn't resist. Despite the misgivings
in her heart, she crossed to him and took his hand. The
largeness of it, rough, strong, tender, swallowed up her
fingers.

"Eva, I have been unkind—"

She started to shake her head but stopped herself.
"Yes. You have. But you have also done what you
thought necessary."

He tilted his head down, his black hair dancing over
his brow. "And if I did something now that I thought
necessary? Would it anger you?"

The scent of spice about him as he leaned closer sent
all her senses clamoring. "It would depend what it was."

He looked as if he were about to speak, but instead he
wrapped his arms about her waist, pulled her to him, and
took her lips in a sudden, white-hot kiss.

At first, she couldn't think. She could only feel. Every
part of her felt this was right. From the way his hands

spanned her back to the feel of his lips over hers, teasing her, to the way he sheltered her in his strong arms.

Without hesitating, Eva grasped his shoulders, pulling him close, desperate to find something beautiful with him. Effortlessly, he swept her up, cradling her against his chest. In two short strides, he took her to the soft hay piled against the stable wall and laid her down against it.

Gazing up at him, she felt safer than she had in a lifetime.

"I've wanted this for so long," he whispered, his voice rough against her ear as he trailed his fingertips down her gown to its hem.

"And I—" She breathed.

At her admission, he slipped his hands under the silken folds and clasped her ankles. "You are so strong, Eva."

She laughed at that, even though his touch on her delicate, stocking-covered skin was delicious torture.

"Don't laugh," he said softly, sliding his hands up to her calves, massaging the muscles lightly. "You are stronger than anyone I have ever known."

Her laughter dimmed and tears filled her eyes. Tears of wonder that, even now, he should see her as someone like that. How could he when she still did not? "I wish I could believe it."

Oh so slowly, he raised her full skirts up her thighs, his rough fingertips skimming the delicate flesh where her hip met her leg. "Then let me believe for you, until you do yourself."

His words were more powerful than any compliment she'd ever received, and in that moment his belief did give her strength. Determined despite the slight remnants of fear, Eva took his hand in hers and slid his fingers between her thighs.

His eyes flared for a moment, but he needed no further urging and he gently stroked the soft flesh in a way she'd never experienced.

Eva gasped, shocked as her body suddenly arched as if his fingers were molten hot. But it was not pain she felt. It was desire. To her own mortification, she parted her thighs further, desperate for whatever it was he could give her.

His fingers teased her opening and he groaned. "You're wet, my darling."

She frowned. She understood what he meant. She could feel that under his fingers she was hot and slick, but she hadn't ever experienced such a thing during her wifely duties.

"I want you so much," he said, his voice tight as if he might shatter just touching her.

As his thumb swept over her, a cry of pleasure wrenched from her throat. "I want you, too." She gasped.

He stared down at her, awe lighting his gaze. "Then we—"

"Eva?" Elizabeth called from the front of the stables.

Eva jolted and sat up so quickly she nearly smacked her face against Ian's shoulder. Carefully, he clasped her shoulders, then lifted a finger, pointed it at himself, and shook his head.

She nodded. Quickly, her body aching with longing, she climbed to her feet. Brushing her hands down her skirts, she strode out into the hall that led back toward Dragon's stall.

Elizabeth stood at the entrance, her gaze sweeping over Eva. "Where have you been? I feared you were caught in the rain."

Eva forced a smile to her lips, though she was sure her cheeks blazed with embarrassment and—God help her—lust. "No. I was here."

Elizabeth nodded, though her gaze drifted toward the back of the stable. "Of course. Well, come, then. The rain has stopped and it's time to take tea."

Eva had no desire to go back to the castle. Every part of her cried out to return to Ian and let him teach her the pleasure he had just begun to promise. "I think—"

"My dear, there is much we must work on." Elizabeth beckoned. "Now, come along."

Eva bit her lower lip, willing the last vestiges of the fire Ian had fanned to life within her to dim. Silently she followed Elizabeth back toward the castle, resisting the urge to look back toward the man who was stealing her heart. All over again.

Eva looked nothing like a lady should.

At least, she looked nothing like the bedecked, girls' school–trained, giggling women of the ton. Where they were beautiful, unthinking, and fairly useless, Eva was a woman come from the world beyond. Or one who had communed with the other side.

The gown of deepest purple moiré silk clasped her slender frame and her skirts belled out over wide crinolines, emphasizing her far too narrow waist. Pale breasts and shoulders were draped by black eyelet lace. Everything about her suggested a specter.

Ian couldn't tear his eyes away. His heart ached at the sight of her. This woman who had been to the brink of undoing made him feel, so deeply. It terrified him. Him. A battle-hardened man. A man who had looked his friend in the face as he'd died and held no second thoughts in his actions.

If he was not careful, he would find himself sinking into unruly emotion. The moment he'd laid her down in the straw and given way to his desires, he'd sunk. Thank God Elizabeth had interrupted them. He would never forgive himself for tasting such temptations when his goal was to see her independence restored.

Even now, as fragile as she appeared, he knew she would not crack as she took labored steps toward the dining room. Her strength was a tempered metal that would withstand the cruelest of blows.

All his heart longed for was to keep her safe from those tests of strength. They would come. Regardless of his wishes, those tests were inevitable. Life was too cold to allow her freedom from them. Unlike all the others who had left her alone, he would be at her side when she faced them. He would give her strength, not take it from her.

He followed her, quietly. Observing each subtle movement as she seemed to drift into the dining room. She didn't even look at the portraits of his family's military exploits upon the walls or glance at the crystal dripping from countless candelabras and the massive chandelier at the center of the room.

Eva was recovering. At the rate she was mastering all her once familiar skills, she'd be able to storm London soon. And given her present progress, he had little doubt of her ability to convince the world she was as sane as anyone. Her beauty alone would strike those about her with awe and admiration.

Eva stood with her shoulders back in queenly posture. The effort tightened her beautiful face, and it was clear she felt as if she were drowning under the weight of her evening gown. But she still prevailed.

One of the footmen held her chair out, and she struggled to maneuver her full skirts under the table. Ian stepped toward her, but his aunt threw him a warning glare. Perhaps in all this she would be the true general.

Slowly, Ian lowered himself into his chair at the head of the table. Eva sat to his left, Elizabeth to his right. They remained thus in perfect silence until at last a footman, in gold and sapphire, brought the soup course forward. The pale cream red lobster bisque filled Elizabeth's bowl, then Eva's, then his.

Ian found himself staring at Eva, waiting to see if she would pick up her silver spoon and finally eat something besides a bite of scone.

Elizabeth ignored the awkward silence, clasping her spoon in her long, aristocratic hand. She dipped the silver into the bisque and said firmly, "Eva, dear, this is one of Mrs. Anderson's best recipes."

"Yes." Eva snapped her gaze up to Elizabeth, anger and something else crackling in her eyes. "Thank you."

For a moment, Ian was certain she was going to stand and march from the room. But even he knew this was no longer about hunger, but will. Eva was hungry again, of course, but she was still not accustomed to the rituals of dining. He was tempted to tell her she didn't have to eat, even though he knew he should hold her down and pour the damn bowl of soup down her gullet, she was so thin.

Eva's clenched hands uncurled. Slowly she reached for her spoon. Every movement took an eternity. She slid the spoon into the bowl, scooping up a small bite with perfect precision. Ian held his breath as she brought the soup to her lips and swallowed.

She shuddered, her fingers tightened about the utensil. At last she looked from Elizabeth to himself. A smile played at her lips. "Am I indeed so fascinating?"

A relieved laugh rolled from his throat. "Yes, Eva. You are." He placed his own spoon down and reached across the table, taking her free hand in his. "You always have been."

As their eyes locked, determination flickered in her gaze. In that moment, he understood that she was pulling herself out of the abyss not only for herself, but for him.

And it rocked his heart with a sudden tenderness.

She curled her fingers around his. The earlier grin twisting into a wry smile. "One could never say I was cause for ennui, I suppose."

"No one could say that about either of you." Elizabeth's brows lifted with amusement as she took a long sip of wine. She patted her curls. "You'll soon see me completely silver, what with all your goings-on."

Eva laughed. "My apologies. A true crime against beauty. I shall endeavor to behave as a model young lady."

Ian couldn't stop himself. His snort was distinct. Instantly his eyes widened, ready to apologize. He was an utter ass. Here she was trying her utmost, and he'd made fun. But only because the Eva he had known had been so wild.

Eva pulled her hand back from his. She rapped his knuckles playfully. "Do you laugh, sir?"

"Indeed, no." He bit his lower lip, admiration and relief warming his heart. "We always expected you to be fascinating, but never quite proper."

Elizabeth nodded with mock seriousness. "Yes. No one would ever believe you to be yourself if you were a stuffy young miss."

"I see. So I may behave as badly as I please as long as I sparkle and my conversation is diverting."

Ian laughed, the first hint of joy and hope sparking inside him. "Exactly."

"And, of course, I must not lose my composure at the mention of Adam."

The mirth around the table died suddenly. Elizabeth's mouth opened and closed wordlessly. Ian's smile faded, the muscles in his face hard with tension. It was the first time she had said her son's name so calmly. So freely.

"No." He breathed softly. "That you cannot do. Though you deserve to."

Eva pulled her hands into her lap. Her gaze fell to the gleaming table. "You must make me a list. Of things I am not permitted to do." Her voice tightened. "Lest people think me mad."

"Eva?" Elizabeth's voice punctured the air. "Why do you say such a thing?"

Eva slowly lifted her face. A white mask of pain. "Because if I do not behave, I will be sent back." She cut her gaze to Ian. "Isn't that true?"

The floor seemed to fall out beneath him. She'd never spoken like this. It was the clarity of her mind coming back. The laudanum was gone now . . . but the hunger for it was not. Her body must ache for it, even as she regained the ability to think and calculate the reality of her situation.

Ian sat forward, desperately wanting her to understand how serious he was. "I will never let that happen."

Eva nodded, though doubt still lingered in her eyes. "So I will keep my side of our bargain. I shan't act mad. And you will have less need to keep me safe. Yes?"

"Yes," he echoed. How he wished he could roar that she needn't pretend that all was well. He couldn't. She was correct. Every moment she acted well was a moment closer to her freedom. "Your wisdom does you credit."

She smiled tightly, then slowly pushed her chair back. She stood with complete dignity. "No, Ian. It is your wisdom that has got me this far. Without you, I would still be scratching at my cell."

Ian's breath stilled, hating the sadness in her voice. "Thank you. But that is undue praise."

She smiled wryly. "I do apologize, but I am tired and will retire. If you insist I eat the remainder of my soup, do send it up. I shall do nothing to interfere with our plans to prove I am not a lunatic."

With that, she turned on her heels and swept from the room.

Ian started to stand, ready to charge after her, to take her in his arms. Every word she'd uttered crashed down on him. Punishing him.

"Wait," Elizabeth urged. "You must let her go."

"I don't wish to." He had to make Eva understand how much she was worth. How nothing could steal away the beauty that had always made her the most special woman in the world. A woman worth giving up one's liberty, one's soul for.

"She is not a child," Elizabeth said as her hand darted out and touched his arm. "Even less so now that the drug has ebbed. You cannot control her."

Ian stared at the empty doorway, wishing he could call her back by the sheer force of his thoughts. He couldn't control her, nor did he wish to. "Of course not."

"If you so desire to help her, let her find herself again." Elizabeth eased her steadying touch and stroked his arm. "She will. I see the fire in her eyes."

Ian gave a single sharp nod. "I wish for her to recover now."

"She must recover at her own pace."

Ian shook his head. "I cannot see her so mistreated again and it is exactly as she says. We must prove her sanity. Officially. With that proof, she will no longer need a guardian. If we cannot, Thomas will be able to send her back. The sooner she is stable—"

"How much simpler things would be if you could simply marry her," his aunt said.

Marry her. The idea rang through his head, sweet and torturous. "That can never happen. Not as long as Thomas is her guardian."

"Indeed, that is true." Elizabeth stood and looked down at him. Her serene face drew into a resolute countenance. "And now I must say something you will not like. You cannot allow Hamilton's death to keep affecting the way you treat her—"

"I will not listen—"

"You will," she replied evenly.

Ian slammed his hands on the table and shoved his chair back. "No, Aunt. Perhaps I am just like Eva. One step from madness." He choked back the sudden pain. "You have no idea about Hamilton—"

"Haven't I?" his aunt said so softly it was barely more than a whisper. "You were always the better of the two. He was a good boy, but he was never like you. Never as strong, nor as true."

Ian couldn't bring himself to look at her or let her words sink too far in. He'd spent months focused on how he'd let Hamilton die. Living for a chance to make amends.

Still, he couldn't forget the part he'd played. Nor the look on Hamilton's face.

Then again, when he had taken Eva in his arms, when he had taken her lips with his, wasn't that exactly what he had done? Forgotten?

"She is not here, my lord." Mrs. Palmer lifted her chin, refusing to allow her failure to induce rashness in her plans. It didn't matter that rage still simmered just beneath the surface of her skin. Burning. Hungry for revenge. Now it was tempered. Ready to strike even the man before her, if necessary.

Lord Carin's thin-lipped mouth narrowed to a slit before he sneered. "Not here?"

Mrs. Palmer glared at him. Did repeating her make what she had said untrue? Or was he indeed as dim as he seemed. No, not dim. Lord Thomas Carin had a lack of personality, which might lead one to believe he was less than astute. But like herself, that was not the case. Surfaces never accurately reflected the person within, she found.

For instance, who would have believed that behind her polite facade lived a woman who would stop at nothing, no matter the blood spilled, to destroy those who humiliated her? Not many. Not even Lord Thomas, who, in her short experience, had a calculation to his action that suited the most intelligent of men.

His pale blue eyes hardened to pinpricks, and that mouth . . . It twisted into a hideous fleshy manifestation of his rage.

A rage she recognized all too well. Now all she need do was turn it to mesh with her own and they would both have their desire: Eva Carin locked in a room and made an example of to her entire asylum. She'd break the woman's mind within a month. A smile pulled at her lips.

"How can you grin?" he snapped. "You've made a damn fool of yourself."

At that, her smile did fade. She took a warning step forward. As intended, he took a step back. Reclaiming the veneer of calm, she locked eyes with him. "I regret that your letter did not arrive sooner." She shrugged a shoulder to suggest the culpability was his, not hers. "Perhaps you should have informed me of this cousin's existence and his problematic nature some time ago."

Lord Carin blew out a furious breath. His dove gray gloved hands fidgeted as if longing to strike something. "Don't mention that bastard."

A touch of distaste crawled along Mrs. Palmer's skin. His control was not as developed as her own. The abject hate under this man's surface was quite something to behold, struggling to come to the front. She couldn't imagine him standing up to the man who had so boldly rescued Eva Carin. But someone with this lord's resources would never have to face an enemy in the flesh. "Do you have anything of use to say?"

His face turned a mottled red. "I am your better, madam."

Ah. She'd struck a nerve, his authority threatened. "You are my equal in this."

"You are the mud beneath my boots."

"Well, this mud will not assist you in retrieving her, if that is how you feel." A lie, of course. Eva Carin was never going to be free. Nothing would stop her vengeance.

"Wait," Lord Carin said, holding up his hands. "We are being hasty. You want her back as much as I. Such desires make us equals. In this at least."

She slowly crossed to her desk, trailing her fingers over an open ledger, adjusting an offending pen back into place. "I have two of my best men tracking them. She should be with us in a manner of days."

"I want her silenced." He wiped a gloved hand over his mouth.

She hesitated, a delicious thrill running down her spine. "Do I understand you correctly?"

Lord Carin's brows lifted. "Silenced. Permanently."

"I have some punishment for her first."

As if it had never occurred to him, he hesitated, then said, "May I watch?"

So that was his game. Perhaps one he was only learning. "You'd like to see her punished?"

A muscle twitched in his cheek. "Yes."

"It will be arranged." She lowered herself onto her chair, lifting her assessing gaze. "And now to the additional funds."

His eyes widened with indignation. "I beg your pardon, madam?"

Was he indeed so naive? Apparently so, from his fluttering lids. "Come, now, good sir. I am putting out quite the expense to ensure you have your permanent silence."

"You lost her," he countered.

"Yes." She leaned back, glaring at the foolish man. Did he truly believe that she would cover for his sins unpaid? "So I did. But if I don't get her back for you, what secrets will she spread?" She glared, daring him to contradict her.

For several moments his face twisted as if struggling with several demons discussing options to a futile problem. At last, he stepped forward and lowered himself into the high-backed chair before her desk, like some strange black bug, pulling in its limbs toward its shell. "Your price?"

A degree of loathing that she felt for only certain guardians washed over her. She turned the page of her ledger, reached for her quill, and dipped it in the black india ink. The man was a rat. A rat that could afford to pay for his indiscretions. "Shall we say one hundred guineas for her safe procurement?"

Lord Carin nodded. "I shall make it one hundred and twenty-five to expedite the matter. I trust the next time I hear from you, you will be able to assure me she has been collected."

"Without doubt." She scratched the name and figure into the perfect columns.

He cleared his throat slightly. "You will summon me then. To watch?"

She didn't look up, but smiled to herself, recognizing in the man before her the need to see others suffer to alleviate his own suffering. "Without fail. I will enjoy an audience."

Still, after she finished writing, she stared at the immaculate page. She could not help but wonder. How far was he prepared to go in all this? Exactly how far had he already gone? She had her suspicions. "I do have one question, my lord."

He cleared his throat, displeasure tightening his features. "Yes?"

"The man." The very thought of him spurred a fresh dose of gall through her veins. "Who came to take her away. He is violent and will not let her go without some struggle. If he were to be caught in the fray?"

Lord Carin stood and brushed at the nonexistent wrinkles in his cloak. A glint of hate flickered in his hard eyes. "I trust you will do what is necessary."

"To ensure Lady Carin's safe return?" She arched a brow. "Of course."

Chapter 21

Eva wasn't entirely certain whether she could continue to bear Elizabeth's continual glances of sympathy. Day after day, the older woman wrapped her up in kindness. Held her hand when she shook, gave her peppermint tea to ease the never-ending return of nausea. And good God, she kept on at her deportment. Her carriage. Her walk. Her speech. Each day was a new lesson in behavior laced with the encouragement a governess might give a three-year-old learning her grammar.

Eva rolled onto her side in her dark room, pulling the blankets up to her chin, and attempted to focus on the fact that each moment brought her closer to reclaiming herself. But Ian's face kept interrupting her list of growing accomplishments.

Lord, how she missed him. Even with him in the same house, she missed him.

The silence between them had not broken since that dinner. She let out a sigh and pressed her face into the down pillow. She should be so grateful. Grateful for this beautiful house and Elizabeth's care. But now all she wanted was to be alone with Ian again. To feel his arms around her and his body bringing hers to life.

It didn't matter even if they yelled and flailed at each other. The powerful feelings that brewed between them could bubble into something stronger, so long as there were no more lies, nor numbing politeness.

Every hour her mind grew sharper, and she knew now that she had reached the worst of withdrawal before she had even arrived at the castle. Oh, she might still cut off her arm for a dose of laudanum, but she no longer felt as if her body would fly apart without a taste of the dream-inducing poison.

Eva pressed her face harder into the pillow, wishing that Mary were in the room. Her friend would have stretched out her delicate hand and stroked her shoulder. They could talk. Talk through everything without the worry of corsets and manners.

A tear slipped down Eva's cheek. What would Mary be doing now? Tied and beaten and drugged, Eva knew. Whatever had her friend done to be put in that place? And why, when she had done something truly terrible, had she been freed and Mary kept imprisoned?

Eva punched her fist into the pillow. It was not right. The world was not right. Even now, she could recall Thomas standing over her bed, railing at her for being so entirely stupid as to take her son out in the curricle. Blaming her mercilessly ... but he'd never truly loved Adam. It was hard to show affection to an infant who had stolen your title.

A jagged breath tore at Eva's chest. Why did she torture herself with memories from before the accident when all she wanted was to forget?

Muffled movement echoed just outside her door and the wood panel creaked open ever so slightly.

Eva drew in a relieved breath. At last. Of course, he would know she still needed his comfort. She lifted her head from the pillow and blinked at the darkness. "Ian?"

Shadows moved into the corner of the room, becoming two separate figures. They didn't speak.

Eva jolted up, opening her mouth to scream.

Before she could, one of the figures darted forward, his dark-clad arm lifting high, a club in his hand.

Ian ripped off his cravat and threw it to the floor. Draining the contents of the glass in his free hand, he staggered toward the window. God damn it. She was only a few rooms away. She might as well be oceans from him. Continents even. He laughed softly as he weaved his way toward the clay bottle half full of whiskey upon the Chippendale table.

He yanked at his linen shirt, tearing the neck as he pulled it over his head. Christ, why were the British so insistent on drowning in clothes? Indian street men went around wrapped in cloth about their waists, freeing their bodies to the elements.

Far more practical. Of course, he'd always been highly restricted in uniform. Still, one could dream.

He stared at the bottle, then at his glass. Also far more practical to drink from the bottle, yes?

Why waste time with glasses when one was going to down the entire contents anyway and end up face-first on the floor. Ian plunked the glass down on the table and glanced out the window.

A wave of self-revulsion washed over him. Hadn't he watched Hamilton drink himself mindless among the other officers, playing cards and laughing at the stupidity of the men in the ranks? The more Hamilton had drunk, the more he had insisted that Indians were little better than the cattle they worshipped or, in the case of the Muslims, little better than the shit that cattle had deposited.

Oh, God. Ian stared at the bottle of spirits, wondering

how such a small thing as liquor could bring back such hideous pain. The fuzziness of his brain repelled him and he shook his head, drowning in the memory of how his friend had disgusted him.

He needed fresh air to wash away the sick feeling swallowing him up. Didn't matter that the fire was burning brightly in his fireplace. He needed the breeze to blow all thoughts out of his head. To get Hamilton out.

Bastard.

He'd assumed that when he'd returned to Blythely and had begun to manage his lands again that India would fade into the black recesses of his thoughts. But the daily books, the riding out to assess fences, sheep, and crops could not beat back the constant recollection of an arid land devoid of justice.

Once, he'd viewed his tenants as something distant, different—human, of course, but still lesser. Now? He couldn't rid himself of the faces of the Indians, made so gaunt by the British Raj. His own people gave not a damn for the lower orders; that had to stop and it would stop with him.

He resolved then and there to start a school for the girls and boys of his tenants, ensuring that future generations had some choice in their livelihood. That they might climb free of the mud and struggle of an existence dictated by the whim of crops and market pricing.

And Eva would help him. She'd claimed as much. With her assistance, he could do it. He could run his estates as they should be run. The fear of fumbling it all disappeared at the idea of her guidance.

Ian looked out the window, ready to drink in the cold air and relax into his new plan and the idea of Eva by his side, but as he looked into the shadowy night, something was moving rapidly along the lawn.

Figures. Two of them. They were carrying something. Something wrapped in white and just the size . . .

He snapped his gaze down to one of the side doors and spotted a footman sprawled on the ground, unconscious or dead.

Ian's senses jolted to life as the situation sank in. He threw the bottle to the floor, and before he could think, he ripped the window open and flung himself out into the night.

Two flights' drop left him bending his knees and rolling. He hit the ground and sprang to his booted feet. Blood pumped like fire through his veins. He narrowed his eyes, focused on the retreating figures. Drawing in slow, even breaths, he charged across the grass, easily closing the distance.

They were large, the two men, and fit, but not as silent as he.

The man running empty-handed glanced back. His eyes widened. "Shite! Dan! Dan!" the thug yelled to his partner.

Ian reached out and grabbed the shouting man. His hands clamped with such force that, as he swung the accomplice around, bones popped. The piece of shite screamed as his shoulder ripped out of its socket and he plummeted to the ground.

Dan glanced back over his shoulder. A fatal mistake. His feet caught on the earth and he flew forward. Eva, wrapped in a white sheet, tumbled out of his grasp.

Christ.

She wasn't moving. Not moving!

Dan, just a few feet from Eva, scrambled back on his elbows. Fear stole over his dirty face. Slowly, Ian stalked forward. He didn't say anything. He didn't have to. He already knew who'd sent them. He knew what they'd intended. So he'd kill them.

Dan pulled a knife, its silver blade flashing in the moonlight. Ian dropped on top of him, his hand going for the weapon.

Dan, equal to Ian in size, bucked. Ian had no idea what demon had taken hold of him, but he slammed his forehead against his opponent's dirty face.

Dan screamed as his nose cracked and blood gurgled in his windpipe. In his shock, his hold loosened on the knife and Ian wrenched it from his hand. Jerking his weight forward, Ian lowered his knee onto Dan's windpipe.

A scream tore through the air and Ian looked back in time to see Dan's partner drive down a knife. Ian twisted his torso, thrusting his arm against the man's wrist. Searing pain flashed through him as the blade skimmed his shoulder.

The force of the move sent the knife flying from the attacker's hand.

"Ian!" Eva shrieked.

Instead of her voice giving him pause, it only pumped the need to save her harder through his veins. Ian drove his knee down onto Dan's neck. He jerked, then stilled.

Dan's partner took a step back, his eyes fixed with horror on the dead man. "You're m-mad."

Ian ignored the blood trickling down his back. He reached out and seized the discarded knife resting on the wet grass. In one swift move, he jumped to his feet. With a knife in each hand, he started forward.

The man shook his head, backing away. "You're bleedin' cracked!"

Ian didn't answer, only took another step forward. He threw the first knife, and it struck the thug's shoulder.

A wild animal shriek tore from the abductor's lips and he staggered under the force of the blow. His hand shot to the wound. "Look, we can come to an arrangement!"

Ian weighted the other knife, trying to decide which bit of soft flesh to cast it into.

The man's throat worked, his eyes flashing with panic. "Please. I'll tell you anything—"

"There's nothing to tell, is there?" What could he say? That Mrs. Palmer had hired him? That they were coming for Eva?

Ian swallowed, glancing at Dan, dead on the ground, and then back to the man cowering before him. Slowly, he lowered the blade. As the heat of bloodlust ebbed from him, it was clear he could not do this. Not in front of Eva. "Run, you prick. Run!"

The thug nodded wildly at his sudden good fortune. Without another word, he spun on his booted heel and ran into the night. The sound of his panting breath faded away, mixed with the thud of his boots on wet earth.

Ian flung his remaining knife to the ground and turned to Eva. On her knees, her thin white chemise was smudged with dirt and wrapped about her thin body. Her skin shone star white in the dark night. Slowly she stretched out a hand to him. Shaking, her fingers hovered, waiting for him to take them.

Ian gasped in a mouthful of cold air, the feeling of his fear releasing him. He rushed to her and dropped to his knees. "Eva." He breathed harshly. His hands reached up, running over her naked arms. "I almost lost you."

In answer, she wrapped her arms around him, pressing her slight body to his hard one, then looked up into his face. Her eyes darted over him. "Never. You will never lose me."

With that, he lowered his mouth to hers, a conqueror's kiss, claiming what was his. What had always been his. What would always be his. She gasped against his mouth, tense for a moment, before she gave herself up to it. Her body molded against his. Her hands clasped his shoulders, pulling him fiercely close.

He tangled his hands in her hair, a sort of desperate desire and need to claim her racing through his veins. She opened her mouth, offering, inviting, and he didn't think twice, driving his tongue into her as much as he wished to drive his cock into her sweet body. To claim her.

For now. This was enough. This melding of souls in a kiss. Out of fear of loss, out of celebration of survival and triumph against their enemies, they kissed. The wild sweetness of it intoxicated Ian, until his thoughts disappeared and a single pulsing word dominated his being. *Mine*.

Her hand trailed to his shoulder and she froze. He winced. Even in ecstasy, he couldn't deny the burst of pain. Carefully, she pulled back from his kiss. When she brought her fingers away, they glistened black in the darkness. "Oh, my lord." She breathed, through kiss-swollen lips.

His breathing began to slow from the ragged, impassioned force it had known just the moment before. "It's nothing."

Eva wiped the blood on her chemise, billowing about her frame in the evening breeze; then she took his face harshly between her hands. "It is not nothing."

She grabbed on to him as though she were certain he might disappear at any moment from her grasp. Her gaze burned with a wild intensity. "They could have killed you. Do you not understand?" Her voice came out on a jagged rumble. Unlike any sound he had heard from a woman. "I could not have borne it. Not again."

"Eva—"

"No." She dropped her hands from him and staggered

to her feet. She stared out into the night. "This happened because of me." She took another staggering step, her bare feet pressing down the grass.

"Stop," he snapped. Unable to bear the pain in her voice. Longing to have her back in his arms, where she belonged. He jumped to his feet, ignoring the slow, pulsing throb in his back.

She swung back toward him, her face taut with fury. "Stop what? Stop telling the truth?" Eva shook her head wildly, her chemise sliding over her shoulder, baring the pale flesh. "You have risked your life too many times already. Too many—"

He strode up behind her, bent his head, and pressed a soft, assuring kiss to the delicate skin where her nape met her shoulder. Afraid of her next words and determined to stop them, he grabbed her shoulders, whipping her toward him. He knew another kiss would change nothing. But he had to try. So this time he took her mouth in a soft, sacred kiss. The instant touch of her flesh awakened that voice once again. That primal voice that would say nothing but *mine*.

She softened under him, seizing his shoulders as if he might disappear into the night. Triumph at her acceptance gave him all the encouragement he needed, and he cupped her face gently, angling her mouth to his.

As their tongues tangled, he held her with a passion that would not be checked. No matter what she or the world said, she was his. Carefully, he drew back, his blood pumping now with the need to mark her as his own. To make love to her. If he could have, he would have laid her down in the field where she'd nearly been taken from him and done so. But she deserved more. She deserved everything he could offer. "You are mine to protect."

"No," she whispered, her voice slicing through the freezing night. "I will not have it. I will not."

Ian stilled under her sharp retaliation, the warmth inside him chilling at her harsh words. "What then?"

"I cannot." She sagged against his grasp. "Too many people have died. Too many."

"I promise," he said firmly. "I will not die."

She lifted her eyes to him; they were as lifeless as they had been in the madhouse. "Do not make promises you cannot keep." She ripped herself back from his grasp. "God laughs at such promises."

Every part of his body urged him to wrap her up in safety. Of course, she was worried for his life. When everyone she had loved had died. But now was not the time for such fears. Now was the time to prepare. "Eva, I want you to stop and think. We cannot stay here."

"Are you not listening?" she hissed. She clenched her fists and lifted them in protest. "I cannot do this to you. I must leave you. Or I will be the death of you."

Ian ground his teeth, knowing exactly what he had to do. "Everything I do is my choice. My choice. You are my choice."

"Am I?" she mocked, her fear turning into something ugly. "Would you be here if not for Hamilton? If you didn't feel guilt?"

The words hit him more cruelly than the open wound stinging upon his back. He stared down at her, knowing the answer she so needed to hear. Knowing it to be the one answer he couldn't give. He stared at her silently, trying not to hate himself for the self-serving bastard that he was. "I don't know. How could I know what might be? All I know is what is."

Her face creased, lips pressing together. She looked away from him, then nodded.

God, she was going to cry. What kind of an animal was he? "Eva?"

She sucked in a harsh breath, then faced him. Soldiers

who marched into battle couldn't match the resignation printed on her countenance. "No. You spoke the truth. We both know why you are here."

"I will protect you," he said, as if that would make up for the unforgivable blow of his earlier words.

She remained silent, her arms hanging softly at her sides, her face a mask, unreadable now to him.

"We must go," he said tightly.

"Of course," she said, her voice devoid of any emotion. "Your wound—"

"No," he cut in quickly, formulating what must be done. "To London. Tonight."

Her brows drew together. "What—? Elizabeth—"

"Elizabeth will understand. She will follow us to London when we send word. But we must get you as far from Blythely as possible." He pointed into the night. "That filth you pleaded for will be back."

"Mercy is for fools. Is that it?"

Ian looked away, then wiped a hand over his face. "Yes. Mercy is for fools."

She nodded. When she lifted her face to him, the bitterest smile tinged her lips. "Then hell awaits us both. Does it not?"

Wincing, Ian took a step forward. Coldness surrounded her. Why had he not realized that she, of all people, desired mercy? "That's not what I—"

She wrenched her hand up, silencing him. Slowly she picked her way through the cold grass, her feet bare. She paused before the man lying broken on the grass. "And him. What shall be done with him?"

Ian lowered his head, knowing exactly what had to be done. Knowing what path they had set on now. "I want you to return to the house. I'll watch to make sure you get there safely. Change into serviceable clothes. Find linen for a bandage. Leave a note for Elizabeth and send a servant for the footman by the castle. Meet me by the stable in twenty minutes. Can you do that?"

"You're serious?" she asked, not lifting her eyes from the dead man.

"They want you back. Badly. And the only hope we have now is to take you before a Chancery Court."

"I'm not ready." She breathed, wiping her hand at the blood still lightly flowing from her temple.

"You will be." He heaved a breath, fighting off the ache in his shoulder. Fighting off the desire to care for her. To ease her pain. But the only way to do that was through decisive action. "Go. Run," Ian ordered as he started for the body.

"Ian?" she asked, her voice unsure.

"I have done far worse. Now go," he growled.

Eva's eyes locked on him for a moment. Confusion filled them. The confusion of being confronted with a stranger. No doubt, Eva had never imagined the things he was capable of now.

She ran, her small form flickering toward the house.

Ian let himself focus upon her retreating body for a moment, wishing so many things. Wishing Hamilton and he had not gone to be toy soldiers in a bloody land. Wishing Hamilton had not revealed such an ugly part of himself. Wishing he himself had not had to choose between justice and loyalty.

Nothing would be the same after tonight. Even if there were dark recesses to their souls, they were bonded in this. Bonded in death and loss.

Slowly, despite the cut along his shoulder blade, he hefted the man's weight over his shoulder. The ocean would be a good enough grave for him.

Chapter 22

They arrived in London to a house swathed in silence. Eva could not recall a more urgent or relentless ride. Not even their coach ride across the country could compare with the way they had taken to horseback and flown toward London as if the devil himself were on their heels.

Cold permeated her skin. She wasn't sure she would ever be warm again. From the damp of the night air to the chill stealing into her soul, the comforts of her body in a state of warmth seemed a distant memory.

It would be only a matter of time before they followed her here as well. She longed to feel safe in Ian's London home, but nowhere was safe. Not anymore.

Hugging herself, Eva glanced around. Eerie in its silence, the house reminded her of an oversized and unloved dollhouse. Waiting for its mistress to come and fill it back with the happiness of imagined worlds.

Not a soul had been in the house since Elizabeth's last visit to town, at least two months previous. Every surface was covered in white sheets. Ian was somewhere looking for candles and coal.

She took a step forward, her feet quiet on the polished wood. Her breath puffed out like cotton before her face. Eva lifted a gloved hand to her lips.

At last, her hands didn't shake. Not in the slightest. This freedom from the ache of life without her laudanum was entirely new. Every part of her wanted to savor the moment. Every part of her also knew that there were far more pressing matters than enjoying the relief of functioning with normalcy.

Ian had killed that man. Every time she closed her eyes she could see Ian's face. The blood streaked against his bare chest. And his eyes. Terrifying to behold. Terrifying in her defense.

Slowly, she turned in a circle, eyeing the circular foyer. Trying to make out objects in the darkness. Shadows danced in every corner. How had she let Ian come to this? Hadn't he deserved to know some touch of peace? Especially after India.

"I've got them," boomed Ian's voice from the hallway to her left. Yellow-gold beams flickered on the cream-colored wall as he neared.

When he stepped back out into the foyer, the light hovered over his features, leaving his face barely visible. Even his dark clothes added to the effect, giving him the air of an avenging spirit.

Eva blinked at her own foolishness. "I'm glad. I'm chilled through."

He started for the stairs, coal bucket in one hand, candelabra in the other. "Come. We must remedy that."

Eva hesitated for a moment. They were moving toward something, something she could no longer stop, and yet she was slightly wary of it. They'd shared so much intimacy already, but even so, her heart pounded at the idea of being completely alone with him with no one to interrupt them. Despite her protests against his involvement, she'd waited for this moment for so long she'd been certain it would never happen, but now she could barely catch her breath. Finally, she moved forward, her stable boy's clothing allowing for easy movement. "Do you need assistance?"

He laughed. "No, love. If there's one thing I am good at, it's carrying. All army men are, you know." In the darkness, the faint glimmer of a smile showed itself. "Don't let them tell you different."

"Well, I shan't, then." She smiled tentatively at his attempt to lighten the mood.

They made their way up the sprawling staircase silently. They had said only those few wild words to each other after Ian had killed the man.

She was grateful to him. So grateful.

But nor could she quite fight the feeling that she was dragging him down into a dangerous world, rather than him pulling her up. It wasn't a pleasant feeling.

"We'll sleep in my room."

She nodded her assent. The very idea of dwelling in one of the spacious town rooms by herself was unthinkable. They paused before his closed door and Eva realized he was giving her the chance to change her mind. To sleep separately if she insisted.

In answer, she reached out to the gold-plated handle and pressed down. It swung open silently.

She walked ahead of him into the unlit room, careful not to run into the darker shadows that were clearly furniture.

"Tomorrow, I'll bring servants and guards in." Ian headed straight to the fire, placed the candelabra on the mantel, then poured in a heap of coal. "Tonight we'll have to make do."

She didn't respond to what seemed the obvious. Instead, she headed toward the four-poster bed and whipped the white duster sheet off in one swift move. The thick goose down coverlet was icy to the touch.

Within moments, the fire crackled heartily. Ian brushed his hands along his breeches and turned toward the bed. "There, now. We'll be warm in no time."

Eva tugged at her cloak string, but it had become absurdly tangled in their wild ride.

Ian's eyes glowed a wicked green in the amber light, his large frame silhouetted by the fire as he came close. He didn't ask. He simply stepped forward and brushed her hands away. Easily, he began to work at the knot.

His close proximity sent a shiver down her spine. They had avoided the slightest contact since their kiss on the lawn. Now his boot tips brushed hers. The scent of horse and light sweat filled her senses. It was surprisingly appealing. The nearness of him urged her to reach out and slide her hands up his strong shoulders. To feel the reality of him beneath her touch.

Ever so carefully, Eva looked up. She'd been so determined to let him go. For his own safety. But now she needed his embrace. She needed the comfort it could give her just as she was certain he needed her touch. Something happened within her when he laid his hands upon her body. Something sacred and sweet and full of healing fire. There was no fear when she was in Ian's arms.

Tonight, she longed for that. Longed to know the fullness of it.

Ian was the only man she'd ever trust. The only man she could ever open her heart to. And if she gave him her heart, how could she deny him her body? She couldn't. Not now.

Gently, she traced her fingertips over his jawline, then cupped his face with her palm. "I want you, Ian."

His face was tense. Yet, under her touch, his gaze softened, heating. Heating with the promise of so much more than pleasure. Slowly, he turned his face, pressing a soft kiss against her palm.

A small, amazed breath escaped her lips at how that soft caress sent shivers of want over her skin. She lowered her hand, offering herself to him. Knowing he would guide her in the mysteries of lovemaking.

A few tugs and slips of the ribbon and her cloak whooshed to the floor. She stood quietly before him in the oversized stable boy's coat and britches.

Eva's chest rose and fell in quick breaths as his sure, strong fingers lingered over her collarbones, tracing them. She wanted him. Desperately. They had been racing toward this moment. They had been racing toward so many things, but this . . .

Slowly, she took his hands and moved them to the thin tie at her throat. Almost daring him to take the next step. To unlace the rough fabric and slip it over her head.

His eyes roved over her face, questioning, burning. "Eva—"

She placed one finger over his lips, then slid her hands down over his broad shoulders. Hard muscles tensed beneath her touch. The feel of him stirred the most powerful emotions within her. But above all was the wish for more. She arched up onto her toes. Taking her courage in hand, she pressed her lips lightly to his.

As though he had been holding back a veritable storm of desire, Ian pulled her against him, his arms enfolding her. The hard feel of his body against hers was always such a shock. Through layers of linen and wool, she could feel the strength of his ribs, the length of his muscled abdomen, and the hardening of his cock.

Sensation swept her up. Completely trusting, she gave herself to it. She wove her fingers into his thick hair. Ian's warm mouth kissed her softly, slowly. Holding her as though he would never let her go, at once he coaxed and ruled her with his kiss. Fleeting, then demanding.

She moaned into his mouth. He stole the opportunity

to slip his tongue between her parted lips. Eva gasped, still astonished by the passion he could fire within her. All else she'd known of lovemaking had been perfunctory. A duty. Something one did lying still in the dark.

Nothing like this.

Now there was no turning back.

They both knew there was no one to interrupt them. To stop this foray into passion. Unlike before when they'd kissed, this passion was slow, a smoldering flame being tended carefully. She opened herself to him, allowing him to gently stroke her tongue, then suck it into his mouth.

Taking up his seductive challenge, she licked at him tentatively, tilting her head to better receive his kiss. Her hands moved from his soft hair to his back, her fingers digging through his coat, pulling him tighter.

In one swift move, Ian had her in his arms, cradled against his chest. Without breaking the hot kiss, he carried her the few steps to the bed and set her down gently. He eased her back, kissing her again and again, in slow, hypnotic movements. Giving. Not taking.

Eva closed her eyes, longing to be lost in sensation. In fire. She wanted to be lost in fire. Burned with desire. Alive. Truly alive at last.

She reached for his coat, shoving at the shoulders. Ian pulled back from the kiss. Never letting his gaze leave her face, he sat back on his heels. Quickly he yanked the garment off and flung it to the floor, flinching only slightly, though his knife wound must have pained him. Without fear or hesitation, Eva sat up, slid her hands to his waist, and tugged his linen shirt free of his trousers.

Ian looked down at her, his eyes half closed, full of wonder. Her fingers brushed the naked skin of his taut abdomen. Instantly, heat coiled down her spine, urging her to work faster. To touch more. She slipped the shirt up and then over his head.

She let her attention drop to his chest. Each of his breaths seemed to come with slow, powerful control. It was beautiful, the way his muscles contracted and expanded with each movement. Little nicks and scars were scattered over his chest. Eva winced at this new revelation. How had he received them? He'd never once mentioned being wounded.

Without thinking, as though she could somehow heal the raised flesh, she leaned forward and kissed a jagged scar just above his ribs.

Ian tensed. Coiling back, he reached down and pulled her away.

They'd both known so much pain. Neither of them wanted to remember. Eva lifted her hand to his face and cradled his jaw. The soft stubble of dark beard scratched at her hand. He was so strong. So strong. Yet it was just below his surface. The pain that drove him.

He curved his face into her palm, his eyes closing. Peace hovered over him for a moment. "Eva." He breathed against her.

God, how she wanted to speak. Wanted to tell him how much of her heart he had stolen. She couldn't. Not yet.

Though she could not give him her love, there was something else she could give. For one ashamed moment, she hesitated. Her body was no longer that of a young girl's. She'd borne a child. . . . Her body wasn't lithe and perfect.

But no matter what she'd been through, no matter what her body had endured, she wouldn't be ruled by fear. Not with Ian.

Deliberately, Eva took handfuls of her shirt and drew it over her head. The fabric dropped from her fingertips. Cold air caressed her skin. She'd changed too fast for a chemise or corset. She was glad of it.

Ian's face lit with desire as his gaze wandered over her body. "I have never seen a more beautiful woman."

She started to laugh, but he shook his head and her laughter vanished.

"Every mark, Eva, every scar . . ." He caressed the lines at her hips and stomach that had formed during her pregnancy. "These are proof of what a strong, beautiful woman you are. A woman, not a girl."

She couldn't draw breath. His words moved her so powerfully. "You truly find me beautiful?" she whispered.

He leaned forward, the power of him urging her back against the bed. It was easy to follow his lead. As she lowered herself back to the bed, he pressed open-mouthed kisses along her neck, nipping ever so slightly at the hollow of her throat.

"Ian?" she said when he didn't answer.

He paused. "Beautiful?"

Eva glanced down at him. Confused.

He lingered over her heart. His dark hair hiding his face. Slowly, he pressed a kiss to the soft flesh. "I feel it beating," he murmured. "Your heart. It beats fast and strong and free. Your beauty begins here."

He pressed another kiss to the spot just above her heart.

Gently, Eva slid her hands to his back, wanting to offer him so much comfort. The kind of comfort he was miraculously giving her.

"But your beauty," he said, "doesn't stop there. It is in every part of you."

She arched toward him, her breasts taut now with need. The tenderness of his touch more erotic than anything she had ever known. His hands caressed her ribs, curving to rest along her sides, teasing at the marred flesh. He stared down at what she'd considered to be so ugly. Pure worship shone on his face. "It is here."

"And it is here," he whispered before he kissed her breasts, then took a nipple into his mouth, teasing it with his tongue.

Eva gasped, shocked he would do such a thing. She dug her fingers into his back, desperate for more. Without even thinking, she curled her legs around his waist. The hardness of him pressed against her core. Eva closed her eyes, no fear, just need.

Ian's careful touch became more insistent, rougher, and then his fingers were working at her breeches. He eased them down, then pulled away from her as he worked his own trousers off.

Completely naked, Eva savored the feel of warm skin on warm skin. She had not been this close to anyone, this loved—

She blinked back tears. This was making love. She knew it with utter certainty. And she had not been loved in so long.

This time, Ian eased himself down farther along the bed. His slightly rough hands caressed her calves. He lifted his eyes to her as he kissed the inside of her thigh. "I want you to look at me." Nodding, Eva bit down on her lower lip, completely alive with sweet anticipation. He massaged her calves as he kissed and nipped his way up her thighs.

It was so tempting to close her eyes. To lose herself in the feeling. Though he had not said it, Eva knew he wanted her to lose herself in him. So she kept her eyes on him. When he pressed her thighs ever so slightly farther apart and lowered his mouth to her, she tensed. Stunned. And then a cry of pure pleasure flew past her lips.

Ripples of shock and hunger rushed through her. As if he couldn't get enough of her, Ian took her hips in hand and kept her in place. His lips and tongue teasing her until she couldn't bear it.

She twisted her hands into the sheets with all her might as pleasure stole through her body. Any moment, she would shatter and disappear.

"Now," she whispered. "Now."

Ian lifted himself and rested his cock between her thighs. Eva's breath hitched and grabbed his shoulders. She felt the need to anchor herself. He pressed his head against her and a moment of alarm swept through. It had been so long. Perhaps she would be too tight. Perhaps it would be pain, not pleasure.

Ian gently rubbed himself along her slick core until she arched against him with hunger. At last, he began to rock against her, not inside, but easing against her tight passage.

Eased with the renewed pleasure he'd created, Eva locked her legs around him, pulling him forward. One smooth thrust and he filled her. The fullness of it, the tantalizing pressure stole her breath away. As he thrust into her body, intense pleasure coiled in her abdomen. With each sure stroke, she climbed higher and higher.

His mouth claimed hers.

Eva gasped, her fingers digging into his back. Somehow. Somehow she wanted to climb inside him. In response, he pulled her torso up off the bed, his arms circling her. The pressure and speed of his tempo increased.

"Please," she whispered. "Please, yes."

"I never want to let you go."

Eva looked into his eyes, her heart so full she didn't know how she could survive it. "Then don't."

A growl tore from Ian's throat and he lowered her back down. He gripped her hips and thrust long and hard. Eva bit her fist, unable to hold back her cries of pleasure.

Finally, Ian circled his fingers over her folds as he simultaneously circled his hips against her.

What was happening to her? The intensity of it threw her from height to height toward something she didn't understand but desperately wanted. She panted, holding on tight to Ian, trusting him. And at last, she couldn't fight the moan of sheer ecstasy as her world spun into perfect joy. Ripple after ripple of pleasure hummed through her.

"Oh, God, yes." He moved faster against her, tilting her hips up toward him. "Yes, Eva." Ian tensed, a harsh groan ripping from his chest as he climaxed.

She stared up at him in wonder. Never had she experienced anything like what had happened between them. She'd never even known such a sensation was possible for a woman. Her heart beat fast and hard with delight that it was Ian who she'd shared such a thing with. It was always meant to be him.

He tried to roll to the side. Eva grabbed on to him, holding his weight to her. It seemed impossible, but happiness washed over her. Pure happiness, as she held him.

It had taken her years to find it. Now she had it in her arms. She smiled into the darkness. Nothing would ever take it from her again.

Chapter 23

The most ridiculous feeling of peace had come over him. For the first time in years, Ian stared into the darkness, trying to understand how the hell it had happened. He flung one arm over his head, the other keeping Eva close to his body. Her cheek rested against his chest. One of her legs was flung over his, possessively.

The way she had touched his scars. It had been shocking and soothing at once. She had no idea how he'd gotten those scars. But what echoed most in his mind was how he had not fought against the men who'd come to kill Hamilton. He'd watched in silence, in understanding as they'd violated Hamilton with a blade the same way Hamilton had violated his soldiers' trust with brutal punishments and dangerous commands, sending them with too few men against untenable odds into the borderlands. But it had been the way Hamilton had harassed young soldiers, driving them half mad with drills that went all hours and verbal abuse that would have broken the hardest dockside tough, that had been his friend's death sentence.

A murdering officer, that's what they'd called Hamilton. Ian had tried to have Hamilton removed from his post, tried to convince him to return to England, but such things were next to impossible in the British Army. It wouldn't have mattered if Hamilton had whipped a man to death, he would have maintained his post. And Hamilton had refused to go home, finding his only power in being an officer of Her Majesty's Army.

Justice over friendship. That was what Ian had chosen, and he would never shake from his mind the look of horror upon his friend's face. Even if Hamilton had deserved what had been done to him.

All he wanted was to keep this feeling of stillness he'd found with Eva. Of wonder. She had given him peace. Eva, who had seen destruction as great as any slaughter. But the thought that Hamilton's wife lay beside him couldn't quite escape him.

What they had done was undeniable. Like the rain that comes in the fall or the sun that insists on rising.

Wasn't it?

He closed his eyes, trying to block out the ugly thoughts. Trying to block out that it had been duty that had driven them apart. He should have told Hamilton's father of his love for Eva. He should have had the courage. Instead, he'd wasted years desperate to make sense of how someone like Hamilton, who had been Ian's closest friend—who had dueled him with sticks and shared his first glass of brandy—could descend to such darkness. He'd wasted those years trying to change his friend.

What a fool he'd been.

Ian swallowed back his disappointment. He'd followed Hamilton halfway around the world to bring him back to goodness. But it hadn't been goodness that he'd discovered in the back of beyond. Rather, he'd found that most men held the canker of destruction within their hearts. Quite simply, he never should have left Eva. Never. Not for any reason. Certainly not to save a man who didn't wish to be saved.

Ian shook the past away and concentrated on the

slender form tucked against him. At long last, she was his. For him alone, her eyes had lit up in surprise and wonder as she reached her pleasure. He could make up for the past. He could make up for all his mistakes.

"Ian?"

"Yes?" he asked, apprehension tightening his chest.

"I think . . . I think it will all be well. Perhaps we can find a way to accept the past. Accept what happened to . . . to them."

"Eva." Pain and a touch of regret instantly lashed him. Christ, she still couldn't really speak either of their names. Adam. Hamilton.

The past that would never let them go.

How he wished he could agree with her, that they might find acceptance. It would be so easy to lie. To open his mouth and ease her with platitudes.

He couldn't do it.

She didn't understand him. She couldn't. He could never explain that her husband had died an ignominious death. And that he had played his own part in it. "I don't know what to say."

"Why?" she whispered.

"We can't." He shifted ever so slightly, the feel of her soft skin rubbing against him. "We can't talk about him."

"But don't you think he would want—?"

"I know exactly what he would want." His throat closed, unable to form the words. Hamilton would be furious, riddled with hate and jealousy, at Ian and Eva's lovemaking.

"Ian, I think we need—"

"Eva, I cannot." Ian swallowed against the sudden burn clawing at his chest. An image of blood and torn flesh flashing before his eyes. "Do you understand?" If he allowed himself, he'd feel the ripped flesh under his hands, those accusing eyes staring up at him, and feel the traitorous knowledge that Hamilton had met the end he'd asked for. "I cannot talk about him."

She nodded against his chest. "I suppose I understand."

A slow sigh of relief escaped his lips. Of course she did. She knew better than anyone what it was to keep silent.

Her chest rose on a long indrawn breath. She started to pull away. Instantly he held harder. "Please don't."

"What?"

"Eva, we need each other." He needed her. He needed her so much. It was a terrifying realization. On this wild journey she had become a part of him. Integral to his existence.

She remained silent. Nothing broke that awful sound of quietude. No clocks, no voices. Not even the fire that had burned down to a low red glow. After a few moments, she relaxed. The silence stretched on. Finally, she nestled against him, her hand gentle and light against his chest.

It was done, then. They'd both agreed. They could continue on like this. Not a word of the past would pass their lips. The unspeakable would remain unspoken.

An ironic laugh escaped Mrs. Palmer's lips. She clapped a quick hand over her mouth. It would not do to lose her composure. Not the proprietress of a madhouse. She set the missive down. Hesitated, then crumpled it until the sheet was nothing but a twisted ball of parchment.

Her carefully orchestrated world was bursting into chaos.

She laughed again, brittle this time; her hand could not silence the sound. As soon as it died in her throat, her stomach churned so hard with fury, vomit threatened to choke her. She swallowed quickly, pressing her trembling fingers even tighter to her lips.

One of her men was dead. Killed by that bastard. If he'd been anyone else, she would have exacted revenge in a moment's notice, buying off magistrates. Men of his standing in society, however, were not so easily handled. Nor so easily disposed of.

No, there was only one way to receive vengeance against him, and it wasn't his quick death. Destroying that which he most cared about was the sure path to revenge. By destroying Eva, she would have all the vengeance she could ever desire.

Now that she knew the extent that man was willing to go to, she would have to take a new tack to achieve her aims. But at this moment, there was no denying it. Eva Carin had slipped through her fingers. The girl was on the fast road to London. If Eva proved she was sane, it would only be a matter of time before questions started being asked about the asylum. She couldn't have that.

Mrs. Palmer leaned over and grabbed the sides of her perfectly polished walnut desk, clenching it so hard that the pain in her flesh brought a sense of calm over her.

Pain. Her own or others', always helped to give her perspective. Soon it wouldn't be hers that set her world to rights. Oh, no. It was that damned woman who would pay for every moment of suffering she and that bastard cousin had inflicted.

Mrs. Palmer stared at the blank cream-colored sheets of writing paper stacked neatly on her desk. There was only one thing left to do.

It was time for Lord Carin to play his part in this game to get back his ward. And once they had her, she'd take Eva Carin apart. Piece by bloody piece.

* * *

"Chancery can bugger itself." Ian's unbridled disgust for the British legal system rang ripe even to his own ears. Several silvered heads, peers all, turned to throw warning glances, shocked that he should so puncture the revered morning silence of the club. Giving a solid tug at his waistcoat, Ian tempered his growing frustration and demanded in a far more appropriate—though still incredulous—tone, "It takes how long before a case is brought to a judge?"

Lord Byron Cartwright, Earl of Wyndham, laughed. A rich baritone that shook the room, once again catching several glances and harrumphs from the more staid members of the club. The man was a barrel-chested devil. He barely came up to Ian's shoulder, but one cross word and the man was as dangerous as a giant.

Wyndham rolled his cheroot between his calloused fingers and leaned back in the leather and brass-studded chair. "Weeks, months. Who knows, old boy? But no time soon."

"Sodding solicitors."

"And barristers." The cheroot crackled slightly as Wyndham lifted a match and lit the tightly rolled tobacco, its tip burning demon red. "Don't forget them."

Ian snorted.

Wyndham arched a russet brow, his impenetrable gaze sparking with amusement. "Someone steal your sheep? Surely the overseer could manage—"

Ian forced himself to lean back in his own wingback, matching Wyndham's easy posture. "The entire world is populated by sheep as far as I can discern."

"Hmm." Wyndham looked up, catching the eye of a passing steward. The man nodded, knowing exactly what the earl wanted. Wyndham waited patiently, blowing small puffs on his cheroot. Within moments, the steward had a bottle of whiskey and two crystal glasses on a tray.

As soon as two glasses had been poured out, Wyndham braced an elbow on the leather armrest and twirled his cigar. "Would you care to divulge the truth of your dilemma?"

Ian gazed about the room. It was early in the day and only a few men were about the room. All reading papers and smoking. "No."

Wyndham blew out a deeper plume of dark blue-gray smoke. "Then there's nothing I can do but drink with you."

Ian eyed Wyndham, determining whether the man could actually be trusted with the details of Eva's situation. It would have been easier if the earl had pushed and prodded, but spies had a damnable way of simply sitting back and waiting for men to spill their guts. Even retired spies like Wyndham. "I've a problem."

Wyndham contemplated his whiskey with great seriousness, then said suddenly, "Baden-Baden."

Ian scowled. "Have you tossed your brains?"

"Hardly." Wyndham shrugged. "Since I can only guess at the problem, I've deduced you can't decide on a vacation spot. Baden-Baden is all the riot these days. Water bathing. Bavarian hausfraus. Can't stand the smell of kraut myself, but they say the pastries are quite—"

"Wyndham, do you really wish me to rip out your throat?"

The earl raised two brows as if completely innocent. "My. And here I am trying to bestow my wisdom upon a fellow soldier in arms. A gentleman. A—"

"A man with a very short fuse."

Wyndham smirked. "I had no idea."

Ian looked down at the whiskey, tempted to toss the damn lot back—or at Wyndham—but a dousing in the old brew wouldn't likely induce cooperation. "Do you recall the former Lord Carin?"

"Hamilton? Of course. Damn bad card player. A bit old guard for my tastes and heard he played butcher with more than one poor chap in India. Could drink a fellow under the table, though."

Ian nodded, trying not to think about how easily Wyndham could recite Hamilton's qualities. Like a laundry list of attributes. How easily he could state Hamilton's ability to send his men to needless deaths in skirmishes or through torment. "Lord Carin had developed . . . a certain taste for discipline," he said carefully. "It was unpleasant to see."

A dry smile played at Wyndham's lips. "Indeed. Some officers can't get it through their heads that dead men don't fight. Carin died most suddenly, as I recall."

Ian locked gazes with Wyndham. "Mmm. Terribly unfortunate."

Wyndham glanced away before nodding. "Yes, yes. Not for the Indians, of course. He was your dear friend, no?"

"All my life." The words felt hollow. Each day in India, Ian's hope had died a little more that they would be able to return to the closeness they had once known. That Hamilton would finally become the man Ian had always hoped he would be.

Wyndham drew in another puff of smoke, the haze leaving a veil between them. "Remarkable how certain traits do reveal themselves most unexpectedly."

Ian stared at Wyndham, wondering how much the other man truly knew. "Yes."

Wyndham poured more whiskey into both their glasses. "Now, what's done is done, and for the best, most likely."

Christ. Wyndham couldn't possibly know how instrumental he, Ian, had been in Hamilton's death. And Wyndham certainly wouldn't approve of it. Would he? He shook the unsettling thought away, forcing himself back to the immediate problem. "His widow. She's in a fair bit of trouble."

Wyndham stilled. "Lady Carin."

"You know of her?"

"Everyone knows of her, old man. She went mad. Like a cuckoo." Wyndham took a long swallow. "Not that she didn't have cause, as I understand." He shook his head, sympathy softening his usually stoic feature. "The heart and mind are such delicate things. One never knows when they're going to snap."

Everyone knew. Everyone. Thomas was a buggering ass. No doubt he'd hung his head at every damn town party and recited the woes of a long-suffering brother-in-law. "What are people saying?"

Wyndham shrugged, those clever eyes of his hard. "Tragedy. Everyone says what a tragedy it was since she was so beautiful, so accomplished . . . so happy. They say that, of course, someone so happy could never survive such losses." Wyndham hooked one leg over his knee, his perfectly polished black boot gleaming in the morning light. "They say she's in a sanitarium somewhere in Europe. Recovering under the watchful eyes of a veritable buffet of doctors and noxious waters."

Just as Elizabeth had thought. "She's not."

Wyndham's eyes widened with exaggerated curiosity. "No?"

The man was such an act. Moving his facial muscles just as one was supposed to at such a bit of information. "What else have you heard?" Ian demanded.

"I've heard that the new Lord Carin, while acting the grieving brother in public, was rather celebratory after his nephew's and brother's deaths." Wyndham smiled tightly. "Not terribly unusual among the ton, but also still rather bad form to go about whoring when your infant nephew is only just dead and his mother shunted off to a sanitarium."

Ian's hands curled into tight fists, the crystal snifter in one hand gripped tight.

"He's not well liked, is Lord Thomas," Wyndham went on.

"Lord Thomas deserves a long walk off a short pier," Ian gritted out.

Wyndham's eyes narrowed. "Does he indeed?"

"I need you to do some digging."

Wyndham laughed again. That barrel laugh piercing the room, shaking the crystal. "My apologies, old man. But I don't do that sort of thing anymore. No, I'm just a retired, idle, pleasure-seeking lord these days. Or have you not heard?"

"How do you feel about madhouses?" Ian said so softly his voice sounded like sifting sand in the silent room.

Wyndham's eyes shuttered. "I beg your pardon?"

Ian leaned forward, deliberate in each word. "Eva was locked in a madhouse that made army prisons look like Carlton House." Ian smiled a tight gallows grin. "Everyone has not heard that, I presume."

"Holy God."

Ian swirled his whiskey in his glass before taking a significant swallow. "In this case, I think God has not involved Himself."

Wyndham rolled his eyes, then set his glass down. "You have her. This is what the Chancery nonsense was about."

"Just two days ago, men attempted to abduct her from my keeping." As if they were discussing nothing of more import than Bertie's ponies for the upcoming races, Ian lifted his glass to the light and contemplated its rich amber color. "They assaulted and incapacitated three footmen to get to her. They were quite skilled."

Wyndham held still, none of his false bravado about him. "You're certain?"

"Thomas wants her dead or locked up," he finally snapped, infuriated that Wyndham didn't seem to be taking his position seriously.

Once again, every graying head turned in their direction.

"Keep your calm." The earl's deep voice belied the ease of his body, which kept the onlookers unaware. For once, it felt as if he was indeed speaking with the real Wyndham.

"It's been damn difficult." Ian exhaled and forced the muscles along his neck and shoulders to relax. "Apparently Thomas will go to great extremes to retain her. More men will likely be in London soon."

Wyndham took a long draw on his cheroot, then idly watched the smoke float up to the ceiling. "And what exactly happened to these men who attempted to take her?"

"One suffered an accident."

Wyndham dropped his gaze back to Ian's. "Did it involve his neck or a rather odd wound?"

"Neck." Ian smiled, filled with a twisted bit of pleasure. "Silly fellow lost his footing and fell under my knee."

"People are inclined to trip." Wyndham shifted in his chair and waggled his brows. "Well, I must admit that makes things interesting."

Ian eyed the spy with a touch of suspicion. Wyndham could occasionally be unhinged. Depending on which way the wind was blowing. "You're an odd bastard."

"Indeed. But this is why you are here speaking to me. Not some poncy-assed bastard who'd act as a proper gentleman should to what you've just told me." Wyndham smoothed a hand carelessly over his excellently tailored gray coat. "I take it she's not in fact mad as a March hare, then?"

"As sane as you or I," Ian clipped, unwilling to mention the laudanum, even if half the women in London were sipping it daily.

"That is not saying a great deal." Wyndham's gaze grew distant in thought.

Ian blew out a frustrated breath. "Chancery is not an option if what you say is true."

Wyndham snorted, the sound full of distaste and experience. "Forget Chancery."

Ian set his glass aside, tired of dancing about the point. "I want another viable option. Now."

"Thomas is her guardian?"

"Yes."

Wyndham nodded to himself. "So if he gets his hands on her, you're sodded, old man."

Ian didn't respond to the obvious truth. He didn't care to hear what he already knew.

"Time is of the essence."

Ian narrowed his eyes. "Thank you for your powers of observation."

Ignoring him, Wyndham said, "We do the only thing that will be completely beyond Thomas's touch."

"And that is?" drawled Ian, his usual amusement at his friend's drawn-out statements now absent.

"Dr. Jenner," Wyndham declared jovially, his eyes lifting back up to Ian's with a renewed vigor.

"Jenner?"

"He was recently appointed as Royal Physician to HRH. If Jenner says she's mentally competent, no one will dare gainsay him." Wyndham smiled wickedly. "It would be an insult to the Queen, now wouldn't it?"

It was so damn simple. So perfect. Almost too perfect.

"It will work, Ian. And then we bring Thomas down like the squealing little pig he is."

A smile tugged at Ian's lips, followed by a laugh to rival Wyndham's. He lifted his glass in salute. "To Her Majesty."

Wyndham lifted his glass in return and winked. "Hail Britannia, old man. Hail Britannia."

Chapter 24

It was utterly clear how Bertha Mason must have felt languishing away in her attic prison while Jane made doe eyes at Mr. Rochester. Eva stared down at the busy street below filled with hackneys, coaches, and, well, every conceivable form of transportation save the railway.

Just below, in the rooms she had sneaked through in the dark with Ian, servants were bustling at a ridiculous speed. Elizabeth had arrived early that morning accompanied by an army of staff. From the shouts and thumping, Eva was certain they'd have the house ready by Ian's return, which of course was no doubt Elizabeth's desire.

Even from the highest, most remote part of the house, Eva could hear the woman shouting like a general. She'd never imagined that genteel Elizabeth could be so vocal.

Sighing, Eva turned and faced the small attic room, gray at this time of the day. Several boxes and trunks dotted the floor.

Ian had claimed it was the only safe place for her. Apparently he'd proclaimed it off-limits to the servants. Earlier Elizabeth had brought up a light repast of toast and tea.

It had been hours since Ian had left. And some time since she'd seen Elizabeth. Well, at least she assumed so from the way the sun had traveled across the floor.

She understood why he'd left her up here. Still, that fact didn't stop her from feeling like a mad old bat locked away from society for its protection, a feeling that, frankly, she'd hoped was behind her. Even so, it was preferable to being out in the open, where Mrs. Palmer's men might spot her.

Damn and blast. She couldn't really be where anyone might spot her. Not yet. Not till she was ready to face the world as a person in her right wits.

The narrow stairs creaked. Instantly, she swung her gaze to the door. The servants weren't supposed to come here, but . . .

She stood her ground, not ready to scurry into the corner like a scared rat.

The small door swung open, creaking on tired hinges.

"Eva?" Ian called up.

She smiled. "Yes."

Ian strode into the room. Wearing the strangest expression. Happiness. Or so it seemed, for he had the largest grin on his face, and his glowing, deep green eyes were full of hope. "I've someone for you to meet."

She darted her gaze past Ian, unease mixing with her own happiness at Ian's good humor. She'd met so few people since she'd been locked away.

A large man, not tall, entered the room, dwarfing it with his strong presence. His russet hair appeared almost black in the dim light, but his eyes—chocolaty with just the hint of whiskey about them—beckoned one to trust him. Perfectly dressed from his dark brown serge coat to his cream trousers and gold cravat, he was the image of a perfect gentleman.

Drawing from some past instinct she could barely recall, Eva stretched out her hand, palm down, offering up her knuckles in a careless manner. "How do you do?"

The man crossed the room in a few short strides and

took her hand in his bearlike paw. He bowed over her enfolded appendage. "My lady. A true pleasure."

Eva stared at him, unsure of her next move in this game. "Might I know your name, sir?"

There was the faintest haughtiness to her voice. She barely recognized it as her own.

His brow lifted in an amused fashion as he looked her over. "My apologies. Blame the silly toss behind you. 'Twas remiss of him to not properly introduce us."

The mockingly pleased tone of the man was catching. As if the fellow were the most important man, the cleverest man in the world, and he knew it.

Eva ventured a smile and looked back at Ian, who looked a bit like an animal trying to assess how its prey had suddenly turned into the predator. "Yes," she agreed, a laugh in her voice. "It is indeed remiss. My lord, will you not introduce us?"

Ian cleared his throat. "Lord Byron Cartwright, Earl of Wyndham. Lady Eva Carin."

It occurred to Eva that this Wyndham fellow was still holding her hand. Slowly she pulled away from his grip.

"Ian, old boy, you led me to believe she was some sort of delicate flower, which one must be careful not to trample."

She drew up, her spine snapping straight as she glared at Ian. "I beg your pardon?"

Ian narrowed his eyes at his friend. "If she is a delicate flower, you are a twinkle-toed ponce. And that is not what I said."

"Do forgive. Poetic license." Wyndham took a step forward, circling Eva like an overzealous dressmaker about to drown her in froths of fabric. "If you're mad, then they'd best lock half the ton away."

Eva eyed the man warily. What ever were they about? "Thank you?"

"Now we must simply proclaim the fact to the world." He grinned, the same sort of grin one might wear three sheets to the wind, dancing a jig upon the topmast of a racing cutter. "And dare them all to contradict it."

Eva frowned, beginning to feel a trifle overwhelmed. She didn't remember most lords being like this man. "Would you care to explain?"

"We're going to have you proclaimed competent," Ian said gently. "Then—" His features softened, clearly aware he was about to say something that would displease her. "Then we're going to—"

"Launch you into society, my dear!" Wyndham boasted. "We shall flaunt you like the latest bauble come from the exotic East, and once we're done and the ton has gazed upon you like an exhibit at the Royal Academy, you shall have reclaimed your crown."

Was he mad? Had Ian found a mad person? "I don't want my crown back," she said firmly. The very idea that her former friends were going to watch her, waiting to see if she would slip up and act like a lunatic among their pomp, was horrifying. "I don't."

Wyndham's smile dimmed and he leveled a look of determination that no doubt would make the fiercest of men quake in their boots. "That is exactly what you want. And Ian, I, and that Wellington of a woman, Lady Elizabeth, will all be there to ensure your success."

Eva turned to Ian. "What is happening here?"

Ian reached out and folded her hands into his. "We are going to make you safe. Safer than you've ever been. Safe from Thomas."

She drew in a slow breath. Though she wished to run down the stairs and out into the street, she nodded. In truth, she wondered whether indeed they could make her safe. Safe from the one thing she needed the most protection from.

Herself.

She lifted her chin. She would face the world. For Ian. For herself. For Mary, who still languished in the asylum.

Her proved sanity might set her friend free.

There were other ways she could make amends for what she had done. Never again would she allow herself to be imprisoned. By building or by man. "When do we start?"

Ian pulled her up against him. "Now, love. We start now."

Wyndham cleared his throat. "Today you will meet many people, my dear. In fact, three of London's most able drapers and seamstresses are downstairs ready to turn you into a bird of paradise."

She glanced over at the earl. "Do you always speak so, my lord?"

He laughed, a powerful, invigorating sound. "Indeed, madam. Why would anyone talk in an uninspired manner?"

Eva laughed. Genuinely laughed. It spilled from her lips in shockingly pleasurable waves. "I have no idea, my lord. No idea at all."

India
Two years earlier

He'd done it again. Hamilton staggered in the dark, his boots kicking at the dusty path back to his bed. He'd lost another five thousand pounds. But luckily his behavior hadn't endangered his commission. He was too successful a soldier. It had taken him only three months to earn the reputation of Mad Bastard. At least, he truly was good at something: mayhem. His last raids had all ended in triumphs for his men, but he'd sacrificed soldiers for those daring successes and part of his madness came from the whispers that he'd butchered his own men for advancement.

He had. The ends necessitated unflinching commitment, and the loss of a few unimportant men meant nothing in the face of victory.

Hamilton peered down the silent alley, wondering whether he should have waited for Ian. No. Ian would have been poor company for his walk home. They never spoke now.

If he could just spill into bed and forget ... and then wake up and start it all again. What would Eva think of him now?

A sort of sharp panic grabbed his guts. She could never know. Never. She wouldn't forgive him if she knew. Would Ian tell? No. Hamilton sucked in a breath. Ian would protect Eva from the ugly truth, just as he'd always done.

As he made a right turn down another, smaller alley, the walls of the houses pressing in toward his shoulders, he scowled. Footsteps shuffled behind him. Hamilton jerked toward them, squinting in the moonlight. Dark hair, sharp features stood out in the dim light, and even in the cold moonbeams Hamilton could make out Ian's green eyes. He let out a sudden sigh of relief.

Yes, Ian would keep his behavior a secret and Eva would still look at him with some degree of love, even if it would never be the love he had so hoped for. He started to smile at his old friend, but then shadows flickered just behind Ian. Hamilton pointed jerkily. "Behind you."

Ian twisted fast. The shine of blade flashed in the night and raked toward his middle.

Someone shouted something in foul native tongue and abruptly the attacker's blade just skimmed Ian's chest.

Hamilton jerked to attention, his shaky gaze desperately trying to discern who was coming out of the shadows.

Two men darted down the dark alley, and before Hamilton's wine-soaked mind could make sense of it, hands grabbed him. He jerked against them, struggling to throw a punch, but before he could, one of the Indians seized his head and slammed it against the stone wall behind him.

The world spun hard and sparked with light.

Hamilton scrambled to get away, but there were two of them and their muscled bodies would not be gainsaid. One of his attackers slammed a palm over his mouth, rendering him silent.

Their sweaty, hulking forms surrounded him, and terror managed to penetrate his wine-muddled thoughts. He could no longer see Ian in the dark. Where was Ian? Where was he?

Someone grabbed his wrists and then he felt a white-hot cut rake his flesh and veins. Sudden clarity rammed through him. This was a death sentence. Hot, slick blood slid down over his fingers. He fought against his assailants, but the wine made him slow and as the blood poured from him he found himself growing weaker.

It was going to look like suicide. But what of Ian?

The men holding him lowered him to the dirt street, and just at that moment a beam of moonlight shone harshly down upon them, bathing an Indian man's face in its icy light. Tears sparked his dark eyes and he lifted a small piece of fabric, a Sepoy's rank stitched to it.

Recognition riddled Hamilton. That rank. It was the same as the boy who had killed himself. Even in his shocked state, Hamilton could see that this man had come for vengeance. "P-please—"

Hamilton looked up into the face of the man hovering over him.

"You killed my son." The Indian's eyes blazed with

broken hate and pain. Shaking, he leaned forward and growled. "You will kill no other sons."

This was about the sodding Sepoy? Hamilton narrowed his eyes and with as much saliva as he could muster he spat in the filthy son of a bitch's face.

Flinching slightly, the native just stared down at him, watching, his dark eyes a void of grief.

Hamilton jerked his gaze away from the unrelenting stare. Uselessly, he struggled against the brutal hands still holding him down. Allowing his blood to flow quickly and freely. He was going to die here. On the dirty ground. At the hands of a native.

In the cold light, several feet away, Ian crouched down, his face a mask of pain and horror. "I warned you. I told you no more deaths. But you couldn't stop."

Hamilton's heart slammed like a wild hammer in his chest. "You're killing your best friend," he hissed.

Ian remained frozen. His voice breaking, he said, "You k-killed my friend. My best friend." Ian's rough intake of breath was audible down the alley before he said, "He's been dead for years."

As the man holding him eased his grip, Hamilton felt his life sliding away, felt his body floating away. He couldn't even draw an easing breath as he locked gazes with his childhood friend. "You son of a bitch."

"I'm sorry," Ian whispered. "So sorry. I tried. I tried to bring you back."

No forgiveness, though. Ian did not ask for it. Nor would Hamilton give it. As the men stared down at him while his lifeblood leaked to the dust, Hamilton wished his father had never taken Ian in or made him promise to come to India. Hamilton wished that Ian had not been such a sycophantic do-gooder. But most of all, he wished that he, himself, had been a better man. Now there would never be the chance. So as he struggled for breath, Hamilton mouthed, "Go to hell, Ian."

Ian nodded and his eyes glimmered with unshed emotion. "I will. So we shall see each other again."

And there on the cold ground, in a foreign land, among the filthy people he loathed, Hamilton breathed out his last.

England
The present

Only a few, harried days later, Eva stood in the Louis XIV salon awaiting her judge. Everything had changed. The gown wrapped about her body was the most beautiful deep lavender moiré silk. It appeared silvery gray in some lights, and sparkling purple in others. The neck bore a simple swath of Irish lace and a cameo from the western shores of Italy. Only her hands and face were exposed. Her dark hair had been woven into an artful little hairpiece at the back of her neck. It almost felt like her own.

The full skirt hid any notion that she might indeed have limbs below her waist.

It was comforting how much Ian believed in her. Right now, she would have given anything to have him holding her hand, adding to her newfound courage. He was waiting in the foyer for Dr. Jenner's arrival. Wyndham had gone to fetch the doctor and they were due any minute.

She had no idea what to think of this new ally in her pursuit of freedom. But he was a welcome burst of light into her dark world. And she knew Ian needed it, too. That faint touch of humor to a world about to crack.

Though she would have preferred Elizabeth to wait with her, Ian had been explicit in his commands. She would be ready for the doctor and not appear as if she needed someone in the room to keep her from topping herself.

A carriage rolled up to the front of the house.

Eva's heart leapt in her chest. She forced herself to take deep breaths as she turned from the window and faced the room designed for a woman.

They had calculated this moment in every degree. Nothing would be left to chance. She would appear as a woman of duty, intelligence, and propriety, in the perfect gown, in a perfect woman's room.

Everything beamed with lightness. In truth, she felt a bit as though she had landed in a sugar confection. The walls were painted blue silk. The furniture: delicate, white-painted wood, gilded and embroidered with roses. She'd come a good distance since that first day at Blythely Castle, when she'd been afraid to contaminate Lady Elizabeth's salon. Today she would not hesitate to sit, even if some part of her still felt as though she didn't quite belong.

Voices carried through the hall, hushed from the foyer. No doubt they were discussing her. Discussing what tactic the good doctor would take.

Footsteps thudded along the wood flooring on the opposite side of the door. It was time. Time to take her place in this illusion. Eva pressed her hands lightly to her skirts and stood by the delicate settee facing the door.

She was bloody well going to do this. She wasn't mad. She may have had everything taken away from her, but insane she was not.

"Lady Carin," a genial voice called as the door opened and a white-haired man crossed the threshold. His thick, silvery beard gleamed and he smiled kindly as he stepped toward her.

Eva swallowed and quickly matched his smile. She lifted her hand, waiting for him to take it.

He did so, bowing over it, his gray suit creasing ever so slightly. "It is a pleasure. I have heard so much about you."

Eva did not let her smile dim as she turned regally and moved, her skirts swaying, to her seat. With great care, she lowered herself, arranging her skirts and crinoline. "Indeed, sir. I am sure my reports are most curious." She gestured to the chair next to her. "Do sit down."

She darted her gaze to the door. Where the devil were they? Ian, Wyndham, and Elizabeth were supposed to have been right behind the doctor. Accompanying him and supporting her.

Dr. Jenner followed her gaze, then sat, sweeping out the tails of his coat. "Pardon, my lady, but I asked that we meet alone. I felt it best if we became acquainted without the pressures of prying eyes."

Or eyes that might tell her what to say and do.

Eva nodded, forcing a smile back to her lips. "Of course. What an honor it is to have you here." She leaned forward, hoping for a slight teasing air. "And all to myself, the Queen's own physician. I am a very lucky woman."

He tsked, his blue eyes twinkling. "Now, now. You flatter me."

Eva shook her head. "I only speak the truth." She lifted her brows just as a lady should when about to offer something. "Might I offer you tea?"

Dr. Jenner eyed her carefully, then nodded. "Please. How kind of you to offer."

Eva stood slowly, allowing her skirts to fall back into perfect place. She took even steps to the fireplace, her back straight, her head high. She tugged on the bellpull, closing her eyes for a moment. She could do this. And even as she said it to herself, she realized it was true. She was entirely capable of this. At last, she turned to him.

Dr. Jenner relaxed slightly in his chair. "Lady Carin, it seems foolish to pretend that I am not here to judge your soundness of mind."

Eva blinked. This was not what was supposed to happen. Then again . . . how freeing to not have to pretend so utterly that nothing was amiss. She laughed softly. "I must confess, it is trying to dance about the subject."

Dr. Jenner nodded. "Please, my dear, sit."

Eva did so, this time angling her knees toward him. Nervous, though thankful they were finally about to begin.

"Now. I would like to ask you, why do you believe your brother-in-law placed you in an institution?"

Eva bit down on her lower lip. Institution? Cesspool, more like. Still, this was not one of the questions she had expected. She folded her hands together, grasping for answers that would be acceptable. Sighing, she lifted her gaze to his. "No doubt, my behavior upset him."

"How so?" he asked gently.

"You see—" Her throat clenched. Could she actually say what she had never said? "You see—" Her voice lowered. "My husband had just been killed in India . . ." It didn't seem possible that she was allowing these thoughts to finally take form. No one had really wished to hear her speak the full truth of the darkness she'd felt. Not really. Not even Ian, for he had his own demons.

"A terrible loss. I am sorry for it."

"Thank you."

"But that is not all?" he urged her.

"No. Of course not," she said factually. "I am sure you heard of my . . . son's death."

"I did. Even Her Majesty voiced her grief."

Tears stung Eva's eyes. "How kind. We received her note."

"You recall it?" Dr. Jenner said, his voice slightly surprised.

"Oh, yes. So many people were so kind, but I could not help but feel—" A tear, traitorous little thing that it was, threatened to slip free, and she blinked quickly. "The tremendous loss of it."

The door swung open and a maid, Alice, quickly scurried into the room. She carried the tray to the little table beside Eva. The girl eyed the two of them, curiosity rolling off her.

"Thank you, Alice," Eva said clearly, yet with an authoritative air.

The girl bobbed a quick curtsy, her brown eyes wide.

"I will call if anything else is required."

Alice snapped her gaze from Dr. Jenner to Eva, a blush spreading over her cheeks. "Yes, my lady."

As the door shut behind the girl, Eva picked up a beautiful porcelain cup painted with blue and gold flowers and simultaneously, as a perfect hostess did, went through the motions of making a proper cup of tea. Neither of her hands shook. "How do you take your tea, Doctor?"

The words came out of her well rehearsed. They sounded bizarre to her own ears. Formulaic and precise, considering she'd just been speaking of her son. Her Adam.

"I take the good leaf as it comes, my dear."

With ease, Eva poured out a cup. No drops or splatters, and she allowed the tea to steep before lifting the strainer. A genuine smile tilted her lips as she passed him the cup and then reached for her own.

"You know," Dr. Jenner began, "the Queen took a particular interest in your situation. She, too, had lost her husband and has so many children of her own. She loves them so dearly that she was touched by the immensity of your tragedy."

Eva's fingers pressed down on the saucer. Visibly, they whitened. "Her Majesty is too gracious."

"She is a remarkable woman and mother. She was sad to hear you had to retire for your health. As you know, Her Majesty, too, has largely retired from society, her mourning for her husband foremost in her thoughts. But I look at you and see a woman who only needs a walk in the park and a bit more cheese and meat on her plate."

Eva laughed, unsure whether she was being granted a reprieve. "That is very good to hear."

"And yet, I must ask you to continue." Dr. Jenner took a sip of tea. "Can you tell me more about Adam?"

The ready smile faded from her lips. "Of course." Eva lifted her cup and took a delicate swallow. Every word was painful and yet cathartic, as if the poison were leaching out of her under his kind gaze. "He was a beautiful boy."

Her voice came out strong. Sure. Completely unrecognizable to her. Slowly, she placed her cup and saucer down on the small lacquered table. "Everything about him reminded me of his father. Everyone said he looked like me, but I only saw Hamilton. Even so young he was fearless. Just a baby, mind you, but he would rock forward and pull himself up onto his little legs. He'd fall, an astonished look upon his face, that he had failed at anything he tried."

Eva bit down on her lip, tears stinging her eyes. "But unlike other babies, he didn't cry when he fell. He would laugh. The slightest, happiest little sound. As if he were defying that invisible thing that had knocked him down. And then he'd rock forward again, ready to try for a step."

"You loved him dearly." It was a statement, not a question.

Eva smiled, even as unstoppable tears slipped down

her cheeks. What would he think of her? "How could I not?"

Dr. Jenner whipped a handkerchief from his pocket. "Take this. It's the least an old fellow like myself can do for making such a beautiful lady cry."

Eva took the handkerchief. Why was he so kind? He had to know the next part of the story. "You know how Adam died?"

"You tell me about it, my dear."

"I had only just received word that Hamilton had died. I needed to go into the village."

"Why?"

Eva frowned. She thought back to that day, the necessity of the letter, Thomas's censure. The driving feeling of danger. "It is all a blur, Doctor."

"That is perfectly normal under such distressing conditions. Do continue."

"Adam was in the curricle with me. I needed him, needed him with me since his father was lost to me. The wheel slipped off in the mud and . . ." She tried to force her mouth around the horrible moment. Pressure began to build inside her. The wildest force until, finally, she burst out: "He was flung from the vehicle. Killed. And it was my fault, do you see? If I had just—"

"My dear lady," Dr. Jenner cut in. "You cannot take the role of God, nor can you claim power over forces of nature and inanimate objects."

Eva gasped for air. She blinked at him. "Pardon?"

"To say you are responsible for your son's death is tantamount to saying it is my fault when my patients die because I cannot get to them in time, or because there is simply no medicine to cure them."

"That must be different," she said. "Thomas told me. He told me again and again."

Dr. Jenner stilled. "Lord Carin?"

She nodded.

"What exactly did he say?"

"That it was my fault. That Hamilton would hate me for what I had done. That I was the most evil of mothers—"

"Your brother-in-law is an insensitive lout and, frankly, the sooner you are out of his guardianship the better, I think."

"But—" It was true, wasn't it? It was her fault. Yet here was this wise man telling her that it was ridiculous of her to contemplate it.

"Now I must ask you a few short questions."

What exactly was happening? It all seemed too rash, so unexpected. She lifted her chin, ready.

"What is your name?" he asked plainly.

She blinked at the simplicity of it. "Eva Carin."

"Who were your parents?"

Clearing her throat, she answered evenly, "Martha and John."

"What is the year?" he asked, his brows lifting with pleasant curiosity.

"Eighteen sixty-five."

"And . . ." He took a deep sip of tea. "What city are we in?"

She laughed at the absurd question, then pressed the handkerchief to her mouth. "Do forgive me. We are in London, of course."

He smiled gently. "They are simple questions, my dear, but important to establishing your awareness to society." He smoothed his fingers over his thick mustache. "Who is your monarch?"

"Queen Victoria."

Dr. Jenner beamed kindly at her. "There, now. We are done."

"We are?" Eva gaped at him. "I don't understand . . ."

"My dear, you are not mad. Nor likely ever were. Grief is a hideous thing. We all need time to recover, and yours was no common loss. I will sign the paper when I leave; it will be registered posthaste with Chancery and the House of Lords. By dinner you should be a free woman."

Eva opened her mouth, then quickly closed it.

The doctor stood and bowed. "I do hope to see you again, though in a social capacity."

At last, Eva smiled up at him. "Thank you. Thank you so very much."

He nodded and headed for the door, but once he reached it, he paused and turned back. "You have not talked of either of them much, have you?"

Eva couldn't quite grasp what he was asking, not in the awe of this moment. "Pardon?"

"You should, you know. Often. It will make the pain lessen. And one day, though it seems impossible now, you will feel only pleasure when you speak of them." He hesitated, his face creasing with consideration. "Forgive me. It may not be my place, but that young man out there, Lord Blake—"

"Yes?"

"He cares very deeply for you. And in my experience, such a thing is not to be passed lightly." He nodded as if confirming his words to himself. "Consider it, my dear."

With that, Dr. Jenner disappeared down the hall.

Eva stared at the empty doorway. Was it so apparent to everyone, the way Ian and she felt such a connection? Lady Elizabeth had intimated such a thing. Dare she give over to her feelings for Ian? Such a thing seemed dangerously close to a betrayal of Hamilton and her son's memory.

But Dr. Jenner seemed to believe that all she need do was talk of her family, not make a martyr of herself to them. Such a task should have appeared Herculean. The last year and a half had been devoted to silence on the subject.

Still, if she allowed herself to think on it, she did feel better. Infinitely better at this moment. Though such relief might be attributed to the fact that she had just been proclaimed sane, she didn't think it the only reason. A weight seemed to have been lifted from her shoulders.

For the first time in months, she felt very nearly free. Perhaps, just perhaps, Hamilton wouldn't hate her. Perhaps it had not been her fault. Perhaps she could smile when speaking of her son. And most surprising of all, perhaps she could open her heart to love.

Chapter 25

"You are free." Relief had Ian floating as he spoke. Finally. It was what they both deserved. What they had so longed for.

Eva beamed up at him, her pale face alight with happiness. "Yes. I am my own woman now."

Own woman. Those two fatal words sucked his relief from him. It was true. She was technically independent. Free of any who would tell her what to do.

"What is it?"

"Eva, you must remember those men."

The light faded from her face. Nodding, she slid her arms from his. "I do."

Thank God she still needed him. He wasn't ready to let go of her yet. To step from her life and allow her to be free of his interference. But then it was likely that she might need him for ages yet. How would she survive in society without him?

Of course she still needed him. He reached out to her, tangling his fingers in hers. "I didn't mean to steal the happiness of the moment."

She turned back toward him, her eyes dark. "Of course you didn't. How could you?"

But he had. He could see it in the way her face had resigned itself. Resigned itself to more fear. More waiting. God, he was a bastard. However, it was true. As long as Thomas was free, she would never truly be. "Wyndham and I will find a way to keep you safe."

"Don't you think Thomas will just leave me to myself now? He has no legal claim."

Ian pulled her back against him, loving the feel of her frame tucked to him. "No." He lowered his head, kissing her hair. "It just doesn't seem possible. Not when he went to so much trouble to imprison you. I cannot see him letting you go. He's an ass."

"That's what Dr. Jenner said."

"Indeed?"

Eva nodded. "Yes. Well, not exactly. I think he used the word 'insensitive' for telling me it was my fault."

"Thomas told you that?"

"Daily. Hourly. There is much I had forgotten. Now, with my head clear, those days are slowly coming back. Lord, I was so drunk on laudanum, it's a miracle I didn't do myself in."

Ian's gut clenched. "Eva, you tried."

A disbelieving laugh rattled from her. "What? That's ridiculous. I would never—"

"Thomas said you were caught by gardeners walking into the lake."

"Well, that would be very foolish of me. I certainly couldn't kill myself that way. Unless it was suicide by pneumonia."

Ian paused. "How do you mean?"

"I'd just have swum, Ian. Unless Thomas says I loaded my pockets down with bricks."

Blinking, he hugged her tighter against him. "You can't swim, Eva."

She glared up at him. "I most certainly can. I didn't spend all my time while you two were in India in my room waiting for you and Hamilton to come back. On my last trip to Bath, I learned. I sea bathe quite well."

A gnawing suspicion started working at him. What was Thomas about? "Eva, why would Thomas have said that?"

"Because as you said, he's an ass. A jealous, vicious ass."

Ian laughed, though the sound was forced. A chill stole over him. It raised the hairs on the back of his neck and gave him the battle-ready feeling he felt under the hot sun, artillery in view. "You're right, of course."

He'd worried her enough. Now was not the time to press her with questions. Come morning light, he'd set Wyndham on the track of those two gardeners. If anyone could find them, the former spy would.

Eva let out a worried sigh. "Do you really think a ball is a good idea?"

Ian snapped his attention back to her. Uncertainty creased her brow. "I do. It will be one more mark against Thomas when you make your triumphant return to society."

"As you say." She lifted her face toward his, a smile playing at her lips. "Care to kiss a free woman?"

Free woman.

Ian brought his palm up to cup her soft cheek. A sudden desire to brand her with his touch seized him. Somehow, with their bodies, he could erase the past from both their minds.

He grabbed her against him, lowering his mouth to hers with fierce need. In response, Eva pressed her body tight into his, her fingers pushing into his back near to the point of pain.

Eva pulled away and lowered herself to the floor. "Make love to me, Ian."

Ian needed no further urging. He knelt down beside her. The light of the fire flickered over her body. She looked like living stone. Alabaster. Perfect. Ready to come alive under loving hands.

There was something restive yet desperate in this moment. She'd offered herself up to him, and he was more than ready to take. But fear clung to his heart. Fear that this was all going to evaporate like a flickering image of palms in the desert.

Happiness was not for men like him.

Instead of immediately covering her body with his, Ian lowered his head and rested it against her silk-covered abdomen.

She remained still for a moment before her hands came to stroke his hair. It was the most tender thing he had felt in his life. The most dangerous.

This was how men lost themselves.

Closing his eyes against the fear, Ian allowed himself to breathe in her scent of roses and soap. What was he doing? "Eva—"

"Shh," she whispered, her hands still slipping through his hair. "Think of nothing but this." She tucked her fingers under his chin and forced his face upward. "Look at me."

He opened his eyes.

Her indigo blue gaze burned with passion. "Don't," she whispered, as if afraid to pierce the silence.

"What?" he asked, unable to tear his gaze from her face.

"Run away." She stroked the side of his face. "I can see it in your eyes. Hear it in your voice. You are on the verge of running from this. From us."

He wanted to laugh. He'd been running for so long now. Was it even possible for him to stop? At last, he leaned forward and looked down into her eyes. "I will never leave you." The words burned in his throat. He meant them. He did. "As long as you need me, I will never go."

"I want to be with you, Ian."

Ian's heart pounded with wonder. Now. Here. He was hers. She was his. And he would not contemplate anything else under the darkness of night.

It wasn't gentleness that set him back toward her legs. Oh, no. It was the need to devour her. The firelight danced over her as he bent and smoothed her silk robe open, exposing her long, pale limbs.

He stared down at the soft skin. Slowly, his breath tightened, coming in shorter, hungrier gasps. Needing to taste her, he bent her knees and knelt between them.

Her eyes were locked on him, her mouth half open. He wanted her wild for him. Thinking of nothing but the pleasure he could give her.

He rubbed his face gently against her inner thigh, then pressed an openmouthed kiss to the velvety flesh before he lightly bit the skin.

She gasped, her hands coming to weave into his hair. Blindly, he pushed her robe open all the way. Ian lifted his eyes to her body, taking in the beautiful curves and hollows of her. With every day she looked healthier, fuller. That alone set his heart beating faster.

The sight of her breasts, small yet taut, pink nipples hard, elicited a groan. He worked his way up her body, savoring every kiss, determined to live in this moment. Determined to pay homage to every part of her body as it deserved.

When he sucked a nipple into his mouth, she arched against him. "Ian—" She gasped. "Don't wait."

He flicked his tongue over the hard peak.

Her hands fumbled at his trousers. Finally she worked

them free. She slipped her hand into the fine wool and wrapped her hand around his hard cock.

A groan tore from his throat. Where had the insecure woman gone? She was fading away. Replaced by this beautiful, enigmatic beauty beneath him. The one who would take what she wanted as she'd done before heartache's cold embrace had found her.

Knowing that she was finding her own strength with him here was intensely erotic.

"Now," she ground out. "Now."

Ian smiled at her passion, though his body was on fire with a pleasure that neared pain. He shoved his trousers down his legs. Gently, he rubbed the head of his cock against her opening.

She moaned and urged her hips up to him.

But he wanted her completely ready. Taking his cock in hand, he slid the head over her most sensitive spot, then up and down her slick core.

Another moan came from her throat. She reached forward and grabbed his buttocks with her hands. Ian positioned himself at her center and thrust forward.

Slick heat welcomed him, wrapping his cock in it. His chest expanded as he sucked in a breath. It was almost impossible to control himself with this woman, he needed her so much.

As if a wild creature had replaced Eva, she pushed herself up onto her elbows and stole his mouth in a long, soul-searing kiss. It nearly sent him pummeling over the edge.

Ian reached down and cupped her bottom, completely tilting her up toward him so that he could thrust deep and hard. To fill her completely.

Eva tore her mouth from his, clinging to his back, nails raking against his flesh.

The feel of her holding on to him, racked with desire, pushed him even harder. Consumed in it, he thrust deep against her, making sure he stroked the spot that would send her spiraling into pleasure.

As he sped his thrust, she dropped back, her legs locked around his waist. Pleasure lit her face. Finally a piercing cry came from her. She grabbed his shoulders, her head back.

Ian focused on the pleasure transforming her face as his cock stroked her tight heat. When she rippled around him, he couldn't hold back any longer. The power of it shook him to his core. "Eva," he moaned, his voice harsh with his passion.

Their breathing slowed almost simultaneously as he lowered himself against her. He couldn't separate himself yet. He needed this feeling of being a part of her. She fit perfectly against him, her slight body curving into his.

It was damn alarming. And he felt more alive than he had in years.

As he tucked her against him, he stroked her back.

She remained silent for several moments. Then she placed her hand against his chest and said gently, "I love you, Ian."

Chapter 26

E va held herself perfectly still. If she moved she would shatter this moment. All would be lost. She would be alone again in the darkness. As she waited longer and longer for him to respond, the darkness encroached a little more into the happiness she'd been so sure she'd finally found.

"Eva," he said softly, his voice full of doubt.

She drew in a shuddering breath, knowing he was not going to say the words she so hoped to hear. "Please don't."

"Wait," he urged.

Eva drew away from him. Coldness clawed itself through her chest. She reached for her robe. "I understand." And she did. God, how foolish of her. How foolish to believe he might love her, too. Who could love her as she was? No matter that she had begun to put the pieces of herself back together. No matter what Dr. Jenner had said, at her core still resided the fact that she had put her son at such risk it had ended in his death.

She swallowed back the sudden foul taste permeating her mouth.

He reached for her, forcing her to stay against him. His skin still slightly damp with their lovemaking. "You don't understand."

"I know I don't deserve—"

"I will not hear that from you," he snapped. "You deserve everything this world has to offer you. But I—" His voice broke.

Eva stared at him, trying to make sense of what he was saying. Shadows played over his face, adding to the mask that had slipped over his features. "Go on," she urged softly.

"Hamilton died."

She tensed, not truly wanting to discuss her late husband in the arms of the man she'd loved since childhood. But hadn't Dr. Jenner told her that talking was precisely what had to be done? Perhaps it was the same for Ian. "I know. But that was neither your nor my fault."

That she knew more than anything.

"It was." His deep voice penetrated the darkness, laden with emotion.

She shook her head against his warm skin, dread pooling in her belly. There was something he wished to say that she did not wish to hear and she was not yet brave enough to bear. So she would do the only thing she could think of to stop him. She would take the blame herself. "Ian, Hamilton went to war out of his father's volition. You know I urged him to stay. Perhaps I should have begged harder."

He laughed, a twisted sound, full of pain and fury. "Sweetheart, it is not you who should have fought harder for Hamilton's life." He rolled over, turning his face and his body toward the fire. "It was I."

She propped herself up onto her elbow, looking down on him. "I don't understand."

His shoulders, those proud, strong shoulders, slumped. "I should have fought harder for him. Don't you see, if I had rescued him as his father wished he would still be alive and Thomas wouldn't have been able to send you to that place."

Eva swallowed, her heart aching at this side of Ian that he had never allowed her to see. "And you would be dead?" she whispered.

"Yes!" he roared. "No. I don't know. But we lost something out there." His voice tore in broken starts. "We lost our friendship and I let him die. Don't you see, if I had fought harder for him or died in his place, he would still be alive. Your son would still be alive. You would never have been sent to that hellhole."

Eva sat in the firelight, his words hitting her with the force of his guilt. For the last year he had been living in this black filth. He'd hidden it so well, her strong Ian. But in the end he was no different than she, racked with guilt at what they had done.

Did she sound as he did when she claimed Adam's death?

There was no doubt in her mind, despite his determined claims: Ian wasn't responsible for Hamilton.

Her eyes blurred and she blinked rapidly. If he did indeed feel the way she did, there was nothing she could say to change his mind. Still, she had to try. Slowly, she lay down beside him, placing her arms around his tense frame. The words she was about to utter were no doubt the hardest she had ever contemplated. They had to be said, though. To bring him back, as he had done everything he could to bring her back. "Do you believe I could have saved Adam?"

"Eva—"

"No. I want to know."

He twisted in her arms, facing her. "You know I don't. It was a dreadful . . . accident." There was a hitch in his voice.

Eva forced herself to remain calm. She sucked in a slow breath, readying herself with false confidence. "There you see."

"See what exactly?" he said tightly. "If you finally see that it was not your fault, then I am happy."

She stared at him for a moment, then dropped her head back. Tired. So tired. "You are not happy. I do not make you happy."

"That's not true—you are everything to me," he whispered.

She bit her lower lip, feeling the truth of the situation. Two lost souls could somehow find their way, could they not? Or would they simply wander, lost in their own separate hells, keeping the other chained in loss? She turned her head back toward him. "Then, if you truly believe me innocent, you cannot claim responsibility for Hamilton."

A muscle clenched in his cheek. "I can." His green eyes turned to two flat rocks, glimmering but almost dead with acceptance. Gently he took her hand and stroked her fingers over the scattered scars along his chest.

"He was responsible for his own actions, Ian."

"Yes, but—"

Her insides tightened at his strange contradiction. "There is no 'but' about it. He—"

"I was there. I watched him die. And I did nothing."

She held her breath, caught up in his sudden intensity.

"He bled to death at my feet. And I didn't stop the man who killed him. In fact, I told him where he might find Hamilton."

She frowned. "That makes no sense. He died in battle."

"That was the report. But it's not what happened. He died in an alley. Most believed it was self-destruction, though his officers did not bring such a thing to light. Some believed it was something more, but Hamilton had made enough enemies that they kept their opinions quiet and they kept his gruesome death quiet, too."

His eyes darted from hers, his face whitening with pain. "But he—" Ian's voice broke. His hand began to shake, the one holding hers, shaking hers right along with it. "It never should have happened. None of it. I never thought to see him change the way he did." His eyes closed. Even with his lids pressed tight, the muscles fluttered as if he were envisioning the nightmare.

There were a thousand things she wanted to say. Anything, really, to break this moment of damnation. At last, there was only one thing: "I know you, and whatever you did, it was the right thing."

He laughed a bitter laugh, then pressed his palms to his eyes.

She'd never seen a man cry. She wished he would. If he did, he might feel some relief. But he wouldn't. Men like Ian didn't allow themselves the luxury.

"You're right." He opened his eyes. No longer dead, they were full of resolve. "He did choose." Without looking back at her, he rolled away. Fastening his trousers, he stared into the fire. "But I chose also. I chose to reveal Hamilton's whereabouts. I chose to stand by while he was killed."

What could Hamilton have done to induce such a thing from Ian? For she knew Ian's heart was too noble to act thusly without reason, even if he might wish her to believe otherwise.

The longer she sat away from him in silence, the more the cold air stung her naked skin. Eva shivered. Her robe was in a pool of white silk about her. Quickly she slipped it on. Wishing it didn't feel as though she were donning armor against the coming moments. "You came back. Alive."

"Too late. Because of what I did, Adam is dead and you . . ."

Eva remained behind him, unable to speak. Whatever

ease had come to Ian in the last days drifted away before her. Replaced by that fatal resolve that had so frightened and assured her. "And?"

"I will not take Hamilton's place. Even if he— No. I can't. Not when I betrayed him. Not when I betrayed you. My heart is not to be trusted with love. I betray those I love."

"I see." Oh, God, did she see. It whipped at her. Worse than the blows Matthew had pummeled her with. Now she would welcome the fiery stripe of the stick lashing down upon her back compared to this hell.

"Thank you," he said quietly.

And though it broke her heart, she curled into his arms, quiet. Praying, praying with all her heart that he would forgive himself. She loved him so much and it took all her strength not to try to make him see the foolishness of his words. If she waited, he would see on his own. Surely, if she waited just a little longer, he would finally be able to embrace love.

Chapter 27

"**B**loody success, don't you think?" boomed Wyndham.

"A coup," Ian said, half stunned by the sheer immensity of Eva's victory. "A veritable coup."

Elizabeth had outdone herself in the decorations. Every member of the ton who was anyone—and a few who weren't—graced the ball. Elizabeth had made sure of that. Between himself, Wyndham, and Elizabeth, they had bullied and ordered like generals to turn the room into a starlit wonderland.

Hung from a hundred golden wires, paper lanterns in the shape of stars swung from the ceiling, and gardenias sprawled everywhere.

Eva was the queen of it all. Despite the gnawing feeling that he was stealing happiness, Ian couldn't stop his own delight. This was all he'd ever wanted for her: to conquer society so that she might be free. But there was one aspect of all this that detracted from the relief he should have experienced.

He'd barely seen her in the last few days. He'd tried to convince himself it was because he was busy. But the truth was he couldn't bare to be around her hope. Expectation fairly shone from her eyes, that at any moment he would utter the words she so longed to hear. But he couldn't.

So he'd swept himself up in the tasks of launching her into society. In all their days together since her return, he'd never felt more adrift. More lost. And with each day that passed, he felt her slipping away. Which was of course foolish. They would never be parted. She needed him.

He studied her, a sweet pain.

Eva stood surrounded by a horde of gentlemen and ladies. Her dark hair had been wound with gold rope and diamond stars. That skin, which had seemed too white for so long, now shone perfect porcelain. The hue that women of the ton virtually poisoned themselves to obtain.

He and Wyndham stood high above, watching near a balustrade, overseeing that nothing should go amiss. Nothing would, of course. Somehow in the midst of all their endeavors, she had grown far out of his reach. He was still trapped in his sorrow. She? Eva was a butterfly born out of her dark cocoon, aflight with glorious color.

Indeed, she turned and laughed at a young fop's sly comment, her green velvet gown, a creation by that atrociously expensive fop, Worth, swishing.

"It's your fault, you know."

Ian continued to keep Eva within his gaze as he said, "Indubitably."

Wyndham threw his head back and let out one of his barrel laughs. "My, don't we feel sorry for ourselves."

Ian tore his gaze form Eva. "I do not feel sorry—"

"Do forgive me. Of course you don't." Wyndham tossed back half his champagne, then inclined his head toward Eva. "She is a goddess."

"I know."

Wyndham lifted his glass and tsked. "Ah. But she is not your goddess."

"She will be," Ian said calmly. They were so close now.

It didn't matter that he couldn't find it in his heart to move past that day in India or his failure of Hamilton. She'd be with him. Even if he couldn't give her the perfect love that all young women desired.

Eva understood. They couldn't betray the past. Honoring it was the only way to atone for how utterly he'd failed Hamilton and the old lord.

"Are you certain? So many worship and adore her. Perhaps she will choose someone less melancholic."

Jealousy, white and hot, instantly tore through him in an unexpected rampage. "And do you worship and adore her?"

Wyndham smirked. "Of course. Who would not?"

Ian stepped forward, grabbing Wyndham's lapel with his gloved hand in a sudden surge of possessiveness. "Whether those buggers down there know it or not, she is mine."

"Here, now." Wyndham brushed at him as if he were an irritating fly. "Don't wrinkle it."

Ian tightened his grip, controlled by some force he'd never felt before, and added a good dose of warning to his stare.

"Please." Wyndham snorted, rolling his eyes rather like a droll stallion. "All right, fine. Fine. She is yours." Wyndham grinned, then said, "For now."

"Do you want to keep your balls?"

"I have no fears. My balls are made of iron. I doubt even you could rip them off. Now stop behaving like a lovesick idiot and detach yourself."

"Oh, I'm sure your balls are impervious to wind and weather, but where there is a will there is a way." He forced a nonchalant expression to his brow and let go of Wyndham's coat before snatching a glass of champagne. "And I am not lovesick. One must experience love to be sick from it."

Wyndham rolled his eyes again so hard it appeared the irises might pop back in his head. "Ah, the lies we tell. You look like a dog irked by someone not paying attention to your piss-marked territory, old boy."

The very thought was disgusting . . . yet accurate. That was exactly how he felt. She was supposed to be his. Under his domain. Under his protection. She'd shared his bed these last several days, but there was something missing. Ian took a long swallow of the bubbling French wine. Sweet and ever so slightly sticky, it tasted of heaven. Of joy. In the last years, the closest he had come to unadulterated joy had been in Eva's arms.

With her hands upon his face, her body loving beneath his. But he couldn't say the words she so longed to hear because, besides his honor, he no longer trusted himself to surrender to those emotions. When he did, his judgment grew unreliable. And Eva needed his judgment to be unshakable.

Once again, he stared down at her. She was the exact picture of what a man wanted. Soon, she would be the queen of the ton—if the women didn't loathe her out of sheer envy. Eva had that slightly reserved presence that suggested that though she was in the world, she wasn't touched by this world.

She would let no man claim her, so every man would try. It was the nature of men. To want what was just out of their reach. Oh, how she kept them out of reach. Even now, she gave a smile, a slight look of warning from her stunning eyes as she laughed at the remark of another young buck pressing for advancement.

"I'm going down there."

Wyndham lifted his finger and poked it into Ian's shoulder. "Behave yourself. So far she's a tremendous success. Don't muck it up."

He curled a lip at the very idea. Hell would bring

down the heavens before he did anything to jeopardize her tentative position.

Eva couldn't quite believe she was this new person. For, surely, her present self had very little to do with the old Eva. That Eva had been bright, laughing, and sparkling, but she? She was reserved, smiling but cool, which seemed to only delight those flocking to her all the more, as if she held the secrets to all their desires. How that made her wish to laugh. In fact, she was on the edge of perpetual laughter at these foolish people.

She half listened to the beautiful tones of the aristocracy, so different from the twisted voices in the asylum and the low tones of the keepers. Eva focused in on Lady Edgington. They'd known each other since they were girls. The other woman was her opposite in every way. Where Eva was dark haired, she was wheat blond, and while Eva was fairly short, Lady Edgington fairly towered. And yet they'd been dear friends. When last they'd spoken, the other woman had been the head of the Committee for Rescue Among the Poor. It had been an admirable pursuit, attempting to find reasonable work for young girls and boys from the East End as servants. But it had been something she'd done not just out of the goodness of her heart but because . . . well, frankly, she'd been bored. They'd all been so bored. All their good deeds had come from a desperation to fill the long hours.

"My dearest Lady Carin, you look divine! Whatever you have been doing, we should all do."

Eva raised her crystal flute in mock salute. "Rest and the waters, my dear. Oh, and a strict discipline."

Lady Edgington tittered, her silky blond curls shaking about her doll's face. "You are terrible! I barely have the discipline to walk about the park, let alone do as you must have done."

Eva inclined her head, her black hair curled deceptively around a gold-roped turban. "Well, it did me a world of good, did it not?"

"A world of good?" A gentleman approached her, a Lord Montague as she recalled, his silver hair flickering in the candlelight. "Madam, you outshine the heavens."

She laughed, a full bell sound. "How naughty of you to tell a lie to a lady, my lord."

He gaped.

And before she knew it a small crowd was gathering about her. All faces she knew. All faces that hovered in the distance of her memory and all faces that meant little or nothing. Where had they been when she'd been shoved into the horrors of her life? They had been absent. All of them afraid to be tainted. But now? They couldn't bear being more than a few feet away.

"Is it true you are having tea with Princess Victoria next week?"

Eva lifted her brows but said nothing. Queen Victoria had paid her undue attention, apparently truly saddened by her loss and the wickedness done against her but, being in deep mourning for her beloved husband, Albert, had sent her daughter to convey her condolences. When Dr. Jenner's report had gone directly before Chancery, Thomas's scandalous behavior had been clear. He'd wrongfully stripped her of her independence, though no one knew the depth of his actions.

Word was that the Queen herself had ordered her officers to look for Lord Thomas and call him upon the carpet for his nefarious behavior.

But where were these people weeks ago? Nowhere. In fact, all of them would have turned against her if she appeared as she had been. No, only Ian had come to her aid. And now he was the one who had faded into the distance while her heart ached for him, but not enough to humiliate herself again.

Lady Prichard, a red-haired beauty with a sprinkling of freckles over her nose, leaned in. "Do tell us how you have achieved such a marvelous shape. Perhaps we should all take the waters."

Eva grinned. "When one does not eat, one diminishes quite remarkably."

They all laughed as if she'd said some tremendous bon mot. "Of course," Lady Prichard said. "I've heard of many marvelous regimes. And I would sell my soul for your coloring."

"Until recently, I kept myself indoors. In truth, I don't recommend it."

Lady Edgington gestured with her fan. "But you are so, so—"

"Glorious," Lord Montague intoned.

"Why, thank you," she said, barely keeping her amusement in check.

"For God's sake, leave the girl alone." The deep, slightly raspy voice came from the left.

Eva turned and couldn't stop her mouth from falling agape. There stood a young lady she'd once known quite well. Her russet hair was curled perfectly over her shoulders and about her pale face, but she didn't look particularly well. In fact, Lady Danby looked as if she might keel over at any moment. Eva smiled carefully.

"Vultures, the lot of you," Lady Danby said tightly.

The group laughed nervously as Lady Prichard leaned in and whispered in Eva's ear, "Consumption."

This one word seemed to contain a certain sort of disdainful sympathy that quirked Eva's ears. She turned to Lady Danby. A wry smile twisted Eva's lips. "We are all birds, Lady Danby, of infinite variety."

A glimmer of recognition occurred as their gazes met. The kind of recognition that occurs between two sympathetic souls. Lady Danby's face softened. "Indeed. And you have escaped your cage?"

"To play with the birds in the park, yes."

Lady Danby's pale lips trembled with repressed laughter. "A pigeon, then?"

A gasp from the surrounding gentlemen filled the air. "A swan, more like," sneered Lord Montague.

Eva grinned. "Pigeons are quite noble creatures. Survivors." Some force moved her and she found her fingers sliding carefully out, hidden by the wide folds of her skirts, to brush Lady Danby's.

When Lady Danby's fingers squeezed hers back, Eva felt a pulse of happiness and a sudden feeling of great sadness.

For she had found that tauntingly unattainable myth. A kindred soul. And the only other woman who had ever touched her in such a way was still locked up in a madhouse, her life an ongoing horror. Mary remained in her heart, and now that Eva had her freedom, she wouldn't forget her. Slowly she pulled her fingers away from Lady Danby's. Desperate. Desperate to give freedom to every woman destroyed by man. But first she had to free herself for good.

Ian headed for the wide staircase. Trailing his hand along the gold wrought-iron railing, he took deliberate steps down to the ballroom.

Hundreds of couples crowded the flower- and star-bedecked room. Several danced, the strands of a Strauss waltz sweetening the air. As he approached, it became clear that Eva was not limiting her attention to men, as some women might do.

Several ladies had joined the circle. It was a veritable

hive of chatter, each little bee busily drinking his or her champagne, attending to every need of the queen.

The women smiled on her, their eyes wide at whatever she said. The rumors were no doubt still alive, but every person in this room wanted to speak with Eva, to see whether she was mad or sane. As they came to her, that enigmatic smile drew them in.

Hooked. They were all hooked on her beauty, her mystery.

'Twas as if she had come alive. Blossomed overnight, leaving the old Eva behind. Finding a new one.

Some small voice within whispered that he was losing her. Already, she'd begun to go out into the parks, smiling and nodding at passersby, finding a kind of enjoyment that had been completely vacant from her before.

Oh, there was still pain in her eyes. It was there in the slight brittleness of her perfect posture and the way her smile didn't entirely light her deep blue eyes. But unlike himself, she'd mastered it, making her able to lavish her attentions on the company of strangers.

It was impossible, the way she was giving herself to these people and absolutely none to him. It hurt to be left alone in the darkness. After all, only she could understand the guilt he lived with hour upon hour.

He walked to the edge of the crowd around her.

The men, all in their perfect black jackets, took one look at him and made way. The women gaped, half smiles on their insipid faces. Many no doubt hoped he had come to ask them to dance.

He ignored them all, just focused on the one thing he wanted. Her back was to him, but she stilled as if sensing his presence.

Ever so slowly, she turned her head in his direction.

Just that faint turn of her head, exposing her fragile neck and her delicate features, stole his breath. God, she was captivating. Full of hidden promise. Her eyes widened ever so slightly, and her pink lips parted in a soft smile of greeting.

Everyone around them grew silent.

It seemed preposterous that the glance between two people could be scandalous. Yet the tension between them crackled with such palpability, he was instantly aware that they were causing what could turn into the greatest gossip the ton had known in weeks—if not years. Just this nearness was enough for them to both stop as though no one were in the room but them.

Everyone recognized it. Sensed it. And turned to it, so they might see it unfurl before them.

At last, Ian stretched out a gloved hand. "Might I have this dance, my lady?"

Eva eyed his hand, her gaze flicking over his body. For one strange moment, he wondered whether she would say no.

Finally, she curtsied ever so slightly, then placed her gloved fingers into his.

The fine fabric of her glove could not hide her slight tension as he clasped her hand in his. Strongly, purposefully, he led her to the center of the floor. Instantly, couples made room for them.

The air pulsed with it. The sudden understanding that they were no ordinary pair. Eyes turned to them, fabric whooshing, voices whispering.

Ian ignored them all, his vision able to bear witness only to the woman before him. Gently, yet firmly, he placed his hand at her waist and took her hand in his. They swayed for the appropriate two counts and were off, swirling about the room. There had been a distance between them since that night. Since he had been unable to return her love. But he knew he could repair it. With care, they would find their way back to the unfettered understanding they shared and break this unease.

For a woman who had not danced in years, she swept across the floor, each step sure-footed. It was absorbing. Hypnotizing, the way her body so effortlessly moved to the music.

Ian stared down at her, but her gaze was askance. He ventured the banal: "You dance very well."

She laughed. "I always loved dancing."

Even now, he could see her flitting about the long gallery at Carridan Hall, her pantalettes flouncing beneath her pink skirts. She'd been so happy as a child. All he'd wanted was to be in her company. Nothing had really changed in the long years that had stretched since then. "I remember."

"You've improved," she said evenly. "You used to be dreadful."

"Practice at least did not make me worse," he teased.

She nodded. After a few moments she cleared her throat. "I must thank you, of course. For the ball, that is."

His chest tightened with a first hint of genuine concern. Why was she acting as if they were strangers?

"Would you care to discuss the weather next?" he said softly, pressing his hand into the curve of her waist, willing her to recall the intimacy between them.

She lifted her eyes up to his face, fire, not sadness, glowing in their depths. "What else did you have in mind? Shall we bring out our ghosts here?"

God, the flame in her burned so brightly now it could heat even the most frigid soul. He longed to drag her against him and devour her mouth with his and feel that warmth. Instead, he pulled her as close as he dare, their torsos brushing lightly together. "Ghosts need never be discussed."

A soft breath of resignation sighed from her before she arched away. "The weather, then."

Christ. It was as though they were back in the coach racing away from the madhouse, a dozen walls springing up between them. If he wasn't careful, they would never come down again. What reason had she to trust anyone? Even himself, who had brought her back.

Ian jerked his gaze above her head, seeing only the other couples as he guided them around the floor. They walked upon the edge of a knife, and it was clear to him that they were either entirely together or entirely apart. "I don't like it," he finally whispered, his voice rough to his own ears.

"What?" She kept her eyes leveled at his perfectly tied cravat.

He leaned his head down, his lips scandalously close to her brow. "The way those men look at you."

"And?" she asked, her mouth parting slightly.

"No one should look at you thus but I." And, God, he meant it. The way he wanted her tortured him with such need he could scarce draw breath. "And you should give no man encouragement but me."

"Encouragement?" she echoed. Her chest lifted, pressing her beautiful breasts together as she drew in a long breath. "I see."

It hit him hard and fast that he'd said something incredibly stupid. Something he could not take back. "What is it that you see?"

A sort of desperation crossed her face as if she were drowning with pain. She narrowed her eyes to accusatory slits. "The future you had in mind for me."

"I don't—"

"You would rescue me. Save me. Indeed you would bring me back from the very dead if necessary." Her words came rushing out. "But then I would be placed safely on a shelf like some porcelain doll. Sometimes looked at, but utterly alone." Her eyes shone with tears and fury. "Unloved. Cold. Hard." Her mouth pressed into a firm line and her fingers dug into his arms. "A figure on a pedestal. A memorial to the—dead."

She stumbled against him. "You will never give yourself to love."

Dread clenched Ian's insides. This was not at all what he'd intended, this passionate anger rolling off her, passing into him. "Eva—"

"No," she hissed, yanking her hands from his. "Take me off the floor."

He wanted to grab at her, suddenly certain that if he truly let her go, she would never be within his reach again. "I don't think—"

She glared at him with the full force of her fury and disappointment. "Now."

There was nothing he could do but comply. Escorting her slowly, with as much dignity as he could muster, he led her out to one of the quiet halls.

The voices and orchestra behind them became a mere din. When at last they stood alone in the hall, their forms barely visible in the sparse candlelight, Ian took her hand gently in his. "That is not what I wish."

She glanced up to the gold-lined ceiling. "Isn't it? I have waited these last days. Certain that you would give in. But with each day that passes, you do not yield. In fact, you grow worse, silently dancing about our dead. You are content to live without loving me but nor do you wish anyone else to." She sighed. "That is what this is." She gestured wildly, arms flung out, displaying herself.

Her reasoning was far too close to his own and it didn't bode well.

The mockery faded as a slow dawning lit her face. "That's it. Isn't it?"

"No," he said firmly, quickly.

"I see it in your eyes," she said softly. She lifted a gloved hand, about to touch his face, but hesitated. "It's there."

He remained silent, having no defense but lies.

Defeated, she dropped her hand. "You will not leap into the breach and take a chance at our love because you are still caught in the past."

He didn't answer. He couldn't. Couldn't, because it was true. That was exactly how he felt.

She shook her head. "All this time . . . All this time, I thought it was I who would never recover from the memories." A wry smile tilted her lips. "But it is you. You are the one condemned to it."

White-hot pain laced through Ian's heart. "It is how I am," he hissed. Unforgivable words pushed their way to his lips. "And if you—"

"What?" Anger tightened Eva's features. "If I would not live? I would not love? I would not laugh? I have paid for my mistakes." She took a strong step forward, her shoulders squared with pride. "I will go on paying for them. Every day, I remember more and it is often more painful than I can bear. But I remember Hamilton, flawed man that he was. I remember my son." Her throat worked and she grabbed his shoulders as she stared up at him. Tears filled her eyes and her voice shook. "Do you not understand? I will not make my memorial to them a living death. I deserve someone who will live in the present. Here. Now. With love freely given."

She withdrew a little, smoothing her hands down her gown. "I will not let you force me to live the cold life you've envisioned."

He attempted to regain the distance between them and reached out. "Eva—"

"Thank you for my freedom," she said softly, backing away. "I will never forget."

She was saying good-bye to him. She was sending him away. Forever. She couldn't. She was still in danger. And she was his whole purpose. "You cannot—"

"I can," she said simply. "You gave me that power. And I will not have those about me who would force me to live in remorse and guilt." For one brief moment, her eyes softened as if she might relent, but then the moment was gone. "Even those I love."

Ian winced, wishing he could seize her, claim her mouth with his, then brand her body with his own. If he could, maybe then she would see that they couldn't be parted. But she would hate him if he attempted such an act now. She'd known too many men who'd forced her to their purpose.

"Now go, please," she said gently. "I don't need you anymore."

Those words ripped him asunder. "What of Thomas and that woman?"

"I will hire men to keep me safe," she replied quickly, calmly, clearly having thought the matter through.

Ian fought back the urge to roar that she was wrong. So wrong. But he couldn't. Not as his own conviction crumbled. She was slipping through his fingers like so much sand, and though he wished to, he could not keep her within his hold. If this was what she truly wanted, he had no choice but to give in.

It was as Elizabeth said: She was not a child. She was a woman. A woman who deserved respect.

His heart cracked against his ribs, bleeding inside. Despite this, Ian cupped her face in his palms, then bent down and pressed his lips so softly to hers it might not have been a kiss at all. In the way one rips a bandage away, he pulled back. "Good-bye, Eva."

He lingered for a moment, praying against all odds that she would beg him to stay. That their mutual desire could be enough.

Silence filled up the space between them. She stood strong, her hands folded before her. Unrelenting.

Finally, it became clear that he could not force himself to retreat. So she turned from him and walked down the hall. Her head high. Her shoulders set.

She did not look back.

Chapter 28

Eva fingered the pistol tucked into her burgundy reticule and the note pressed next to it. Every breath she took stung as she resisted the urge to read it yet again. And yet? Her fingers danced over the small, folded parchment and she whipped it out.

Eva,

    I have information pertaining to Adam. I have let you and society believe a lie these years. Meet me and I will disclose the story. It will ease your heart, but if you do not come, a bullet shall find its way through Ian's brain. Do not test me. Come posthaste with the carriage that shall come to collect you. Bring no one. Tell no one.

                               Thomas

Come alone? Thomas was mad himself to think she would come with no defense. But perhaps it was because her heart had leapt at the possibility of news of her son. She'd never seen his body. She'd never kissed him goodbye. What lie could he mean? Could he . . . ? Did she dare hope that the lie was that Adam had not died? She'd heard sordid stories of heirs being spirited away so that a relative might inherit.

Her heart pounded wildly, mixing with the clop of the

horse's hooves beating along the cobblestones. Tucking the note deep in her reticule, she caressed her weapon once again, drawing assurance from its cold metal.

It would never occur to Thomas that she would carry a pistol. Not when he had controlled her so fiercely for so long. Not when she'd been so weak the last time they'd seen each other. No doubt he assumed she would do whatever he said, docile as sheep herded over a cliff. He was arrogant enough. And it most definitely would never occur to him that she'd enlist the aid of a man like Wyndham. She resisted the temptation to glance out the rain-specked window and look for the big lord who'd promised to assist her.

She should have gone to Ian. But she couldn't. Not after what had transpired between them. Wyndham had been quiet and understanding and had attempted to persuade her to speak with Ian. Her adamant refusal had secured his promise that he would not be far behind her.

The carriage rolled through the packed streets, struggling to find its way.

Each jostle of the vehicle wore at her nerves. She'd been exhausted after having been on display all evening at the ball, but she had not once closed her eyes in slumber last eve. Over and over again, she'd gone over the note. What secret could there be? The thoughts repeated in a cruel, unending cycle, wearing down her mind through the waning hours.

She shouldn't dare hope for the impossible. But she did. Her rational self knew it was far too fantastical, but her heart? Her heart would not listen to reason.

Most likely, Thomas would relay some horrid detail of her son's death meant to drive her to the edge. That was the most likely conclusion. Even so, she could not force herself to believe it.

Yet so many things surrounding the day Adam had

died danced in her head unresolved. Once he'd been flung from the curricle, she'd never seen him again. It was a detail she'd not considered under the haze of laudanum. She didn't even know what he'd truly died from. And she could have sworn that Thomas had hated her son.

She sucked in a sharp breath in realization. The letter. That's what the letter had been for. She'd written to Ian, begging him to return, no longer trusting her and Adam's safety to Thomas. She'd had to deliver it by hand because the servants—all under his employ—couldn't be trusted to deliver it for her.

It came back to her in a pummeling tide, as did the sudden recollection of her begging to see her child, begging to see his body but not being allowed. Horror shook through her as she felt Thomas's bony hands holding her down as a doctor had poured laudanum into her mouth.

The hackney turned down a narrow alley, leaving the choke of people behind. Tall brick walls pressed in on the little way, blocking out the daylight.

Lord, how she wished Ian were here with her. With one look, he'd wipe her fears away. He'd help her make sense of her assaulting memories. But she'd sent him from her life.

The driver made some inarticulate noises and the hackney began to slow.

Eva's heart took to life, pounding at her breastbone. It was all well and good to be brave in the safety of one's room. Or with Ian at her side. Here, she was alone.

Well, not entirely alone. She'd not been stupid, thank God.

She wound the strings of the reticule about her wrist, leaving it a little open so she could reach the pistol swiftly.

The hackney swayed as the driver jumped down. His

shoes clacked against the cobblestones. Eva closed her eyes for a brief moment. She could do this. Whatever it took. She'd lived enough of her life afraid. She wouldn't be ruled by fear. Nor by Thomas. Not anymore.

When the door swung open, Eva climbed down with a confidence she didn't truly feel, her calm hands guiding her full skirts through the door.

She paused and looked about. The driver, in his black coat and dusty trousers, stood just a few feet off.

He gave her a shaky smile. "This is the place, ma'am. The gent asked me to drop you here."

Eva nodded sharply. The fellow probably was used to dropping people in bizarre locales. "I assume you have been paid?"

He tugged at his sandy forelock. "Oh, yes. All taken care of." Quickly he shut the door, then started patting his front. Puffs of dirt flew into the air. "It's about somewheres."

Eyeing him cautiously, she tried to stay alert to her surroundings. The walls stretched on in both directions, largely uninterrupted by windows or doors.

The cab driver pulled out a rumpled piece of paper. "I can't read it. But the gent asked me to give it to you."

Eva stretched out her gloved hand and took the twist of paper.

Without a word, he climbed back up onto the black hackney, cracked his whip, and trotted off down the alley.

Standing entirely by herself in the dark alley, Eva let her eyes drop to the note in her palm.

Find the door with the mark. I'll be waiting.

She looked down the alley and crumpled the note in her fist. There were two doors to her immediate left. She took a few quick steps, unsure whether she was headed in the correct direction.

There on one of the peeling brown doors was a white chalk stripe. Taking courage in hand, she strode up to the door. Her mouth dried ever so slightly as she reached for the iron handle. For one brief moment, her hand refused to obey her will, all the fear that Thomas had invoked in her pulsing through her veins. As if she could defy that very domination of fear, she twisted the circular latch and pushed.

The heavy panel opened into darkness. Somewhere ahead was the faint, flickering glow of candlelight. She followed the dirty light and crossed over the threshold.

The door swung shut behind her, the iron hinges groaning.

"Welcome, Eva," Thomas called from the darkness.

Swift movement flashed in the corner of her eye. She jerked to the right just in time to avoid the club aimed at her head. She ripped the pistol from her reticule.

Thomas stumbled when the club dashed through the air and met contact with the wall, crushing the plaster. Crushing it into white shards ... just as it would have done to her skull.

Eva leveled the pistol at him, her hands shaking slightly. "Not exactly how you had planned, now, is it?"

Thomas caught his footing, his face a mask of shock. He looked at her as if he had never seen her before. "No." He swallowed, placing the club down on the floor. Lifting his hands in supplication, he shifted back on his shining boots. "Not exactly."

Chapter 29

Eva's heart sank.

Thomas would not stop until she and now, most likely, Ian were dead. It had all just been a lure to bring her here. And fool that she was, she'd come. Adam was dead. But she could still save Ian and herself from Thomas's unhinged passions.

Keeping the pistol aimed at his heart, she demanded, "What were you going to do with me?"

"Since you seem so inexplicably difficult to kill"—Thomas's gaze flicked up from the barrel—"I was going to toss you in a trunk and throw it in the river."

"You didn't think I'd ever escape that place," she said. "You wanted me to die there."

Glancing up and down her slight frame, Thomas arched a disdainful brow. "I had doubts you would survive."

Good God, he was an evil bastard. "Murder by chance, then?"

Thomas's pale green eyes widened as if the answer were obvious. "Blood and I have never been friends."

Eva laughed dryly, the sound painfully sharp in the small space. "No. How foolish of me to forget."

Thomas was the kind who howled if he'd nicked a knee or bloodied his hands from a fall. No wonder he'd chosen to brain her, a relatively clean way to attack someone. "I'm going to leave now," she said evenly.

Carefully, she inched a foot toward the door, worried he might do something very foolish. "I'm going to the authorities. Then hopefully some modicum of justice might be done."

Thomas licked his lips, his hands still stretched out, his gaze fixed on her pistol. "I don't think you will."

Eva straightened her arm, tempted to become a monster herself and simply caress the trigger. "Why not?"

His pink tongue darted out to lick his dry lips. "Because you came here to discuss your son."

"You negated such discussion when you attacked me."

Thomas blew out a heavy breath. His gaze darted from the pistol to her face. "I was hoping to avoid showing my hand."

That feeling of possibility came back to her. What could he have that was such a great secret he would lock her away or try to send her abroad? She dared not give way to fanciful hopes. "Why?"

"Well, the very nature of the information is incriminating to myself." Thomas smiled faintly. "Luckily, you will never use it to harm me."

From the smug gleam in his eyes, she saw that the little power she had was about to slip away, and she couldn't let that happen. "Out with it, Thomas."

Thomas lowered his hands. "I want you to give me the pistol."

This time a laugh poured from her, full bodied with disbelief. "Why on earth would I do that?"

"Because you would do anything to keep your son safe," he snapped, his face growing rigid with impatience.

Keep your son safe. Terror and hope clutched at Eva

in one swift assault. It was a hypnotic moment, the world stopping with cruel promise. "Adam?"

"Yes," he said simply. "He's still alive, Eva."

Her heart stopped beating at that moment. Everything stilled as an intense longing for her baby swept over. "Don't lie."

Thomas shook his head, confidence replacing his earlier wariness. "Why would I lie? Such information would steal the title from me. Why would I give it to you if it weren't true?"

"To ... to silence me, to take advantage of this situation," she said tightly, not daring to let herself begin to believe. Lord, she could not bear it to have Adam taken from her again.

"Yes. That is exactly what I will do. But it is true, Eva."

It wasn't true. It couldn't be true. No God would offer such impossible hope.

"Believe it," he urged. "But if you kill me, you will never find him."

An image of her son danced before her, his small arms reaching up, face back, laughing as he waited to be lifted into her embrace. A guttural hiss of rage ripped from her throat. "What did you do?"

"You never saw the body." Thomas shifted, squaring his shoulders. "You fainted and they brought the both of you back to the house. He'd been knocked unconscious and had a broken arm." A faint hint of disgust curled Thomas's lip. "The driver brought him back, but I stopped him in the stable. I took the boy and hid him, to see if he'd live or not." Thomas blinked, the muscle below his right eye tightening slightly. "He lived."

"My God," she gritted. She couldn't even imagine what Thomas would have had to do. Loathing filled her. Thomas would have had to carry the little body, place it in some hay-filled basket. Or perhaps he'd just slung

Adam down like a sack. Then he would have had to callously wait and watch through his own nephew's pain. "Thomas, if one of us is mad, it is you."

"No." He took a shaky step toward her. "It was the perfect opportunity to have what I always wanted. What I always deserved." Thomas's eyes flared, his gaze sparking with a frightening passion. "Don't you understand? All my life, I watched. I watched you and Ian fumble at love and Hamilton's pathetic attempts to be good enough for you both and our father. I was never going to be that fool. I learned after Mother died how important it was not to become attached. Not to care. So I kept myself separate. And when you're separate, doing what I did is very simple. Easy. No looking back."

Eva's insides twisted at his admission. Was that what he had been doing when they were children? Keeping himself distant, so he'd have no conscience in this world? And no affection. He'd closed his heart to any sort of love, so he would never understand the love she felt for Ian or her son. Her heart sank.

Thomas smoothed his trembling hands down his creased waistcoat, the moment of emotion gone. "Money will buy a person anything, Eva, including silence. I paid off the servants who spotted the boy."

Again her finger itched to pull the trigger and kill him. But she couldn't. Not while he held her future in his hands. "Where is he?"

Thomas lifted a finger and wagged. "No. He is my one insurance against you. If you do not let me go now, you will never see him again. He will be lost and Lord knows what will happen to a friendless child." Thomas tilted his head to the side, his eyes narrowing. "You've seen the beggar children on the streets, Eva. What they're willing to do for a scrap of bread. Can you imagine that befalling your son?"

"What you did to me was unforgivable, Thomas." Her voice broke in her rage, but she kept on. "What you have done to Adam? You shall burn in the depths of hell forever."

"The afterlife doesn't overly concern me." Thomas stretched out his hand expectantly. "Now, if you would hand me the pistol?"

Eva glared at him, wishing to God she could think of something. Anything to save her from this impossible situation. If she killed the bastard, she would never see her son again. If she gave him the pistol, he would have complete control over her.

Where the hell was Wyndham? He was supposed to have followed her. And his imminent arrival would have been most welcome. He'd promised to be close behind her. But there was no sign of him.

"It doesn't really seem like much of an exchange," Thomas said lightly. "The knowledge your son is alive weighed against your little life."

Eva closed her eyes, her throat closing. The feelings racing through her were the strangest mix she had ever known. Joy. Perfect joy at her son's survival. She had not killed him. Somewhere out there he was playing a child's games, laughing a little boy's laugh, and he would grow into a beautiful man. It was more happiness than she could bear.

But then there was Ian. She hadn't gone to him for help. She'd cut him from her life brutally. After all he had done for her, how could she have condemned him so harshly?

Even after all she had said, she knew Ian would have been there for her in a moment. Ready to hold her hand, to make her heart feel at ease. To protect her from the evils of this world.

Despite all his faults and his fears, she loved him more

deeply than she could love anyone, save her child. And now she most likely would never see him again.

There was no choice. She had spent the last two years in anguish over her son's death. Now that she knew he was alive, she could never give up Adam's safety.

She couldn't.

There was only one thing she could do. She'd cling to the knowledge that even though her son wouldn't grow up knowing his true parents, he would grow up.

And that—that was all that mattered.

Eva slowly closed the small distance between them. "I will do whatever you ask," she said.

"Good." Thomas grinned. "Now—"

Eva lifted the pistol and rammed the muzzle into his heart, then cocked the pistol.

Thomas let out a squeal of horror. "What?!"

"I will do whatever you ask . . . after you tell me where Adam is." In that moment, her weapon shoved into Thomas's flesh, she knew with utter certainty what a fool she had been to send Ian away. She should have kept him at any cost. Love was far too valuable to cast it away as she had. Now there was no turning back. "Tell me."

"I can't."

She shoved the muzzle deeper against his soft muscle. Her finger slid against the trigger, only wanting a little more pressure to do what it was created to do. "Tell me!"

A crash of noise echoed through the small room. The door swung open, letting in a burst of dingy sunshine.

It had to be Wyndham!

Eva's gaze whipped to the square of light. Her blinded eyes squinted at the figures in the door. Thomas shouted, then reached forward, wrenching her arm and snatching the pistol out of her hands. "I lied, you little bitch," he hissed.

Eva twisted back to Thomas. "What?"

"The gardener drowned your son in the lake," Thomas growled. "Dead. Just like you will be."

A pistol cracked.

Pain tore through her body. White-hot, torturous pain. She screamed and fell to the floor.

Shadowy figures raced into the room.

Through the haze of agony, she spotted Ian, a pistol in his hand.

The room blurred, but she had to say something. Had to get it out.

She heard a snarl and then more shots. Sparks exploded in the dark room.

As he knelt down beside her, Ian's voice split the space. "Eva!"

Tears slicked her cheeks.

It was over.

Ian's face, so strong, so determined, hovered over hers, creased with fear. He had come for her.

But now Adam truly was lost forever.

Chapter 30

Ian couldn't tear himself away from the bed.

Each breath she drew in and successfully blew out seemed to sustain him, giving him his own life. There was no peace to her sleep. 'Twas as if the laudanum had returned. Beneath their lids, her eyes flickered.

Every single wince stabbed at his heart.

Christ, how he wished he could force her back to him. To assure her that all would be well. That nothing would separate them ever again. Especially not his own idiocy.

Soft steps lingered in the doorway.

Ian shoved a hand through his hair before turning to see who it was.

Wyndham stood on the threshold, his shirt neck open, a glass of whiskey in hand. "May I?"

Ian wanted to tell him no. He'd felt momentarily betrayed when the spy had conveyed Eva's meeting with Thomas. But that sense of betrayal had vanished when he realized Eva would have gone with or without Wyndham's help. Ian's desire to protect Eva would never cease, but now he would never attempt to stop her from doing as she wished, not when his perverse sense of control had meant he'd almost lost her.

All he longed for was to spend the rest of his life with her, and every day he'd say a damn prayer of thanks to Wyndham.

If not for him, Eva would be dead. But it had nearly killed him. Eva had gone to Wyndham and asked for his help. All because Ian had been a complete fool.

Wyndham sauntered into the room, shadows under his eyes. "How is she?"

Ian stared at Eva, wishing he knew. "She hasn't woken up."

Wyndham sat in a chair on the opposite side of the bed. He gazed at Eva. "She will. She's a strong one."

Ian opened his mouth to agree. His throat cut off any sound. A tremor shook through him. God, how foolish could a man be? He'd been willing to throw everything away. For what? For someone who had proved a disappointment as a man and as a friend?

Ian curled his hands into fists. It was like waking from a paralyzing dream. The realization that Eva was right. He had tried to put Eva on a high shelf away from love. And he'd chosen pain and guilt over embracing love. Because of his obsession, he'd wanted to treat their love like something to be ashamed of instead of flaunted to the world. That obsession had almost cost him Eva's life.

"Don't," Wyndham's voice cut in. "I see it on your face. Don't beat yourself up for the mistakes you made."

"I almost lost her. In more ways than one," he whispered. He could still envision it. The look in Thomas's eyes as he pulled the trigger. He didn't think he'd ever be able to put Eva's prone, bleeding body from his mind. "I almost—"

"Yes, almost. But you didn't. I don't think you ever truly let her go."

Ian wiped a hand over his face, his palm coming away slightly damp. Jesus. He was crying. A ridiculous tear had betrayed his usually unshakable nature. "Well, I think I fooled her. I'm sure she thinks I just walked away."

"We all have paths we must finish when we mourn. You were mourning your mistakes and your friend in the only way you knew how."

The weight of Wyndham's wisdom eased his guilt ever so slightly. But not enough. "I very nearly ended up mourning Eva."

"You have the chance to live free of it." Wyndham fingered his glass. "Now, if you lose that, then you're a fool."

Nodding, Ian reached his hand out and took Eva's limp one in his. She stirred. Ian tensed, willing her to awaken.

Very gently, her eyes flickered, then opened. For one moment there was a look of peace on her features. Instantly it vanished. She gasped. "I've lost him." A sob racked her body. "I've lost him."

Struck with alarm, Ian climbed onto the bed, gently pulling her into his arms, taking extreme care not to jostle the wound in her shoulder.

Wyndham sat frozen in his chair, completely at a loss.

Ian eased her head back and looked into her pain-stricken eyes. "Lost who, darling?"

She looked away, her whole body shaking violently. "Adam." She sucked in a jagged breath. "Oh, God, I've lost him again."

Ian took her face gently in his hand and forced her to look back at him. Of course, she was full of grief. Full of wild regret. "No. You have not."

"Wh-what?" Her deepest blue eyes lit with confusion. Her face twisted. "Thomas said—"

Wyndham cleared his throat. "That sod? He wouldn't have known the truth if it had bit him in the arse."

Eva twisted and narrowed her gaze at the earl. She seemed to calm slightly, realizing they were not alone. "I—I didn't even realize you were here."

Wyndham smiled, though it was clearly forced. "Ever the sneaky bastard."

Eva didn't smile.

Wyndham shifted uncomfortably on his chair.

"We found the driver and the gardener that Thomas bribed," Ian said gently.

"You did?" Her voice was a gentle note of hope tinged with fear.

"You didn't think I was just going to stand entirely by, did you?"

She frowned. "No, I suppose not. But does that mean—?" She licked her lips. "Does that mean—?"

Ian nodded toward Wyndham. The earl strode quickly to the door and leaned out into the hall.

"Ian," she whispered.

"Wait just a moment." Ian cradled her close.

The shuffle of footsteps echoed down the hall. Then a man entered, his scruffy clothes hanging about his wiry frame. The man kept his gaze down as he entered.

Eva gasped. "I know you."

He tugged at his forelock. "Aye, my lady. The name's Johnny."

"You're one of the gardeners," she said softly.

"I am, at that. And . . ." He hesitated, sneaking a glance at Ian.

Ian nodded. The man had been terrified when Ian had found him and his wife. "Go ahead."

Johnny's hands fidgeted a moment before he lifted his gaze and looked Eva full in the face. "I've been a father to your son these last years."

"Adam?" Eva cried, her voice rich with emotion.

"Yes, my lady. I saw what Lord Thomas was up to and I couldn't bear it. I went into the stables and stole the child off. Adam's been with my wife and me ever since." A smile pulled at Johnny's lips. "He's a beautiful boy.

Always was. Always had my heart in his little hands. That's why I couldn't just stand by."

Ian waited, having no idea how she would react.

A laugh so full, so pure, bubbled from her. She beamed. "Thank you—" Tears of joy slipped down Eva's cheeks. "Thank you so much."

As her laughter faded, she winced. "Good God, that hurts."

"Bullet wounds are usually thought to be painful," quipped Wyndham.

Eva ignored him. "I'm going to see my son again," she marveled.

"Yes, Eva," Ian said. "As soon as you're recovered."

She smiled a smile so full, its beauty shone from within her. "I can't believe it."

Johnny shuffled his feet for a moment. "You won't— you won't take him away right away now, will you, my lady?"

Eva's smile deepened, her eyes full of love. "I should never take him from the family that loved him so much. That saved him. But will you and your wife come to live with me?"

Johnny smiled a fast, relieved smile. "Yes, my lady. The boy should know and love you, good lady that you are."

With that, Wyndham opened the door and Johnny quickly made his departure, a lightness to his step.

"Thomas is a bastard," Ian said tightly.

"A dead bastard," Wyndham added brightly.

Eva's smile dimmed. "Are you safe, Ian? The courts. They won't prosecute—"

Wyndham snorted. "There is a flood of confessions happening these days. Ian and I found the driver as well. He and Johnny both confessed to what Thomas did, hiding the boy. We both witnessed Thomas's attempt to kill you . . . The man is lucky his body hasn't been chucked in a dung heap."

Ian stilled. He didn't quite know how to say this to Eva, but he knew how important it was. "Wyndham has gone to Palmer's asylum."

Eva's gaze swung from Ian to Wyndham. "Mary?"

Ian shifted his gaze to the earl. "She's not there."

"What?" She gasped.

"Apparently," Wyndham said, "your friend is quite the young woman. She's escaped."

"We must find her," Eva pleaded. "Will you help, my lord?"

Wyndham bowed. "For you, Eva, anything."

"Thank you," she said, full of hope. Her face positively radiated. "I have so much to thank you both for."

Wyndham batted his lashes. "Please. All in the day's work for a chivalrous—"

"I do beg your pardon, Wyndham, but is there a reason you're still here?" Ian asked, pierced by the need to have Eva entirely to himself.

"I was telling . . ." Wyndham glanced from Ian to Eva, then nodded. "Right. I see how I'm loved."

"You are indeed," Eva said, but at the same time she wove her fingers around Ian's. "I shall always be grateful to you."

Wyndham smirked at them, then made a quick exit.

"And you, Ian. You've given me back my son."

Ian drew in a long breath. It would be so easy to focus on the events at hand, but at long last he was ready to say what truly needed to be said. "I must ask for forgiveness."

"For what?"

"I wasted so many years trying to earn the love of an old man with a promise that never should have been given. I loved Lord Carin, but I never should have put his memory before us."

"Oh, Ian." Eva's eyes shone with tears of amazement as she looked at him. "How do I thank you for being such a wonderful soul?"

God, he didn't deserve her gratitude. He didn't deserve her. But he would never let her go again. "You can forgive me? Please. For being such a fool."

She arched a dark brow. "We've both taken turns at playing the fool."

Ian stroked her cheek. Anticipation touched with a hint of apprehension filled him. What if she told him to sod off? She had every right. "There's another role I'd like to play."

"Yes?" Eva asked, her voice soft.

"Lover." His heart beat furiously in his chest as he waited before he said, "Husband. Father."

Eva opened her mouth, ready to reply, but then she frowned. "I have to ask. What about India and Hamilton?"

"What I did in India had to be done. If I hadn't acted, Hamilton would have sent more men to their early graves . . . And it doesn't matter anymore." Ian clasped her hand, loving its warmth and the feel of its smallness in his. "I've been so dim."

She grinned. "You have indeed."

"Will you help me, then?"

"With what exactly?"

"To be my partner in living life with as much joy as we can grab on to?"

Eva lifted her hands to his face and gently pulled him down to kiss her. "Let's grab on now," she whispered.

"Absolutely, my love. Absolutely."

Epilogue

Adam dashed straight into the shallow waves, the salt water soaking his short pants. A shriek of happiness rippled from him as he looked back, a smile dimpling his cheeks.

Eva waved at him, resting on a blanket stretched out on the sand. He was growing so fast. Soon he'd have to have a pony to ride upon at the seaside.

Ian rose from the blanket and sprinted toward Adam. The little boy's mouth opened wide. He turned and darted onward on his short little legs, loving the game.

"I'm going to get you, lad!" Ian shouted, chasing after him. "Don't you doubt it!"

Johnny and his wife, Emma, sat a few feet away from her on their own blanket. Their hands were entwined as they grinned and watched Adam and Ian dart about over the sand.

Eva couldn't hide the smile that so often warmed her cheeks these days. It was a miracle really, the way Johnny and Emma had whisked her son away and raised him as their own. She'd not known what to expect when she saw Adam for the first time in years. But he was a happy boy. Chubby cheeked, and eyes alight with mischief. 'Twas clear as anything how much the couple loved him, and so they'd happily come with Adam into Eva and Ian's new home, that the boy wouldn't be parted from his loved ones ever again.

Gently Eva placed a hand on her growing middle, savoring the feel of new life. It had taken time, but they were a family now. All five of them. Adam was full of adventure and laughter, Johnny and Emma having raised him with a remarkable degree of care.

Now he was Ian's son, too.

No one could have risen to the task with such zeal as her husband.

They'd both risen to it.

And soon they'd be six.

Sometimes, she still woke in the night with thoughts of Mary darkening her joy. But she knew her friend was out there somewhere and Wyndham would find her.

All Eva needed to shake off those rarer and rarer moments of fear was to touch her husband or to glance upon the innocent face of her son.

They'd faced the storm. Weathered it. Been tempered by it. Finally all the fear had been left behind. Eva drank in the sight of her husband and her son playing like two carefree creatures. When the fear had vanished, all that was left in its wake was love.

Perfect, enduring love.

Read on for a preview of Máire Claremont's
compelling new novel

LADY IN RED

"You can't stay here, Mary."

The breath withered from her chest, replaced by gripping panic. She desperately searched Yvonne's face. Sincerity marked it. Yvonne didn't jest in her declaration and that meant only one thing. The streets. And all the dangers it possessed. "Please," she choked. "I'll do whatever—"

"It is not that I wouldn't protect you. But your father ... This is one of the first places he will look." Yvonne paused. "Am I right to think he will seek you?"

Mary's knees buckled.

Regardless of the weakness in such a gesture, Mary crumpled to the floor. Sitting naked in a pool of sheets so soft she wanted to bury herself in them, she swallowed back the realization that she had traveled for days for nothing. Foolishly, she hadn't even realized that her papa, the Duke of Duncliffe, would find her. Not when all she'd been concerned with was escape and coming to Yvonne.

How utterly stupid. How very, very stupid. Of course, he would pursue her here. The moment he learned of her disappearance, she would be hunted down like a base criminal. When he found her, he would send her back. Back to that place where each day had been a nightmare of pain.

"What is this plan of yours?" she whispered, though she couldn't imagine any plan at this moment that would save her.

Yvonne crossed to a pink marble-topped table, laden with cut-crystal bottles of liquor. She poured out two stout matching glasses of amber liquid. Holding her counsel, she crossed her chamber. As she lowered herself before Mary, the folds of her gown and hoops whooshed over Mary's legs.

"Take it." Yvonne held out one of the glasses.

Mary clasped the cool crystal in her hand. "What do you propose?"

Studying her glass, Yvonne cleared her throat. "Mary, my dear, I know you have been through a great trial, but I must ask." She took a long swallow of her drink, and once she had eased the snifter to her lap, she inquired bluntly, "Do you think you could bed a man?"

Mary flinched. An image of large fists hitting and yanking assailed her. Then searing pain. She forced the nause-ating recollection back into the trunk in which she kept all such terrifying memories. Before they could come to full life.

"I can see that you have been forced into pleasuring others with your body."

What on earth was she to say to that? That yes, she had been degraded and treated less than human? The words wouldn't pass her lips. Not ever. If she didn't speak them, perhaps one day she could truly pretend and come to believe they weren't true.

Mary lifted her own glass and swallowed. Hard. Sev-eral swift gulps allowed her to savor the heat of the spicy brandy trailing down to her stomach. "It was horrid," she said simply, then added, "It was punishment."

"I am sorry. Though most likely not to the same level of hurt as yourself, I too have been forced." Yvonne laughed hollowly, her eyes haunted with imprisoned memory. "In my profession one cannot go long without receiving ... unwanted attentions. Especially when one is first starting out and must subjugate oneself to a pimp."

Mary frowned at this revelation. If Yvonne had been ... "How can you do what you do now, then?"

Yvonne raised a hand and brushed it gently over Mary's lips, possibly ridding herself of the bad taste of unpleasant memories before she smoothed that hand along her softly curled hair. "I was fortunate. I found a gentleman who worshipped me, set me up, and then gave me this house." The displeasure that had painted her features turned to a gentle fondness. "He was very kind. He taught me that I could enjoy my body again. He liberated me from fear and pain."

Mary could not imagine such a thing. The best she hoped for was to never have to contemplate her body in relation to a man's again. Perhaps then she could be happy.

Yvonne eyed her carefully. "I think the Duke of Fairleigh could be *your* liberator."

Was Yvonne mad? She had no wish to be liberated from the fear that kept her in the constant and valid awareness of men's dangerousness, brutality, and capability of the utmost trickery. "I do not think that likely."

"You feel this way now, Mary. Of course you do—"

"I will always feel like this." Her hand, still holding the sheet in place, dug through the silk until the bite of her nails pierced her palm. "Why do you think *he* can steal my fear away?"

"There is much scandal surrounding his family and his cold demeanor is his answer to the disdain of the world. But he is a duke, Mary." She paused, letting the information take its full effect before adding, "And exceptionally wealthy. Such a man—"

"Could protect me from my father," Mary finished, a dull acceptance seeping into her heart. And yet, Edward had made her feel something she'd never felt before . . . powerful, herself.

"If your father comes here, I will lose you within moments." Yvonne allowed no kindness in her countenance to ease the painful truth. "But if you were to go to the Duke of Fairleigh as his mistress, he might be able to keep you hidden or, if it came to it, safe."

Once again, she would be putting herself into a man's power. The world was such an unjust place. Could she never save herself? Could she only throw herself from one man's whim to the next?

Mary squeezed her eyes shut against the anger inside her. No matter how hard she wished it, this world didn't belong to women, and she did indeed need a man's help. Edward's help. "But how can you be certain he'd wish to keep me?"

"Because I have not seen him so curious about a woman in the years that I have known him."

"You will tell me what I must do?"

"Of course."

"I don't know if I can"—she grimaced searching for words that would be acceptable to her ears—"couple with him."

"When the time comes, I will ensure you will be able to. And he will not force you. He is not that kind of man. Quite the opposite in fact."

"Fine, then." Even as she spoke, Mary couldn't quite hide her fear. He hadn't hurt her. In fact, he had seemed fixated on assuring her she was safe, but he was still a man and a stranger. And despite the unfamiliar feelings he had evoked, she cared for neither.

But to keep herself away from that place . . . from her father, she would go to Edward. What choice had she?

Yvonne took her empty glass. "Good, then. I shall arrange it. I'm sure we can find you a pleasing frock somewhere. And in the meantime, let's drink to the moon, eh? And your protection." She leaned forward, her eyes full of hope. "I am so glad you shall be safe."

But Mary no longer trusted hope. It was a fool's emotion, and she was tired of being a fool.

ETERNAL
ROMANCE

FIND YOUR HEART'S DESIRE..